THE PREGNANT WIDOW

MARTIN AMIS

The Pregnant Widow

INSIDE HISTORY

ALFRED A. KNOPF
NEW YORK · TORONTO
2010

THIS IS A BORZOI BOOK
PUBLISHED BY ALFRED A. KNOPF
AND ALFRED A. KNOPF CANADA

Published in the United States by Alfred A. Knopf,
a division of Random House, Inc., New York,
and in Canada by Alfred A. Knopf Canada,
a division of Random House of Canada Limited, Toronto.
www.aaknopf.com
www.randomhouse.ca

Originally published in Great Britain by Jonathan Cape,
a division of the Random House Group Ltd., London.

Grateful acknowledgment is made to Random House, Inc.,
for permission to reprint an excerpt from "The Geography of
the House" from *Collected Poems* by W.H. Auden,
copyright © 1965 by W.H. Auden.
Reprinted by permission of Random House, Inc.

Library of Congress Cataloging-in-Publication Data
Amis, Martin.
The pregnant widow / by Martin Amis. — 1st ed.
p. cm.
ISBN 978-1-4000-4452-8
1. College students—Sexual behavior—Fiction. 2. British—Italy—
Fiction. 3. Nineteen seventy, A.D.—Fiction. 4. Memory—Fiction.
I. Title.
PR6051.M5P74 2010
823'.914—dc22   2009041689

Library and Archives Canada Cataloguing in Publication
Amis, Martin
The pregnant widow / Martin Amis.
ISBN 978-0-676-97781-3
I. Title
PR6051.M58P74 2010   823.'914   C2009-905307-1

Manufactured in the United States of America
First North American Edition

To IF

The death of the contemporary forms of social order ought to gladden rather than trouble the soul. Yet what is frightening is that the departing world leaves behind it, not an heir, but a pregnant widow. Between the death of the one and the birth of the other, much water will flow by, a long night of chaos and desolation will pass.

ALEXANDER HERZEN

narcissism: n. excessive or erotic interest in oneself and one's physical appearance.

Concise Oxford Dictionary

Now I am ready to tell how bodies are changed
Into different bodies.

The Metamorphoses
(TED HUGHES, *Tales from Ovid*)

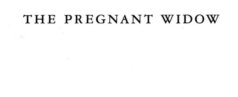

THE PREGNANT WIDOW

2006

Introductory

They had driven into town from the castle; and Keith Nearing walked the streets of Montale, Italy, from car to bar, at dusk, flanked by two twenty-year-old blondes, Lily and Scheherazade . . .

This is the story of a sexual trauma. He wasn't at a tender age when it happened to him. He was by any definition an adult; and he consented—he comprehensively consented. Is *trauma*, then, really the word we want (from Gk "wound")? Because his wound, when it came—it didn't hurt a bit. It was the sensory opposite of torture. She loomed up on him unclothed and unarmed, with her pincers of bliss— her lips, her fingertips. Torture: from L. *torquere* "to twist." It was the opposite of torture, yet it twisted. It ruined him for twenty-five years.

When he was young, people who were stupid, or crazy, were called *stupid*, or *crazy*. But now (now he was old) the stupid and the crazy were given special names for what ailed them. And Keith wanted one. He was stupid and crazy too, and he wanted one—a special name for what ailed him.

He noticed that even the kids' stuff got special names. And he read about their supposed neuroses and phantom handicaps with the leer of an experienced and by now pretty cynical parent. I recognise that one, he would say to himself: otherwise known as Little Shit Syndrome. And I also recognise that one: otherwise known as Lazy Bastard Disorder. These disorders and syndromes, he was pretty sure, were just excuses for mothers and fathers to dope their children. In America, which was the

3

future, broadly speaking, most household pets (about sixty per cent) were on mood drugs.

Thinking back, Keith supposed that it would have been nice, ten or twelve years ago, to drug Nat and Gus—as a way of imposing ceasefires in their fratricidal war. And it would be nice, now, to drug Isabel and Chloe—whenever they weaponised their voices with shrieks and screeches (trying to find the limits of the universe), or whenever, with all the freshness of discovery, they said quite unbelievably hurtful things about his appearance. *You'd look a lot better, Daddy, if you grew some more hair.* Oh really. *Daddy, when you laugh, you look like a mad old tramp.* Is that a fact . . . Keith could imagine it easily enough: the mood-pill option. *Come here, girls. Come and try out this lovely new sweet.* Yeah, but then you'd have to consult the doctor, and trump up a case against them, and go and queue in the striplit pharmacy in Lead Road . . .

What was wrong with him? he wondered. Then one day (in October 2006), when it had stopped snowing and was merely raining, he went out into it, into the criss-cross, into the A to Z—the sodden roadworks, the great *dig* of London Town. And there were the people. As always, now, he looked from face to face, thinking, *Him*—1937. *Her*—1954. *Them*—1949 . . . Rule number one: the most important thing about you is your date of birth. Which puts you inside history. Rule number two: sooner or later, each human life is a tragedy, sometimes sooner, always later. There will be other rules.

Keith settled in the usual café with his Americano, his unlit French cigarette (a mere prop, now), his British broadsheet. And here it was, the news, the latest instalment of the thriller and tingler, the great page-turner called the planet Earth. The world is a book we can't put down . . . And he started reading about a new mental disease, one that spoke to him in a haunting whisper. It affected children, the new disease; but it worked best on grown-ups—on those who had reached the years of discretion.

The new disease was called Body Dysmorphic Syndrome or Perceived Ugly Disorder. Sufferers of BDS, or PUD, gazed at their own reflections and saw something even worse than reality. At his time of life (he was fifty-six), you resigned yourself to a simple truth: each successive visit to the mirror will, by definition, confront you with something unprecedentedly awful. But nowadays, as he impended over the basin in the bathroom, he felt he was under the influence of a hellish

4

hallucinogen. Every trip to the mirror was giving him a dose of lysergic acid; very occasionally it was a good-trip trip, and nearly always it was a bad-trip trip; but it was always a trip.

Now Keith called for another coffee. He felt much cheered.

Maybe I don't actually look like that, he thought. I'm just insane— that's all. So perhaps there's nothing to worry about. Body Dysmorphic Syndrome, or Perceived Ugly Disorder, was what he *hoped* he'd got.

When you become old . . . When you become old, you find yourself auditioning for the role of a lifetime; then, after interminable rehearsals, you're finally starring in a horror film—a talentless, irresponsible, and above all low-budget horror film, in which (as is the way with horror films) they're saving the worst for last.

Everything that follows is true. Italy is true. The castle is true. The girls are all true, and the boys are all true (Rita is true, Adriano, incredibly, is true). Not even the names have been changed. Why bother? To protect the innocent? There were no innocent. Or else all of them were innocent—but cannot be protected.

This is the way it goes. In your mid-forties you have your first crisis of mortality *(death will not ignore me);* and ten years later you have your first crisis of age *(my body whispers that death is already intrigued by me)*. But something very interesting happens to you in between.

As the fiftieth birthday approaches, you get the sense that your life is thinning out, and will continue to thin out, until it thins out into nothing. And you sometimes say to yourself: That went a bit quick. That went a bit quick. In certain moods, you may want to put it rather more forcefully. As in: *OY!! THAT went a BIT FUCKING QUICK!!!* . . . Then fifty comes and goes, and fifty-one, and fifty-two. And life thickens out again. Because there is now an enormous and unsuspected presence within your being, like an undiscovered continent. This is the past.

Book One

Where We Lay Our Scene

I

FRANCA VIOLA

It was the summer of 1970, and time had not yet trampled them flat, these lines:

> Sexual intercourse began
> In 1963
> (Which was rather late for me)—
> Between the end of the *Chatterley* ban
> And the Beatles' first LP.
>
> —Philip Larkin, "Annus Mirabilis"
> (formerly "History"), *Cover* magazine, February 1968

But now it was the summer of 1970, and sexual intercourse was well advanced. Sexual intercourse had come a long way, and was much on everyone's mind.

Sexual intercourse, I should point out, has two unique characteristics. It is indescribable. And it peoples the world. We shouldn't find it surprising, then, that it is much on everyone's mind.

Keith would be staying, for the duration of this hot, endless, and erotically decisive summer, in a castle on a mountainside above a village in Campania, in Italy. And now he walked the backstreets of Montale, from car to bar, at dusk, flanked by two twenty-year-old blondes, Lily and Scheherazade . . . Lily: 5' 5", 34-25-34. Scheherazade: 5' 10", 37-23-33. And Keith? Well, he was the same age, and slender (and dark, with a very misleading chin, stubbled, stubborn-looking); and he occu-

9

pied that much-disputed territory between five foot six and five foot seven.

Vital statistics. The phrase originally referred, in studies of society, to births and marriages and deaths; now it meant bust, waist, hips. In the long days and nights of his early adolescence, Keith showed an abnormal interest in vital statistics; and he used to dream them up for his solitary amusement. Although he could never draw (he was all thumbs with a crayon), he could commit figures to paper, women in outline, rendered numerically. And every possible combination, or at least anything remotely humanoid—35-45-55, for instance, or 60-60-60—seemed well worth thinking about. 46-47-31, 31-47-46: well worth thinking about. But you were always tugged back, somehow, to the archetype of the hourglass, and once you'd run up against (for instance) 97-3-97, there was nowhere new to go; for a contented hour you might stare at the figure eight, upright, and then on its side; until you drowsily resumed your tearful and tender combinations of the thirties, the twenties, the thirties. Mere digits, mere integers. Still, when he was a boy, and he saw vital statistics under the photograph of a singer or a starlet, they seemed garrulously indiscreet, telling him everything he needed to know about what was soon to be. He didn't want to hug and kiss these women, not yet. He wanted to rescue them. From an island fortress (say) he would rescue them . . .

34-25-34 (Lily), 37-23-33 (Scheherazade)—and Keith. They were all at the University of London, these three; Law, Mathematics, English Literature. Intelligentsia, nobility, proletariat. Lily, Scheherazade, Keith Nearing.

They walked down steep alleyways, scooter-torn and transected by wind-ruffled tapestries of clothing and bedding, and on every other corner there lurked a little shrine, with candles and doilies and the lifesize effigy of a saint, a martyr, a haggard cleric. Crucifixes, vestments, wax apples green or cankered. And then there was the smell, sour wine, cigarette smoke, cooked cabbage, drains, lancingly sweet cologne, and also the tang of fever. The trio came to a polite halt as a stately brown rat—lavishly assimilated—went ambling across their path: given the power of speech, this rat would have grunted out a perfunctory *buona sera*. Dogs barked. Keith breathed deep, he drank deep of the ticklish, the teasing tang of fever.

He stumbled and then steadied. What was it? Ever since his arrival, four days ago, Keith had been living in a painting, and now he was stepping out of it. With its cadmium reds, its cobalt sapphires, its strontian yellows (all freshly ground), Italy was a painting, and now he was stepping out of it and into something he knew: downtown, and the showcase precincts of the humble industrial city. Keith knew cities. He knew humble high streets. Cinema, pharmacy, tobacconist, confectioner. With expanses of glass and neon-lit interiors—the very earliest semblances of the boutique sheen of the market state. In the window there, mannequins of caramelised brown plastic, one of them armless, one of them headless, arranged in attitudes of polite introduction, as if bidding you welcome to the female form. So the historical challenge was bluntly stated. The wooden Madonnas on the alleyway corners would eventually be usurped by the plastic ladies of modernity.

Now something happened—something he had never seen before. After fifteen or twenty seconds, Lily and Scheherazade (with Keith somehow bracketed in the middle of it) were swiftly and surreally engulfed by a swarm of young men, not boys or youths, but young men in sharp shirts and pressed slacks, whooping, pleading, cackling—and all aflicker, like a telekinetic card trick of kings and knaves, shuffling and riffling and fanning out under the streetlamps . . . The energy coming off them was on the level (he imagined) of an East Asian or sub-Saharan prison riot—but they didn't actually touch, they didn't actually impede; and after a hundred yards they fell like noisy soldiery into loose formation, a dozen or so contenting themselves with the view from the rear, another dozen veering in from either side, and the vast majority up ahead and walking backward. And when do you ever see that? A crowd of men, walking backward?

Whittaker was waiting for them, with his drink (and the mailsack), on the other side of the smeared glass.

Keith went on within, while the girls lingered by the door (conferring or regrouping), and said,

"Was I seeing things? That was a new experience. Jesus Christ, what's the *matter* with them?"

"It's a different approach," drawled Whittaker. "They're not like you. They don't believe in playing it cool."

"I don't either. I don't play it cool. No one'd notice. Play *what* cool?"

"Then do what they do. Next time you see a girl you like, do a jumping jack at her."

"It was incredible, that. These—these fucking *Italians.*"

"Italians? Come on, you're a Brit. You can do better than *Italians.*"

"Okay, these wogs—I mean wops. These fucking beaners."

"Beaners are Mexicans. This is pathetic. *Italians,* Keith—spicks, greaseballs, dagos."

"Ah, but I was raised not to make distinctions based on race or culture."

"That'll be a lot of help to you. On your first trip to Italy."

"And all those shrines . . . Anyway, I told you, it's my origins. Me, I don't judge. I can't. That's why you've got to look out for me."

"You're susceptible. Your hands shake—look at them. And it's hard work being a neurotic."

"It's more than that. I'm not nuts, exactly, but I get episodes. I don't see things clearly. I misread things."

"Particularly with girls."

"Particularly with girls. And I'm outnumbered. I'm a bloke and a Brit."

"And a het."

"And a het. Where's my brother? You'll have to be a brother to me. No. Treat me as the child you never had."

"Okay, I will. Now listen. Now listen, son. Start looking at these guys with a bit of perspective. Johnny Eyetie is a play-actor. Italians are fantasists. Reality's not good enough for them."

"Isn't it? Not even this reality?"

They turned, Keith in his T-shirt and jeans, Whittaker in his horn-rims, the oval leather elbow-patches on his cord jacket, the woollen scarf, fawn, like his hair. Lily and Scheherazade were now making their way towards the stairs to the basement, eliciting, from the elderly all-male clientele, a fantastic diversity of scowls; their soft shapes moved on, through the gauntlet of gargoyles, then swivelled, then exited downward, side by side. Keith said,

"Those old wrecks. What are they looking at?"

"What are they looking at? What do you think they're looking at?

Two girls who forgot to put any clothes on. I said to Scheherazade, *You're going to town tonight. Put some clothes on. Wear clothes.* But she forgot."

"Lily too. No clothes."

"You don't make cultural distinctions. Keith, you should. These old guys have just come staggering out of the Middle Ages. Think. Imagine. You're first-generation urban. With your wheelbarrow parked in the street. You're having a little glass of something, trying to keep a grip. You look up and what do you get? Two nude blondes."

". . . Oh, Whittaker. It was so horrible. Out there. And not for the obvious reason."

"What's the non-obvious reason?"

"Shit. Men are so cruel. I can't say it. You'll see for yourself on the way back . . . Look! They're still there!"

The young men of Montale were now on the other side of the window, stacked like silent acrobats, and a jigsaw of faces squirmed against the glass—strangely noble, priestlike faces, nobly suffering. One by one they started dropping back and peeling away. Whittaker said,

"What I don't get is why the boys don't act like that when *I* walk down the street. Why don't the girls do jumping jacks when *you* walk down the street?"

"Yeah. Why don't they?"

Four jars of beer were slewed out in front of them. Keith lit a Disque Bleu, adding its smoke to the sulphurous snorts and sneezes of the coffee machine, and the ambient mist of superstitious distrust: the bar-goers and their cataract gaze, seeing and dismissing, seeing and not believing . . .

"It's your own fault," said Whittaker. "Not content with being naked—you're blondes."

The girls were still quietly colouring and bristling, and blowing the stray strands from their brows. Scheherazade said,

"Well we're sorry about that. And next time we'll wear clothes."

"And we'll wear veils," said Lily. "And why blondes?"

"See," he went on, "blondes are the opposite of their pious ideal. This gets them thinking. Brunettes are hopeless—they're Italians. They won't fuck you unless you swear you're going to marry them. But the blondes. Blondes'll do *anything*."

Lily and Scheherazade were blondes, one a blue-eyed, one a brown—

they had the transparent complexions, the candour of blondes . . . Scheherazade's face, Keith thought, now had about it a look of quiet surfeit, as if she had hurriedly but successfully eaten something rich and greedy. Lily seemed pinker, puffier, younger, the eyes inward, reminding him (as he kept wishing she wouldn't) of his little sister; and her mouth looked taut and underfed. They were both making the same movement, beneath the brow of the table. Smoothing their dresses kneeward. But the dresses wouldn't go.

"God, it's almost worse in here," said Scheherazade.

"No, it's worse out there," said Lily.

"Mm. At least in here they're too old to leap up and down."

"And too hoarse to yodel in your face."

"They hate us in here. They want to lock us up."

"They probably hate us out there too. But at least they want to fuck us."

"I don't know how to break this to you," said Whittaker, "but they don't want to fuck you out there either. They're fruits. They're all terrified. Listen. I'm friends with the top model in Milan. Valentina Casamassima. Also a blonde. When she comes to Rome or Naples and they all go crazy, she turns on the biggest guy there and says, *Come on, let's fuck. I'll suck your cock here in the street. I'm going down on you* right now."

"And?"

"They quail. They back off. They crumple."

Keith uneasily turned his head away. And felt a shadow cross the harlequinade—the harlequinade of his time. Near the centre of this shadow was Ulrike Meinhof, strolling nude in front of the Palestinian recruits (*Fucking and shooting,* she said—*they're the same*), and even further in there was Cielo Drive, and Pinkie and Charles. He said,

"That's too high a price."

"Meaning?"

"Well they're not *really* trying to pull you, are they, Lily. I mean, that's not how you set about it, is it. Their only hope," he said, "is to stumble on a girl who dates football teams." This was perhaps obscure (and they were staring at him), so he went on, "That's what Nicholas calls them. My brother. I mean, there aren't many of them, but they do exist. Girls who like dating football teams."

"Ah," said Lily, "but by pretending to like dating football teams, Valentina proves that they don't even want girls who like dating football teams."

"Exactly," said Keith (who was in fact quite confused). "Still. Valentina. Girls outtoughing the boys like that. It's . . ." It was what? Overexperienced. Uninnocent. Because the young men of Montale were at least innocent—even their cruelty was innocent. He said helplessly, "Italians are play-actors. It's all a game anyway."

"Well, Lily," said Whittaker, "now you know what to do. When they whoop and leap, you know what to do."

"Vow to go down on them."

"Yeah. Vow to do that."

"I was in Milan in the spring, with Timmy," said Scheherazade, leaning back. "And you didn't have to vow to go down on them. You got stares and whistles and that gurgly sound they make. It wasn't a . . . a circus, like here."

Yes, thought Keith, a circus—the highwire, the trapeze, the clowns, the tumblers.

"You didn't get crowds. You didn't get *queues*."

"Walking backward," said Lily. Who now turned to Scheherazade, and said with a solicitous, almost a motherly urge, "Yes. But you didn't look like you look now. In the spring."

Whittaker said, "It isn't that. It's Franca Viola."

So the three of them attended to Whittaker, with the reverence due to his horn-rimmed gaze, his fluent Italian, his years in Turin and Florence, and his unimaginable seniority (he was thirty-one). There was also the fact of Whittaker's *orientation*. What was their attitude to homosexuals, around then? Well, they accepted them utterly, while also congratulating themselves, every couple of minutes, for being so amazingly tolerant. But they were moving beyond that now, and homosexuality had the glamour of the vanguard.

"Franca Viola. Incredible girl. She changed everything."

And with a proprietorial air Whittaker told the tale. Franca Viola, Keith learnt, was a Sicilian teenager who had been kidnapped and raped by a rejected suitor. Which was one thing. But kidnap and rape, in Sicily, provided the alternative route to confetti and wedding bells. Whittaker said,

"Yeah, that's right. What the penal code calls *matrimonio riparatore*. So, Keith, if you ever get tired of playing the guitar under the balcony with a flower in your mouth, and if the jumping jacks don't work, remember there's always another way. Kidnap and rape . . . Marrying the rapist. That's what Franca Viola's family was telling her to do. But Franca didn't go to the church. She went to the police station in Palermo. And then it was national news. Incredible girl. Her people still wanted her to marry the rapist. So did the village, so did the islanders, so did half the mainland. But she didn't. She pressed charges."

"I don't understand," said Scheherazade. "Why in the world would you marry the rapist? It's prehistoric."

"It's tribal. Shame and honour. It's like Afghanistan. Or Somalia. Marry the rapist, or your menfolk'll kill you. She didn't do that. She didn't marry him—she put him *in jail.* And she changed everything. Now Milan and Turin are partly civilised. Rome is beginning to get better. Naples is still a nightmare. But all that shit is draining southward. Sicily will be the last to go. Franca was sixteen when it happened. Incredible girl."

Keith was thinking that his sister Violet, another incredible girl, was also sixteen. In any kind of shame-and-honour arrangement, Violet would have been murdered long ago—by Keith himself, and his brother Nicholas, and his father, Karl, with the moral and logistical support of Uncle Mick and Uncle Brian. He said,

"What happened to her, Franca?"

"She got married properly a couple of months ago. To a lawyer. She's your age now." Whittaker shook his head. "Incredible girl. The balls on that girl. So when we go outside again, and the boys swoop down on you, you'll have two choices. Go with Valentina Casamassima. Or think of Franca Viola."

They drank one last beer and talked about the May Events, in France in 1968, and the Hot Autumn, in Italy in 1969—and the slogans. Never Work. Never trust anyone over twenty-five. Never trust anyone who hasn't been to prison. The Personal is Political. When I think of revolution, I want to make love. It is forbidden to forbid. *Tutto e subito:* All and Now. The four of them agreed that they would settle for that. They would all now settle for All and Now.

"That's how babies feel," said Keith. "Apparently. They think: I am nothing and I should be everything."

Then it came over them that it was now time to go, to go out there, and Whittaker said,

"Oh yeah. Another thing that drives them crazy is that you're almost certainly on the Pill. They can't get over it—what that means. Contraception is still illegal. And abortion. And divorce."

"How do they get around that?" said Scheherazade.

"Easy. Hypocrisy," said Lily. "Mistresses. Backstreet abortions . . ."

"How do they get around contraception?"

Whittaker said, "They're meant to be great experts at coitus interruptus. Great artists of timely withdrawal. Oh, sure. I know what that means."

"What?"

"They come up your arse."

"Whittaker!"

"Or all over your face."

"*Whitt*aker!"

And Keith felt it again (he felt it several times a day): the tingle of licence. Everyone could swear now, if they wanted to. The word *fuck* was available to both sexes. It was like a sticky toy, and it was there if you wanted it. He said,

"Yeah, Whittaker, I've been meaning to ask you. You say *ass* just like we say *arse*. Without sounding the *r*—*ahce.* Lily and Scheherazade say it like that, but they grew up in England. Like you say *lahndscape.* And those *aunts* that bothered you at the picnic. Those aunts crawling up your shorts. That gave *me* the horrors. What's that accent?"

"Boston Brahmin," said Scheherazade. "Posher than the Queen. Now if we may be excused . . ."

As the girls moved off again Whittaker said,

"I think I see how it's going to go. Out there. What happened? Earlier. Tell."

"You know, boys are so cruel. And so fucking *rude.*" Keith said that the mimed rampage, out there, the sexual revolution, was also a kind of plebiscite. "On the girls. And guess who won. I found myself thinking, Would you please insult Lily too?"

"Mm. Would you have the common courtesy to treat Lily like a stripper in a bear pit?"

"Scheherazade's the people's choice. By acclamation . . . She's transformed, isn't she. I haven't seen her for a few months, and I barely recognised her."

"Scheherazade, in general, is absolutely glorious. But let's face it. It's her breasts."

". . . So you understand about Scheherazade's breasts."

"I like to think so. I paint, after all. And it's not the size, is it. It's almost despite the size. On that wandlike frame."

"Yeah. Precisely so."

"I read something the other day," said Whittaker, "that made me warm to breasts. I saw them in a different light. In evolutionary terms, this guy says, breasts are there to imitate the arse."

"The arse?"

"The breasts ape the arse. As an inducement to having sex face to face. When women evolved out of oestrus. You must know what oestrus is."

Keith knew. From Gk *oistros* "gadfly or frenzy." Heat. Whittaker said,

"So arselike breasts sweetened the bitter pill of the missionary position. Just a theory. No, I understand about Scheherazade's breasts. The secondary sexual characteristics in their Platonic form. Plan A for the tits. I understand—in principle." He looked at Keith with affectionate contempt. "I don't want to squeeze them or kiss them or bury my sobbing face in them. What d'you guys *do* with breasts? I mean they don't lead anywhere, do they."

"I suppose that's true. They're sort of a mystery. An end unto themselves."

Whittaker glanced over his shoulder. "I can tell you they're not universally admired. Someone I know had a very bad reaction to them. Amen."

"Amen?" Amen—pronounced *Ahmun*—was Whittaker's reclusive Libyan boyfriend (who was eighteen). Keith said, "What's Amen got against Scheherazade's breasts?"

"That's why he never goes down to the pool any more. He can't take her breasts. Wait. Here they come."

Did this mean—could this truly mean—that Scheherazade, down by the pool (as Lily had hinted), sunbathed topless? There was still time for Keith to say, "Are you seriously telling me her tits look like an arse?"

He himself paid a quick visit to the basement—before they all filed out into the street . . . The Italian toilet, and its negative sensual adventure: what was it trying to say? Southern Europe in its entirety had it like this, even France, the grime-scored crouchpads and flowing knee-high stopcocks and the fistfuls of yesterday's newspaper wedged between pipe and brickwork. The stench that threaded acid into the tendons of the jaw, and made the gums sting. Don't flatter yourself, the toilet was saying. You are an animal, made of matter. And something in him responded to this, as if he sensed the proximity of a beloved beast, moist and leathery in the spiced darkness.

Then they all filed out into it—past the female mannequins in the boutique windows, and into the swirling oestrus, the pitiless verdict, the mortifying unanimity of the young men of Montale.

So they drove from town to village—to the castle, perched like a roc on the mountainside.

You know, I used to have a lot of time for Keith Nearing. We were once very close. And then we fell out over a woman. Not in the usual sense. We had a *disagreement* over a woman. I sometimes think he could have been a poet. Bookish, wordish, letterish, with a very peculiar provenance, a committed romantic who, nonetheless, found it fairly difficult to get any kind of girlfriend—yes, he could have been a poet. But then came his summer in Italy.

2

SOCIAL REALISM
(OR SLAG FOR LOVE)

Keith lay between the sheets, up in the south tower. He was thinking, not very constructively, about the frayed burlap sack Whittaker had slung over his shoulder as they left the bar. *What's that?* Keith asked. *Mail?* Italian mailbags, he assumed, like English mailbags, were manufactured in the nation's prisons; and Whittaker's burlap sack did indeed look felon-woven (it seemed most disaffectedly thrashed together), with a sociopathic, faintly purplish tint somewhere in its weft. Keith found, these days, that his thoughts often turned to law enforcement. Or, rather, to its absence, its inexplicable laxity . . . *Not mail,* said Whittaker. *Mail gets delivered direct. In here is—the world. See?* And there it was, the world: *Time*s, *Life*s, *Nation*s, and *Commentary*s, *New Statesman*s, *Listener*s, *Spectator*s, *Encounter*s. So it was still out there—the world. And the world already seemed very quiet and very distant.

"So I suppose you agree," said Lily in the dark, "with the young men of Montale."

"No I don't," said Keith. "I wanted to do a jumping jack at you. To tell you so."

". . . Have you any idea what that was like? For me?"

"Yeah, I think I have. I get that when I'm with Kenrik. They don't do jumping jacks at him, but they—"

"Well he is beautiful."

"Mm. It's hard to take, but remember. The world has bad taste. It goes for the obvious."

"*What's* obvious?"

"Come on, you know what I mean. The superficial. Her looks may please the vulgar, Lily. But you're much cleverer and more interesting."

"Mm. Thanks. But I know what's going to happen. You're going to fall in love with her. Not that you've got a hope, of course. But you will. How could you not? You. You fall in love with anything that moves. You'd fall in love with female football teams. And Scheherazade. She's beautiful and sweet and funny. And madly grand."

"That's what puts me off. She's irrelevant. She's from another world."

"Mm. Actually you do know when you're outclassed," she said, making herself more comfortable on the bolster of his arm. "An A-one berk like you. A chippy little guttersnipe like you." She kissed his shoulder. "It's all in the names, isn't it. Scheherazade—and *Keith*. Keith's probably the most plebeian name there is, don't you think?"

"Probably . . . No. *No,*" he said. "The earl mareschals of Scotland were Keiths. There was a line of them, each called Lord Keith. Anyway, it's better than Timmy." He thought of gangly, lackadaisical Timmy, in Milan, with Scheherazade. "*Timmy.* Call that a name? Keith's a better name than Timmy."

"*All* names are better names than Timmy."

"Yeah. It's impossible to think of a Timmy ever doing anything cool. Timmy Milton. Timmy Keats."

". . . Keith Keats," she said. "Keith Keats doesn't sound very likely either."

"True. But Keith Coleridge? You know, Lily, there was a poet called Keith Douglas. *He* was posh. His middle name was Castellaine and he went to the same prep school as Kenrik. Christ's Hospital. Oh yeah. And the K in G. K. Chesterton stands for Keith."

"What's the G stand for?"

"Gilbert."

"Well there you are then."

Keith thought of Keith Douglas. A war poet—a warrior poet. The fatally wounded soldier: *Oh mother, my mouth is full of stars . . .* He thought of Keith Douglas, dead in Normandy (a shrapnel wound to the head) at twenty-four. Twenty-four. Lily said,

"All right. What would you do if she vowed to go down on you?"

Keith said, "I'd be surprised, but I wouldn't be shocked. Just disappointed. I'd say, Scheherazade!"

"Yeah, I bet. You know, I sometimes wish . . ."

Keith and Lily had been together for over a year—with a recent, term-long hiatus, variously known as the Interregnum, the Intermission, or simply Spring Break. And now, after the trial separation, the trial reunion. Keith owed her a great debt of gratitude. She was his first love, in this particular sense: he had loved many girls, but Lily was the first who loved him back.

"Lily, it's you I love."

The nightly interaction, the indescribable deed, now took place, by candlelight.

"Was it fun?"

"What?"

"Pretending I'm Scheherazade."

". . . Lily, you keep forgetting how high-minded I am. Matthew Arnold. *The best which has been thought and said.* F. R. Leavis. *Felt life in its full creative force.* Besides, she's much too tall for me. She's not my type. You're my type, Lily."

"Mm. You aren't as high-minded as you used to be. Anything like."

"Yes I am . . . It's her character. She's sweet and kind and funny and bright. And she's *good.* That's the real turn-off."

"I know. It's nauseating. And she's grown about a foot too," said Lily, now indignantly wide awake. "And almost all of it's in her neck!"

"Yeah, it's quite a neck all right." Lily had already said a good deal about Scheherazade and her neck. She compared her to a swan and sometimes—depending on her mood—an ostrich (and, on one occasion, a giraffe). Lily said,

"Last year she was . . . What's *happened* to Scheherazade?"

Scheherazade awoke one morning from troubled dreams to find herself changed in her bed into a . . . According to the famous story, of course, Gregor Samsa (pron. *Zamza*) was transformed into *an enormous insect,* or alternatively *a giant bug,* or alternatively—and this was the best translation, Keith felt sure—*a monstrous vermin.* In Scheherazade's case, the metamorphosis was a radical ascension. But Keith couldn't fix on the right animal. A doe, a dolphin, a snow leopard, a winged mare, a bird of paradise . . .

But first the past. Lily and Keith broke up because Lily wanted to act like a boy. That was the heart of the matter, really: girls acting like boys was in the air, and Lily wanted to try it out. So they had their first big row (its theme, ridiculously, was religion), and Lily announced *a trial separation.* The words came at him like a jolt of compressed air: such trials, he knew, were almost always a complete success. After two days of earnest misery, in his terrible room in the terrible flat in Earls Court, after two days of *desolation,* he phoned her and they met up, and tears were shed—on both sides of the café table. She told him to be evolved about it.

Why should boys have all the fun? said Lily, and blew her nose into the paper napkin. *We're anachronisms, you and me. We're like childhood sweethearts. We should've met ten years from now. We're too young for monogamy. Or even for love.*

He listened to this. Lily's announcement had left him bereaved, orphaned. That was what it meant: from Gk *orphanos* "bereaved." Keith was actually born bereaved. And the suspicion that this would remain his natural state was clearly far too readily available to him. Desolate: from L. *desolare* "abandon," from *de-* "thoroughly" + *solus* "alone." He listened to Lily—and of course he knew it already. Something was churning in the world of men and women, a revolution or a sea change, a realignment having to do with carnal knowledge and emotion. Keith did not want to be an anachronism. And I think I can say that this was his first attempt at character management: he decided to get better at not falling in love.

If we don't like it, we can always . . . I want to act like a boy for a while. And you can just go on as you are.

Thus Lily had her hair restyled, and bought lots of miniskirts and cut-off culottes and halter tops and see-through blouses and knee-length patent-leather boots and hoop earrings and kohl eyeliner and all the other things you needed before you could act like a boy. And Keith just stayed the same.

He was better placed than her, in a way: he had some experience of acting like a boy. Now he took it up again. Pre-Lily, before Lily, he often encountered a difficulty more associated with acting like a girl: his emotions. And he didn't always see things clearly. He got it completely wrong, for instance, about what everyone was calling *free love*—as a succession of horrified hippies could quietly attest. He thought it meant what it said; but it wasn't love that was on offer from the mushroom-pale flower-daughters of the capital, with their charts, tarot cards, and Ouija boards. Some girls were still saving themselves for marriage;

some were still religious—and even the hippies were only very slowly going secular . . .

After Lily, post-Lily, the new rules of engagement seemed more firmly emplaced. The year was 1970, and he was twenty: to this historic opportunity he brought his minimal handsomeness, his plausible tongue, his sincere enthusiasm, and a certain willed but invigorating coldness. There were disappointments, near things, there were some miraculous acquiescences (which still felt like *liberties,* in the shame-and-honour sense: involving impudence, overfamiliarity, taking advantage). Anyway, the free-love business certainly worked best with girls who were acting like boys. New rules—and new and sinister ways of getting everything wrong. He acted like a boy, and so did Lily. But she was a girl, and could do more of it than he could.

Come with me, said Lily, three months later on the phone, *come with me to Italy for the summer. Come with me to a castle in Italy with Scheherazade. Please. Let's have a holiday from it. You know, there are people out there who don't even* try *to be kind.*

Keith said he would call her back. But almost at once he felt his head give a sudden nod. He had just spent a night of almost artistic misery with an ex-girlfriend (her name was Pansy). He was frightened and bruised and, for the first time, obscurely but intensely guilty; and he wanted to return to Lily—to Lily, and her middleworld.

How much will it cost?

She told him. *And you'll need spending money for when we go out. The thing is, I'm no good at being a boy.*

All right. And I'm glad. I'll start borrowing and saving up.

His ridiculous row with Lily. She blamed him, basically, for confusing and therefore corrupting Violet with Christianity when she was a little girl. Which was true enough as far as it went. *I tried to de-convert her when she was nine,* he explained. *I said,* God is just like Bellgrow: your imaginary friend. *And yet she stuck with it.* Lily said, *And you'd think religion would make her behave. And it's had the opposite effect. She's sure she'll be forgiven for everything because she believes in a fool in the sky. And it's all your fault.*

Lily was of course an atheist—an open-and-shut atheist. Keith argued that this position wasn't quite rational; but then Lily's rationalism wasn't rational in the first place. She hated astrology, naturally, but she hated astronomy too: she hated the fact that light bent, that gravity slowed down time. She was especially exasperated by the behaviour of subatomic particles. She wanted the universe to behave sensibly. Even Lily's dreams were quotidian. In her dreams (this was rather shyly disclosed), she went down the shops, or washed her hair, or had a snack for lunch while she stood by the fridge. Openly suspicious of poetry, she had no patience with any work of fiction that strayed from the sternest social realism. The only novel she unreservedly praised was *Middlemarch*. Because Lily was a creature of the middleworld.

Come with me to a castle in Italy with Scheherazade. It should be said that the Scheherazade section of Lily's proposal, so far as Keith was concerned, was neither here nor there. Scheherazade, when he last saw her, around Christmas, was as usual the frowning philanthropist in flatties and spectacles; she did community service, and CND and VSO, and drove a van for Meals on Wheels; and she had a loose-limbed boyfriend called Timmy, who liked killing animals and playing the cello and going to church. But then Scheherazade awoke from troubled dreams.

Keith was assuming that social realism would hold, here in Italy. And yet Italy itself seemed partly fabulous, and the citadel they occupied seemed partly fabulous, and the transformation of Scheherazade seemed partly fabulous. Where was social realism? The upper classes themselves, he kept thinking, were not social realists. Their modus operandi, their way of operating, obeyed looser rules. He was, ominously, a K in a castle. But he was still assuming that social realism would hold.

D oes she still do all that stuff with the old wrecks?"

". . . Yes, she does. She misses it."

"Where's her bloke, anyway? Where's 'Timmy'? And when's he coming?"

"That's what *she* wants to know. She's quite cross with him. He's supposed to be here by now. He's in Jerusalem doing God knows what."

". . . Her mum's the one I fancy. Oona. Nice and little." He thought about Pansy. And thinking about Pansy necessarily involved him in thinking about her mentor, Rita. So he said, "Uh, Lily. You know I said Kenrik may be coming down this way. He's going camping with the Dog. Sardinia, supposedly."

"What's the Dog's real name? Is it Rita? . . . Describe."

"Well. From up north. Rich working-class. Very big eyes. Very wide mouth. A redhead. And no curves at all. Like a pencil. Could we put them up for a night, Kenrik and Rita?"

"I'll ask Scheherazade. And I'm sure we can make room," she said, yawning, "for a nice titless ginge from up north. I'll look forward to it."

"You'll marvel at her. She's a real expert at acting like a boy."

Lily turned on her side, making herself smaller, wholer, more complete and compressed. He always felt for her when she did this, and he followed the relays of her jolts and twitches, these tiny surprises on the way to oblivion. How could she find it, without embracing the irrational? . . . Lily sometimes liked to hear his voice as she trembled off, into the religion of sleep (he usually summarised the novels he was reading), so he moved up close, saying,

"There'll be enough novels later. Listen. The very first girl I ever kissed was taller than me. Probably just a few inches but it felt like about a yard. Maureen. We were at the seaside. I'd already kissed her in the bus shelter, sitting down, and I had no idea how we were going to kiss goodnight. But there was a drainage pipe on the ground by her caravan, and I stood on that. Nice kisses. No tongues or anything. We were too young for tongues. It's important not to do things you're too young for. Don't you think?"

"Scheherazade," said Lily thickly. "Get her near a drainage pipe." Then, more clearly, "How, how could you not be in love with her? You fall in love so easily and she's . . . Goodnight. I sometimes wish . . ."

"Goodnight."

"You. Such a slag for love."

When we wake up in the morning (he thought), it's the first task that lies ahead of us: the separation of the true from the false. We have to dismiss, to erase the mocking kingdoms made by sleep. But at the close of the day it was the other way round, and we sought the untrue and the fictitious, sometimes snapping ourselves awake in our hunger for nonsensical connections.

It was true what she said, or it used to be. Slag for love. To do with his peculiar provenance. He fell in love with girls so easily—and he went on loving them. He still loved Maureen: he thought of her every day. He still loved Pansy. Is that why I'm here? he wondered. Is that why I'm here with Lily in the castle in Campania? Because of the tragic night with Pansy, what it said, what it meant? Keith closed his eyes and searched for troubled dreams.

The dogs in the valley barked. And the dogs in the village, not to be outdone, barked back.

Just before dawn he went up and smoked a cigarette on the watch-tower. The day was coming in like a current. And there it was suddenly, over the flank of the massif, God's red rooster.

3

POSSIBILITY

We are trapped by the truth, and the truth was that it all built *very slowly . . .*

"There's one boring thing," Scheherazade said on the first afternoon as she led him up the tower.

But it wasn't boring yet. For some fifteenth-century reason, the steps were bracingly steep, and on the half-landings, when she swivelled, Keith could see up her skirt.

"What's that?"

"I'll show you when we get to the top. We've got a while to go. It's endless."

High-mindedly, Keith averted his gaze. Then he looked. Then he looked away (and beheld, through the slit in the stone wall, a pale horse with its flanks shuddering). He looked, and looked away—until, with an audible click of the neck, he locked into position and went ahead and *looked.* How was it that he had never taken due note of this—the beauty, power, wisdom, and justice of women's thighs?

Scheherazade said over her shoulder, "Are you a great seer of sights?"

"I'm on for anything."

"What, mad keen?"

He already seemed to be in a film—a salacious thriller, perhaps—in which every line of intersexual dialogue was an irresistibly smutty pun. They kept climbing. Now he searched for a single entendre. "Keen enough. I've got all this reading to do," he said. "Catching up. *Clarissa. Tom Jones.*"

"Poor you."

For the record, Scheherazade's lower undergarment was workaday and pale brown (rather like the kind of pants Lily used to wear—

before). As against that, its hem was loosely neglectful of the right but-
tock, providing a slice of white in the crux of all that churning bronze.
She said,

"There's talk of the Passo del Diavolo."

"What's that?"

"The Devil's Pass. Very twisty and scary. So I'm told. Right. Now
you two are in this turret. And I'm in that turret." She gestured on
down the passage. "And we share the bathroom in between. That's the
boring thing."

". . . Why's it boring?"

"Lily refuses to share a bathroom with me. We've tried it. I'm just too
messy. So she'll have to go halfway down the tower and turn right. But I
don't see why *you* should. Unless you've got a thing about messiness too."

"I haven't got a thing about messiness."

"Look."

The skylit bathroom was long and narrow and L-shaped, its left-
hand turn presided over by a burnished towel rack and two wall-sized
mirrors. They moved through it. Scheherazade said,

"We share. So here's the drill. When you come in from your room,
you lock the door to my room. And when you leave you unlock it. And
I do the same . . . This is me. God I'm a slob."

He took it in, the white nightdress aslant the tousled bed, the heaps
of shoes, the pair of starched jeans, trampled out of, all agape, but still
on its knees and still cupping the form of her waist and hips.

"It always staggers me," he said. "Girls' shoes. Girls and shoes. So
many. Lily's brought a whole suitcaseful. Why are girls like that about
shoes?"

"Mm, well, I suppose the feet are the only bit of you that can't possibly be pretty."

"You think that's it?"

They looked down at the ingenuous occupants of Scheherazade's flip-
flops: the curve of the insteps, the visible flex of the ligaments, the ten
daubs of crimson in five different sizes. He always found it affecting—
that girls bothered with that dot on the outer toe. The pinkie toe, like
the runt of the litter. But you couldn't neglect it, obviously—each little piggie needed its red beret. He said,

"*You* have pretty feet."

"Not too bad." The ten toes gave a self-conscious ripple. "As feet go.
Feet. They're such dumb-looking things."

"I suppose. Some people claim it's quite complicated. Girls and feet. May I?" He picked up the left-sided representative of a pair of shoes he knew to be characterised as *court*. "What could look *less* like a foot than that?" He meant the degree of stylisation or contrivance. "With that arch and that heel."

"Mm. Feet. And to think some people have a fetish about feet."

"Imagine what that says about you."

"Terrifying. It's very easy," she said, as they came back through the already significant bathroom, "to forget to unlock. Everyone does it all the time. There's even a little bell—see? If I'm locked out, I ring it." She rang it: a soft but determined purr. "You've got one too. I always forget. Which is boring of me."

Scheherazade gazed his way with her peculiar directness, the golden, idealistic eyes, the very level brows. When that look fell on Keith, he had the feeling that she had already dealt with every matter concerning him—birth, background, appearance, even stature. Important, too (he disconnectedly thought), was the fact that she called her mother Mum, and not Mummy (like all the other female members of her class). This spoke to Keith of her essentially egalitarian soul. But the strangest thing about Scheherazade was her smile, which was not the smile of a beautiful girl. There was too much collusion in the softly rippled lids—collusion in the human comedy. The smile of a beautiful girl was a sequestered smile. *It hasn't sunk in yet,* said Lily. *She doesn't know.* And could that really be? Keith said to Scheherazade,

"I'm not easily bored. Nothing's boring. Looked at in the right way."

"Oh I know that line," she said. "If it's boring, it's interesting because it's boring."

"That's right. Being boring's interesting."

"And it's interesting that nothing's boring."

Aren't they nice, the young? They've stayed up till dawn for two years drinking instant coffee together, and now they're opinionated—they have opinions.

"Still," she said, "repetition's boring. Come on, it is. Like this weather. Sorry about that."

"Never apologise for the weather."

"Well I want to swim and sunbathe. And it's rainy. And it's almost *cold* . . . But at least it's sweaty."

"At least it's sweaty. Thank you for having me. It's fabulous here. I'm entranced."

Keith knew of course that the psychological meaning of *feet* was itself twofold. These brutal trotters were a permanent reminder of your animality, your unforgiven, non-angelic status as a human being. They also performed the menial task of connecting you to solid ground.

So here was the castle, its battlements kept aloft on the shoulders of the four fat-girthed giants, the four towers, the four terraces, the circular ballroom (with its orbital staircase), the domed pentagonal library, the salon with its six sets of windows, the baronial banqueting hall at the far end of the implausibly and impractically long corridor from the barnyard-sized kitchen, all the antechambers which receded, like facing mirrors, into a repetitive infinity. Above was *the apartment* (where Oona spent almost all her time); below was *the dungeon floor,* half submerged in the foundational soil, and giving off the thinnest mist of what smelled to Keith like cold sweat.

"There's an old word for the way she regards you, Scheherazade," he said to Lily in the pentagonal library. He was up on a ladder, almost at dome level. "You'll think it just means being patronising. But it's a term of praise. And humble gratitude. *Condescension,* Lily." From eccles. L., from *con-* "together" + *descendere* "come down" ("together" was the important part). "Her being a Lady and all."

"She's not a Lady. She's an Honourable. Her dad was a viscount. You mean she treats you," said Lily, "for all the world as if you aren't a berk."

"Yeah." He was talking about the class system. But he was thinking about the looks system—the beauty system. Would there ever be a revolution in looks, where those who were last would now be first? "I suppose that's about the size of it."

"And you only give the nobs praise and gratitude because you know your proper place. You're a good berk."

Keith wouldn't like you to think that he was forever oiling up to the girls of the aristocracy. In recent years (I should point this out) he had spent the vast majority of his spare time oiling up to the girls of the proletariat—and then the girls, or the girl, of the professional intelligentsia (Lily). Of the three strata, working-class girls were the most puritanical. Upper-class girls, according to Kenrik, were the most promiscuous, the *fastest,* as they themselves put it, faster even than the girls of the middle class, who, of course, would soon decisively outspeed them . . . He returned to the leather-decked davenport, where he was reading *Clarissa* and taking notes. Lily was on a chaise longue, and had before her something called *Interdiction: On Our Law and Its Study.* He said,

"Ooh, you didn't like that, did you. Dear oh dear."

"You're a sadist," said Lily.

"No I'm not. You'll notice that I have no quarrel with other insects. Not even wasps. And I actually admire spiders."

"You tramped down to the village to get the spray. What's wrong with the swat?"

"It leaves a horrible smear when you use the swat."

The fly he had just fatally drenched was now stretching its back legs, like an old dog after a long nap.

"You like the lingering death, that's all."

". . . Does Scheherazade act like a boy? Is she promiscuous?"

"No. I'm far more promiscuous than she is. Numerically," said Lily. "You know. She did the usual amount of necking and getting felt up. Then she took pity on a couple of dopes who wrote her poems. And regretted it. Then nothing for a while. Then Timmy."

"And that's it?"

"That's it. But now she's blooming and restless and it's given her ideas."

According to Lily, Scheherazade had an explanation for her particular metamorphosis. *I was a pretty sixteen-year-old,* she apparently confided, *but after my father got killed I turned plain—I suppose because I wanted to hide.* So her exterior, her outward semblance, was depressed or retarded by the death of the father. Came the plane crash, and then the years passed. And the fog slowly thinned and cleared, and her physical talents, stacked and circling in the sky, could now approach and make their touchdown.

"What sort of ideas?"

"Spreading her wings. But she still doesn't know she's beautiful."

"Does she know about her figure?"

"Not really. She thinks it's going to go away. As quickly as it came. How come you've never read one?"

As well as a sexual trauma, Keith also had a suitcaseful of remedial reading ahead of him. "Never read what?"

"An English novel. You've read the Russians and the Americans. But you've never read an English novel."

"I've read *an* English novel. *The Power and the Glory. Vile Bodies.* I've just never read *Peregrine Pickle* or *Phineas Finn.* I mean, why would you? And *Clarissa*'s killing me."

"You should've thought of that before you changed subjects."

"Mm. Well I was always more of a poetry man."

". . . A poetry man. Who tortures insects. Insects feel pain too, you know."

"Yeah, but not much." He looked on as his buzzing victim twirled and drilled on its axis. "We are to the gods as flies to wanton boys, Lily. They pluck us for their sport."

"You say you don't like the smear. But you just like to watch them squirm."

Were *all* flies hated by Keith Nearing? He liked butterflies and fireflies. But butterflies were moths with antennae, and fireflies were soft-bodied beetles with luminescent organs. He imagined, sometimes, that Scheherazade would be like that. Her organs would glow in the dark.

Keith took to going up to the tower, around noon, to read an English novel—and to get a little peace. This visit to his bedroom tended to coincide with the shower that Scheherazade tended to take before lunch. He heard it, her shower. The heavy beads of water sounded like car tyres on gravel. He sat there, with the morbidly obese paperback on his lap. Then he waited for five pages before going in to wash his face.

On the third day he unlatched and pushed on the bathroom door and it didn't give. He listened. After a moment he reached for the bell with a ponderous hand (why did this feel so significant?). More silence, the click of a distant latch, a shuffling tread.

Scheherazade's warmed face now emanated out at him from the folds of a thick white towel.

"See?" she said. "I told you."

The lips: the upper as full as the nether. Her brown eyes and the balance of their gaze, her level brows.

"It won't be the last time either," she said. "I promise."

She swivelled, he followed. She turned left and he watched the three of them retreat, the real Scheherazade and the simulacra that slid across the glass.

Keith remained in the L of mirrors.

. . . Dud, Possible, Vision. How many hours, how many very happy hours he had spent, with his mother Tina, playing Dud, Possible, Vision, in the Wimpy Bar, the coffee bar (the Kardomah), the art-deco milk bar.

What about those two over there by the jukebox, Mum?

The boy or the girl? . . . Mm. Both of them are Low Possibles.

And they graded not just strangers and passers-by but everybody they knew. One afternoon, as Tina ironed, it was asserted by him, and confirmed by her, that Violet was a Vision—fit to take her place along-side Nicholas. And Keith, who was eleven, said,

Mum? Am I a Dud?

No, dear. Her head went back an inch. *No my love. You've got a* face *face, that's what you've got. It's full of character. You're a Possible. A High Possible.*

. . . All right. Let's do a womie.

Which womie?

Davina.

Oh a Vision.

Mm. A High Vision. What about Mrs. Littlejohn?

But in fact he had more or less resigned himself to ugliness (and he stoically answered to *Beak* in the schoolyard). Then this changed. The necessary event came to pass, and this changed. His face changed. The jaw and especially the chin asserted themselves, the upper lip lost its niblike rigidity, the eyes brightened and widened. Later he came up with a theory that would disquiet him for the rest of his life: looks depended on happiness. A disinclined, a hurt-looking little boy, he suddenly started to be happy. And now here was his face in the rippled and speckly mirror in Italy, pleasantly unexceptionable, firm, dry. Young. He was happy enough. Was he happy enough to survive—to live with—the ecstasy of being Scheherazade? He also believed that beauty was mildly infectious, given close and prolonged contact. It was a universal presumption, and he shared it: he wanted to experience beauty—to be legitimised by beauty.

Keith rinsed his face under the tap, and went down to the others.

Chill, moist clouds swirled above them, and all around them—and even beneath them. Slivers of grey vapour detached themselves from the mountaintop and slid lollingly down the slopes. They seemed to lie on their backs, resting, in the grooves and culverts, like exhausted genies.

Keith actually went and waded through one of these dropped cloudlets. Not much bigger than Scheherazade in her thick white towel, it reclined on a low terrace beyond the paddock. The steamy, smoky presence stirred and altered under his tread, and then flattened out again, with the back of its hand placed long-sufferingly across its brow.

A week went by, and the new arrivals had yet to avail themselves of the Olympian swimming pool in its grotto setting. Keith decided that it would do his heart good to see the girls enjoying themselves down there—particularly Scheherazade. Meanwhile, *Clarissa* was boring. But nothing else was.

I often wish," said Lily in the dark, "I often . . . You know, I'd give up some of my intelligence for a bit more beauty."

He believed her and he felt for her. And flattery was futile. Lily was too intelligent to be told she was beautiful. This was the form of words they had settled on: *she was a late developer.* He said,

"That's—Lily, that's old-fashioned. Girls are supposed to be clever careerists now. It doesn't all depend on how good a husband you can pull."

"You're wrong. Looks matter even more. And Scheherazade makes me feel like a duck. I hate being compared. You wouldn't understand, but she's torturing me."

Lily once told him that when girls turned twenty their beauty, if they were due any, would be coming in. Hers, she hoped, was on its way. But Scheherazade's was in, it was here, it was just off the boat. The physical prizes being doled out to her—what Grammys and Tonys and Emmys, what Palmes d'Or. Keith said,

"Your beauty will be along very soon."

"Yes but *where is it?*"

"Let's think. Less intelligence, and more beauty. It's like the line— What would you rather? Look cleverer than you are, or be stupider than you look?"

"I don't want to look clever. I don't want to look stupid. I want to look beautiful."

He said slackly, "Well, given a choice, I'd like to be rougher and cleverer."

"How about *shorter* and cleverer?"

"Uh, no. I'm already too short for Scheherazade. She's way up there. How could I ever get it started?"

Lily came closer and said, "Easy. I'll tell you how to do it."

This was becoming the regular prelude to their nightly act. And necessarily or at least helpfully so, because Lily, here in Italy, for reasons that were not yet clear to him, seemed to be losing her sexual otherness. She was like a first cousin or an old family friend, someone he had played with as a child and known all his life. "How?" he said.

"You just lean across when you're on the floor playing cards with her last thing. And start kissing her—her neck, her ears. Her throat. Then you know that loose little knot she has on her shirt when she's showing off her brown midriff? You could just pluck at that. And it'll all fall open. Keith, you've stopped breathing."

"No, I was just suppressing a yawn. Go on. The little knot."

"You pluck at that, and then her breasts'll just tumble out at you. Then she'll hoick up her skirt and lie back. And arch herself so you can peel off her pants. Then she'd go on her side and unbuckle your belt. And you can stand up, and it won't matter that she's taller than you. Because she'll be safely down on her knees. So you needn't worry."

When it was over, she turned away from him, saying, "I want to be beautiful."

He held her. Hold to Lily, he told himself. Hold to your level. Don't—don't—fall in love with Scheherazade . . . Yes, it was safest to walk the middle ground, content to be a Possible. That was the thing to hope for. Possibility.

"You know, Lily, with you I'm myself. With everyone else I seem to be acting. No. Working. With you I'm myself," he said. "Effortlessly myself."

"Mm, but I don't want to be myself. I want to be someone else."

"I love you, Lily. I owe you everything."

"And I love you too. I've got that at least . . . Girls need looks even more now. You'll see," she said. Then she slept.

4

THE DEVIL'S PASS

So there were trips (a resort and then a fishing village on the Med, some ruined temple, some national park, the Passo del Diavolo), and there were visitors. Like the current trio: the Dakotan divorcee, Prentiss; her quite recently adopted daughter, Conchita; and their friend and help-mate Dorothy, known as Dodo. It would not be seemly, I think, to give their vital statistics, but we can disclose the most vital statistic of all: Prentiss, Keith guessed, was "about fifty" (i.e., somewhere or other between forty and sixty), Conchita was twelve, and Dodo was twenty-seven. In addition, Prentiss was a Possible, Conchita was a Vision, and Dodo was a Dud. Little Conchita came from Guadalajara, Mexico, and wore clothes of mourning—for her father, Keith was told.

Prentiss, who was waiting on the outcome of a will, her grand-mother's (on which their European tour partly depended), was tall and angular. Conchita was actually a bit on the tubby side (with a curva-ceous pot belly). And Dodo, a trained nurse, was stunningly fat. Keith was dismayed by the size of Dodo's head—by how small it was or seemed. Her head was almost an irrelevance, like a teacup on an ice-berg. The visitors all slept up in Oona's vast apartment.

He was not a very typical twenty-year-old, Keith, but he was typical in this one regard: he thought that everyone was placidly static in their being—everyone except twenty-year-olds. But even he could tell that the lives of the three visitors were subject to drama and flux. There was of course the matter of Conchita's bereavement. There was Prentiss's legacy, and the resolution of various feuds and tensions with her par-ents, her many uncles and aunts, her three brothers and her six sisters. And there was even some suspense involving Dodo, whose corpulence, in tendency, was not deliquescent but all stretched and taut; her flesh had the tensile quality of a stiffly inflated balloon. Would Dodo, during her stay, actually burst? Or just go on getting fatter and redder in the face? These were real questions.

"If only the sun would come out," said Scheherazade, as they ate breakfast in the kitchen. "Because seriously fat people adore swimming pools."

"Do they?" said Keith. "What for?"

"Because they're lighter by the weight of the water they displace."

"That's a lot of water," said Lily. "I can't decide whether or not I want to see her in a swimsuit. Think of her poor knees."

There was a silence, spent in sympathy for Dodo's knees. Then Keith said ponderously,

"When I look at her, I feel I'm staring at the size of an unhappiness."

"Mm. Or d'you think it's glands?"

"It's not glands," said Lily, "it's *food*. Did you see her last night with the goose? She had thirds."

"And Conchita tucked in too."

"It makes you think, though, doesn't it. Dodo."

"Doesn't it. It puts your own worries," concluded Lily, "in some kind of proportion."

Servants served the castle, a team of them coming in every day from the village. Keith had never before been in the regular company of servants.

Both his biological parents were of the servant class, his mother a maid, his father a gardener. Keith in any case had his leftist sympathies (very tame compared to those of the fiery Nicholas), so of course he had a kind of relationship with the castle servants, a relationship of nods and smiles and, surprisingly, bows (formal inclinations of the upper body), and a few words of Italian, especially with Madonna, who among other things made all the beds, and with Eugenio, number two with the roses and the lawns. They were both about twenty-five and were sometimes seen laughing when they were briefly alone together. And therefore Keith started to wonder if love would come to them, to the tender of beds and the tender of flowers. And Eugenio saw also to the terraces, and the growing of fruit.

It was transparent, then, the style of his thinking. But by now he had read enough to know about the bitterness of servants, the helpless rage nursed by servants. And he hoped he hadn't inherited it; he reasoned that the bitterness solidified later in servant life, when they got older, which his parents had failed to do . . . Keith was brought up to think that all this—his provenance—was not that important, was not *that* important. And for the time being he agreed. He had always known, incidentally, that Tina was not his mother, that Karl was not his father. This information was his lullaby. *You are adopted and we love you,* crooned Tina, for at least a year before he began to understand. Provenance wasn't so very important. And he thought he'd say a word or two to Conchita about it before she went on her way north.

Conchita had two cuddly animals, Patita (a duck) and Corderito (a lamb), and she loved *to colour;* she was twelve and she still loved to colour. *I'm dying to colour* (pron. *collar*), she would say as lunch drew to an end. *May I be excused* (pron. *ess-cuced*)? *I'm dying to colour.* And she would go to the library with her colouring books. Seasides, cars and buses, girls' clothes, and of course all kinds of flowers.

Lily approached him as he sat at the circular stone table on the upper-most shelf of the east garden. It was warmer now, but still overcast, with the bilious, low-pressure light that augurs thunder. Scents were detectable in the sallow air: *il gelsomino* (jasmine), *il giacinto* (hyacinth), *l'ibisco,* and narcissus, narcissus . . . Keith was still processing the events, or non-events (he couldn't tell), of the journey through the Passo del Diavolo with Scheherazade at his side. He couldn't tell. Who could he ask?

"You're going from one to the other," Lily noted.

"Well it's the only way of getting through it. Not *Tom Jones. Tom Jones* is great. And Tom's my kind of guy."

"In what way?"

"He's a bastard. But *Clarissa*'s a nightmare. You won't believe this, Lily," he said (and he had, incidentally, decided to swear more), "but it's taking him two thousand pages to fuck her."

"Christ."

"I know."

"But honestly, listen to you. Usually, when you read a novel, you go on about things like, I don't know, the level of perception. Or the depth of the moral order. Now it's just fucks."

"It's not *just* fucks, Lily. One fuck in two thousand pages. That's not *just* fucks."

"No, but it's all you go on about."

There weren't any serpents in this garden, but there were flies: in the middle distance, vague flecks of death—and then, up close, armoured survivalists with gas-mask faces. And there were silky white butterflies. And great drunken bees, throbbing orbs that seemed to carry their own electrical resonance; when they collided with something solid—tree bole, statuary, flowerpot—they twanged back and away, the positive charge repelled by the positive. Lily said,

"Two thousand pages was probably how long it took. When?"

"Uh—1750. Even then he has to get her stupefied on drugs. Guess what she does afterwards. Dies of shame."

"And it's meant to be sad."

"Not really. She goes out babbling about how happy she is. I'll be uh, *rejoicing in the blessed fruits of His forgiveness . . . in the eternal mansions.* She's very literal about it. Her heavenly reward."

"Her reward for getting fucked on drugs."

"Lily, it was rape. Actually it's pretty clear she fancied him something rotten from the start. They're all in a fever about violation." She was looking at him receptively, now, so he continued, saying, "Girls can fuck in *Tom Jones*—if they're yobs or nobs. A milkmaid. Or a decadent hostess. But Clarissa's bourgeois, so she has to get fucked on drugs."

"Because then it's not her fault."

"Yeah. And she can go on claiming she didn't want to. Anyway, she did hold out for two thousand pages. That's a million words, Lily. Did you hold out for a million words? When you were acting like a boy?"

Lily sighed and said, "Scheherazade's just been telling me how frustrated she is."

". . . Frustrated how?"

"Sexually. *Ob*viously."

He lit a cigarette and said, "Does she know she's beautiful yet?"

"Yes. And she knows about her tits too. In case you're wondering."

"And what does she think of them?"

"She thinks they're just fine. But they're very tender now and they're making her extra frustrated."

"She has my sympathy. Still. Timmy'll be along in a chapter or two."

"Maybe. She just got a letter. He can't tear himself away from

40

Jerusalem. She's cross with him now all right. And she has high hopes of Adriano."

"Who's Adriano?"

Lily said, "You're not expressing yourself very clearly. Don't you mean, Who the fuck is Adriano?"

"No I don't. You're following a false lead, Lily. Who's Adriano? . . . All right. Who the fuck is Adriano?"

"There. It goes better with your scowl." Lily laughed sharply and briefly. "He's a notorious playboy. And a count. Or one day will be."

"All Italians are counts."

"All Italians are poor counts. He's a rich count. He and his dad have a castle *each.*"

"Big deal. I didn't realise until yesterday. There are castles everywhere in Italy. I mean, there's one every few hundred yards. Did they have uh, did they have a long brawling-baron period?"

"Not particularly," said Lily, who was reading a book called *Italy: A Concise History.* "They kept getting invaded by barbarians. Hang on." Methodical Lily consulted her notes. "The Huns, the Franks, the Vandals, the Visigoths, and the Goths. Then the Keiths. The Keiths were the worst."

"Were they. And when do we meet Adriano?"

"That's what she needs. Someone of her own station. And did you thrill," said Lily, "to the Devil's Pass?"

In the back seat of the Fiat, he was placed between Prentiss and Scheherazade—while Lily rode in what was called *the cabriolet* (a smart red convertible) with Oona and Conchita. In the back seat Prentiss stayed exactly where she was, but Scheherazade swayed into him, swooned into him, on every tight turn. It was raining hard, and all they did, in the Passo del Diavolo, was steer through it and stare out at it. Keith, anyway, was attending to a riot of sense impressions: he was like the young men of Montale, each of his glands and hormones a Jocopo, a Giovanni, a Giuseppe. Her arm and thigh coming to press against his arm and thigh. Her golden aromatic hair gathering, folding, for a moment, on his chest. Was this usual? Did it mean anything? *Hey, Prentiss,* he wanted to say. *You've been around. What's all this then? Watch. Scheherazade keeps . . .*

"It was good," he said. "Very twisty and scary."

"Mm. Scary. I bet. With Dodo wedged into the front seat."

"And always on the side of the precipice—thanks very much."

"God. You must've been terrified."

In the car Keith was telling himself that Scheherazade was simply half-asleep. And for a couple of minutes, just before they turned back, she did go under—with her head resting trustfully on his shoulder. Then she snapped to, coughed, and glanced up at him through her lashes with her unreadably generous smile . . . And it all began again, her arm against his arm, her thigh against his thigh. *What d'you think, Lily? Gaw, you should have seen her in the bathroom the other day. Another lapse with the lock, Lily, and there she was in blue jeans and bra. Is she trying to tell me something?* Or maybe her habits of thought had not quite drawn level with the facts of her transformation. In the full-length mirror she still sometimes saw the mousy philanthropist in sensible shoes and spectacles. And not a winged horse in blue jeans, and a white brassiere with the narrowest trim of blue. He said,

"Whittaker seemed always to be fighting the wheel over to the left."

"That's why I went with Oona. Your front right tyre looked completely flat."

"I kept thinking the car'd just give up and flip over. How was it for you, the Devil's Pass?"

"All right. Conchita dozed. And the roof leaked."

He closed his eyes. The bruiser bees twanged and fizzed. He sat up. A crouched fly on the stone tabletop was staring at him. He waved it away but it returned, and crouched there, and stared. Little skull and cross-bones . . . In this matter of Scheherazade, the butterflies, as Keith saw it, took his side. The butterflies: party toys, doll-scale fans and hankies—hopeless optimists, twittering dreamers.

Unusually for a twenty-year-old (the privilege followed from his peculiar situation), Keith was aware that he was going to die. More than that, he knew that when the process began, the only thing that would matter was how it had gone with women. As he lies dying, the man will search his past for love and life. And this is true, I think. Keith was good on the big picture. But the immediate situation, the immediate process—this he often saw with unreliable eyes.

My God, they've got *every*thing here," he said. He meant the library, from whose shelves he extracted a copy of *Pamela* (subtitle: *Virtue Rewarded*), by the author of *Clarissa,* and a copy of *Shamela,* by the author of *Tom Jones. Shamela* was a parodic attack on *Pamela,* and sought to expose its false piety, its penny-wise vulgarity, and its incompetently sublimated lechery—*lechery,* ult. of W. Gmc origin and rel. to *lick.*

"So Prentiss's rich now," he said. "Or richer."

"Richer. I think," said Conchita.

She got up from the desk and went and stood by the window. The shapely curve of her abdomen in the shapeless black smock. In her anomalously deep voice she said,

"I want to get the exact colour of the roses."

Thea sacked collar . . . He said, "How did you come here from America, Conchita? I mean by boat or by plane. Plane? What class?"

"Prentiss in the front. Us in the back."

"So how did Dodo manage? I'm thinking of the meals. The tray."

The twelve-year-old returned to her desk and picked up the pencils of mauve and purple, saying, "Dodo pulls it down as far as she can, and fills the"—she made the shape of a V with her straightened hand—"and fills the gap with magazines. And puts the tray on that."

Maga-sceence . . . Keith looked forward to passing this on to Lily (fatso know-how for the jets), but not as keenly as he would have done—before. He still owed Lily a great debt of gratitude. Gratitude was what he was good at. It was his one emotional talent, he believed. Sitting, now, he was grateful for the chair beneath him, the book before him. Grateful, and pleasantly surprised. He was grateful for the ballpoint in his hand, pleasantly surprised by the cap on the ballpoint. Conchita said,

"Then she eats everything. Even all the butter."

As he had intended to say, he said, "I might not see you tomorrow before you go. Did you know I'm adopted? Being adopted—it's all right."

Her head didn't move but her irises came up off the page, and he was immediately ashamed, because he realised that being adopted (as a minor existential burden) was not very high on the schedule of Conchita's troubles. She said,

"It's all right."

"I meant later on." For a moment he contemplated her, the lunar purity of her brow, the hectic dusk-and-rose of her cheeks. "I meant later on. I'm sorry about your parents. Goodbye."

"*Adiós. Hasta luego.* I think we're coming back."

*M*a's *out, Pa's out, let's talk dirt. Pee po belly bottom drawers.* That's what his mother and her sisters used to chant (she told him), back in 1935 . . .

"I can assure you I'm no stranger," said Keith, "to Islamic talent. They're the best-looking people on earth, don't you think?"

"Yes I do. The whole crescent."

He and Whittaker were playing chess on *the sunset terrace*—facing west. Whittaker had been telling him about the dos and don'ts of being in love with Amen. The don'ts were by far the more numerous. Keith said,

"Me, I went out with two Muslim chicks. Ashraf. And little Dilkash."

"What nationalities? Or don't you distinguish."

"Ashraf from Iran, Dilkash from Pakistan. Ashraf was great. She liked a drink and she came across on the first night. Dilkash wasn't like that at all."

"So Ashraf was a do. And Dilkash was a don't."

"Yeah. Dilkash didn't." Keith twisted in his seat. The truth was that he had a bad conscience about Dilkash. "I never asked Nicholas and I still can't work it out. So I'll ask you."

Whittaker in fact bore close affinities with Nicholas. They both talked in formed sentences—even in formed paragraphs. They both knew everything. And at first you thought they looked not unalike. As a pupil for many years in a British boarding school, Nicholas had naturally had his gay period. But there was political will in Nicholas, now: what politicians, at least, called *steel.* And this didn't hold for Whittaker, with his elbow patches and his thick glasses. Keith said,

"Ashraf, Dilkash. Iran, Pakistan—what's the diff? I mean, they're both Arabs. Aren't they? No. Wait. Ashraf's an Arab."

"No, Ashraf's not an Arab either. She's a Persian. And the diff, Keith," said Whittaker, "is that Iran is a decadent monarchy and Pakistan is an Islamic republic. At least in name. More wine. Oh, sorry. You don't, do you."

"I do a bit. Go on then . . . Round at Dilkash's place her parents drank pop in the evenings. Can you credit it. A grown man and woman, in the evenings, drinking pop. Does Amen drink?"

"Drink? To him that's just—oh, unbelievably gross. He smokes hash. On the other hand."

"Ashraf was great, but with Dilkash I never . . ." Keith paused. "Now what's this drama," he said, lighting a cigarette, "about Amen and Scheherazade's breasts?"

"Amen," said Whittaker, with his face low over the chessboard, "is much queerer than I am. *Much.*"

"So there are degrees. Yeah, that makes sense. Of course there are."

"Of course there are. And Amen's *very* queer. Hence the seriousness of the problem he's having with Scheherazade's breasts."

"I never see him any more."

"Nor do I. It's worse than ever."

"The exercises."

"The exercises."

"Too thin."

"Too fat. He was too thin until about Monday afternoon. Now he's too fat."

Whittaker ate most of his meals with them, but he was not a castle-dweller. He and Amen shared a modern studio further down the slope. Keith thought of Amen, eighteen years old, and piratically handsome with his missing upper incisor; and the fuzzy eyelashes that scrolled all the way up and over, like harem slippers. He didn't want to say so—but Keith quite fancied Amen. Whenever he saw him he felt a fleeting pressure on his chest. It was nothing like the alpweight continuously applied by the presence of Scheherazade; still, it was there. Keith said,

"He's such a lovely colour. And with those muscles, he looks like he's wearing armour. Golden armour. *Lily* thinks she's not thin enough. Puppy fat. Six months ago she had what she called *a puppy-fat attack.*"

"She should come over. Amen's turned the whole upper floor into an orthopaedic ward. All these weights on strings. There are bits of his body he doesn't like. He's *furious* with bits of his body."

"Which bits?"

45

"It's his goddamned forearms, it's his goddamned calves. It's the proportions. He's artistic and it's the proportions. The relationship."

"Is that his quarrel with Scheherazade's breasts? The relationship?"

"No. It's more basic than that."

They sat under the shadow of their sister mountain. Above and beyond, the clouds sought the gothic colours and buffoonish configurations they would be needing, in readiness for the thunderstorm—now long-awaited. Whittaker said,

"It's like with the gaping yokels in the bar in Montale. Only more extreme. Amen, Keith, grew up in the Sahara Desert. The women he's used to all look like bowling balls. Then one afternoon he's down at the pool, he comes up for air, and sees a six-foot blonde. Topless. And there they are, staring down at him. Scheherazade's breasts."

So it's true, thought Keith. "Topless," he said nauseously. "You're kidding. I thought Lily was just teasing me."

"No. Scheherazade down at the pool—topless as nature intended. And now, with Amen, it's become a negative obsession."

"Mm. I'm trying to see them from his point of view."

"It's complicated. He's artistic and it's complicated. Sometimes he says they're like a terrifying sculpture called *Female*. And not stone—metal. And get this. Sometimes he says they belong in a thick glass jar. In a backroom at the lab. With all the other freaks."

"That *is*—that's formidably gay . . . Me, I expect to take them in my stride. I think I'm pretty clear-headed about breasts. I was bottle-fed, see. No topless period in babyhood."

Corpulent raindrops began here and there to fall.

"It might be less trouble," said Whittaker, "if we all looked like bowling balls. Amen's sister, Ruaa, she's not fat, I don't think, but she's . . . She looks like—what's that horror film with Steve McQueen? Oh yeah. *The Blob*."

The thirty-two pieces on the sixty-four squares were now reduced to seven a side.

"Draw?" said Keith. "Here's a tip for Amen. The next time he sees Scheherazade's breasts, can't he just pretend they're an arse? Are there bits of *your* body Amen doesn't like?"

"He doesn't like any of it. I'm thirty-one. You guys are all kids. Too big, too small, too this, too that. When are you ever going to feel good about your bodies?"

After dinner he played an hour of cards with Scheherazade on the thick-rugged floor of a distant chamber (*the den* or *the gunroom,* with its moose's head, its crossed cutlasses, its miniature cannons on either side of the grate). Keith had spent most of the evening in conversation with her mother, so he was now well placed (Scheherazade's fanned cards were six inches from his chin) to see what youth was. Her face was actually narrower than Oona's, but the flesh itself was full and plump. And it had a self-magnifying quality, her flesh—the plump peel of youth . . . There was much laughing and, on her part, some beaming; every now and then she beamed at him. Just before twelve they climbed the tower by lanternlight.

"I'm Scheherazade," said Lily in the dark. "This is Scheherazade lying here. But she's been drugged. She's completely at your mercy. She's helpless on drugs."

"What kind of drugs?"

"She can't speak. She's helpless. Do your worst!"

Later Lily said,

"No. Stay. Have it by the window. Lean out."

He leant out, and smoked. The night was starless, with silenced cicadas . . . Seventeen years ago to the hour, on July 15, 1953, he was allowed down to see the stranger in his parents' bedroom. Karl was now also present, and there was a midwife packing up, and his mother's face on the pillow was flushed and moist and wise. Keith was not quite four. With a suddenly flaring heart he approached the cradle—but no, in his mind it wasn't a cot or a basket: it was a bed, and on it lay a creature the size of an established infant, with thick, damp, chest-length blonde hair, and warm cheeks, and the knowing smile of sleep. A false memory (or so he always assumed), touched up or restored by facets and lustres that awaited her in the future—because he had seen a newborn baby or two, meanwhile, and he had no illusions about how they looked. But now (leaning out, smoking, thinking) he decided that this impossible vision, his formed sister, was what he actually saw, in his hallucinatory state, smashed on love and protectiveness.

No stars and no cicadas. Just a quarter-moon, lying on its back and at an expectant angle, like a baby girding itself for the bottle or the breast.

"Where's our storm?" said Lily as he joined her.

Keith sank back. Lily too was like a foster-sister to him . . . All will be decided here, he thought. All will be decided in the castle in Italy. Right from the start, as he scaled the tower with his bags, three steps below Scheherazade (the segment of white in all that churning bronze), he strongly intuited that his sexual nature was still open to change. For a while it worried him: he would go gay and be swept off his feet by Amen; he would fall for one of the prettier ewes in the field beyond the paddock; at the very least, he would develop a sick thing for, say, Oona, or Conchita—or even Dodo! . . . This is the climax of my youth, he thought. All will be decided here.

Then it came, an hour later, two hours, three hours. Amateurish, tinny, like a pantomime shotgun. You could almost see the bearded villain in his frock coat, and the flabby smoke ring widening over his blunder-buss. Amateurish—and neolithically loud.

"You?" Lily suddenly said.

"Yes," he said. "Me."

"Mm. Tomorrow all your dreams will come true."

"How's that?"

"After the storm. We display ourselves. Her. Down by the pool."

FIRST INTERVAL

The Me Decade wasn't called the Me Decade until 1976. In the summer of 1970 they were only six months into it; but they could all be pretty sure that the 1970s was going to be a me decade. This was because all decades were now me decades. There has never been anything that could possibly be called a you decade: technically speaking, you decades (back in the feudal night) would have been known as thou decades. The 1940s was probably the last we decade. And all decades, until 1970, were undeniably he decades. So the Me Decade was the Me Decade, right enough—a new intensity of self-absorption. But the Me Decade was also and unquestionably the She Decade.

It was all being arranged, history was arranging it—just for Keith. Or so he sometimes felt. It was all being done with Keith in mind.

Among the poor (according to a distinguished Marxist historian), *women went out to work after 1945 because, to put it crudely, children no longer did so.* Then higher education, with the female share of university places set to double from a quarter to a half. Also, and never for a moment forgetting Keith's needs: antibiotics (1955), the Pill (1960), the Equal Pay Act (1963), the Civil Rights Act (1964), the National Organization for Women (1966), "The Myth of the Vaginal Orgasm" (1968), the National Abortion Rights Action League (1969). *The Female Eunuch* (love and romance are illusions), *Women's Estate* (the nuclear family is a consumerist hoax), *Sexual Politics* (bottomless insecurity drives the man's will to dominate), and *Our Bodies, Ourselves* (how to emancipate the bedroom) all appeared in 1970, back to back, and with perfect timing. It was official. It was here, and just for Keith.

.   .   .

Not until the year 2003 did the year 1970 catch up with him.

The date was April 1, or April Fool's Day, and he was fresh from the most extraordinary encounter with his first wife. Keith's immediate response, when the encounter ended, was to call his second wife and tell her about it (his second wife thought it was outrageous). When he got home, he gave a more detailed version to his third wife, and his third wife, who was nearly always insanely cheerful, thought it was very funny.

"How can you laugh? It means my whole life is meaningless."

"No it doesn't. It just means your first marriage was meaningless."

Keith looked down at the backs of his hands. "My second marriage isn't looking too clever either. Suddenly. Talk about a rebound."

"Mm. But you *can't* say that. Think of the boys. Think of Nat and Gus."

"That's true."

"What about your third marriage?"

"That's looking all right. Thanks to you, my darling. But all that time I was just . . . Now I'm feeling even worse. In my head."

The doorbell buzzed. "That's Silvia," she said (meaning her grown-up daughter). "Be positive about it. You should thank God you never had any children with that mad old bitch."

. . .

There was a beautiful girl, called Echo, who fell in love with a beautiful boy. One day, when he was out hunting, the boy strayed apart from his companions. He called out to them: Where are you? I'm here. *And Echo, watching him from a cautious distance, called back,* I'm here. I'm here, I'm here, I'm here.

I'll stay, *he said.* You come to me.

Come to me. To me, to me, to me.

Stay there!

Stay there, *she said in tears.* Stay there, stay there, stay there.

He stopped and listened. Let's meet halfway. Come.

Come, *she said.* Come, come, come.

. . .

Our Marxist historian writes:

Why brilliant fashion designers, a notoriously non-analytic breed, sometimes succeed in anticipating the shape of things to come better than professional predictors is one of the most obscure questions in history; and, for the historian of culture, one of the most central.

What, then, was the sartorial commentary on the period under review? For the Italian trip, Keith was careful to standardise his not very extensive wardrobe: jeans, shirts, T-shirts, and his only suit. But you should have seen him in the spring, trolling up and down the King's Road, with an identically dressed Kenrik, in high-heeled snake-skin boots, elephant loons, a belt as bulky as a grappling hook, paisley-patterned shirt, a military tunic with gilt epaulettes, and a grimy silk scarf knotted round the throat.

As for the girls, well, take Scheherazade, for instance: the modest Cleopatra sandals (with kitten heels), and then a vast expanse of bare brown calf and thigh, the two firm stems going up and up and on and on, and up, and on, until, at the last possible instant (the suspense was killing everybody), the corolla, in the form of a light summer skirt hardly broader than a watchstrap; next, starting persuasively low on the hips, another expanse (the moist concavity of the navel), ending in the gathered loop of the transparent top, and finally the unsupported gulch of the cleavage.

To summarise and approximate: the boys were dressed as clowns, as they eagerly (and quite rightly) signed away about a third of their estate *without conditions*. And the girls? Was it—all the display—was it meant to sweeten the pill of the transfer of power? No, because they were going to get the power anyway. Was it a form of saying thanks? Maybe, but they were going to get the power anyway. Now he thinks that the display was a display, not of female power, quite, but of female magnitude.

. . .

Keith stood over the sink in his study or studio at the far end of the garden, tending to the wound on the back of his hand. This wound had been sustained in early March, when his knuckle came into unemphatic contact with a brick wall. The injury was now on its third scab, but he was still tending to it, dabbing it, blowing on it, cherishing it—his poor hand. These little hurts were like little pets or potted plants you were abruptly given the care of, needing to be fed or walked or watered.

As you pass the half-century, the flesh, the coating on the person, begins to attenuate. And the world is full of blades and spikes. For a year or two your hands are as nicked and scraped as a schoolboy's knee. Then you learn to protect yourself. This is what you'll go on doing until, near the end, you are doing nothing else—just protecting yourself. And while you are learning how to do that, a doorkey is a doornail, and the flap on the letterbox is a meat-slicer, and the very air is full of spikes and blades.

. . .

It was April 10, 2003, and in the caff Keith was reading the paper. Baghdad had fallen. This new struggle, between Islam and Christendom: Keith's infantile but persistent thought (which came from the squashed poet in him) was something like, But we used to get on so well, the believers and the infidels . . . It wasn't really a fight between different religions, or between different countries. It was a fight between different centuries. What would future historians call it? The Time War, perhaps, or the War of the Clocks.

The secret police of the regime that had just been deposed went by the name of Jihaz al-Haneen. This included the torture corps—whose operatives were scholars of pain. Yet Jihaz al-Haneen translated as *the instrument of yearning.* The only way the phrase made any sense to him was as a description of the human body.

. . .

He had his wound coming, a different kind of wound, in the castle in Italy. It was the sensory opposite of torture: her pincers of bliss, her lips, her fingertips. And what remained in the aftermath? Her manacles, her branding irons.

It was here and all around them. What were they to do, the young ones? The response to the sea change, the realignment of power: this was the thing they were beginning to feel their way through, along with hundreds of millions of others. It was a revolution. And we all know what happens in a revolution.

You see what goes, you see what stays, you see what comes.

Book Two

Dreamball

I

WHERE WERE THE POLICE?

Under the burning axle of the parent star, he sat topless, poolside, his face inclined over the pages of *Peregrine Pickle*. Peregrine had just attempted (and failed) to drug (and ravish) Emily Gauntlet, his wealthy fiancée . . . Keith kept looking at his watch.

"You keep looking at your watch," said Lily.

"No I don't."

"Yes you do. And you've been down here since seven."

"Eight thirty, Lily. Beautiful morning. And I wanted to say goodbye to Conchita. You know, I have a bond with Conchita. And it's more than us both being adopted . . . Anyway, I wasn't thinking about the time. I was thinking about drugging girls. They're *all* at it."

Lily said, "What's the time got to do with drugging girls? I suppose drugging girls was your only hope—back then. That was how you did it."

"Yeah." He thought, now, of another ex-girlfriend: Doris. "Yeah. Instead of going on at them about the sexual revolution. Bending their ear about the sexual revolution . . . Have you decided yet? Whether to get your top brown?"

"Yes. And the answer's no. Put yourself in my position. How would you like to sit here naked with Tarzan?"

He stood up and strolled to the water's edge. Oona and Amen had independently come and gone—their morning lengths; and Keith was wondering about the unreliable optics of the swimming pool. Its walls and floor were a metallic grey. When the water was still, its surface shone solidly and impenetrably, like a mirror; when the water rippled, or when the light changed (from shadow to dazzle, but also from dazzle to shadow), it became translucent, and you could see the fat plug at the bottom of the deep end, and even the odd coin or hairclip. He wondered at it, this grey new world of glass and opacity, and not the wobbly, slippery, ribbony blue of the pools of his youth.

"Here she comes."

Scheherazade was decanting herself downward through the three tiers of the terraced gradient, and now moved through a bower-and-hothouse setting as she neared the water, barefoot but in tennis wear—a quilted skirt of pale green, and a yellow Fred Perry. She twirled off the lower half of it (he thought of an apple being pared) and tugged herself out of the upper; and then she made wings of her long arms and unclipped the upper half of her bikini (and it was gone—with the merest shrug it was gone), saying,

"Here's another boring thing."

Of course, this wasn't boring either. On the other hand, it would have been disgracefully callow and bourgeois (and uncool) to take the slightest notice of what was now on view; so Keith had the difficult task of looking at Lily (in housecoat and flip-flops and still in the shade) while simultaneously communing with an image that was fated, for now, to remain in the loneliest wilderness of his peripheral vision. After thirty seconds or so, to ease the trapped nerves in his trapped neck, Keith stared up and out—at the gold slopes of the massif, echoing in the pale blue. Lily yawned, saying,

"What's the other boring thing?"

"Well, I have just been informed—"

"No, what was the *other* boring thing?"

Lily was looking at Scheherazade. So Keith did too . . . And this was the thought, this was the question they awakened in him, Scheherazade's breasts (the twinned circumferences, interproximate, interchangeable): *Where were the police?* Where on earth were the police? It was a question he was often asking himself, in these uncertain times. Where were they, the police? Scheherazade said,

"Sorry, I'm not with you."

"I mean, what was the *first* boring thing?"

"The bathroom," said Keith. "You know. Sharing it. The bell."

"Ah. Now what's the *second* boring thing?"

"Let me just get wet."

Scheherazade stepped forward and kept going and dived . . . Yes, the

inexpressible tedium of the shared bathroom, where, the previous afternoon, Scheherazade appeared with her bent knees pressed together, and
her fists closed tight on the hem of a pink T-shirt, as with short shuffling steps she backed laughingly away . . . Now she surfaced and
climbed out with tensed tendons, covered in bright beads of water. And
it was all laid before you. Topless as nature intended. And yet to Keith
the spectacle seemed anti-natural—seemed unsound, like a slippage of
genre. The cicadas turned their volume up, and the sun glared. She said,

"Just cold enough. I hate it when it's soupy. You know. Blood-heat."

Lily said, "Is the second boring thing more boring than the first boring thing?"

"About the same—no, more boring. We're being *joined.* Oh well.
These things are sent to try us. Gloria," said Scheherazade, lying back
with her hands behind her head. "Gloria. Jorquil's great throb. She's in
disgrace and she's being packed off to purdah—here. With us. Gloria
Beautyman. Beautyman. Spelt like *beauty,* spelt like *man.* She's older
than us. Twenty-two. Or twenty-*three.* Oh well, what can we do? It's
Jorq's castle."

Keith had encountered Jorquil, or been in his presence for a minute
or two—Jorquil, Scheherazade's thirty-year-old uncle (it was that kind
of family). Now Keith said, "Good *name.* Gloria Beautyman."

"Yes it is," said Lily cautiously. "But does she live up to it? Does she
carry it off?"

"Sort of. I don't know. I think she's an acquired taste. Rather peculiar
figure. Jorq's besotted. He says she's the best thing out. He calls her
Miss Universe. Why is Miss Universe always from Earth? He wants to
marry her. I don't quite get it. Jorq's normal girls look like film stars."

"Jorq?"

"Yes, I know. He's no Adonis, Jorq, but he is very rich. And very
keen. And Gloria . . . She must have hidden depths. Still. Poor Gloria.
After two weeks at death's door from a *single glass* of champagne, she can
almost sit up in bed."

"What's she in disgrace for? What kind of disgrace? Do we know?"

"Sexual disgrace," said Scheherazade with a greedy look as her teeth
caught the light. "And I was *there.*"

"Oh do tell."

"Well I did vow not to. I really oughtn't. No, I can't."

"Scheherazade!" said Lily.

"No. I really can't."

"Sche*h*erazade!"

"Oh all right. But we mustn't . . . God, I've never seen anything like it. And it was so out of character. She comes across as a bit prim. She's from Edinburgh. Catholic. Ladylike. And she almost died of shame. Let's wait for Whittaker. He loves this kind of thing."

In espadrilles, khaki shorts, and a frazzled straw hat, Whittaker advanced down the path, leaving behind him, among the saplings on the second level, the barely distinguishable but plainly terrified figure of Amen. Keith considered. Obsession—positive, negative. From L. *obsidere* "besiege." Amen, beleaguered by Scheherazade's breasts.

"I thought they'd gone to Naples," said Lily, "to pick up Ruaa. You know. The Blob."

Scheherazade said, "You're not to call her the Blob in front of Whittaker. He thinks it's disrespectful . . . What's wrong with Amen, Whittaker? He looks so haunted."

But Whittaker answered her nothing, and just sighed and sat.

"Sexual disgrace, Whittaker," said Keith soothingly. "Someone lady-like almost dies of shame."

"Oh she's all right, Gloria," said Scheherazade. "The thing was, she did these paintings for a sex tycoon. And we—"

"No, wait," said Lily. "How do you mean, a sex tycoon?"

"The one who does sex revues but not *Oh! Calcutta!* . . . You see, Gloria's mainly a dancer. Royal Ballet. But she's also a painter. And she did these little paintings for the sex tycoon. Ballet dancers at it in mid-air."

"In mid-air?" said Lily, with some impatience. "In mid-*air?*"

"Ballet dancers at it in mid-air. And the sex tycoon had a big lunch party in Wiltshire, and Gloria was asked, and we were only sixty miles away, so we went. And she disgraced herself. I've never seen anything like it."

Keith sank back. The sun, the cicadas, the breasts, the butterflies, the caustic taste of coffee in his mouth, the fiery treat of his French cig-arette, the narrative of sexual disgrace that did not involve his sister . . . He said,

"Spin this out, Scheherazade, if you wouldn't mind. Any chance details. Don't stint us."

"Well. The first thing she did was almost drown in the indoor pool.

Wait. Jorquil dropped us off. He said, *You be chaperone. And for God's sake don't let her drink anything.* Because she doesn't. She can't. But she seemed very flustered. And so of course I went to the loo and when I came back she was finishing a huge flute of champagne. I've never seen anything like it. She was unrecognisable."

"Is she little?" said Keith. "That can sometimes happen when they're little."

"She's *quite* little. She's not *that* little. Afterwards she was violently sick for days and then completely bedridden. We really did. We really did think poor Gloria was going to die of shame."

"And I suppose the whole place anyway," said Lily, "was crawling with slags."

"Not really. I mean, there were a good few hunks and pin-ups round the pool. You know. People who look like they're made of pale chocolate. But there were rules. No toplessness. No sex. And Gloria wasn't topless. Not topless. Oh no. She was bottomless. She lost her bikini bottoms just before she nearly drowned. She said they got sucked off by the jacuzzi."

". . . They got sucked off by the jacuzzi," said Whittaker. "That's awfully good."

"Her exact words. *They got sucked off by the jacuzzi.* So the chap, the polo pro, when he fished her out, he had to hold her upside down by the ankles and give her a good shake. That was a sight. Then the minute we got her clothes back on she was off upstairs. And on the dance floor they were swinging her from man to man and feeling her up. And she looked like someone in a dream. And they were feeling her up. I mean *really* feeling her up."

Keith said, "Really feeling her up how?"

"Well. When I went back in she had her dress round her waist. Not just that—it was tucked into her garter belt. To keep it there. And guess what. The man with his tongue in her ear was stroking her arse with both his hands *inside her pants.*"

There was a pause.

Whittaker said, "That's also first-rate. Inside her pants."

"These two great hairy mitts inside her pants . . . And it was so out of character."

"*In vino veritas,*" said Lily.

"No," said Keith. But he said nothing more. Truth in wine? Truth in

Special Brew and Southern Comfort, truth in Pink Ladies? So Clarissa Harlowe and Emily Gauntlet, when drugged, were behaving *truthfully*? No. But when the girl raised the potion to her own lips (Gloria, Violet), then you could claim that it was *veritas*. He said uneasily, "You'd think she'd know that about herself. Gloria Beautyman."

"You would. There's more. The bathroom upstairs with the polo pro."

Over the poolside a pensive silence formed.

"Bit of a disappointment, frankly, after all that. Jorquil came, around four, and no one could *find* her. We went upstairs and all the bedrooms were locked. House policy. Then—in the passage. There were these two huge bunnies or pets or playmates. Ex-centrefolds, these huge madams. Incredible creatures. Like retired racehorses. They'd been trying to control her all day. They were banging on the bathroom door saying things like, *Are you* coming, *Gloria? Have you* flushed *yet, Gloria?* Then the door opened and she stumbled out. Followed by the polo pro."

". . . How did Jorquil like that?"

"He stormed off. He didn't see it."

They waited.

"Well they were only in there for a couple of minutes. The polo pro said it was all perfectly innocent. You know, a bit of cocaine. I think they just had a snog. There was lipstick on the polo pro's neck. Not a smear, either. A little smiling mouth. You could even imagine the little smiling teeth . . ."

Whittaker said, "That *is* disappointing."

"I know. Still, she cried her heart out in the car. And she's been suicidal ever since."

Scheherazade rubbed her eyes with her knuckles, childishly . . . According to an English novel he had read, men understood why they liked women's breasts—but they didn't understand why they liked them *so much*. Keith, who liked them so much, didn't even know why he liked them. Why? Come on, he told himself: soberly enumerate their strengths and virtues. And yet somehow they directed you towards the ideal. It must be to do with the universe, Keith thought, with planets, with suns and moons.

The young are perpetually running a light fever; and it is a mistake easily made by the memory, I think—to suppose that twenty-year-olds are always feeling good. Minutes after the conclusion of Scheherazade's bedtime story, Keith arose (the simple act of straightening up, sometimes, gave him the bends) and made his excuses. Had he been back at home, in the old days, he would have called out piteously for Sandy, their gentle Alsatian, her coat grained in black and yellow; and Sandy would have joined him on the blanket with her frown, and licked the insides of his wrists . . . Twenty-year-olds are fighting the weight of gravity, and they suffer decompression, with classic symptoms. Pain in the muscles and joints, cramps, numbness, nausea, paralysis. After a tragic doze in the tower, Keith again straightened up, and went next door and put his head under the tap.

Any minute now, he was sure, he would resume being happy. Where did it come from, the happiness that reshaped his face? Unlike most people, Keith had had to fall in love with his family, and his family had had to fall in love with him. It worked with his mother Tina, it worked with Violet—Violet was easy. But it never really worked with Karl, his father. And, for almost ten years, it didn't work with Nicholas. When Keith appeared, when he staggered on to the scene, aged eighteen months, the eyes of the five-year-old Nicholas, Tina told him, had the dead light of the betrayed. And Nicholas made a kind of hobby of it, the roughing up, in words or deeds, of his little brother. And Keith accepted this. This was life.

Two weeks after his eleventh birthday, Keith was doing his maths in the breakfast room. A sick wasp was climbing up the window pane, and always dropping down, and climbing up, and dropping down. He felt Nicholas materialise behind him. Things were better now (largely thanks to Violet, with her tearful intercessions); still, he tensed. And Nicholas said, *I've decided I like having a younger brother.* Keith nodded without turning, and all the figures on the page swam away and then swilled back again, and he started to be happy.

2

LOOK HOW HE LIT HER

"I can't find my gyms. My tennis shoes."

He was coming down from the tower (having left his headache behind, in the significant bathroom). Scheherazade wore her pale green skirt and her yellow top. And Keith received her penetrating address, and her tone of amused accusation, now, as if, in fact, Keith had hidden them—had hidden Scheherazade's tennis shoes. He halted one step above. He was six foot two. He said,

"Who're you playing with?"

"Local toff." She shrugged. "Meant to be the great Italian playboy. So you know. The usual greaseboat."

"You mean greaseball. Or do you mean dreamboat?"

She frowned and said, "I thought I meant greaseboat. Or do I mean dreamball?"

"Are you any good?"

"Not really. Quite decent form. I had lots of lessons and the chap said it was all to do with how you shaped. The important thing is how you look. Then it all follows."

He was six foot two. He said, "By the way—rightly are you called Scheherazade. The disgrace of Gloria Beautyman. Gloria Beautyman's day of shame. I hope you'll tell me many more stories like that."

"Oh I was very bad. She begged me not to. Gloria wept and *begged* me not to."

For a moment Scheherazade's eyes went liquid, as if she had brought Gloria's tears with her all the way to Italy. Keith said,

"Well you couldn't very well not tell."

"No. We all want to hear about boundaries, don't you think? She said, *Please, oh* please, *don't tell Oona*. Mum was just off to the airport." Scheherazade folded her arms and leant sideways against the wall. "But she knew about her being locked in the bathroom with the polo pro. Jorq was raging around the place. And it's awkward, because they're practically engaged. *Don't tell Oona.* The lipstick stain and the hands inside the pants."

"And the bikini bottoms getting sucked off by the jacuzzi. So what did you tell your mum in the end?"

"Well she grilled me the minute I got here. I'm not a very good liar, and it helps if a bit of it's true. The cocaine was true. He was offering it to everyone. So I just said Gloria was taking cocaine in there. With the polo pro. And Mum didn't particularly mind."

"So Gloria's in the clear."

"But now I've gone and told all you lot. And when she comes we'll be smirking. And she'll know."

"But we won't do that. We won't smirk. You train Whittaker not to."

"All right. And you train Lily. All right. Good."

She passed him. She turned. She was six foot six. He said,

"Have you actually seen those miniatures she did?"

"Yes I have. The sex tycoon had them up on the wall on the stairs. Ballet dancers floating around doing God knows what. An arm there, a leg here. I've seen them. And I thought they were rather sweet."

Keith was trying to work out where he stood on the chain of being. She turned again and climbed yet higher. He shut his eyes and saw her complete, in her coating—in her catsuit of youth.

That afternoon they went down the steep little lane towards the village, to stroll and hold hands and be a couple together: Lily and Keith. The deep streets, the crushed cobbles, the fig-dark shadows, all silent in the siesta hour, which was given over to the faint trickles of digestion. The graffito, daubed in white: *Mussolini Ha Sempre Ragione!* Mussolini Is Always Right! Above their heads, visible from almost any vantage, stood the arthritic neck of Santa Maria. It was five o'clock, and the bells wagged and swung. A chance to stroll and hold hands and be a couple, while there was still time.

"Look at it," he said. "It's not a dog. It's a rat."

"No it's not," she said. "It's a perfectly decent little dog."

"It doesn't even *want* to be a dog."

"Don't. You're embarrassing it."

". . . Actually it does look a bit embarrassed."

"It does. Poor little thing. Some sort of dachshund. Or a terrier. I think it might be a cross."

"That's possible. Its mum was a dog but its dad was a rat."

The pet shop was proudly double-fronted: in the left window, a sectioned menagerie (kittens, squirming hamsters, a single stunned rabbit); in the right, with the whole bay to itself, the rat in its smart blue collar, plus the plastic bone, the wicker basket, and the red velvet cushion on which it habitually perched. This was not the first time they had paused to marvel at it. Rat-sized, its grey coat both close and coarse, with twitching whiskers, malarial eyes, rosy snout, and a tail like a fat garden worm. Keith asked,

"How many rats do you know that live in this kind of style? That's why it looks so embarrassed."

Lily said suddenly, "They're playing on the court at his castle. He's meant to be a great athlete. She says if she likes him even the tiniest bit she's definitely going to consider it."

Keith heard himself say, "No. Is this fair to Timmy?"

"Well it's Timmy's fault in a way. He ought to be here. I told you how frustrated she is. She's desperate."

"Desperate?"

"Desperate. Look. It's embarrassed again."

He said, "See? A dog wouldn't be embarrassed. Then I don't understand about Scheherazade. Only a rat would be embarrassed."

"What don't you understand? A dog would be embarrassed. If everyone kept mistaking it for a rat."

He turned and said, "Six months ago she was a lollipop girl helping schoolkids cross the road. And ferrying dinners around in a van. I wouldn't even *swear* in front of her."

"But she's different. She's changed. You should hear her now—sex, sex, sex. There's so much more woman in her now."

He remembered Lily's description of her, Lily's, first time, with the French student in Toulon, and her *walking on the beach the next morning, and thinking, God, I'm a woman* . . . Awakened to womanhood. This was what psychologists called an *animal birthday*: an animal birthday is when your body *happens* to you. It wasn't like that for boys, the first time: the first time was just something you got out of the way. A feeling of helplessness went through him, and he reached for Lily's hand.

"Oh yeah," he said. "When Gloria Beautyman comes, you've got to pretend not to know about her day of shame."

"Violet's a bit like that when she drinks, isn't she."

"Yeah, but she's a bit like that when she doesn't drink too. Remember. We're not to *traduce* Gloria. You know what that means, Lily—*traduce*?"

"Go on then."

"From Latin *traducere*. 'Lead in front of others, expose to ridicule.' " Traducement was what happened to tragic heroes. Get your laughing done with, get your staring done with. "So we won't traduce Gloria."

"See, it's barking. It's a dog."

"What it wants is to go back to being a rat." It wants to walk away from it all. No fanfare: a discreet return to the rodent kingdom. "It wants to walk away from the velvet cushion and the plastic bone. It wants to run up a drainpipe."

"You're so horrible. See, it's barking. That proves it's a dog."

"That's not a bark. That's a squeak."

"It's a definite yap. You're embarrassing it. You're traducing it. It's barking at you. That's its way of telling you to fuck off."

They had started along the lane that scrambled up the slope (and ducked under the road, and scrambled clear on the other side) when they saw Scheherazade, who was in the process of alighting from a cream Rolls Royce. She briefly bent herself over the window frame, with her green skirt outthrust; then she stood there waving at it as the machine surged onward. Keith thought for a moment that the car was driverless, but now a bronzed forearm appeared, and was lazily brandished, and then withdrew.

"So?" said Lily as they joined Scheherazade at the gates.

"He told me he loved me."

"*No*. At what stage?"

"In the first game of the first set. It was fifteen-all. He's coming to lunch tomorrow. And he's full of plans."

"And?"

"He'd be absolutely perfect," said Scheherazade, with a cry-baby face. "Except for just this one little thing."

N*ow I am ready to tell how bodies are changed Into different bodies.*

I agreed with Keith when he decided that her beauty was in, it was here, it was just off the boat . . . Seven or eight years ago Keith said to his sister, *You're growing so fast now, Vi. Let's stare at your hand for a moment and try and catch it as it grows.* And they stared and they stared, until her hand did seem to give a palpable outward throb. Scheherazade's talent was still coming in, still pulsing in. It was just off the boat, but every day there was more of it. She turned to go, back up the wharf, and the stevedores cried, *Signorina, signorina*—and there was another trunkful of silks and dyes and spices. An English rose, but one invigorated by what was unmistakably the American—the *American,* something harder and brighter: the influx of precious metals from the New World. There was hardly enough room in her to put everything—no one knew how they were ever going to get it all in.

And Keith too was changing—but not outwardly . . . Here in the castle, when you walked down the length of its stone passages, the echo was louder than the footfall, and you faced the disjunctions caused by the pitiful sloth of the speed of sound. The syncopated footfall. *Hello. Echo.* And you kept seeing your reflection, too, in unexpected places, in rich and ripply mirrors, of course, but also in silver bowls and tureens, in the blades and tines of weighty cutlery, in sheets of armour, in thick leaded windows after dark.

Inwardly Keith was changing. There was something in him that wasn't there before.

"Come on. What's wrong with Adriano?" he asked Lily, that evening, in the salon.

"I'm not telling you. You'll have to wait and see. All I'm saying is that he's very handsome. With an exquisitely chiselled body. And very cultured."

Keith's eyes moved sideways in thought. "I know. He's got a terrible laugh or a very high voice." Solemnly Lily shook her head. He thought on, and said, "I know. He's nuts."

"No. You're nuts. And you're not even warm."

Keith went to the kitchen. "What's the thing that's wrong with Adriano?" he asked Scheherazade.

"I promised Lily I wouldn't tell."

"Is it uh, insurmountable? The thing that's wrong with him?"

"I'm not really sure. I suppose we'll see."

"Is it because he's—"

"No more questions. Don't tempt me. Or I'll crack. I've done it once before today already. Blabbed."

At dinner that night he conducted a thought experiment, or a feel experiment: he looked at Scheherazade, for the first time, with eyes of love. As if he loved her and she loved him back. While he made himself agreeable to Lily and Oona and Whittaker, as often as he dared he looked at Scheherazade, with eyes of love. And what do they see, those eyes? They see the equivalent of a work of art, they see wit and talent and gripping complication; for minutes on end he believed himself to be in a private screening room, bearing witness to a first performance of unforgettable spontaneity. Behind the scenes of this motion picture, the director, a troubled genius (and probably Italian), would be wisely sleeping with his great discovery. Of course he was. Look how he lit her. You could tell.

Keith dropped his head and gazed at the grainy murk in the bottom of his coffee cup. There was something in him that wasn't there before. It was born when Lily said the word *desperate*.

It was hope.

Here they were in the She Decade—but they were all of them in the cusp of Narcissus. They were not like their elders and they would not be like their youngers. Because they could remember how it was before: the lighter weight on the individual, when you lived your life more automatically . . . They were the first that ever burst into that silent sea, where the surface is a shield that burns like a mirror. Down by the grotto, down by the bower, they lay there near-naked, in their instruments of yearning. They were the Eyes, they were the *I*s, they were reflections, they were fireflies with their luminescent organs.

3

THE HIGHEST
THRONE ON EARTH

My dear Little Keith,

I send bad news about our unbelievable little sister (how bad <u>is</u> it, would you say?), so I'll try to put a smile on your face before I take it off again:

My heart leaps up when I behold. The Heart Is a Lonely Hunter. Heart of Oak. Heart of Darkness. Bury My Heart at Wounded Knee. Then burst his mighty—

"What's so funny?" said Lily, who was putting marmalade on the toast and pouring herself a second cup of tea.

"It's a game we play. Me and Nicholas. Come and look."

". . . I ask again. What's so funny?"

"You've got to substitute *dick* for *heart*. As in, now cracks a noble . . ."

She said, "*The Heart Is a Lonely Hunter.* Isn't that by a woman?"

"Ah, but you don't use *dick* when it's a woman. You use *box* instead."

"Bury My . . . It's a bit puerile, isn't it?"

"Yes. Very." He explained that when you grew up in an enlightened household, where everything was allowed and forgiven, where nothing was judged, except judging, you got keen on the subversive. "We've always done it. And there are tons more."

"Maybe they should have been *less* enlightened. With your unbelievable little sister."

"Mm. Maybe."

The letter was on the breakfast tray. And the breakfast tray—laid and heroically borne aloft by Lily—carried information of its own. There was no longer any doubt about it: Lily and Keith were now in a sibling relationship—a sibling relationship only marginally enlivened

68

by the nightly crime of incest. And no crime, no act of applied endogamy, had been perpetrated the night before. It was rescheduled—this being the paraphrasable content of the tea, the toast, the quartered oranges. He said,

"I suppose you want to read the rest of it now. Leaning over my shoulder. Well you can't."

"Don't be mean."

"All right. But not until you tell me what's wrong with Adriano. And why Scheherazade feels so unbearably sorry for him."

"We all have a little blemish."

"That's true. And his is?"

"But I want it to be a lovely surprise."

He said, "Okay. But no interrupting."

The night before last I took Violet to a party at Sue and Mark's. Among other points of interest, there was a duck waddling round the floor and shitting everywhere, and there was a witchy girl waddling after it, in a crouch, with a toilet roll in her hand. So, the standard hippie hell (and freakfest and goons' rodeo), and Vi behaved much as we've come to expect. The unusual thing was what happened on the way there.

"Oh and I suppose Nicholas never messes around in hippie hells."

"Sexually? No. He doesn't. Hardly. Because he's so left-wing. I keep telling him. *You're interested in the wrong revolution, mate.* But does he listen?"

"And you think he ought to. Mess around."

"No, I'm just surprised. Girls are always making passes at him. And he never comes across. Molly Sims made a pass at him."

"Molly Sims? No."

"Yes. A pass so graphic, he claimed, that she wrote him a note of apology the next day."

"But she's famous for hardly sleeping with anyone. Molly Sims? Bullshit."

"That's what I said. He crashed at her place after a party and she came to say goodnight. In a babydoll. And she sat like this, with her knees up."

"So what could he see?"

"*A cassoulet of pussy.* According to him."

"Bullshit."

"That's what I said. But he insisted. *A farting cassoulet of pussy.* I didn't believe him either. Then he showed me the note. That's extreme, that is. As a pass."

"Very . . . You know, last night I dreamt you'd read Sex at Oxford. Everything was completely normal. In my dream. Except that you'd read Sex at Oxford."

"What degree did I get?"

"A two-two. I hate dreams."

"You're interrupting."

I collected her around ten from some wine bar in Notting Hill. I was with the poet Michael Underwood. Have you met him? Anyway, in the taxi (how can I put this?), I suddenly got the feeling that I'd grown a moustache. It wasn't my moustache. It was Michael's. So I just said, No thanks, Mike, and we went back to talking about William Empson and I. A. Richards. He's gay, you see. Not prancing and whinnying, quite, but obviously and contentedly gay.

Now. Violet had some girls with her, and we needed two cabs for the next leg, and she climbed in with Michael. At the other end (and it wasn't that far) he scrambled out looking as though he'd just come through the Battle of Stalingrad. As he stood there, with his hair all over the place, and tucking his shirt back in and retrieving his tie from between his shoulder blades, he said (note: he rolls and swallows his <u>r</u>s, like Denisov in <u>War and Peace</u>), "I say, your sister's jolly ghrandy, isn't she?"

"Ghrandy?"

"Randy." This was one of the things he liked about Lily: she read at the same speed he did (and she knew all there was to know about his little sister). "Randy. Like Scheherazade's supposed to be. According to you."

It seemed quite funnily symmetrical at the time, and it was only the next day that it started preying on me. So I called Michael and we had a drink. Intermission:

Love Is a Many Splendoured Thing. I Love Lucy. If music be the food of love. Love in a Cold Climate. Love is of man's life a thing apart. Love Me Tender. God is love. The Spy Who Loved Me. Stop! In the <u>name</u> of—

"Love is a . . . What's he going on about now?"

"Well with this one," said Keith, "when *love*'s a verb, you substitute *fuck,* and when it's a noun you substitute *hysterical sex.*"

"Stop! In the *name* of . . . Can't you finish this later? Then in a while we can join the turtle-doves in the grotto."

"Mm. I'm impatient to set eyes on him. Wait. Jesus."

"Finish it later. Adriano, close your eyes. I'm Scheherazade."

"Wait."

Lily said, "Stop! In the name of . . ."

"Before you break my—"

"Stop!"

Afterwards, Keith and Lily went downstairs and were introduced to Adriano over coffee in the salon. They talked about castles. Adriano's castle wasn't like Jorquil's castle—a fortress on a mountainside. Adriano's castle (as Keith would soon see for himself) gathered a whole village in its arms. Then Keith returned to the tower.

His mission, up there, did not befit a romantic hero—or even the anti-hero he was destined to become. It was beneath him, all this. Only what could he do? *The man who occupies the highest throne on earth,* said Michel Eyquem de Montaigne in—what?—1575, *is still sitting on his arse.* Human beings, atom-splitters and moon-striders, serenaders, sonneteers, they want to be gods, but they are animals, with bodies that once belonged to a fish. In short, Keith Nearing sat on the cold bowl. He was of course impatient to be with Adriano; still, Adriano would understand.

Keith was not reading Sex at university—or not any more. These days he was reading *Pamela* and *Shamela.* And yet, for his first four terms, Sex was what he read. Not just Sex; he also read Death, he read Dreams, he read Shit. According to the neo-Freudianism that was dominant in his era, these were the cornerstones of the self—sex, death, dreams, and human ordure, or night soil. Montaigne could have gone further: the highest throne on earth has an oval cavity in it, and there's a toilet roll close to hand.

There *was* one boring thing about the bathroom—the bathroom that linked him with Scheherazade. It had no window. Only a skylight, hopelessly distant. Compared to the average male inhabitant of England, Keith was, he considered, positively debonair about defecation. But its meaning could not but sadden him. And he assented to the

valiant condolence offered by the great Auden in the final stanza of
"The Geography of the House":

> Mind and Body run on
> Different timetables:
> Not until our morning
> Visit here can we
> Leave the dead concerns of
> Yesterday behind us,
> Face, with all our courage,
> What is now to be.

That helped. And so did this: as he would one day say to his two
growing sons, *Boys? Here's some fatherly advice about shits when you're shar-*
ing a bathroom with a girl. Light a match afterwards. Light two. Because
it wasn't the smell, really, that humiliated you; it was the humiliating
emanation of decay.

Keith lit his third match. While it would be inaccurate to say that he
didn't mind if Lily had to breathe his heat, his dead concerns, his yesterdays, he was quite unable to bear the thought of Scheherazade and her
delicately alerted nostrils. So he stayed on afterwards, with *Roderick*
Random or *Peregrine Pickle,* sometimes for half an hour, just to make
sure. He was twenty, remember, and still young enough—still osmot-
ing with his fluids and nostalgias. *Nostalgia,* from Gk *nostos* "return
home" + *algos* "pain." The return-home pain of twenty years old.

Also young enough (he was taking his leave of the bathroom with a
final dubious sniff) to have all but an hour or two of every day quite poi-
soned by the awareness of a physical insufficiency. Oh, how the young
suffer for a nose, a neck, a chin, a pair of ears . . . The bit of his body
Keith hated was the bit that wasn't there. He suffered for his height.

Poet and seeker, farting air-gasper and blood-pumper (cosmic cham-
pion, cringing cur), he slipped into his trunks and climbed on to his
flip-flops, and strolled down the descending terraces to the pool, ready
to face, with all his courage, what was now to be.

Ah," said Adriano, addressing Scheherazade with an elegant undula-
tion of his open palm, "bring me the sunflower mad with light!"

The open palm withdrew, and closed on the bunny-eared bow of the silk cord that secured the waist of his creamy trousers (the creamy colour, perhaps, was meant to match his car). Keith sat on a metal chair and watched—as *il Conte* showily disrobed.

When he first got wind of Adriano, Keith imagined a grand seducer, a purple genius of the chamber and the boudoir—glutinously virile, with heavy lids, plump lips, and sebum visibly pooling in every pore. Then came Scheherazade's proviso: *He'd be absolutely perfect,* she said. *Except for this one little thing.* And Keith spent a happy night defacing his posterboy, the greaseboat or dreamball. Dribble, stutter, asphyxiating BO. But Adriano wasn't like that.

He disrobed, Adriano: off came the snowy slacks, the bobbled loafers, the shantung shirt, all the way down to the curious ribbing of his sky-blue swimsuit, which, nonetheless, bulged eventfully . . . Adriano was equipped with perfect English, or near-perfect English: he sometimes said *as* instead of *like* (and for some reason he couldn't say *Keith*—he never once got it right). Adriano would inherit an ancient title and a limitless fortune. Adriano was densely muscular and classically handsome, with something coinlike, something silvery and Caesary, in his noble brow.

On he came, to the sunbed of Scheherazade. Adriano sat, and with formidable insouciance he slid his hand between her moistened calves.

"Ah," he resumed. "I know how Tereus felt when he first spied Philomela. As a forest when a drought wind turns it into a firestorm."

It was not the voice of a small man, which was remarkable in its way. Because guess what. Adriano was four foot ten inches tall.

"I thought you'd've finished that," said Lily, as Keith joined her in the shade, "while you were having your shit."

"Lily!" Nobody was supposed to know for sure about his shits. "Actually I tried, but I lost my nerve. Come on, read it with me. No interrupting."

When I woke up the next day, feeling very seedy <u>indeed</u>, I found
1) a strange girl in my bed (fully dressed, including gumboots),
2) Violet, under an old curtain and a tattoo-bespattered skinhead on the sitting-room floor, and, most derangingly, 3) a fucking <u>duck</u> doing laps in the bathtub. Yes, well, an average kind of

evening. But what stayed with me was the business with Michael Underwood.

We—

"The duck," said Lily (he could feel her breath on his neck). "That must have been *very* bad. Ooh. See? He's making progress."

Keith stared out into the yellow glitter. Adriano had worked his way up the sunbed, and now sat face to face with the supine Scheherazade; he was leaning forward and his right hand rested on the far side of her waist.

"He's torturing her," said Keith. "Look at her face."

And it was true, he thought. Scheherazade had the expression of a woman cajoled on to the stage by a professional magician or hypnotist or knife-thrower. Amused, embarrassed, deeply unconvinced, and about to be sawn in half. Lily said,

"I see a smile. Look. He's almost resting his chin on her tits."

"Wait till they stand up at the same time. That'll put things in perspective. Now shsh. You're interrupting."

"Adriano—what happened to his neck?"

We met after work, and Michael was unusually quiet—all loath and diffident. I had to sneak up on the subject. A couple of drinks later he said—Christ—he said he'd never been set upon so wildly and so insensately (this was the word he used) in all his life. And he reminded me, again with some diffidence, that during his art-school years he was known as Dockyard Doreen. And consider this. Michael isn't pretty. So, my dear Little Keith, please, your thoughts.

"Insensate?"

"Senseless. Without sense. Or sensibility. Without feeling." And he thought: Impy! He thought of the Violet boyfriend called *Impy.* "Maybe I'll talk to Whittaker . . ."

"What happened to Adriano's thigh?"

You do see the weirdness of it, don't you? When I felt Michael's moustache on my lips, all I had to say was no thanks. Imagine if he'd kept on coming all the way there. So, Keith, please, your thoughts.

PS. A jiffy bag came for you from the Lit Supp. I'll get the office to smother it in stamps and send it on.

PPS. It looks as though Kenrik <u>will</u> be going camping with Rita. Their destination is Sardinia, and I suppose it's conceivable that they'll get as far as Montale. I gave him the number. Is it really a castle? Kenrik insists that he and Rita are just good friends and he intends to keep it that way. I dutifully—but I think point-lessly—repeated your words of advice. I said, "Whatever you do, <u>don't</u> fuck the Dog."

"Why shouldn't he?" said Lily. "If he wants to. I'm not sure I under-stand."

"No one understands. Not really. But everyone knows that you mustn't."

"Ah, but Rita'll be having a say in that, won't she. And she acts like a boy. She's *bound* to try her luck. Kenrik's heaven—he's a dream. He's like the young Nureyev. Mmm . . . What's this thing from the *Lit Supp?*"

"When you left me, Lily, I—"

"I didn't leave you. It was mutual."

"When you left me, Lily, I began to think about my future." And he wrote to the *Lit Supp,* asking for a book to review on trial. He wanted to become a literary critic. And a poet (but that was a secret). He knew he could never become a novelist. To become a novelist, you had to be the silent presence at the gathering, *the one on whom nothing is lost.* And he was not that kind of observer, not that kind of I. He couldn't read a sit-uation; he was always misconstruing it. "Scheherazade!" he called out. "A parcel sent here from England! How long?"

"It varies!" she called back. "Between a week and a year!"

"Look," said Lily. "He's reading her palm now. She's laughing."

"Yeah. He's tracing her loveline. Hah. Some hope."

"Short men try harder. What happened to his foot? Are you going to tell your mum?"

"About Violet? Let's not talk about Violet. It'll be an absolute disas-ter," Keith said thoughtfully, "if Kenrik and Rita get here and they aren't just good friends."

At noon Whittaker arrived with the coffee tray, and the party re-gathered in the sun. Beyond, three columns of smoke fumed skyward from the valley, olive-coloured and silvery-blue at the edges. Below, on the upper slope of the nearest foothill, you could see the two monks who often walked there—in impassioned conversation but without gesture, walking, pausing, turning, with hidden hands. Whittaker said,

"Adriano. I hear you're a man of action."

"It would be futile to deny it. Why, my body, as the map of a battle, itself tells the tale of my love of adventure."

And it was true: all over his ripply little frame Adriano bore the wounds of his commitment to the good life.

"So your left foot, Adriano. What happened there?"

Two lesser toes had been sheared clean off by the propeller of a speedboat in the waters of Ceylon.

"And this . . . discolouration on your neck and shoulder?"

The result of a helium blaze on a hot-air balloon, six miles above the Nubian Desert.

"How about these black studmarks on your hip and thigh?"

Out hunting wild boar in Kazakhstan, Adriano succeeded in graping himself with his own shotgun.

And the knee, Adriano?

A toboggan smash on the elevated run at Lucerne . . . Other mementoes of hazard were written on his body, most of them the result of numberless tramplings on the polo field.

"Some call me accident-prone," Adriano was saying. "Only the other day—well, I was recovering from a forty-floor elevator plunge in the Sugar Loaf Plaza in Johannesburg. Then some friends bundled me onto a jet to Heidelberg. We survived the landing, in dense fog, thanks to heroic work by my co-pilot. And we were just taking our seats for *Parsifal* when the balcony collapsed."

There was a silence, and Keith felt himself being taken, being slid out of genre. He thought the upper classes had ceased to be this—had ceased to be the source of unsubtle social comedy. But here, contending otherwise, was Adriano. Keith said, "You should be more careful, mate. You should just stay indoors and hope for the best."

"Ah, Keethe," he said, trailing a little finger down Scheherazade's forearm, "but I live for hazard." He took her hand, kissed it, smoothed it, returned it with slow care. "I live to scale the impossible heights."

Now Adriano rose up. With some pomp he approached the diving board.

"It's very bendy," warned Scheherazade.

He marched to the end of it, turned, measured out three long paces, and turned again. Then the two-step advance, the springing leap (with right leg coyly cocked). And like a missile catapulted by a siege engine, with a rending twang Adriano shot sunward. There was a moment, halfway up, when you glimpsed a look of swollen-eyed alarm, but then he bunched and balled and twirled, and vanished with an almost inaudible splash—a gulp, a swallow.

". . . Thank God for that," said Lily.

"Yes," said Scheherazade. "I thought he was going to miss. Didn't you?"

"And hit the concrete on the far side."

"Or the hut. Or the rampart."

"Or the tower."

After another twenty seconds the board stopped juddering and the four of them climbed spontaneously to their feet. And stared. The surface was almost entirely undisturbed by Adriano's ramrod splashdown, and all they saw was sky.

"What's he doing down there?"

"Do you think he's all right?"

"Well he did land in the shallow end."

"It was quite a drop anyway. Can you see any blood?"

Another minute passed and the colour of the day had time to change.

"I saw something."

"Where?"

"Should I go and look?"

Adriano burst up like the Kraken, with a tremendous snort and a tremendous swipe of his silvery quiff. And he didn't seem like a small thing, the way he stirred the whole pool as he pounded back and forth, the way he whisked the whole pool with his golden limbs.

But it was true—what Lily said in the dark that night. And Keith wondered how the two of them managed it. Thereafter, during lunch, tea, drinks, dinner, coffee, cards, Scheherazade and Adriano never once stood up at the same time.

As they were trying to go to sleep Keith said,

"Adriano's cock's all balls. I mean his cock's all bullshit."

"It's the material. Or it's just the contrast of scale."

"No. He's got something down there."

"Mm. As if he'd upended a fruitbowl into it."

"No. He's got a hi-fi set down there."

"Yes. Or a drumkit."

"It's just the contrast. His cock's all balls."

"Or maybe it's not."

"He'd still be ridiculous."

"There's nothing ridiculous about a big cock. Believe me. Sleep well," said Lily.

4

STRATEGIES OF DISTANCE

Dear Nicholas, he thought, as he insomniated by Lily's side. Dear Nicholas. Do you remember Impy? Of course you do.

It was this time last year, and we had the house to ourselves for the weekend, and Violet came earlier than you did, on Friday afternoon, with her new beau.

Violet: "Keith, say hello to Impy." *Me:* "Hello, Impy. Why are you called Impy?" *Violet* (in whom, as you're aware, there is no aggression, no malice, no ill will): "Because he's *imp*otent!"

And Impy and I stood there, unsmiling, while Violet lost herself in symphonic laughter . . . Soon afterwards she came into the garden with two glasses of fruit juice.

Me: "Vi, listen. *Don't* call Impy Impy." *Violet:* "Why not? It's better to make a joke of it, don't you fink? Otherwise he'll get a complex."

This being her sense of what it was to be modern. She was sixteen. You know, I often used to wish I had a girlfriend who looked exactly like our sister. An idea unavailable to you. Blonde, soft-eyed, white-toothed, wide-mouthed, her features and their soft transitions.

Violet: "He likes being called Impy. He thinks it's funny." *Me:* "No. He *says* he likes it. He *says* he thinks it's funny. When did you start calling him that?" *Violet:* "On the first night." *Me:* "Jesus. What's his real name?" *Violet:* "Feo." *Me:* "Well call Impy Feo. I mean Theo." *Violet:* "If you say so, Key." *Me:* "I say so, Vi."

Why does she still have trouble with the *th* sound? Remember her transpositions? *Ackitt* for attic. *Kobbers* for because. Navilla ice cream.

Me (thinking I had to spell it out): "Make a real effort, Vi, and call Impy Theo. You should build him up. Then you might find there's no *reason* to call Theo Impy. Call Impy Theo." *Violet* (quite wittily):

79

". . . Should I start calling Impy Sexy?" *Me:* "It's too late for that. Call him Theo." *Violet:* "Feo. All right, I'll try."

And she was very good. During dinner that night, and all the next day, did you *once* hear her call Impy Impy? Me, I held out high hopes for Impy. Slender and tremulously Shelleyan, with vulnerable eyes. I could imagine him reading or even writing "Ozymandias." I looked to Impy as a force for good. Then came Sunday afternoon.

You: "What's going on?" *Me:* "I'm not sure. Theo's in tears upstairs." *You:* "Yes, well some bloke, some shape, just knocked on the kitchen door. One of those guys who's very fat but hasn't got an arse. Vi said, *See you, Impy,* and off she went. What does *Impy* mean?"

Oh Nicholas, my dear—I'd been hoping I wouldn't have to tell you.

Me: "So that's why she calls him Impy." *You:* ". . . All right, she's young. But you'd think *she'd* want to keep that reasonably quiet." *Me:* "I know. I mean, if it was the other way round." *You:* "Exactly. Meet my new girlfriend. I call her Fridgy. Would you like to know why?" *Me:* "Impy's worse than Fridgy. I mean, a girl can pretend not to be frigid. And a boy . . ." *You:* "I'm going to talk to her." *Me:* "I already have. She just keeps saying how keen she is for him not to get a complex." *You:* "And what does she say when you tell her the obvious?" *Me:* "She says, *Well he is impotent.*" *You:* "Yeah I bet he is."

And we agreed: no talent for it, no feel for it. So what does she want from it? What does she want from the modern?

And now, one year on, what does Violet do? She rapes fruits—or she tries. I'll ask Whittaker about this.

Hear the sheep?

Dear Nicholas, oh, brother, the girl here she . . . When she dives, she dives into her own reflection. When she swims, she kisses her own reflection. She works her way up and down the pool, with dipping face, kissing her own reflection.

It's hot at night. Hear the sheep, hear the dogs?

Scheherazade was flat on her back in the garden—upper terrace. She held a book, interposed between her eyes and the evanescent sun. The book was about probability. Keith sat four or five yards away, at the stone table. He was reading *Northanger Abbey.* Several days had passed. Adriano was a good deal around.

"Are you enjoying that?"

"Oh yes," he said.

"Why, particularly?"

"Well. It's so . . . sane." He yawned and, in a rare spasm of unself-consciousness or candour, he stretched, in his director's chair, with pubic bone outthrust. "The beautiful intelligence," he said. "And so sane. After Smollett and Sterne and all those other mad sods." Keith couldn't be doing with Sterne. He clapped *Tristram Shandy* shut on about page fifteen, when he came across the adjective *hobby-horsical*. But he forgave Smollett everything for his osmotic translation of *Don Quixote*. You see, he was still having these thoughts, for a little while longer. "No, I'm loving Jane."

"Isn't it all about marrying for money?"

"I think that must be a myth. This heroine says that marrying for money is *the wickedest thing in existence.* Catherine. And she's only sixteen. Isabella Thorpe wants to marry for money. Isabella's great. She's the bitch."

"Gloria Beautyman was supposed to come today. But she's had a relapse."

"Another glass of champagne."

"No, she's still recovering from the first one. She's not faking it either. Jorq's got her in the Harley Street Clinic. She lacks a chemical. Diogenes. It's obviously not diogenes. But something that sounds nearly the same as diogenes."

"Mm. Like the Eskimos. Like the Red Indians. One shot of whisky and that was it. All they could do was hang around the forts. There was a kind of sub-tribe of them. Known as the Hang Around the Forts."

"That's all we do, isn't it. Hang around the forts."

Scheherazade was referring to their recent outing—from one castle to another castle, from Jorquil's castle to Adriano's castle. Keith said,

"And you, are you enjoying yours? What is it?"

"It's about probability. Quite. The paradoxes. Or do I just mean the surprises? It's fascinating in its way. But a bit low on human interest." Scheherazade herself now yawned hungrily. "Time for a shower, I think."

She stood. "Ow," she said, and for a moment she examined her upturned foot. "Trod on a burr. Adriano's coming to dinner again. With a hamper. Meals on Wheels. Do you mind him?"

"Mind him?"

"Well he can be a bit much. And you . . . Sometimes I think you mind him."

Keith felt it for the first time: the flooding need for passionate speech, for poetry, for avowals, for tears of tenderness—for confession, above all. It was official, it was authorised. He was painfully in love with Scheherazade. But these abstract adorations were part of his history, and by now he felt he could manage them. He cleared his throat and said, "He *is* a bit much. But I don't mind him."

She looked up towards the shoulder of the field, where the three horses grazed. "Lily tells me you hate flies."

"This is true."

"In Africa," she said in profile, "all day you're looking at these poor black faces. They have flies on their cheeks and their lips. Even in their eyes. And they don't brush them away. Just used to them, I suppose. Human beings get used to them. But horses never do. See their tails."

And of course he watched as she turned and moved off—the mannish khaki shorts, the mannish white shirt only half tucked in, the tall walk. Her shirt was damp and there were grass halms on her shoulder blades. Grass halms gleamed in her hair. He sat back. The frogs, massed in the wet ground between the walled flowerbeds, gurgled and comfortably grunted. It came to his ears as a stupor of self-satisfaction—like a clutch of fat old men reviewing a lifetime of probity and profit. The frogs in their shallow swamp, in their stupor.

The yellow birds laughed in the garish tenement of the elm. Higher up, the crows, with famished and bitter faces, faces half carved away (he thought of the black knights on the chessboard). Higher still, the Homeric strivers of the upper air, dense and solid as magnets, and in formation, like the blade of a spear, aimed at a land far beyond the horizon.

Twenty pages passed. Odd how a watched sky seems changeless; but then a paragraph later that swordfish has disappeared, to be replaced by the British Isles (an arrangement surprisingly popular with Italian clouds) . . . Lily now sat silently opposite. *Public Order and Human Dignity* lay unopened on her lap. She sighed. He sighed back. The two of them, Keith realised, were diffusing a dingy and neglected air. On top of everything else, they were experiencing the demotion that a settled couple will tend to feel when there are romantic awakenings near by. Lily said frowsily,

"She's still toying with the idea."

Keith said even more frowsily, "It's grotesque."

". . . Tom Thumb wants to take her to a bullfight in Barcelona. In his helicopter."

"No, Lily, you mean his aeroplane."

"Not his aeroplane. His helicopter. Tom Thumb's got a helicopter."

"A helicopter. That would be certain death. As you well know."

". . . If you could stretch him out he'd be very attractive."

"But you can't stretch him out. And besides. He's not just a midget. He's a ridiculous midget. I can't think why we don't all just laugh him off the property."

"Come on. He's got a lovely little face. And he's charismatic. It's impossible to take your eyes off him, don't you find? When he's diving or on the exercise bar."

The exercise bar was a fixture that Keith had barely noticed until now. He'd assumed it was some kind of towel rack. These days, Adriano was always twirling and snorting around on the exercise bar. Lily said,

"You can't look away."

"That's true." He lit a cigarette. "That's true. But only because you're so sure he's about to fuck himself up—you know, he's making me feel very left-wing."

"That's not what you were saying last night."

"True." Last night he was saying that every upper-class prick should model himself on Adriano. It would mean eternal peace in the class war. All that trouble and expense Adriano went to, in search of fresh damage—why bother to string up Adriano? Just give him a rope, and show him a tree or a lamp post. "Yeah. But he's still walking, isn't he, Tom Thumb. That's the trouble. He's not Tom Thumb. Or Mighty Mouse or Atom Ant. He's Tom in *Tom and Jerry*. He's got nine lives. He keeps recovering."

Several pages passed.

"You're upset about Violet."

"Why should I be upset about Violet? Violet's all right. She doesn't date football teams or anything like that. Let's not talk about Violet."

Several pages passed.

". . . The impression he gives of deserving it all—that's what I can't bear. You'd think that being four foot ten," Keith went on, "would teach the little bastard a bit of humility. *Oh* no, not Tom Thumb."

"God, you really don't like him, do you."

Keith confirmed that this was the case. Lily said,

"Come on, he's sweet. Don't be chippy."

"And I hated his fucking castle. With an ancient footman behind every chair. With an old pez in a dragoon outfit standing behind your chair and hating your guts."

"And all that yelling down the length of the table. Still. What about the starlets?"

In Adriano's open-plan *piano nobile* (an area about the size of a London postal district) they were led to a deep sideboard on which were ranked a couple of dozen framed photographs: Adriano, seated or recumbent, with a succession of able-bodied beauties in various opulent or exotic settings. Keith now said,

"That didn't mean anything. All he ever does is loll around with rich wasters. He's bound to be quite near a girl every now and then. Someone takes a photograph. So what."

"Then where does he get his confidence from? And come on. He *is* confident. And he has a reputation."

"Mm . . . Frailty, thy name is woman, Lily—it's the money and the title. And the bullshit charm . . . I hate the way he's always kissing her on the hand and the arms and the shoulder. Scheherazade."

"You're not seeing it straight. He's actually very tentative. He talks a lot, and he's Italian, he's tactile, but he hasn't even made a pass. They're never alone. You're not seeing things clearly. You don't always, you know."

"Putting olive oil on her back . . ."

After a pause, Lily said, "All is explained. How predictable. Mm. I see it. You're painfully in love with Scheherazade."

"You sometimes amaze me," he said, "by how wrong you get things."

"Then it's just class resentment. Pure and simple."

"What's the matter with class resentment?"

In fact it was not that painful, it was not yet all that painful. And he was often thinking, You have Lily. You're safe with Lily . . . He was certainly disquietened by what had started going wrong with him in bed. Not only one-time students of psychology might notice the coincidence: Keith was worried about his sister, and his sister was what Lily had seemed to become. But the meaning of the connection, if any, eluded him. And he still looked at Lily ten times a day and felt grateful and surprised, gratefully surprised.

"She's trying to drum up some charity work in the village. She says doing good makes you high, and she misses it."

"There you are. Still a saint." He tossed *Northanger Abbey* on to the table and said, "Uh, Lily, listen. I think you should go topless at the pool . . . Why not?"

"Why not? Why d'you think? How'd you like to sit there with your cock out? Next to Tom Thumb—with *his* cock out. Anyway. Why?"

Actually he had several reasons. But he said, "You're nicely made up there. They're shapely and elegant."

"You mean they're small."

"Size doesn't matter. And Adriano's cock's all bullshit."

"Yes size does. That's what it comes down to. She said it might be all right if he was just four inches taller."

Four inches? he thought. That's still only five foot *two*. He said, "Being five foot two, or six foot two, wouldn't stop him being ridiculous. How can *you* bear him? You like social realism."

Lily said, "He's very fit. And she's read somewhere that it's quite different. With someone who's very fit. And you know what a noodle Timmy is. I told her, *Small men try harder.* Imagine how hard *you'd* try if you were four foot ten. He wants to take her to St. Moritz. Not for the snow. Obviously. Mountaineering . . . Close your eyes for a second and imagine how hard he'd try."

Keith disguised a soft groan in an exhalation of Disque Bleu. His squashy white packet carried no health warning. The fact that smoking was bad for human beings: this was now widely suspected. But he didn't mind. Typically, I think, in this regard, Keith was still young enough to assume, in certain moods, that he wouldn't live that long anyway . . . He closed his eyes for a second and saw Adriano—brutally shod, with alpenstock and alpenhorn, with pitons and eye bolts—readying himself to conquer the south face of Scheherazade. He glanced down at the flattened outline in the grass, where her shape had lain.

"Well tell her not to do anything hasty," he said, picking up his book again. "She shouldn't let herself down. It's really Timmy I'm thinking of."

So far, the new rhythm of the weather was answering quite accurately to his inner state. For four or five days the air would steadily thicken and congeal. And the storms—the storms, with their African vociferousness, were timed for his insomnias. He was making friends with hours he barely knew, the one called Three, the one called Four. They racked him, these storms, but he was left with a cleaner morning. Then the days began again to thicken, building to another war in heaven.

I don't know what you're complaining about, Lily was on record as saying. *You still sit up half the night playing cards with her. I saw you that once— down on your knees together. I thought you were getting married. Plighting your troth.*

When we kneel, we're the same height. Why's that?

Because her legs are a foot longer than yours from the knee down. What d'you play anyway? said Lily, who hated all games (and all sports). *Old Maid?*

No, they played Pope Joan, they played Black Maria and Fan-Tan and Stud Poker. And now (better, much better), on the rug in the gun-room (the rug was a sprawled tiger), kneeling opposite one another, they played Racing Demon . . . Racing Demon was a kind of interactive Patience. As card games went, it was almost a contact sport. There was a lot of snatching and taunting and laughing and, almost always, a shimmer of hysteria towards the end. He wanted to play the games called Skin and Cheat. Is that what he wanted? He wanted to play Hearts. Hearts: that, perhaps, was the trouble.

Did they mean anything, those smiles and glances? Did they mean anything, those exhibitions, in the shared bathroom, those exhibitions of riveting disarray? Keith read, and sighed, and wished he was a yellow bird. Because it would have horrified him beyond computation—to take her undesigning friendliness and smear it with his hands, his lips.

Keith grew up in cities, in small coastal cities—Cornwall, Wales. Cornwall, where the island dips its toe into the English Channel; Wales, with its arms reaching out to embrace the Irish Sea. The only birds he knew well were city pigeons. When they took to the air at all (and it was invariably a last resort), they flew for fear.

Here in Italy the black *cornacchie* flew for hunger, the high *magneti* flew for destiny, and the yellow *canarini* flew for joy. When the wind came, the dervish tramontana, the yellow birds neither rode the gusts nor fought them; they didn't fly, they didn't float, they just *hung*.

The castle received other male visitors during this anxious time. There was an unforgivably young and handsome army major called Marcello, who seemed much taken with Scheherazade; but he was instantly fingered by Whittaker *(Why can't hets tell?* he said. *Marcello's unusually gay).* There was an eloquent and erudite apparition by the pool, Vincenzo, who seemed much taken with Scheherazade; but he talked a lot about church restoration, and when he sat down to lunch he was wearing a dog collar. Adriano's only departure from gridiron stereotype was his mild anti-clericalism *(I think people who worship should worship alone).* So did this constitute the historic opportunity? It was occurring to Keith that he was the only secular heterosexual in the entire region who was over four foot ten.

He had never been unfaithful to Lily. He had never been unfaithful to anyone. I think it is important to remember that Keith, at this stage (and for the very short-term future), was a principled young man. With girls, his transgressions, his known wrongs, were so far derisory in number. There was his commonplace negligence (a sin of omission) in his dealings with Dilkash. There was the far more complicated felony (a sin of commission, this time, and often repeated) in his dealings with Pansy—Pansy, acolyte of Rita. He thought about them hourly, the two girls, the two wrongs.

At an early stage in his religious period (eight to eleven), as he was collecting the bibles after class, his RI teacher, the hideous but compelling Miss Paul (a secret tippler, he had since decided), said dreamily, *You see, Keith my love, every one of us has nine stars in the firmament. And each time you tell a lie, one of your stars go out.* And a sober Miss Paul wouldn't have said that (*go out*—a sober Miss Paul would have got that right). *When all nine are dead—then your soul is lost.* And over the years Keith somehow transferred this notion to his future: his future with girls and women. He had seven stars left. Of course, the wisdom of the drunken Welsh spinster was offered (and then distorted by him) long before the sexual revolution. And now, he felt, everyone would be needing many more stars than nine.

He hung around the fort, and he was safe with Lily . . . The mountains they looked out on configured themselves in three echelons, three strategies of distance. Nearest were the foothills, pocked and dappled and sparsely forested. Beyond the foothills were the humpbacked cliffs, ridged, tensed, like the spines of dinosaurs. And in the far distance stood a world of crests, of snowcaps and cloudcaps, of sun and moon, a world of crests and clouds.

SECOND INTERVAL

Find a mirror you like and trust, and stick to it. Correction. Find a mirror you like. Never mind about trust. It's too late for that—it's too late for trust. Stand by this mirror, and be true to it. Never so much as glance at another.

Actually things aren't *quite* that bad. Correction. Actually they are. But this is a truth we will have to postpone for many pages and then creep up on . . .

Beyond a certain age you no longer know what you look like. Something goes wrong with mirrors. They lose the power to tell you what you look like. All right, they do tell you, probably. But you can't see it.

Beyond a certain age, then, you have neither the means nor the opportunity to find out what you look like. All the mirror will give you (in at least two senses) is a rough idea.

.   .   .

The first clause in the revolutionary manifesto went as follows: *There will be sex before marriage.* Sex before marriage, for almost everyone. And not only with the person you were going to get married to.

It was very simple, everyone knew it, everyone had seen it coming for years. In certain quarters, though, sex before marriage was a distressing development. Who was distressed by it? Those for whom there had *not* been sex before marriage. Now they were saying to themselves, *So suddenly there* will *be sex before marriage? On what basis, then, was I told that there will* not *be sex before marriage?*

Nicholas, when he was coming of age in the mid-1960s, found himself involved in a series of long, boring, repetitive, and in fact completely circular arguments with his father. It began to happen about

89

every other night. *Why doesn't he go away for ever?* Nicholas used to say. *Or, failing that, why doesn't he go away for a very long time and then go away again as soon as he gets back?* The same sort of thing was happening to Arn, to Ewan, and to all Keith's other friends (except Kenrik, whose father died before Kenrik was born).

The circular arguments were ostensibly about various limits to be imposed on Nicholas's freedom and independence. In fact they were about sex before marriage. But there was never any mention of sex before marriage (rendering the arguments circular). And this was Professor Karl Shackleton, sociologist, positivist, progressivist. Karl was all those things—but he hadn't had sex before marriage. And, looking back, he liked the idea of having sex before marriage. We may parenthetically note that it is the near-universal wish of dying men that they had had much more sex with many more women.

Keith indulged himself by feeling slightly hurt when it became clear that Professor Shackleton was not going to repeat this pattern with his foster-child (and Karl, already embrittled by his first minor stroke, his first minor cancellation, wasn't about to take on Violet). It was only Nicholas, his male flesh and blood, that Karl really envied. And *envy,* the dictionary suggests, takes us by a knight's move to *empathy.* From L. *invidere* "regard maliciously," from *in-* "into" + *videre* "to see." Envy is negative empathy. Envy is empathy in the wrong place at the wrong time.

.   .   .

"The boys have won," said his stepdaughter, Silvia. "Again."

"I hate to hear it," said Keith.

"I hate to say it."

Silvia had studied Sex (in the sense of Gender) at Bristol University. And she was now one of those "child" journalists who already, at twenty-three, wrote a much-discussed weekly column in one of the broadsheets. Keith first met her when she was fourteen—1994, when he sold his large duplex in Notting Hill, and moved into the house above the Heath. Silvia had inherited her mother's looks, but not her insane cheerfulness; she was one of those torpid wits who made everyone laugh except herself.

"So, against your better judgement," she said torpidly, "you find yourself spending the night with a young man. And they're all the same. Doesn't matter who. Some replicant in a City suit. Some stinkbomb in an Arsenal shirt. And the next morning, out of habit, you say, you know, give me a call sometime. And he stares back. As if you're a leper who's just proposed marriage. Because *give me a call* is emotional blackmail, see. And commitment's not allowed. The boys have won. Again."

Had his sons won, Nat and Gus? Had his daughters lost—Isabel (nine) and Chloe (eight), had they lost?

Keith grieved for his own youth, but he didn't envy his children. The erotic world they faced (Silvia had more to say about this) he would find unrecognisable. So he could partly understand the consternation of the fathers, as their own world fell away.

> Full fathom five thy father lies;
> Of his bones are coral made;
> Those are pearls that were his eyes:
> Nothing of him that doth fade,
> But doth suffer a sea change
> Into something rich and strange.
> Sea-nymphs hourly ring his knell.

He thought, Go forth, my children. Multiply as and when you please. But go forth. And thank you, you sea-nymphs, for your knells. And in your orisons, too, be all my sins remembered.

. . .

In an attempt to alleviate the chronic sexual problems he suffered throughout the 1970s (and throughout the 1980s, and beyond), Keith spent several lunchtimes in a succession of Mayfair escort agencies, where, hovered over by genteel madams, he sat in parlours resembling miniature airport lounges, with stacks of brochures on his lap. The girls, in their hundreds, were attractively photographed, and you could read about their vital statistics and other attributes. He was looking for a certain shape, a certain face. Keith didn't go through with it in the end. But he learnt something, and something literary: why you can't write about sex.

Leafing through the glossy pages, he felt the brothelgoer's mad power—that of choice. Power corrupts: this is not a metaphor. And writers were instantly corrupted by the mad power of choice. Authorial omnipotence did not go well with the definingly fallible potency of the male creature.

But the summer in Italy wasn't art, it was only life. No one made anything up. All this really happened.

.   .   .

It was April 19, 2003, and he was holed up, now, in the studio at the end of the garden. He didn't want to come out, but he sometimes did come out. Then on April 23 he started sleeping there. His wife stood before him with her fists on her hips and her strong legs planted well apart; even so, he started sleeping there. He needed to escape from sanity—not just for eight, but for eighteen hours in every twenty-four. Rearrangements were being made in the sources of his being.

Opening his eyes, waking, taking leave of the mocking kingdom made by sleep, getting out of bed and standing upright: this seemed to consume the lion's share of what remained of the day. As for getting shaved, shat, showered: this was a Russian novel.

.   .   .

Then, at the meeting point, Echo stepped carefully into the clearing. She raised her hands to greet the glassy boy. He looked at her pretty body, but he shook his head and turned away, saying, No. I would rather die than let you touch me.

And what could Echo do, left alone? What could she say? Touch me, *she said as she fell to her knees.* Touch me, touch me, touch me.

.   .   .

How slowly time moves when it's only twenty years old.

Keith was now well launched on the bullet train of his fifties, where the minutes often dragged but the years tumbled over one another and disappeared. And the mirror was trying to tell him something.

He was never a likely candidate for vanity, and had always thought himself free of it. But age, ever prodigal with its gifts, grants you vanity. It tricks you out with vanity, and just in time.

.   .   .

When he talked to his children Keith noticed that *cool* was pretty well the lone survivor from the lexicon of his youth. His sons used it, his

daughters used it, but the word had lost its grace-under-pressure con-
notation and just meant *good.* Accordingly, you never heard its opposite:
uncool.

For someone born in 1949 the word brings additional difficulties.
Getting old is very uncool. Pouches and wrinkles are very uncool. Deaf
aids and walking-frames are very uncool. Sunset homes are *so* uncool.

. . .

He had other things on his mind, but he kept thinking about the
encounter with his first wife—in the public house called the Book and
Bible. What a price he had paid for everything, for the summer of
1970. What a price he had paid.

Book Three

The Incredible Shrinking Man

I

EVEN IN HEAVEN

"Amen," said Whittaker, "can understand companionship. He can understand sex with a stranger in the afternoon. But he cannot understand the love affair."

"Well, they're tricky," said Keith. "Love affairs."

"Among fruits I'm a freak. I want monogamous cohabitation. On the het model. A quiet dinner. Sex every other night. And Amen—Amen says you should never even think of sleeping with anyone twice. So, as you see, our views subtly diverge."

Keith said, "I keep glimpsing him on the terrace. He's edging nearer. What's happening? Is he coming to terms, at last, with Scheherazade's breasts?"

"No. Not at all. In fact it's worse than ever. But he braves Scheherazade's breasts for the sake of Adriano."

". . . Amen fancies Adriano." Keith lit a cigarette. Earlier, the complacent gurgle of the frogs; now, the settled neurosis of the cicadas . . .

"He doesn't *fancy* him exactly. As you so charmingly put it. He admires him as a specimen. I do too. Adriano's perfection, in his way."

"Mm. Well he's worked at it, hasn't he."

"I guess they all tend to do that. Little people. They can't make themselves taller. So they make themselves wider . . . I keep thinking I'm watching *The Incredible Shrinking Man*. At about the point where he starts getting scared of the cat."

"Early on, remember, when he goes to kiss his wife and now she's taller than he is?"

"Mm. Some say *The Incredible Shrinking Man*'s an anxiety dream about the American hard-on. Potency. The rise of women."

They played on, exchanging, simplifying.

"Okay," said Whittaker. "*How* gay was the gay poet?"

"How gay? Well, obviously gay, Nicholas said. Contentedly and obviously gay."

"Mm-hm. And does he have the gay coloratura? The drawly singsong. Like me."

"I don't know. The fruit accent . . ."

"The fruit accent's no mystery. Bear in mind that our lovelives have only just been legalised. We need the fruit accent. To make things clear to other fruits. Now uh, Violet. There's no aggression in her?"

"None. I mean, I don't know about her in bed." And he leadenly resolved to ask Kenrik about it, if and when Kenrik came. "But other-wise — none."

"*Low self-esteem.* That's what a professional would say. She seeks reas-surance by the quickest path. You know all that. But coming on so hard to a fruit . . . I'm sorry. And I'll go on thinking about it. But I keep coming up against a dead end."

"That's what I keep coming up against. Draw? This board's so quiet."

"Yeah. Our games aren't good. Why is that?" He looked up and his horn-rims were full of curved light. "It's because we're both in love. Nothing left over."

"I'm not sure I'm in love." What is it, this "love"? "*You're* in love."

"Yes I'm in love. Amen, when he plays, Amen's ferocious. He smashes the pieces down. Amen's definitely not in love."

The mad, ratcheting cackle of the cicadas — was that how insects laughed? Keith said, "Amen in the garden. He reminds me of Bagheera in *The Jungle Book.* The panther. Staring anxiously through the leaves. Monitoring Mowgli."

"And if he's Bagheera," said Whittaker, "you're Bambi. When you gaze at Scheherazade. No. You're Lady, gazing at the Tramp."

"*Lady and the Tramp.* Remember their first date — the Italian restau-rant? Dinner for two at an Italian restaurant."

"That's not a very typical first date for dogs. Then Lady and the Tramp go and gaze at the moon. No howling, just gazing . . . Keith, a word of fatherly advice. When you gaze at her at dinner. Your eyes get wet. And you have a *wronged* look. Careful with that."

Keith said, "This is nothing. I used to get myself bedridden with crushes when I was a kid. The teacher'd call, and my mother'd have to nurse me through it. This is nothing."

"I thought—aren't adopted people supposed to be cautious about love?"

"Yeah, they usually are. But I'd had this huge success early on, with Violet. And I must've thought, I don't know, I must've thought I could make girls love me. All I had to do was love them, and they'd love me back . . . Scheherazade's nothing. I just admire her from afar."

"Look on the bright side," said Whittaker, with some amused cruelty in the line of his lips. "She's Lily's best friend. So at least Lily wouldn't mind."

Keith coughed and said, "She's Lily's *second*-best friend. There's Belinda. She's at Dublin. It's academic anyway. But Scheherazade's Lily's *second*-best friend."

Amen, Keith learnt, was back on the bus. And heading furiously for Naples. He was very exercised about his sister. And who wouldn't be? Amen had heard that Ruaa sometimes loosened her veil in the market, disclosing her mouth and her forelock. Whittaker said,

"Do that one more time and it's over."

"Good. Stalemate."

"Uh, no. Stalemate is an endgame thing. Where the king can't move except into check. This is just a draw by repetition."

You've got to try, Keith thought. A draw by repetition: you don't want that. They're laughing at you, the cicadas, the crazy little scientists in the garden. The yellow birds are laughing at you. When a girl looks like Scheherazade, and she's desperate, you've got to at least *try.*

So you're not sleeping, Lily told him, *and you're not eating. You're just wasting away.*

At the end, of course, the incredible shrinking man, having survived the cat and the spider, just gets smaller and smaller, and wanders off— into the cosmos of the subatomic.

So, Oona," said Lily. "What do you think? Will Adriano win the heart of Scheherazade?"

"Adriano?"

This was a change of subject. Oona sat correcting proofs on the cleared dining-room table, and she was taking it seriously (she deployed a style manual, a dictionary, and a stack of diaries and photographs). Her maternal aunt, Betty, had completed a memoir before her recent death; and Oona was seeing it into print—*for a vanity house,* she said. But it turned out that old Betty had much to recommend her: a patron of the written arts, a traveller, an erotic adventurer. Keith had earlier spent half an hour with it, Betty's life and times. Yachts, diabolical divorces, tycoons, drunken geniuses, car crashes, spangled, stratospheric suicides . . . Whittaker and Scheherazade were in the nearest anteroom, playing backgammon with great violence (there was much use of the doubling-dice), for a lira per point. Adriano was not of the company, having been called away to some fresh deathtrap (featuring potholes or parachutes). Oona, who had the most experienced eyes Keith had ever seen, said meticulously,

"Well he's very keen, Adriano. And persistent. And we're impressed by persistence—women are. But he's wasting his time."

And Lily said, "Because he's too um, petit?"

"No. She might even look kindly on that. Being so soft-hearted. It's the Italian extravagance that offends her. Too theatrical. She says Timmy needs teaching a lesson. But she'll forgive Timmy. Times change, but types stay the same, and she's not the type. I *was* the type. And I know. Keith dear, what's the literal meaning of *pandemonium*? Is it like *pantheon* but the opposite?"

During dinner Keith had made a conscious effort not to gaze at Scheherazade, and he was surprised by how straightforward he found it—and surprised by how suavely he jawed and quipped and wielded his irons. Until he did in fact take an angled glance. Her face was already fixed on his: unblinking, decidedly particular, as always, decidedly personal, and (he thought) quietly enquiring. With her mouth in the shape of a levelled longbow. And from then on, and throughout, not gazing at her became as onerous as anything he had ever attempted. How to deny yourself vital essence? When it's there in front of you. How to do it? Now he said,

"Oona, why do you keep slashing away at the tops and the bottoms?"

"Widows and orphans," she said. "The lone word at the top of the page. The lone line at the bottom. I'm a widow."

"And I'm an orphan."

She smiled and said, "Do you remember?"

"The orphanage?"

He said no, he didn't remember . . . He remembered another orphanage, and another orphan. Every weekend, for a year or two, they drove there, the whole family (it was the sort of thing this family did), and took him out for the afternoon—little Andrew. And the orphanage was like a Sunday school or a seminary that went on for twenty-four hours a day: blocklike wooden pillars, benches laid out in lines, and assemblages of eerily silent little boys. Andrew himself was largely silent. There were many silences, in the Morris 1000, in the seaside tea shop, in the market-town museum—the kind of silences that roar in a child's ears. Then they dropped him off again. Keith remembered the silent quality of Andrew's pallor, on his coming out, on his going back in.

"You don't mind talking about it?"

"No." And he thought, It's about *me,* isn't it? "Being an orphan's not nothing. But it's not everything. Nowhere near. It's just—*there.* Christ. Is that Frieda Lawrence?"

"Mm. Oh they came here several times. In the Twenties. I was a little girl, but I remember them."

Keith had in his hand a soft photograph—Frieda's ripe, rural, misleadingly honest face. And D.H. in quarter-profile, with his stubborn, bloody-minded chin and his black beard cut close and dense. The two of them were standing in front of the fountain. The fountain down there in the courtyard. Keith said,

"The Lawrences, *here* . . . I read the Italy trilogy just before we came. In the books he calls her *the q-b.* The queen bee."

"Well in life he called her *the shitbag.* In public. That's right. He was very advanced. Betty was fascinated by Frieda. You know, Frieda betrayed him *every day.* Frieda. One of nature's infidels. But she did it on principle. She thought free love would free the world."

Lily said, "Where did they sleep when they were here?"

"In the south tower. Either your room or Scheherazade's."

"Christ," said Keith. A little later he thought of Mexico (and of Germany—Frieda Lawrence, née von Richthofen), and he said, "I wonder how Conchita's doing. I hope she's all right."

"Conchita?" said Oona, with something like suspicion in her frown. "Why shouldn't she be?"

"No reason." He was thinking about Conchita in Copenhagen, in Amsterdam, in Vienna—in Berlin, where two world wars were made. "I just wondered."

Eleven o'clock had not yet struck, but the evening started coming to an end—out of deference to Oona, who would soon be leaving them, for Rome, for New York. There would be no Red Dog, no All Fours, with Scheherazade, no Racing Demon, not tonight. Holding a lantern, under a skull-like moon, Keith went with the two girls to the dark tower.

Does it bother you, Keith? his father asked him more than once—he meant the afternoons with orphan Andrew. *Would you rather not go?* And Keith said, *No. We ought to* . . . He was nine and not yet happy; but he was an honest and sensitive little boy. And went on being honest and sensitive when happiness came—honest and sensitive. One of these two attributes, or perhaps both, would now have to give.

*B*aa, said the sheep. *Gaa. Daa* . . .

He was in the process of making love to Lily.

When Keith inveigled her into going topless at the pool, he had three objectives. First, it would lessen his unease when he looked at the breasts of Scheherazade (mission accomplished); second, it would fractionally increase her resemblance, when naked, to Scheherazade (mission accomplished); third, he thought it might be good for her sexual confidence, so diminished, he felt, by the constant proximity of Scheherazade (outcome unclear).

He was in the process of making love to Lily.

The arms and legs of his spectral sister still went where they went, where they used to go, the hands smoothed, his two tongues explored her two mouths . . .

He was in the process of making love to Lily.

Years ago he had read that sexual union without passion is a form of suffering, and also that *suffering isn't relative.* Is pleasure relative? Compare a dance hall with a prison, compare a day at the races with a day in the madhouse. Or if you want to see them both in the same place, pleasure and pain—a night in a brothel, a night in the delivery ward.

He was in the process of making love to Lily. *Paa. Maa. Nah!* . . .

"Jesus," said Lily, later, in the dark.

"The sheep. What's the *matter* with them. Traumatised."

"Traumatised. By Tom Thumb."

Adriano, two nights ago, had come to dinner by helicopter. And until two nights ago the dreadful cries of the sheep on the upper terrace had done no more than express boredom: the entirely understandable boredom (ragged, end-of-tether) that went with being a sheep. Sheep don't bleat. Sheep yawn. But then Adriano, like a furious asterisk, came clattering and battering down on them from out of the starry night . . .

"They don't sound like sheep any more," said Keith. "They sound like a crowd of mad comedians."

"Yes. Like *impressions* of sheep. And completely overdoing it."

"Completely overdoing it. Yeah. Sheep aren't *that* bad." He said, "See? It's easier, or quicker, for Tom Thumb to get here by helicopter. Rather than by Rolls Royce. And now we're all being tortured by the fucking sheep."

"Do you know how tall Tom Thumb was? I mean the real Tom Thumb. The one in the story? . . . Okay. Multiple choice. Four inches, five inches, or six inches?"

Keith said, "Four inches."

"No. Six inches."

"Oh. So not too bad. Comparatively."

"As tall as his father's thumb . . . I've thought of one," she said. "Alone of All Her Hysterical Sex."

"That's not a proper one, Lily. The gentler hysterical sex. The weaker hysterical sex. It doesn't work like that. Okay—Courtly Hysterical Sex. That's a proper one. Yours isn't a proper one."

Naa, said the sheep. *Nah. Nah!*

Making love to a fragrant twenty-year-old girl, in summer, in a castle, in Italy, while the candle wept its light . . .

> Action is transitory—a step, a blow.
> The motion of a muscle—this way or that—
> 'Tis done, and in the after-vacancy
> We wonder at ourselves like men betrayed:
> Suffering is permanent, obscure and dark.
> And shares the nature of infinity.

Making love to a fragrant twenty-year-old girl, in summer, in a castle, in Italy.

Christ, even in heaven they couldn't stand it. Even in heaven they *couldn't stand it another second,* and made war. Just under half of them: angels and archangels, virtues, powers, principalities, dominations,

thrones, seraphim and cherubim—they couldn't stand it *another second.*
Even in heaven, strolling the impurpled pavements soft with smiling
roses, lolling on ambrosial clouds, and quaffing immortality and joy—
even in heaven they *couldn't stand it another second,* and rose up, and gave
battle, and lost, and were hurled over the crystal battlements, and top-
pled down into Chaos, there to raise the black palace of Pandemonium,
the place of all devils, in the Deep of Hell. Satan, the Adversary. And
Belial (the worthless), and Mammon (the covetous), and Moloch (the
child-eater), and Beelzebub, whose name means Lord of the Flies.

They were on the floor of the gunroom, stacking cards in the wooden
box, Scheherazade in a thin blue dress, sitting side-saddle, Keith in shirt
and jeans, sitting Indian-style. Keith was remembering that at home,
for a while, he and his brother were known as the Two Lawrences. He
was D. H. and Nicholas was T. E.. Thomas Edward (1888–1935);
David Herbert (1885–1930). The golden archaeologist and man of
action; the tubercular son of a Nottingham miner. Lawrence of Arabia
and Lady Chatterley's Lover. Keith said,
    "It's an exciting thought. I mean historically. David and Frieda
sleeping in the tower. I wonder which turret."
    "From the sound of it," said Scheherazade, "Frieda slept in both."
    "Depending on who was in the other one."
    "Mum said she used to brag about how quickly she seduced David.
After fifteen minutes. While her husband poured sherry in the other
room. Not bad going for—when?"
    "I don't know, about 1910? Scheherazade. There's something I
must . . ." He lit a cigarette. He sighed and said . . . Some sighs can
drift away on the leaves of the trees. Some sighs can dissipate themselves on flags of stone, on grass, on grains of sand. Some sighs seep
down to the crust, some to the mantle. The sigh Keith needed would
have to go as close to Hell as possible. But he couldn't reach it, and just
sighed and said, "Scheherazade, there's something I must say to you. I
ask in advance for your forgiveness, but there's something I must say."
    Her brows were as level as the floor they sat on. "Well," she said.
"You're probably forgiven."
    ". . . I don't think you should get involved with Adriano."

"Oh," she said. And blinked slowly. "Well I'm *not* going to get involved with Adriano. All right, I'm cross with Timmy at the moment, it's true. But I'll probably stop being cross with him once he comes. Adriano's always on about love. And I don't want all that. He'd've been much better off just making a tactful little pass. And then I would've found out how I felt."

The pivot of the hips, the swivel of the thighs. She knelt, she stood (it was over).

"I just wonder how I'm going to extricate myself without . . . Poor Adriano. He's started to appeal to my pity, and I'm an absolute sucker for that. There's a trip to Rome he's planning. For some surprise. I'll tell him then. And I'll feel freer in my mind . . . Oof. Bit exhausting, saying all that. Let's go to bed. Now if you get those glasses over there I'll bring the lamp."

2

BODY PARTS

The neck of the loved one resembled those cylindrical shafts of light you saw in uncertain weather, when the rays of the sun began to find their way through the colander of the clouds. Like a tall lampshade of white lace. . . . This style of thought, Keith knew, was of no help to him, and he turned his attention elsewhere.

"It's too big," said Lily. "Much too big."

"I feel as if I'm seeing it for the first time," said Scheherazade. "And it's absolutely enormous, isn't it."

"Absolutely enormous."

". . . And you wouldn't call it fat exactly."

"No. And it's—quite high up."

"It's high. And it's not a bad shape."

"As far as one can tell."

"No. There's just too much of it," said Scheherazade.

Lily said, "*Much* too much."

Keith listened. It was good, hanging around with girls: after a while, they thought you weren't there. What were they talking about, Lily and Scheherazade? They were talking about Gloria Beautyman's arse . . . On the exercise frame, utterly unregarded, Adriano coiled, whirled, and stretched, his legs outthrust and rigid to the very nails of his toes.

"It's so out of proportion," Lily resumed, staring at it from under her hand. "It's like those tribes on TV. The ones who have big arses on purpose."

"No. I've seen them in the flesh—the arses that are big on purpose. And Gloria's—Gloria's . . . Maybe it *is* as big as the arses that are big on purpose. She's a dancer. I suppose it's a dancer's arse."

"Have you ever seen anything that size in a leotard?"

Gloria Beautyman, in a petalled bathing-cap and a slightly furry dark-blue one-piece, was under the pool hut's external shower: 5' 5", 33-22-37. She was a dark, pained, and grimly self-sufficient figure, with a frown fixed above the bridge of her nose like an inverted V (lower-case and italicised). This one-piece of Gloria's continued on downward for an extra couple of inches, like a not very daring miniskirt; and its awkward modesty, hereabouts, made you think of bathing machines and dipping-stools . . .

"She's turning round again," said Scheherazade. "Whew, it's a whopper, isn't it. She's lost weight and it really sticks out at you. Awful swimsuit. Virginal."

"No, spinsterish. What are her tits like?"

"There's nothing wrong with her tits. They're almost the prettiest tits I've ever seen."

"Oh are they now. Describe."

"You know, like the upper bit of those dessert glasses. For um, parfait. Just full enough to have a touch of heaviness. I wish I had tits like that."

"Scheherazade!"

"Well I do. Hers'll last. And I don't know how long mine'll be able to keep this up."

"Sche*her*azade!"

"Well I don't. You'll see them when Jorquil comes. He'll be wanting to show them off. Poor Gloria. She's all atremble about Mum. Who doesn't know the half of it."

Lily said, "You mean she only knows about the one hairy mitt inside her pants."

"Impossible to imagine, isn't it. Look at her. Almost frumpish."

"Like a sensible young wife. Very . . ."

"Very Edinburgh. Look. Oh no. She's had all her hair cut off too. And I liked it long. That's why her head seems so small in comparison. More penance. More sackcloth and ashes. No, it's not the tits."

"No. It's the arse."

"Exactly. It's the arse."

Adriano still twirled like a catherine wheel or a propeller on the upper bar of the exercise frame. Keith thought, I'll wait till he comes down from there—then I'll go and tower over him for a while. And Lily, not quite prepared to leave things as they were, said conclusively,

"It's a *farcical* arse."

The day extended itself in unmediated heat—not a cloud. Lunch, *Pride and Prejudice,* tea, *Pride and Prejudice,* a conversation with Lily on the lawn, Scheherazade and Adriano returning from the tennis court, showers, drinks, chess . . . At dinner, Gloria Beautyman of course drank nothing, and said very little, her square but heart-shaped face humbly lowered over the tablecoth. Oona, continuously expected, did not appear; with every shift in the aural atmosphere, Gloria tensed and stopped chewing; then she stopped eating. While the rest of them were reaching for the fruit, she went off with a double candle, seeking, no doubt, the castle's most distant and desolate wing. Her shorn head, her smocked shape receded down the passage. You thought she might be intending to empty the alms boxes on the way, or make her last rounds of the lepers in the cellar.

"This early exit," said Whittaker, following the clank of a heavy but distant door, "will cast a pall over the evening."

"She suffers for love, I think," said Adriano.

"Not for love," said Scheherazade. "She's just dreading Mum."

"Hang on," said Keith. "Did you tell Gloria what you told Oona? That with the polo pro she was only taking cocaine?"

Adriano looked up suddenly (alerted, perhaps, by the mention of a polo pro), and Scheherazade said,

"Well, I was going to but she kept giving me these truly terrible looks. As if I'd just murdered all her children. So I thought, Well, I'll let her get on with it."

"Trust me," said Adriano contentedly. "She suffers for love."

"It *isn't* love."

"Ah. Then I must continue to suffer alone. *L'amor che muove il sole e l'altre stelle.* Love that moves the sun and the other stars. Such is mine. Such is mine."

"It's the opposite of love."

Keith went off after dinner to the pentagonal library with his notebook. And he made a list, headed "Reasons." It went as follows:

1) Lily. 2) Beauty. <u>Sche</u> has a daily beauty in her life that makes me ugly. And beauty cannot <u>want.</u> Can it? 3) Fear of rejection. Of

scandalised rejection. 4) Illegitimacy. In the general and the particular sense. The presumption needed is above my reach to know. 5) Fear of not seeing things clearly. Those displays in the bathroom maybe mean nothing in a world where Frieda Lawrence once put herself about. Fear of the fatal misreading.

. . . He had acquired some understanding of it, by now — this business of making passes at girls. You were alone in a room with the wanted one. And then two futures formed.

The first future, the future of inertia and inaction, was already grossly familiar: it was just like the present. It was the devil you knew.

The second future was the devil you knew nothing about. And it was a giant, with legs as tall as steeples, and arms as thick as masts, and eyes that beamed and burned like gruesome jewels.

It was your body that decided. And he was always awaiting its instructions. On the thick-rugged floor he sat with the wanted one, and as each game reached its climax they both rose to their knees, with their faces separated only by their breath.

At such a moment you needed despair — and that he had. He had despair. But his body wouldn't do it. He needed that coating to seep down over his eyes; he needed to become reptilian, and receive the ancient juices and flavours of the carnivore.

Now he returned to his list, and added a sixth item: 6) Love. And he found the poem with no trouble at all.

> Love bade me welcome; yet my soul drew back,
> Guiltie of dust and sinne.
> But quick-ey'd Love, observing me grow slack
> From my first entrance in,
> Drew nearer to me, sweetly questioning,
> If I lack'd any thing.
>
> A guest, I answer'd, worthy to be here:
> Love said, You shall be he.
> I the unkinde, ungratefull? Ah my deare,
> I cannot look on thee.

The poem, which was essentially a religious poem, continued, and there was a happy ending. Forgiveness, and miraculous acquiescence:

Love took my hand, and smiling did reply,
Who made the eyes but I?

Truth, Lord, but I have marr'd them: let my shame
Go where it doth deserve.
And know you not, sayes Love, who bore the blame?
My deare, then I will serve.
You must sit down, sayes Love, and taste my meat:
So I did sit and eat.

But it was love that was the trouble. Because that was what he had, and that was what she didn't want. He was shrinking and she was growing. He was the incredible shrinking man. The cat, the spider, and then the subatomic—the quark, the neutrino, something so tiny that it met no resistance as it passed through the planet and out the other side.

Correct me if I'm wrong," he said, "but is Scheherazade wearing your pants?"

"*Due caffè, per favore* . . . How did you see Scheherazade's pants?"

"How did I see Scheherazade's pants? Lily, I'll tell you. I glanced in her general direction when she was sitting on the sofa before dinner. That's how I saw Scheherazade's pants."

"Mm. All right."

"I mean it's no great feat to see Scheherazade's pants, is it. Or yours. I think you might have to get up a bit earlier in the morning to see Gloria's pants. Or Oona's. But it's no great feat to see Scheherazade's pants. Or yours."

"Stop *wheedling* . . . No, it's true. Nowadays pants are part of what girls wear on the outside."

After breakfast in bed, followed by the boundary violation they both knew so well, Keith and Lily walked down to the village. *Dating your sister,* of course, was a synonym for boredom. Having sex with your sister, on the other hand (he assumed), would be unforgettably terrifying. Having sex with Lily was not unforgettably terrifying. Nor was it boring, once it began. And yet his mind and his body were not in concord. The only link he could find between his two sisters was *low self-esteem.*

Lily loved Keith, or so she said; but Lily didn't love Lily. And perhaps that was what girls would be needing, in the new order—a strenuous narcissism. It sounded weird, but it was quite possibly true: they had to want to go and fuck themselves. He said,

". . . *I am a boy. This is a girl.*"

"Don't do that," said Lily.

"Why are they staring? *This is a shirt. This is a skirt. This is a shoe.*"

"Stop it! It's rude."

"Staring's rude too. Anyway. Is Scheherazade wearing your pants?"

"Yes."

"I thought so. It gave me a shock. There she sat, wearing what are arguably your coolest pants."

"I gave her a pair . . . I showed her my pants and she liked them. So I gave her a couple of pairs."

He now imagined the following sequence: Keith showing Kenrik his pants, and Kenrik liking them, and Keith giving Kenrik a couple of pairs. Lily went on,

"She said my pants made hers look like gym knickers. Or female Y-fronts. Or bunion pads . . . You've got a thing about pants."

He said, "I have suffered much at the hands of pants."

It was actually a theme of some delicacy—Lily's pants. When she left him, in March, she walked out of the door in functional underwear. When she returned, she returned in cool pants. What goes through a girl's mind, he wondered, when she makes the switch to cool pants?

"Doris," he said with perhaps inordinate bitterness.

"When was Doris?"

"Long before your time. I went to bed with her every night for five months. It took me ten weeks to get her bra off. Then I came up against the pants. And they weren't cool pants either. The cool thing about cool pants is you know they're coming off. That's all. They put your mind at rest."

"Even then you had a thing about pants."

"No, *Doris* had a thing about pants." She rose with her pants on. She turned in with her pants on. Keith wanted to say to her: Doris, you have a thing about pants. You have pants on—different pants on, but pants on—twenty-four hours a day. "I kept telling her, *It's 1968, for Christ's sake.* I kept bending her ear about the sexual revolution . . . You know I gave up Psychology because of pants. When I read Freud on pants—as a fetish. He says your mother's pants are the last thing you see before the trauma of discovering that she doesn't have a penis. So you fetishise them." And he thought at the time, If that's true, then the whole human project should be quietly abandoned. "I changed to English the same day."

"That's enough about pants."

"Agreed. But then there's Pansy."

"Christ. Who's Pansy?"

"I told you. A friend of Rita's. In fact a protégée of Rita's." With Pansy, Lily, I suffered the tragic night of the pants. "Don't look like that. When are you going to tell me about Anthony? And Tom? And Gordon?"

". . . And all this," said Lily, "because I happened to give Scheherazade a few pairs of pants."

He folded some banknotes under the saucer. "Let's have a quick look at the rat."

"Perhaps it's been sold. Perhaps, even as we speak, it's being cherished in a lovely little home somewhere."

"Guess what happens at the end of *Northanger Abbey.* Frederick fucks Isabella. He doesn't marry her. He just fucks her."

"Was she drugged?"

"No." But he thought, Yes she was, Isabella, in a way: Isabella was drugged on money. "She persuades herself that he's somehow going to marry her. After."

"So she's ruined. She's lost."

"Utterly. Anyway. Why does Scheherazade suddenly want cool pants? Why is she going around," he persisted, "in what are debatably your coolest pants?"

"To be at her very best for Tom Thumb."

And he allowed himself a silent chortle as they moved off down the sunken street. Still, it was also occurring to him that he and Adriano were caught in the same contradiction: they were retrograde, they were counter-revolutionary. Under the old regime, love preceded sex; it wasn't that way round any more.

"There it is. Grim as death. It knows it's not going anywhere. Ever."

"You're so unkind."

"I'm not unkind enough."

"It's just a rather small dog with a funny face."

"You should give up on this dog angle, Lily. And praise it as a rat. With all the usual rat virtues." Among these strengths would be a lustier embrace of life—a lustier embrace of life at the level of *nostalgie. Nostalgie de la boue:* the return-home pain for the mud, the trash, the shit. "Rats get around more."

"You're so horrible. It's a dog."

. . . When the binary moment came, and you chose between two futures, and you chose the unknown, and acted, something mysterious had to happen first. The wanted one, far from becoming more intensely herself, had to become generic. The body parts, the this and the that of her, had to retreat, and lose outline and individuality. She had to be everywoman, everygirl. And Scheherazade just wouldn't do that.

3

MARTYR

Adriano had many cars, including a racer that seated only one, like a canoe; at its wheel, in his goggles, he resembled a badger motoring its way through a children's book. But today, at noon, it was the high-slung Land Rover that waited in the gravel drive at the castle's gate—the size of a Sherman tank, it seemed, with Adriano standing on the driver's seat, or the dashboard, and poking his head through the sunroof and waving his thick-gloved hands in the air. Scheherazade, Lily, and Whittaker climbed aboard; and off they drove to Rome.

Keith went down to the pool with the idea of befriending Gloria Beautyman. Family history, after all, had conditioned him to be kind to girls in disgrace. Some might say (and Lily was among them) that this was part of the difficulty: Keith and his family were no good at disgrace. They had neither the talent nor the stamina for it. They found it less trouble to forgive. And some might say, further, that Violet, after transgressions far more chaotic and multiform than Gloria's intriguing lapse—well, you could tell by her eyes: Violet was wondering how much more disgrace she'd have to sit through, before getting back to transgression.

"May I? Do you mind?"

". . . No. No not at all."

Now he calmly and personally settled himself, and *Northanger Abbey,* at Gloria's side. How do we explain the poised airiness of his mood? Well, Keith was looking forward to the disposal of Adriano (*I'll feel freer in my mind*). And he had a new project or policy. Carnalisation. Falling out of love with the loved one. I can say (between ourselves) that this was going to be a very bad day indeed for Keith's interests—his interests as he saw them. But for now he was happy, he was freshly showered, he was twenty years old. Gloria said,

"You gave me a fright. I thought you might be Oona." She drew in breath; and comprehensively exhaled. "Is it always this hot?"

"It builds and builds. And then there's a storm."

Gloria, too, had a book on her lap, which she now put aside, marking the page with the stub of a train ticket. She seemed to prepare herself for sleep, but after a while, with closed eyes, she was surprisingly saying,

"Am I correct in thinking that Scheherazade has gone to Rome to buy a monokini this afternoon? I heard her announce such an intention."

Am I curraict in thinking . . . The voice itself was warm and civilised; and the strict enunciation — what they called *cut-glass* — seemed consonant with Edinburgh, the city of economics (and political philosophy, and engineering, and mathematics), the city of hard thought. He said,

"Yes she did, didn't she."

"I know — the gaiety of nations. And all that. But frivolity has its limits. It's a three-hour drive. I've just done it."

Keith agreed that it was a long way to go.

"A monokini. What did she think she had on this morning?"

Her eyes were still closed, and so he looked: the squarish face whose chin came to a delicate point, the narrow line of the mouth, the full Celt-Iberian nose, the boyish black bob. Her eyes opened suddenly and roundly. He said,

"Uh, she had a bikini on this morning."

"Yes. A bikini that she'd thrown away the other half of. In other words, she had a monokini on this morning. Ninety-five miles. Are monokinis less dear than bikinis? Are they half the price? Perhaps I'm very old-fashioned. But honestly."

A silence developed and he attended to *Northanger Abbey.* He was going back to check whether Frederick Tilney did, in point of fact, fuck Isabella Thorpe. The novel became partly epistolary, and it was hard to be exactly sure. And this was, after all, the novel's one cataclysmic event. He tried to feel the weight of this: a single sexual act that held vicious meaning for your whole existence . . . Keith supposed that gallantry obliged him to stick up for Scheherazade, and tell Gloria that there were other reasons for the trip to Rome. For example, tea at the Ritz with Adriano's father, Luchino. Keith happened to know, too, that Scheherazade, not content with the purchase of a monokini, planned to spend *a hundred dollars on underwear* (she would be giving Lily a few pairs). What's happening? he thought. There was a time when he would have disapproved of this — would have looked up from the pages of *The Common Pursuit* or *The Liberal Imagination,* and wondered aloud how the money could be more sensibly spent. Gloria said,

"Am I a prig or has it all gone a bit too far? This obsession with *display.*" And looking past him she said to herself with a flat smile, "Ah, here it is. *For the thing which I greatly feared is come upon me . . .*"

Keith turned. On the upper lawn, with a pair of secateurs in each hand, Oona was browsing through the roses.

"*And that which I was afraid of is come unto me.* Watch. Watch how she's spinning it out. Ooh, I'm for it now. You know why, of course?"

Lily was always telling him, as if in sincere reproach, that he had no talent for lying. *You're hopeless,* she would say, throwing her hands in the air and slowly shaking her head. *It's truly pathetic. And that's why you're no good at flattery and you're so easy to tease . . .* Keith stayed silent (he was planning to say something artful), and Gloria said,

"Should I just wait? Or should I go up and present myself for execution?"

"Oh, I wouldn't worry about Oona. Oona doesn't mind about a bit of cocaine."

For a moment he felt great powers of scrutiny coming to bear on him. "What do you mean?"

"Oh, sorry. I heard you got caught taking cocaine in some bathroom at a party. That wouldn't bother Oona. She's seen it all, that one."

Again, the shaft of intense examination. Then this passed, and she sat back.

"All right. Let the time be of her choosing." She picked up her book again. She even started to hum. Minutes, pages, went by. She said, "Where were we?"

"Uh, display. It's all gone too far . . . What has? Sexual—emancipation?"

"There's just been a fuss in London," she said, "because they've started showing pubic hair."

"Who have?"

"Women. Oh you know. In the men's magazines."

"That's hardly a feminist decision."

"I never said it was. I think it demeans everyone, don't you? But there it is. It's a sign of the times . . . Gentle Jesus. Meek and mild. All right—do your worst."

Oona was descending. She came to a halt on the middle terrace, then turned with a sharp inclination of her head. Gloria gathered herself in a towel; her small feet inched — crept, stole — into their flip-flops.

"Pray for me," she said, and shuffled off in her white pleats.

The book on the empty chair turned out to be a popular biography of Joan of Arc. Joan of Arc, a warrior and a standard-bearer — leading armies, capturing cities, lifting sieges — at the age of seventeen. Violet's age . . . He turned to the last chapter. The Maid of Orleans, he learnt, was put to death for heresy, but the judicial pretext had to do with a biblical stricture about clothing. Her crime of the wardrobe was perpetrated in order to thwart another kind of crime: rape. They incinerated her, in Rouen in 1431 (she was not yet twenty), for dressing as a boy.

Keith moved into the shade. His talk with Gloria had given him his first pang of homesickness. He wanted to go back to England, and get hold of a men's magazine . . . And again he felt it, the tremor in the air, the wind-borne scent that makes the wildebeest flock and hurtle. It kept astonishing him — how weak the prohibitions always turned out to be, and how ready everyone was to claim the new ground, every inch of it. An automatic annexation. What was called, in children, *self-extension,* as they stockpiled each dawning power and freedom, without gratitude, without thought. And now: where were the hinderers, the wet blankets, where were the miseries, where were the police?

He closed his eyes. When he opened them again, the angles of the shadows had discreetly steepened, and Amen was in the pool, gliding through it soundlessly. Just the head, and its mirror image. When Adriano swam, he seemed to fight the water, kicking and kneeing it with his legs, smashing it with his fists (and moving through it, you had to admit, at an unbelievable speed). Perhaps it was his own reflection Adriano wanted to destroy . . . Now at the far end Amen rose, smooth and silent. He paused. He called out,

"*Ça va?*"

"*Bien. Et toi?*"

Would there be cards tonight? And how far would he get with his other new project? His other new project or policy: willed reptilianisation. He would summon it, the raptor, with its locked eyes, its moronically acquisitive grin, its dripping teeth. Once conjured and activated, of course, the tyrannosaur would then be dismissed. And Keith could love. He would change his shape, no longer reptilian or even mammalian, no longer a man, even, but the gentlest of angels.

The cherubim, they said, were full and perfect in their worship of God. It was the seraphim who were the gentlest of angels, who eternally trembled and aspired, like tongues of flame. So that's what he'd be. The rapt seraph, that adores and burns. Keith slept.

It wasn't Amen, drifting across the grey surface, now, but Gloria. The black orb swivelled, and he could see at once that she was lighter. Lighter, of course, by the weight of the water her body displaced; but lighter in the eyes, lighter in the line of her mouth. She dipped under and then surfaced beneath the shadow of the diving board.

"Mm. *I* could do with a sleep . . . And by the way. Forget what I said about Scheherazade. She can have her monokini. With my blessing."

He watched her dripping form as it climbed the metal steps; and it briefly occurred to him that she was two different women joined at the waist. Yes, a dancer's body, he supposed, with the muscles of the calves, the thighs, pushing upward, striving upward . . . Gloria's poolwear: today's swimsuit (Lily and Scheherazade agreed) was even worse than yesterday's; the lower boundary resolved itself, not in a beltlike skirt, but in the beginnings of a loose and fibrous pair of shorts.

"*Let* her be a prodigal," she said, dabbing an ear with her towel, "and an exhibitionist."

He lit a cigarette. "What explains this radical change of heart?"

"Oh, irony, is it. Oh yes. You clever young men. No. The dear girl's been a better friend to me than I thought she'd be. That's all."

"Well I'm glad."

And for the first time Gloria smiled (showing teeth of savage strength, and ideally white, with the very faintest tinge of blue). She said,

"What's it like for you then? All this looking. Come on. At your age. She's a bit of an eyeful, isn't she?"

"Who? Scheherazade?"

"Yes. Scheherazade. You know, the tall one with the very long legs and neck and the highly developed chest. Scheherazade. You've got Lily, of course, but you're used to Lily. What is it, a year? Yes, you're used to Lily. Scheherazade. What does she imagine is going through your mind? What?"

"You're amused."

"Don't you see what I'm saying? There's you. And that Italian. You're young men. The sun is hot. What are you supposed to be thinking?"

"You get used to it."

"Do you? And how does uh, Whittaker like it? And that other one I saw skulking about? Who's obviously a Muslim. If one's going to flaunt oneself like that, then one should consider one's audience."

"And that's why you're more discreet. You yourself."

"Well partly," she said, settling on the wicker chair, and reaching for Joan of Arc. "It only came up about a year ago, all this. It wasn't something you had to think about before. Jorquil insists sometimes, but I decided I wouldn't. Display."

"Modesty."

"There's another reason. Also to do with one's boyfriend."

He said cautiously, "If it's the reason I think it is, then I see your point."

"What's the reason you think it is?"

"I don't know. Devaluation. Demystification."

"Well yes," she said, and yawned. "You do lose the element of surprise. But it isn't that." She gave him a friendly but scornful glance. "I suppose there's no harm in telling *you*. How old are you? 'Nineteen'?"

"I'll be twenty-one in a couple of weeks."

"Then perhaps we should wait until you're of age. Oh all right." And she gave a cough of polite introduction: "Huh-*hm*. Some women want to get their breasts brown. And I don't."

"And why's that?"

"I want to be able to prove I'm a white woman . . . I'm not horrible and prejudiced or anything. And of course I'm devoted to Jorq. But when I'm starting up with a *new* boyfriend, I might want to prove I'm a white woman. You'll see how dark I get."

"You're already very dark," he said, and crossed his legs. They were talking about degrees of bodily display, and Gloria was pretty, perhaps very pretty. But she was in purdah ("veil, curtain"), in occultation, and she transmitted no sexual charge. None. He said, "I don't understand. Gloria, unless you sunbathe naked, you'll always be able to prove you're a white woman."

"Yes, but I might want to prove it sooner than that. You know. At an earlier stage."

They read in silence for half an hour.

"It's vulgar," she said. "It's just vulgar. And anyway, who *told* them to?"

By half past nine he was out on the loveseat of the west terrace, with the transient fireflies (like cigarette butts flicked through the air), and, by his standards, fairly drunkenly reading *Mansfield Park*. Taking the smoothest route to the reptile house, he thought, might involve a certain amount of medication. He couldn't drug Scheherazade—but himself he could disorder and anaesthetise. And two whole glasses of wine, perhaps, would lead to the rediscovery of his glorious reptilian heritage . . . Oona, earlier, had taken a sandwich up to the apartment; and Gloria Beautyman, in a housecoat of brown duffel, wordlessly picked at a bowl of green salad while she stood over the kitchen sink.

Fiction was kitchen-sink, he was deciding. This was the conclusion he was coming to. Social realism was kitchen-sink. The thing being that some sinks, and some kitchens, were much more expensive than others.

He heard the gravel scrape, and then the jeep with its moody rumble, he heard the doors open and then gulp shut again, Whittaker's low tenor, the rattle of gravel. He read on. It seemed most unlikely, at this point, that Henry Crawford would fuck Fanny Price. So far, though, there tended to be one fuck per book. At any rate, *one fuck per book* was how he expounded it to Lily. But it would be more accurate to say that in every book you *heard* about a fuck. This never happened to the heroines. Heroines weren't allowed to do that, Fanny wasn't allowed to do that. And no one had any drugs . . .

Ten minutes later, with an inconvenienced expression on his face, Keith was pacing down the stone staircase. Its damp slate again diffused the cold sweat of late June. In the hallway he could make out the dropped shopping bags, which gleamed with rigid expensiveness, ice-white. He stepped into the courtyard, where the chill, joining a palpable dew, thickened into mist. Would it hold, kitchen-sink—would social realism hold? He was a K in a castle, after all: he had to be ready for change, for category mistakes and shape-shiftings and bodies becoming different bodies . . .

For a moment the figure on the far side of the fountain loomed like a large and complicated animal, of uneven mass, and many-limbed. And he had the brief impression that it was feeding, giving or transferring sustenance . . . It was Lily and Scheherazade in a static but urgent embrace. They weren't kissing or anything like that. They were crying. He moved forward. Then Lily opened her eyes and closed them again with a shiver of her chin.

"Why?" he repeated in the dark. "Come on, Lily, this is . . . How bad can it be? *What?"*

By now, Lily was no longer shedding tears; she merely rasped and groaned every few seconds. How bad could it be? What desolation had awaited them in the bijou boutique, in the Ritz?

"It was the most awful thing ever."

Keith was concluding that there must have been an accident: the world reduced to what happens in headlights, the school bus and the express train . . . He heard a thick gulp, a bubbling sniff, and Lily spoke again. It was a thin, circling sound—the voice of a little girl, helplessly circling her bitterest care.

"And it's *so* much more terrible for Scheherazade . . ."

"Why?"

". . . Because it means she *has* to now."

"Has to what?"

". . . There's no choice. Everything's changed with Adriano."

He waited.

Another groan, another gummy, sticky sniff, and then she said miserably, "He's a martyr. He was born in 1945. So she has to."

Late the next morning Keith left behind him a decidedly quietened castle and went past the pool and down the slope to apply to Whittaker.

"Let's take a walk."

"Where to?"

"You should get out more, Keith, and breathe some fresh air. Instead of sitting in your room all day reading English novels. Just a stroll."

"Yeah but where to? . . . Begin from the beginning. Imagine I don't know anything at all."

"It was one of the most extraordinary things I've ever seen . . . Okay. We did the shopping."

They did the shopping. And went to the hotel to be reunited with

Adriano. They rode the elevator to the penthouse—Whittaker, and Lily and Scheherazade, with their creels and caskets, their monokini, their gaiety, their youth, in summer dresses. The door slid open and there was Luchino.

"I don't know what we were expecting exactly. It's funny. None of us had given it a moment's thought. Isn't that odd. Anyway."

Luchino was six foot three. Also present was Adriano's younger brother, Tybalt. Tybalt was six foot six. Also present, of course, was Adriano. Adriano was four foot ten. Whittaker went on,

"And you wanted to say, *Hi. What the fuck happened to* him?"

"And you couldn't do that."

"You couldn't do that. It was like a stage set. Or a tableau. Or a dream. I kept expecting to get over it. Or get used to it."

"That's what Lily said."

"But none of us did. The tension, the pressure, was beyond anything. You could *hear* it."

"Then the tea."

Keith lit a cigarette. They were following the path that encircled the foothills of the opposite mountain, where the valley crashed like a wave against the heights.

"Where are we going?"

"Nowhere. We're walking. The tea was all laid out on the roof— very Anglo-style, like they are. Lace doilies. Cucumber sandwiches with the crusts cut off. And there were tables but no chairs. No chairs. Luchino, Tybalt—both disgustingly handsome. And then you thought how handsome Adriano was too. But he was all the way down there."

"And he played his part."

"He played his part. A very determined little guy, Adriano. And it was all kind of nuts. Why not talk about it? Find a form of words. Maybe even joke about it. Christ, I don't know."

"Yeah." Yeah, he thought. Laugh about it: in case Adriano started getting a complex. "Then drinks."

"Then drinks. Both girls asked for whisky. Unusual, no? I sat between them on the sofa and I could feel their hearts beating. Both their hearts. Ah. Here are the inamoratos."

They came to a halt. The two monks were striding down the narrow trail towards them on sandalled, skirted feet, talking, turning, nodding. *Buon giorno. Buon giorno.* They moved on through the scrub and the jagged outcrop, concernedly gesturing, but with hidden hands.

"Ah, they're *so* in love. I had ten minutes with Luchino," said Whittaker. "He gave me a wise smile, and we talked. Or he did."

"Adriano was born in 1945."

"Yes. The saddest story. Adriano was born in 1945 . . . On the way back, in the jeep, no one said a word. Except Adriano. The usual stuff. Hang-gliding smash-ups. Rafting spills . . . *Incubo.*"

Which meant *nightmare.* Whittaker said,

"He was tremendously precise, Luchino. Very uh, condensed. Not rehearsed exactly. Crystallised. He'd found a form of words."

"Can you remember any of it?"

"Oh yes. He said, *If, God forbid, Adriano should die before I do, then at last, in his coffin, my son will be as other men are.*"

"He did, did he."

"And this. *Not a moment passes without my praying for such episodes of joy as he will ever experience. Moments of love and life. Heaven defend the angels of mercy who grant him as much.*"

". . . Did you tell Scheherazade all that?"

4

SANE DREAMS

It was, without any doubt, the saddest story. A story from another genre, another way of doing things. Social realism had failed to hold. And what was the form of words?

The child was conceived in May, 1944. And for all but the first and last few days of her pregnancy Adriano's mother was in prison. The crime she was guilty of was being married to her husband. Luchino had been drafted into what they were calling the New Army, Mussolini's New Army; and Luchino evaded it, this draft, with his wife's blessing; they both feared, with good reason (according to Whittaker), that Luchino would sooner or later be trucked off to a labour camp in the Reich. *Lucia was adamant,* said Luchino. *We knew—everyone knew—that the worst possible prison was less lethal than the best possible camp. What we didn't know was that Adriano was alive inside her.* Tybalt was born in 1950. And Lucia died in 1957, when Adriano was twelve.

So Keith was sad about that. To give him some credit (which he will soon be needing), I can say that Keith was duly harrowed by his imaginings of the enwombed Adriano. Fully fifteen years later, in 1984, when he saw his first child on the paediatrician's monitor, delightedly busying itself like a newt in a millpond, all ashiver with festive and apparently humorous curiosity, Keith's first thought was of Adriano and his hunger: the hunger of the enwombed Adriano. The tiny ghost and his face of pain. And this pain would clothe him for the rest of his life. Four foot ten. Five foot six could make a semi-educated guess at four foot ten. And how *near* the war was . . .

So Keith understood why the girls cried. But now the rules had been rewritten, and the generic proprieties no longer obtained. The question had to be asked again. What were heroines allowed to do?

You're very gloomy. Come on, you should be happy to oblige."

With gloomy couples, in gloomy weather, whole days pass like this. With gaps, mugs of coffee, silences, brief disappearances, cups of tea, yawns, vacancies . . . Later on, Lily and Keith would have to go down to the village and *represent the castello:* Oona had signed them up for some ceremonial jumble sale at Santa Maria.

"I don't mind that," he said. "Except it means going to church. No, I'm depressed about Tom Thumb."

"Don't call him Tom Thumb."

"Okay. I'm depressed about Adriano. Were you expecting his dad to be a—to be a bit on the short side?"

"I expected, I don't know, someone below average. A titch. Like you. Not a giant. And then the giant brother. That's when she melted. You know how soft-hearted she is."

Like a dream, said Whittaker. All this is like a dream. He said, "*Will* she, d'you think?"

"Well. Two birds with one stone. A lovely boost for him, and it'll stop her being desperate. She'll feel her way into it."

Keith lay on the bed—he lay on the bed with *Emma.* Lily was undressing for the shower: not a lengthy operation. She leant towards him and slid down her bikini bottoms with her thumbs. Over the weeks, the parent star was daubing Lily to its taste, the flesh browner, the hair blonder, the teeth whiter, the eyes bluer. She kicked off her flip-flops and said abruptly,

"Who fucks Fanny?"

"What? No one fucks Fanny." They were resuming their discussion of *Mansfield Park.* Keith tried to concentrate—to concentrate on the world he knew. With a show of liveliness (talking was better than thinking), he said, "She's a heroine, Lily, and heroines aren't allowed to do that. Anyway. Who'd *want* to fuck Fanny?"

"The hero. Edmund."

"Well, Edmund, I suppose. He marries her, after all. I suppose he gets round to it in the end. He *is* the hero."

In her green satin housecoat, Lily sat herself at the dressing table with her back to the three mirrors. She took up a cardboard nail file and said, "So you don't fancy Fanny."

"No. Mary Crawford's more the thing. She's a goer too."

"How can you tell?"

"There are ways, Lily. Mary's talking about admirals, and she makes a joke about *vices* and *rears*. In Jane *Austen* . . . But *Mansfield Park*'s not like the others. The villains are Visions and the goodies are Duds. Resurgence of old values. Jane becomes anti-charm. It's a very confused novel."

"And there aren't any fucks."

"No. There are. *Mansfield Park*'s got *two* fucks. Henry Crawford fucks Maria Bertram. And Mr. Yates fucks her sister Julia. And he's an Honourable."

"What were *they* drugged with?"

"That's a good question. I don't know. Unloving parents. Boredom."

"Scheherazade's drugging herself with pity."

He thought this was true. The Adriano project had become a form of social work or community service. "Sex as a good deed. Yeah. Tell that to Jane Austen."

"She thinks about him growing up with Tybalt. And then Tybalt overtaking him. Tybalt growing. Swelling into this great towering god. She wishes . . ."

In fact they could hear her in the intervening bathroom — the taps, the quick tread.

"If only she'd met Tybalt first. She could fuck him. But she can't. She's got to fuck Tom Thumb instead. And she thinks she's found a way."

So Lily whispered, and stared. And was gone, out of the door and down the steps in her robe.

And Keith attempted to return to Emma, and Miss Bates, and the life-altering picnic on Box Hill.

"You know what they looked like?" said Lily, reappearing with one towel swathed around her and another twirled up in a cone on her head. "Tybalt and Adriano? When they stood there at the bar side by side? They looked like a bottle of Scotch and a miniature. The same brand and the same label. The bottle and the miniature."

Lily was now getting dressed. All was familiar to him. Familiar, and irrational, like the thoughts that bracket sleep. Was her flesh just the clothing of her blood, her bones? Then she sat at the table before the three mirrors, to dress her face, the eyes in violet, the cheeks in rouge, the lips in pink. He said,

"Should you tong your hair when it's wet? Are you sure? . . . Tybalt *would* be six foot six, wouldn't he. Not five foot eleven or anything like that."

"Actually I admire Scheherazade's attitude. She's trying her best to be positive. She thinks she can see her way to some sort of dirty weekend. The kind where you never go out. Or even get up. So they're never perpendicular at the same time."

"All right, Lily. Describe the horizontal weekend."

Keith listened with a wandering mind . . . Adriano would drive her to the capital and park near—or preferably under—one of its premier hotels; adducing discretion, Scheherazade would proceed alone to the booked suite; there she would bathe, and perfume and moisten herself, and lay her long body, coated in some deliquescent negligee, on the white sheets—for him! for Adriano! The man himself would then dramatically appear; standing before the bed, perhaps, he would reach with lingering fingers for the furled bow that secured his white slacks, and, with a stern smile . . .

"After that," said Lily, "you just use room service. Nothing in public, where they're both standing up. It's that that makes her die of self-consciousness. She's ashamed of herself, but there it is. She keeps thinking about what *he's* thinking about. And she gets the creeps."

Keith agreed that it wouldn't be any good if she got the creeps.

"Her attitude's this. If she fancies Tybalt so much, then she must fancy Adriano. Sort of. And anyway. She's getting more and more desperate." Lily rose to her feet and smoothed her hands floorward. "Come on. It's time."

And he thought suddenly, This is the world I know, this is my place, among the wide-awake—with her. He rolled off the bed saying, "I've been meaning to tell you. You look really lovely, Lily. And we won't break up. We'll stay together. You and me."

"Mm. Mm. I suppose you're in love with *her* now."

"Who?"

"Emma."

"Oh, definitely. She's a bit flash, Emma, but I fancy her, I admit. *Clever, handsome, and rich.* It's a start."

"Ah, but has she got big tits? . . . Does Jane Austen *say* if they've got big tits?"

"Not in so many words. Or not yet. Any moment now she'll probably say, *Emma Woodhouse had big tits.* But not yet."

"You said, you said Lydia Bennet had big tits. The one that runs off with the soldier."

"Well she has. Or a big arse anyway. Catherine Morland has big tits. Jane Austen more or less tells you that. It's in code. See, Lydia's the tallest and youngest sister—and she's *stout*. That's code for a big arse."

"And what's code for big tits?"

"*Consequence*. When Catherine's growing up she gets *plumper* and her *figure gains consequence. Consequence*—that's code for big tits."

"Maybe it's simpler than that. The code. Maybe *plump* is tits and *stout* is arse."

Keith said that she could very well be right.

"So Scheherazade's plump, and Gloria's stout. But you wouldn't call Junglebum stout exactly, would you."

"Junglebum? No. But words change, Lily. Arses change."

"Listen to him. First it was all moral patterning. And felt life. Then it was all drugs and fucks. Now it's all tits and arses. Hang on. I've got one. Hysterical Sex and the Single Girl. With Natalie Wood. That's a proper one."

"No, Lily. That's not a proper one." He thought for a moment and said, "Hysterical Sex Story. With Ali MacGraw. That's a proper one."

"But she died. And anyway, we hated it."

"I know we hated it. Is Tom Thumb coming to dinner?"

"Don't call him that. Yes. By helicopter."

"Christ, I'm going to talk to him about this. The sheep are just about halfway back to normal."

"Talk to Scheherazade. She says she loves to think of Adriano flying free . . ."

Keith said, "You know, I reckon that's how he pulls, Adriano. If four foot ten doesn't do it on its own, he takes them to his dad's and wheels out Tybalt."

". . . 1945's the key. The war's the key. Then she can tell herself she's doing it for the troops."

"For the troops?" he said with a crack in his voice. "But he was on the wrong side!"

"What?"

"Italy was an Axis power. So Tom Thumb was a fascist." Keith went on to impart the two remaining facts in his possession about Italy and the Second World War. "Mussolini introduced the goose step. And when they finally strung him up, he was in a German uniform. Nazi to the last."

"Calm down . . . And don't tell Scheherazade all that."

The evening began noisily enough. First, the grinding turmoil of Adriano's rotors. And then they were all heckled and barracked off the west terrace, in the rosy dusk, by the screams of the sheep. But dinner was in fact strangely quiet—or did he mean quietly strange? Whittaker, Gloria, and Keith, facing Lily, Adriano, and Scheherazade. Adriano, then, was not at the head of the table, but he seemed to lead the talk, with his sense of entitlement fully refreshed, saying,

"We clinched the championship with a bitterly fought victory in Foggio. Yet more silverware for our trophy room! Now soon we face the rigours of pre-season training. I'm chafing to begin."

Keith, again, happened to know that Scheherazade had instructed Adriano to stop talking about love, which Adriano, ominously, had at once agreed to do. On the other hand, this left him short of conversation. So he spoke, at perhaps exorbitant length, about his rugby team, *I Furiosi,* and its reputation, in what was already the harshest of leagues, for exceptionally uncompromising play.

"Where do you go, Adriano? On the field."

This was Scheherazade, who wore a new smile on her face. Meek, sorrowful, all-comprehending, all-forgiving. Keith listened on.

"Ah. My position. In the very centre of the fray."

Adriano was the hooker, and did his work in the fulcrum of the pack. How he especially relished it, he said, at the commencement of a scrum, when the six heads came smashing together! It was normally the hooker's job, Keith knew, to backheel the ball into the tread of the ten-legged melee that strained at his rear. But it was a different story, apparently, with *I Furiosi:* as the clash began, Adriano simply raised and crossed his little legs, so that the men behind him (the second row) could rake their studs down the knees and shins of the opposing front line. He said,

"Most effective. Oh, I can promise you. Most effective."

". . . But doesn't anyone put a stop to it?" said Scheherazade. "And don't they take their revenge?"

"Ah, but we are equally famed for our indifference to injury. I am the only *Furiosi* forward with an unbroken nose. The lock is blind in one eye. And neither prop has a tooth in his head. Also, both my ears still hold their shape. Not yet even calcified. Which, again, makes me stick out as a sore thumb from my confrères."

"And after the match, Adriano?" said Lily.

"We celebrate our victory. And in no uncertain fashion, rest assured. Or, once in a blue moon, we are consigned . . . to drown our sorrows. All night—always. There is much broken glass. We are veritable lords of misrule!"

". . . Who was it who said," said Whittaker, "that rugby is a game for hooligans played by gentlemen?"

And Keith said, "Yes, I've heard that. And football is a game for gentlemen played by hooligans."

"I lived in Glasgow till the age of ten."

This was Gloria, and they all turned to her because she so seldom spoke. Meeting no one's eye, she said,

"One thing is clear. Football is a game *watched* by hooligans . . . When Celtic play Rangers it's a war of religion. Unbelievable. They should go in the army. Adriano. *You* should go in the army."

"Oh, Gloria, don't think I didn't try! But there are certain restrictions and, alas . . ."

Falling silent, he bunched the white napkin in his bronzed fists. And for five minutes the room silently churned. Then Adriano straightened his back and said,

"A game for hooligans? How wrong you are, Whittaker. How very wrong you are."

And Adriano proceeded to assure the gathering, with possibly excessive chapter and verse, that *I Furiosi* were all of gentle birth, belonging to exclusive sports clubs that charged very high entrance fees; when they drove to their away fixtures, he said, why, they did so in a fleet of Lamborghinis and Bugattis; he even took the trouble to note the deluxe, five-star quality of the hotels they despoiled and the restaurants they wrecked. Adriano sat back, his point made.

They then sat through the gradual formation of a hopeless vacuum. Lily's stare implored him, and so Keith said,

"Uh, I used to be just like you, Adriano. I was mad about rugby until I was thirteen. Then one day . . ." There was the usual maul. Exactly the sort of thing he used to love diving into and coming out of covered in blood. "And I . . ."

"You lost your nerve," said Adriano understandingly, and even reached out and patted Keith's hand. "Oh, my friend, it happens!"

"Yeah. I lost my nerve." But there was another thought in his mind, on the significant Saturday morning—and a thought behind that, and a thought behind that. He said to himself, in 1963: From now on, nothing is renewed. You will be needing everything. *You will be needing everything. For the girls.* "So I stopped diving in. People noticed. I was dropped."

Adriano said, "But Kev. How did you tolerate the shame? And the universal contempt?"

Lily said, "I think that's very funny, Adriano. If I may say so."

"How did I tolerate it? I told everyone I did it for my sister." Violet was eight, nine; she used to get upset when he came home covered in welts. *I'll give it up because of you, Vi* . . . This was true, in a sense. He did it for the girls. "Anyway. She was very grateful."

"It's straightforward," said Scheherazade, folding her mat. "You didn't want to be hurt any more."

Adriano stayed in his seat as the table cleared around him, to be rejoined, in due course, by Scheherazade.

He sank back, his fraternal duty done. Lily said,

"That was fantastic."

"Wasn't it. Stunning. Will it be like that every night?"

"Impossible. We'll all die or go mad. I kept pinching myself. Not to stay awake. To make sure I wasn't asleep. And dreaming."

"You don't get dreams as mad as that."

He lay there, and ran an errand of love—but for the last time. For the last time he conjured Scheherazade and imagined that all his thoughts were her thoughts and that all her feelings were his feelings. But as love said its farewells, lingering, kissing its fingertips, it told him that someone as solid, someone as broadly convincing as Scheherazade would not, could not, entwine herself with someone as unbelievable—and obscurely fraudulent—as Adriano. While Lily wafted off in search of sane dreams, Keith hoped and believed that Adriano too would waft off, would melt as the dawn melts the stars, and that Scheherazade would go on being more and more desperate.

But it was the war that presided over his insomnia. For the first time in his life, perhaps, he felt its size and weight. *That* was not a war in heaven. It was a war of the world.

How near the war was, and how vast.

The war was so near to them and they never really thought about it — the six-year earthquake that killed a million a month (and took Italy, and ground and pestled its mountains against one another).

The war had made its application to the courage of their mothers and fathers, and they were all its children, its tiny ghosts, like the enwombed Adriano.

The war was so near to them and it was not a shadow. It was a light. The colour of the light was a fecal brown.

THIRD INTERVAL

Like everyone else alive during the period under review, Keith was a vet of the Nuclear Cold War (1949–91): the contest of nightmares. In 1970, a twenty-year tour lay behind him. A twenty-year tour lay ahead of him.

He was conscripted—he was *impressed*—on August 29, 1949, when he was ninety-six hours old. This was the date of the birth of the Russian bomb. As he lay sleeping, historical reality stole into the ward at the infirmary, and gave him the rank of private.

Growing up, he didn't feel resentful about military service exactly, because everyone else alive was in the army too. Apart from crouching under his desk at school, when they practised for central thermonuclear exchange, he didn't seem to have any duties. Or no conscious ones. But after the Battle of Cuba, in 1962 (for its duration, its thirteen days, his thirteen-year-old existence became a swamp of nausea), he entered into the spirit of the contest of nightmares. In his mind—oh, the obstacle courses, the sadistic NCOs, the fatigues, the lousy chow, the twirling potato skins of kitchen patrol. In the Nuclear Cold War, you only saw action when you were sound asleep.

During this period, physical violence was somehow consigned to the Third World, where about twenty million died in about a hundred military conflicts. In the First and Second Worlds, the shaping strategy was Mutual Assured Destruction. And everyone lived. There, the violence was all in the mind.

Keith lay in his bed, trying to understand. What was the outcome of the dream war and all that silent combat? Everything could vanish, at any moment. This disseminated an unconscious but pervasive mortal fear. And mortal fear might make you want to have sexual intercourse;

but it wouldn't make you want to love. Why love anyone, when everyone could vanish? So maybe it was love that took the wound, in the Passchendaele of mad dreams.

. . .

What a very compassionate book it is, the *Concise Oxford Dictionary*. Take, for example, the entry on *neurosis*. He rang his wife and read it out to her.

"Now listen. *A relatively mild mental illness,* my love, *not caused by organic disease.* Here's an even better bit. *Involving depression, anxiety, obsessive behaviour, etc.*—that et cetera's great—*but not a radical loss of touch with reality.* There. That's *so* understanding, don't you think?"

". . . Come to the house."

He went to the house. It was April 28, 2003, and he crossed the garden under a dishevelled sky. And things were going fairly well, he thought: he was sitting at the table with a glass of orange juice, and doing a reasonable impersonation of Keith Nearing. Then the girls came down for their lunch.

He and his wife had four main epithets for their daughters: *the flowers, the fools, the poems,* and *the rats.* Keith chose the third.

"There you are, my poems."

And they greeted him and came to him, little Isabel, tiny Chloe.

Now, there was a domestic tradition: when the girls were freshly bathed, and had washed their hair, Keith would offer up his nose to the thick wet coils and say (as he savoured the cleanliness, the youth, the scent of pine), *Mmmmm . . .*

So Isabel meant it kindly enough, no doubt. Keith was just out of the shower, so she leant over her father's scalp (rapidly greying and radically thinning, its few remaining shreds rigidified by styling gel) and said,

"Mmmmm . . . No, in fact, Daddy, I think you'd better go and have another try."

And that's what he did. That's what he did—even though he was quite drunk and very frightened of falling over in the shower. You'd think that being a stone or two overweight might give you some extra ballast; but it's hard, he told himself, to balance a potato on toothpicks, especially when you're dealing with a slippery surface. He got through that all right. But he didn't go back to the house.

"So you're smoking," said his wife as he slipped out of the back door (he quit in 1994, on the day after their wedding). "Isabel said you smelled like the bus station in Kentish Town."

"All this won't last too long," he said.

. . .

The second item of business on the revolutionary manifesto ran as follows: *Women, also, have carnal appetites.*

Immemorially true, and now of course inalienably obvious. But it took a while for this proposition to be absorbed. In the no-sex-before-marriage community, the doctrine was that good girls didn't do it for lust—and bad girls didn't do it for lust either (they did it for fleeting leverage or for simple gain, or out of a soiled and cobwebbed lunacy). And some of the young ones themselves never quite came to sober terms with it, with female lust. Kenrik, Rita, and others, as we shall soon discover.

There will be sex before marriage. Women, also, have carnal appetites. So far, so good. But there were other clauses in the manifesto, some of them written in fine print or invisible ink.

. . .

Touch me, touch me, touch me, touch me, touch me . . .

These were Echo's last words, but it took her a long time to die. Love was fixed in her body, envenoming everything. Her pretty form faded away. But she wasn't turned into something else (a very common and not necessarily unpleasant fate in the world where she lived)—into a bird, say, or a flower. She just faded away. All that remained was her voice and her bones.

Her stony bones became part of the humus. Her voice wandered off by itself, invisible in the forest and on the bare mountainside. Touch me, touch me, touch me . . .

Of course, the glassy youth lived on in his glassy beauty. Until another boy, another supplicant (also once mocked and spurned), lifted his head to heaven. "Let him love and suffer, as he has made us love and suffer."

> "Let him, like us, love and know it is hopeless.
> And let him, like Echo, perish of anguish."
> Nemesis, the corrector,
> Heard this prayer and granted it.

. . .

Keith's stepdaughter Silvia once said (having listened to him complain about his exercise class) that old age wasn't for sissies. But the suspicion was building in him that it was all much simpler than that. Old age wasn't for old people. To cope with old age, you really needed to be young—young, strong, and in peak condition, exceptionally supple and with very good reflexes. Your character, too, should be of no common stamp, but should blend the fearlessness of youth with age-old tenacity and grit.

He said, "Literature, why didn't you tell me?" Old age may bring you wisdom. But it doesn't bring bravery. On the other hand, you've never had to face anything as terrifying as old age.

Actually, war was more terrifying—and just as unavoidable, it seemed, for human beings. In the local caff he sat with *The Times* trembling in his hands. *This* was avoidable (or at least postponable). Why was no one identifying the true *casus belli*? It was obvious. American presidents, in wartime, are always re-elected. There would be regime change in Baghdad, in 2003, so that there would be no regime change in Washington, in 2004.

Nicholas, who supported it, tried to instil in him some courage about the Mesopotamian experiment, but Keith, just now, couldn't begin to bear the thought of flying iron and mortal flesh, and what happened when the hard machine met the soft.

. . .

Like rats, flies love war, love battlefields. At Verdun (1916), there were donkeys, mules, oxen, dogs, pigeons, canaries, and two hundred thousand horses. But only the rats and the flies (the flies in their scores of millions) were there because they liked it. The flies were huge, black, silent. Huge. The rats, too, were bloated, like war profiteers . . .

In his studio Keith stared at the colourless sky and enjoyed "the view": the vista of his own corneal crud, asperities, excrescences, which swilled and slopped when he moved his head. His eyes were Petri dishes, with their cultures of dirt and death.

What to do, he thought, now that the flies live inside my eyes?

. . .

Oona told them that all her life she had instinctively headed south. *But now,* she said, *I feel the wrongness of the sun.*

136

They didn't heed her (and they all got away with it, so far as he knew).

For them, it was a cook-out or a fry-up. They sat in the sun, slick with extra virgin, the whole day long. And how resinous they became, in their gold peel of youth.

Another time Oona said to him, with what seemed to be unalloyed admiration and respect, "You're *young*." And even then he wondered about it, the drastic promotion of youth . . . There was 1914–18, then 1939–45—with a twenty-one-year gap. Thus in 1966, according to the schedule established over two generations, it was time to send the youth of Europe up the line to death: into the winepress of death. But history broke the pattern. The young weren't going to die; they were going to be loved. Youth sensed this, and became self-aware. The only war they knew was the one they fought when they were asleep. Everything and everyone might suddenly disappear. So, yes, *tutto e subito.* All and Now.

"Well, thanks, Oona," he said, and gazed across the terrace at the fireflies—little visitors from another dimension. The fireflies, the luminescent beetles, were the colour of Venus. Fire, with a photon of lemon in it.

His entire life, he was already sure, would be determined here.

.   .   .

When he went out into the streets of London, he had the near-continuous feeling that all beauty was gone. And what had taken its place?

Beauty is truth, truth beauty. This was beautiful, perhaps. But how could it be beautiful? It wasn't true. As he saw it. Beauty, that rare thing, had gone. What remained was truth. And truth was in endless supply.

Book Four

The Desiderata

I

GIRLS AND THE BUTCHERS

There were comings and goings, now, and additions and subtractions, and rearrangements. Kenrik and Rita were coming, and Ruaa was coming, and Oona, after a short absence, was again going. Would Prentiss, Dodo, and Conchita be returning? Jorquil was quite possibly coming, and Timmy, perhaps, was coming. Most inauspiciously, for now, Scheherazade would soon be vacating her turret, on the far side of the shared bathroom, to be replaced by Gloria, summoned up from her vault. Scheherazade would occupy the apartment—to be replaced in her turn, quite possibly, by Gloria and Jorquil.

They were sitting at the bar's only pavement table and he was telling her that everything would be fine so long as Kenrik and Rita, when they came, were still just good friends.

"What type of person," asked Lily, "is the Dog?"

"Wait," he said. "I'm getting overloaded with all these nicknames. One night it'll just pop out." He was thinking of the trackless voids that now opened up over the dinner table. "I'll say, *Junglebum, tell Tom Thumb about the time you drank the . . .* Let's get used to calling her Rita."

"Okay. What kind of person is Rita?"

"Type?" And he told her: rich working-class (the daughter of a coin-op king), sports car, she ran a large stall (costume jewellery) in Kensington Antique Market. "She's older than us," he said, "and very experienced at acting like a boy. It's her mission. She's like an anti-policewoman. There to make sure everyone breaks the law."

"Well, if Kenrik doesn't fuck the Dog," said Lily, "maybe he can fuck the Blob."

"Lily!"

"Or maybe he can fuck *me*."

"*Lily!*"

"Well someone's got to."

"*Lily!*"

Someone's got to . . . This was a not very erotic remark about a not very erotic situation, and Keith's reply to it was not very erotic.

"Come on, someone does it almost every night. Me. Or in the morning."

"Yes, but not properly."

"Not properly." His fingernails craved his armpits. "I still love you, Lily."

"Mm. *You* may love me. But your—"

"Don't come out with it. That's what Rita always does. She always comes out with it."

He ducked into the bar—a kind of carpentry workshop, with a fridge and a line of dust-greyed brandy bottles up on the shelf. Yes, and what have we here: Italians other than Adriano. In their black fleeces they stood in silence at the counter, like slabs of granite to which the local sculptors had yet to apply their tools, their bodies asleep, their minds and faces formed, it seemed, in the brief interval between two crushing blows to the head. Keith sympathised. Making love to Lily was no longer repetitive, exactly, because it got more treacherous every night. Men have two hearts, he thought, the over, the under. And as Hansel applied himself to Gretel, his overheart was full, it beat, it loved, but his underheart was merely (and barely) functional— anaemic, insincere. And this, of course, was getting noticed.

"Rita's a character," he said as he set Lily's sparkling wine before her. "A real character."

"Not another one. And with Jorquil on the way. Not to mention Tom Thumb. And you were *wrong* about the war." She tapped the book in front of her. "Italy surrendered in 1943. Then the Germans invaded."

"Did they? Shit . . . No. Nothing."

"The fighting was the partisans *against* the fascists. Luchino fought the fascists while the mum starved in prison. So Adriano *was* on the right side. And Scheherazade *can* fuck him for the troops."

Keith lit a cigarette. "How's that actually going? They stay up late enough."

"She says it's like being fifteen again. You know. Stages."

Keith knew all about stages. With his teeth locked together, he said, "Which one are they on?"

"Just kisses so far. With tongues now. She's building up to tits."

Keith drank his beer. Lily said,

"You know. First with his hands outside her top. Then inside. She's quite looking forward to it if she can keep her nerve."

Keith asked why this was.

"Well they've grown a lot in the last six weeks. They feel different. Much more sensation. All throbby and tickly. And she wants to try them out."

"Try out her tits."

"Try out her tits. On Adriano." Lily paused and said, "Then go forward bit by bit and do the same with her box."

Keith threw his pen on to the metal tabletop and said, "You know, this whole thing's completely sick. And she's miserable—you can tell. She can't drug herself with pity. It's, it's . . . You ought to use your influence."

"Where's that bloody fool Timmy? It's so hurtful, because he's obviously just having a marvellous time. He loves the work with the born-again people, but the thing is, every weekend he goes hunting."

"What's there to hunt in Jerusalem?"

"He goes to Jordan. He hunts with the Jordanian royal family."

"Oh I see. Why didn't you say? Well, we mustn't begrudge Timmy his fun. Killing animals with a king."

"I did think about sending him a telegram. Saying she's pining."

Keith said from under his eyebrows, "I don't think you need go that far . . . You know, I sometimes feel Adriano's not what he seems." And what he *seemed* seemed outrageous enough. "Him on her lap. Like a ventriloquist's dummy. It's unreal."

"Poor little chap."

"Rich little chap. Come on." He rose and said dutifully, "I suppose we ought to go and pay our usual respects to the rat. Just talk to her, Lily. You ought to, you know. You owe it to her. Don't forget she's your best friend."

Scheherazade was miserable, and you could tell. The superstitious castle, the fierce mountain, the raw blue sky—everything was numbed by it. Aware of the terrible rule about looks and happiness, Keith expected her to suffer a loss of light in the face, a slight crimping, perhaps, of the mouth. There *was* a new frown, a new fold (which formed the shape, incidentally, of a corporal's double stripes). But suffering just made her more painterly. In painterly Italy. You felt the weight, the downward tug on her heart. Compared to Scheherazade, even Gloria, with her cropped head, her dun smocks, her workshirts and tartan trews, her bricklike leather sandals with the inch-thick toe holes, seemed merely professionalised in her penitence and grief.

Oona left for Rome in a chauffeur-driven jeep. Whittaker went to Naples in the Fiat to pick up Amen and Ruaa. Conchita sent a postcard, with very round *a*s and *o*s, from the Hague.

On their upper lips, on their brows, plump globules of sweat, like strips of translucent bubble wrap. Even their sweat was plump. It gathered under their eyes like the tears of inconsolable five-year-olds. Glands seeped, eyes saw, hearts beat, flesh glowed. They were the colour of peanut butter. But when Keith closed his eyes he saw himself as a scarecrow, stalled in a standstill of frost.

What next?"

"What next? What honestly will be next?"

Lily and Scheherazade, down by the pool, were discussing Gloria's latest swimsuit.

"I know," said Lily. "A frogman outfit. A—what are they called? A bathysphere."

"Yes. Or a kayak. Or a submarine," said Scheherazade. "Gloria wearing a whole submarine."

Every five or six seconds you heard a wrenching creak with a *whump* in the middle of it. This was Adriano, plunging and then soaring to treetop height on the new trampoline—his personal gift to the property. Adriano's trampoline had in fact received mixed reviews. Scheherazade herself disdained all use of it (*Don't tell him,* she said to Lily, *but it hurts. And I bet it's very unflattering),* and Lily asked to have it explained to her—the point of just jumping about like that; Gloria somehow managed to look quite elegant as she dropped and rose (landing on her split legs and scissoring back again); and Amen, on his return, became an enthusiast (he had long and noisy sessions in the very early morning); and Keith once or twice clambered up and messed around on it for five minutes. But the principal exponent and virtuoso of the trampoline was of course none other than Adriano, twanging and twirling himself into extraordinary altitudes, his veins and tendons like cords and cleats, the human being lashed together very tight.

Lily said, "Miss Scotland, no, Miss Glasgow. 1930."

"My God, where does she *find* them?"

Gloria's latest swimsuit, for the record, was grey and featured a pale orange skirt of petal-shaped panels; the top half was made out of wool, the bottom half out of plastic.

"It's not even plastic," said Lily.

"No, it's not even plastic," said Scheherazade. "It's lino."

"Why? What's the point? It's as if we're all absolutely *dying*," said Lily, "to see the exact shape of her arse."

Keith read on for fifteen pages *(Wuthering Heights)*. When he looked up again, Lily had replaced Gloria under the poolhouse shower, Adriano was still on the trampoline—and Scheherazade was working two handfuls of olive oil into her breasts . . . Well she was. This had the humble merit of being true.

"Oh, Scheherazade," he said with a sigh. Yes, he was a moral being, apparently. He was still a moral being. "I think I might've misled you the other day," he began. "Adriano was on the right side in the war. I've just spent an hour in the library. See, fascism was discredited, and Mussolini fell in the summer of 1943. Then the Germans . . ."

But bear in mind, Scheherazade, that it was not among Italy's war aims (he kept wanting to stress); it was not among the war aims of the Axis powers, Scheherazade, that you, one day, would try out your tits on Adriano. He concluded,

"The country suffered horribly. 1945 was its year of sorrow."

She said, "History terrifies me . . . Our parents were the ones who had to go through all that. We're lucky. The only thing we've got to worry about is the end of the world. Everything might just—stop."

He reminded himself that Scheherazade actually *did* things about the end of the world—marches, rallies. Whereas all his protests were subliminal. Everything stopping. Now, for instance, he looked out at the grotto, daubed with its flesh and youth, and for a moment the grotto was grotesque. Grotesque, from Ital. *grottesca* "a painting resembling something found in a grotto"; grotto, from Gk *krupte-* (see CRYPT). "And how are we supposed to feel about that?" he said. "I mean everything stopping."

"Mum says that's why the young are at it all the time. You know, *carpe diem*. Gather ye rosebuds."

He was seeing her avid teeth for the first time in days; but then the smile flattened out into meekness as Adriano sternly returned to her side.

. . . Keith excused himself and went up to her room to say goodbye to it. Scheherazade would be moving the next day. And the bathroom: was that the last time—a couple of afternoons ago, when she appeared in the short silk housecoat (limply fastened at the waist), and she looked dazed and bumped into things and didn't seem to notice him and was giving off a thick sleepy warmth of womanhood? Probably. There would be no more encounters, no more spectacles of disarray, in the intervening compartment. She was never as naked, there, as she was by the pool; but she seemed much more so, because only his eyes saw her . . .

He entered Scheherazade's Tudorbethan chamber with the leaded windows and the splintery black beams. As before, it was eloquent of hurry, absent-mindedness, of better things to do. The temptation to snivel over her discarded clothes, to slide, for a moment, into her unmade bed, to sit at the dressing table and usurp her reflections in the triple mirror—the temptation was there, but no. On the bed was a towel, still damp and indented, and shaped in a semicircle with a shallow ridge round the back of it, where she must have sat and dried, not an hour ago. This he passed over and, instead, half smothered himself in one of her pillows.

As he was leaving, he consulted her royal-blue passport—renewed as recently as October, 1969. And the photo. For a while he seemed to be staring at something in a provincial newspaper. The face of a girl who had distinguished herself on the harpsichord, or clocked up five thousand miles for Meals on Wheels, or rescued a cat from that great oak behind the guildhall.

Ruaa," said Whittaker, "does not 'meet,' as they put it. She hasn't even 'met' *me*. Except when she's sent up here to get something, she's confined to the kitchen. Where I'm no longer allowed to go unless he comes too."

Whittaker attended to his glass: Black was drinking Tio Pepe. White (who was also smoking) sipped on an experimental glass of Scotch.

"Incredible," said Keith, who genuinely found it so. "Incredible. Even little Dilkash 'met' all right. She had a job. Temping. And as for Ashraf . . . Okay," he said (he was trying to cultivate or encourage a certain brashness in his attitude to women). "Okay. I've got a true story for you. Pass it on to Amen."

"Amen'll profit from it?"

"Yeah, it'll put things in perspective about the—about his sister." Keith squared up. "Now. A couple of summers ago, in Spain, a gang of us, we had a picnic with a lot of wine and went swimming in this mountain lake." Keith, Kenrik, Arn, Ewan. Yes, and Violet, who had just turned fourteen. "And Ashraf came wading out of the water in her white two-piece. And we all called out, *Come on darling, give us a flash. Come on, gorgeous, give us a butcher's.* And she—"

"Butcher's?" said Whittaker.

Keith told him it was rhyming slang. Butcher's hook: look. "Why's that funny?"

"I'm just thinking. *Give us a butcher's.* Not the most obvious inducement to a Muslim. I mean, they have a different approach to butchers. They—"

"D'you want to hear this story or not? No offence and I know you're gay and everything, but there's Ashraf—big girl, mind—coming out of a mountain lake half-naked, and you want to talk about butchers."

Whittaker opened his hands and asked Keith to proceed.

"Well. *Come on, sweetheart, come on, give us a gander.* And she reached behind her back and . . ." Then came a shrug, and a silence. "And there were these two fucking volcanoes staring you out. And this was years ago. Long before they all started doing it." 1967, Spain, Franco, and the Guardia Civil policing the beach (and the ban on bikinis) with their half-raised machine guns. "Okay. Now where does it say a Muslim chick can do that?"

Whittaker said urbanely, "Oh, there's probably some obscure teaching somewhere or other. You know. When infidels gather as you bathe, and cry out for a butcher's, reach behind your back and . . . So what moral is Amen supposed to take from Ashraf?"

"Uh, it'll make him loosen up about the Blob. Sorry. Ruaa. Jesus. I'm a little the worse for . . . I was raised to respect all cultures. And I respect Ruaa. But religion—religion's always been my enemy. It teaches girls to be a drag about sex."

"You know, Keith, there might be a moral in Ruaa for *you*. Actually I like having her here. It means he can't just disappear. That's my situation. I love someone who could just disappear."

Keith thought of Ashraf—a Muslim of discos and miniskirts, a cool-pants Muslim whose evening drink was Chivas Regal. He thought of Dilkash, with her orangeade and her sensible trouser suits. Yet she too had powers of surprise. The shock of Ashraf's presentation, at the lake, was not that much greater, relatively, than the shock Dilkash had given him, after a month of chaste friendship, when she took off her cardigan and revealed her bare arms . . . Had he humiliated Dilkash? Humiliated Pansy? He couldn't get any of them out of his mind, any of them—he was like the very sick old man he would one day become, needing to know how it had gone, all his life, with women and love.

"What about the Ruaa approach to Violet? With you as Amen. Never leave her alone with any man who isn't a close relative. Shame and honour, Keith. Shame and honour."

"A different approach," he said. "Draw?"

. . . Don Quixote, talking of his imaginary girlfriend, Dulcinea del Toboso, told Sancho Panza, *I paint her in my fancy, according to my wish.* Keith had done too much of this with Scheherazade, and made her into someone above his reach to know. She would have to come down, to condescend, in his imagination.

Love did have the power to transform—as it had once transformed his newborn sister. He remembered that page, that short chapter of his being, with all his body. Not only his mind remembered it. His fingers remembered it, his breastbone remembered it, his throat remembered it.

And he had read that men were beginning to see women as *objects.* Objects? No. Girls were teemingly alive. Scheherazade: the inseparable sisters who were her breasts, the creatures that dwelt behind her eyes, the great warm beings of her thighs.

2

THE FALL OF ADRIANO

Mid-morning, now, and Scheherazade was packing her things: Keith had already sadly helped her with a suitcase and a stack of books. At noon, he came up with a mug of coffee and heard the clatter of the shower . . . He reached for his novel (he was still listlessly rooting for Catherine and the fixed lour called Heathcliff) . . . Now came a flurrying, rustling sound, and just then, too, the cicadas started up. The rhythmless marracas of the cicadas . . . As he listened, Keith felt his face go damp and flabby, like a face marooned and immobilised over a critically hot bath. Now silence.

He tried the door. Thank God, he thought wearily; and he pressed a fatalistic forefinger to the bell.

"You know what I suffer from? Clinical amnesia. Well what d'you think? Next week there's an official dinner he wants to take me to, and Mum said I ought to go to anything like that if I can bear it. Adriano. Will there be dancing? Imagine."

Scheherazade was in a gown that her great-aunt Betty might have worn, or actually did wear, in New York, in 1914. Heavy silk of Sherwood green, with the deep pleats starting just above the waist. He said,

"Give it up, Scheherazade. For your own good."

She turned her back to him. "I'm not thinking of my own good. Could you uh . . . ?"

So Keith stood behind Scheherazade, whom he had never reached out and touched—the babyish fist of her coccyx, the long range of her spine, the wing-cases of her shoulder blades. And for a moment he thought he might honestly be capable of reaching in and around with his warm young hands; but then she drew aside the main body of her hair, between finger and thumb, revealing the long, downy, aromatic nape (exactly level with his nose). And all he wanted to do was rest his brow against her shoulder, rest it, cool it, ease it.

"What do I do—I just . . . ?"

He slid the zip northward; he joined the plush little buttons; he fixed the clasp. The clasp of her gown, no bigger than a fairy's paperclip, presiding over that empire of green and all it contained.

Keith said, "I suppose this is the last time. You forgetting."

"I suppose." She turned. "But if Jorq comes I'll be moving back. So you never know."

After two or three seconds she turned again, and walked. He locked the door after her—Scheherazade, in Sherwood green, and rustling like a tree. Green giantess of the frightening forest. Maid Marian. Who takes from the rich and gives to the poor.

He offered a sigh—a sigh directed, perhaps, as far as the Moho: the discontinuity between the lower mantle and the oceanic crust . . . Instead of helping her out of her clothes, he was helping her into them. It will happen, he thought. It won't go on being the wrong way round.

Keith stood there among hooks and racks. The tub, he saw, contained two inches of barely tepid water, very slightly clouded yet almost mirror-like with its slick of oil. He thought about climbing into it; he thought about drinking it; but he just pulled the plug and watched the little maelstrom writhe into being.

N ow the real heat began. The shadows, rich, sharp, and (he thought) distinctly furtive, yes, with a distinctly paranoid look about them— the shadows could no longer hold their ranks, and cowered inward, while the sun bulged and dropped and repositioned itself directly overhead as if to stare and listen. In the afternoons the gustatory and intestinal odours of the village rose up in layers of salt and gravy. A metal chair, down by the pool, would clasp you in its fire like an instrument of torture; coffee spoons could bite or sting. The nights were still damp but the air was thick and motionless. The dogs no longer barked (they whimpered) and the sheep's blares of rage and boredom quailed and dried in their throats.

"He's normal," said Lily in the dark.

". . . No he isn't. What's normal about Adriano?"

"His arrangements. Down there."

"You mean she's seen it?" He swallowed as silently as he could. "I thought he was still outside her top."

"He is, or outside her bra. He's in between her top and her bra. Which is coming off any night now. But she saw the shape in his white trousers. And it's normal. It's not like it seems in his swimsuits. She thinks his swimsuits are made out of baseball mitts. Don't be alarmed by his driving."

"What? Why should I be?"

"He's one of those people who think they have to look at you when they talk to you. So he memorises the road ahead and turns around and has a chat. He hardly took his eyes off Scheherazade all the way to Rome. I was in the back. And he drove all the way in profile. Did you know she's never gone down on anyone? Even on Timmy?"

"No, Lily, I didn't know. How could I tell?"

"That's part of it, you see. She just got *three* letters from college friends, and they're all busy acting like boys. She wants to try new things. Which for her means anything that isn't the missionary position."

". . . Why's it called the missionary position?"

"Because the missionaries," said Lily, "told the natives to stop doing it like dogs and start doing it like missionaries."

"Christ, the nerve of it. No, really. The nerve of it. Still. Fascinating. You mean in all this time she's never once gone down on Timmy?"

"That's sort of why she's feeling left out. She's kissed it. She says she's kissed it, whatever that means."

"Yeah. What's that mean?"

"Just a peck, I suppose. Or maybe she French-kissed it—on the tip."

"Lily . . ."

"She's kissed it but she's never sucked it. She's never put it in her mouth and really sucked it. She said, *Is that how you do it? You put it in your mouth and you suck it as hard as you possibly can? . . .* What'll happen if Kenrik and Rita aren't still just good friends?"

"If they're lovers? Simple. They'll be hating each other."

"Mm. Which we could never do."

On Sunday, under a percussive sky that seemed to hum like a cymbal, Adriano kept his promise and took the four of them out to lunch—Keith, Lily, Gloria, Scheherazade—at a starred restaurant in a place called Ofanto, which was twenty miles away.

They went there in the motorised drawing room of the Rolls Royce, eerily piloted by Adriano. Keith's unease seemed to be more basic than Lily's. Even on the return journey he failed to convince himself that Adriano could actually see over the dashboard, except perhaps through the upper segment of the steering wheel. And when he talked to Scheherazade in the back seat, screwing his head around the full half-circle without moving his shoulders (as Linda Blair was soon to do in *The Exorcist*), all you could make out was one arched eyebrow and the expanse of his silvery frown.

"The truffles," he kept turning and saying. "You must have the truffles, Scheherazade. Mmm—as a taste of ambrosia." The head creaked round again. "The truffles, Scheherazade. Quite divine."

Ofanto drew near. Confirming his ability to see out of the side window at least, Adriano muttered wonderingly (and you could tell that this was most retrograde to his hopes and wishes),

"So many people! It used to be a market town. Just a sleepy market town. And now?"

And now there is industry, and clumps of workers, each with his singlet and his cigarette, and cuboid medium-rise flatblocks, and insect nests of aerials, and distantly swearing dogs aswivel on trapped balconies—and where there is all this, all that, there is also the presence of young men . . .

"Just a sleepy market town. And now—I don't know. I don't know."

At this point we should jump ahead to six thirty that evening. There are sour drinks on the castle's west terrace. Sour drinks in the sour dusk. Adriano, perfunctorily asked up, had perfunctorily declined, and drove on. So the four of them are arranged out there, their faces averted in the private trials of digestion. The usual sunset colours, with a shading or grading of turbulence, as Jupiter's stomach rumbles, in some other valley, under some other mountain.

"*Well,*" said Scheherazade.

And Keith turned to her. Because something was the matter with the film she used to be starring in. Was it the light? Was it the continuity? Was it the dialogue—was the whole thing dubbed all along?

Well what?

"Well," said Scheherazade.

For a moment, sitting there on the swing sofa, she seemed average— average in the eyes. There was a good reason for this. And Keith partly understood her need to go to the table and pour out that second helping of white wine; her glass, already half empty, rested at an angle on her print-flowered lap . . . Those average eyes of hers were fixed on Gloria Beautyman, who stood by the French windows, poking with her finger at the ice cubes in her Pellegrino. Scheherazade said,

"Well. Your backside gathered quite a following this afternoon."

Gloria seemed to swallow something suddenly. She said, "Meaning?"

"Meaning? Meaning your rear end and the stir it caused."

"And the same went for you," said Gloria, swallowing again, "and your—your *bust.*"

"Well if you're going to cram it into those cords . . ."

"You told me to. I was going to go in a smock but you said wear something else. So I wore cords. They're just *cords.*"

"Cords. Skintight and bright red. With your arse like a prize tomato."

"Hark who's talking. With *that* top on."

And Keith was wondering. What were heroines allowed to do?

As Lily, Keith, Scheherazade, Adriano and Gloria walked across the dusty grey piazza, and down the length of the endless avenue, the young men of Ofanto staged their choreographic referendum on the attractions of the three girls. Here they came again. Drawn like iron filings in obedience to magnets of varying power, the young men squirmed and milled and then divided—with graphic candour—into two columns: one in front of Scheherazade, and one behind Gloria Beautyman. One group walking forward. One group walking backward. And Lily? . . . I can say that her figure, when it came, turned out to be impeccably symmetrical, not top-heavy, not bottom-heavy—classic, without fetish. But this of course would have pulled little weight with the young men of Campania, faithful to the sacrament of the twinned and rolling orbs.

It was here that Adriano made his terrible mistake. It was such a little thing. All he did was reach out with his hand.

"What are we supposed to do?" asked Gloria on the rosy terrace. "Swaddle ourselves like Ruaa?"

And Scheherazade laughed tinnily and said, "At least you had the sense to refuse that glass of champagne. Otherwise—well I shudder to think."

Gloria glanced quickly from face to face. And two tears leapt from her eyes: you could see them whitely glitter as they leapt and fell . . .

Now Lily stood up into the silence.

"To be really popular in Italy," she said with slow emphasis, "this is what you'd need. *Your* tits. And *your* arse."

"You know," said Keith wildly, "you know my tutor Garth, Lily—the poet? He says the female body has a design flaw. He says the tits and the arse should be on the same side."

". . . *Which* side?"

Keith thought for a moment. "I don't think he's fussy," he said. "Though I suppose you'll tell me he was fussy in the first place. The front. To get the face. It would have to be the front."

"No, the back, surely," said Scheherazade (as Gloria turned and went inside). "If it was the front, her legs would be pointing the wrong way."

Lily said, "She'd walk backward. And the boys in the street—I'm trying to work it out. Which way would they walk?"

That night, dinner was dead, killed by the reeking fungi of Ofanto: no one attempted it. Lily and Scheherazade were closeted in the apartment, so Keith went stumbling down the slope to use up time with Whittaker—and with Amen, who silently produced a large sliver of the blackest and greasiest hashish.

"Jesus, it's a bit strong, isn't it?"

"*C'est bien de tousser,*" said Amen. "*Et puis le courage. L'indifférence.*"

"Whittaker, what's all this?"

He meant the images in the paintings that were fanned out on the floor. Whittaker said,

"Cataloguing. My Picasso period."

The figures in the canvases were all bassackward or inside out, and after a while Keith was asking whether it would be any good if *men* were sexually rearranged, with the cock and the arse on the same side, and maybe the head wrenched round, too, like Adriano's in the Rolls . . .

"You know Tom Thumb called me *Keef* today?" he said, some time later. "He called me *Kif.* And it's true. I just smoked a whole death-pipe of kif with Amen."

Lily said, "You fool. You know you can't cope with drugs."

"I know. You look amazing." And she did, too, in the candlelight. She looked like Boris Karloff. "*Assassin* comes from hashish. Or the other way round."

"What are you going on about?"

"It's just . . . It's just impossible to believe that they smoked this stuff to make them *brave.* I was shitting myself on the way back. I still am. And guess who I bumped into in the dark. Literally. The Blob!"

"Come on, it's one o'clock."

"Christ, I thought it was about half past nine."

"Because you're a drugged fool," said Lily. "That's why."

He did as he was told. Ruaa, like the feathery night made solid. *Oof . . .* And then as he drank a quart of water in the kitchen he heard a footfall—and felt a rush of fresh fear at the thought of Scheherazade. Fear? Scheherazade?

"Okay, I'm calmer now. I'm cool. So tell."

"It was an absolute catastrophe for Tom Thumb."

"Yeah, I could see that," he said contentedly as he drew a sheet over the hive of his chest.

"When he took her hand."

Because that's what he did, Adriano. As soon as they got out of the car, and the riot, the revolution began, Adriano strode to Scheherazade's side and took her hand. And looked out and up at the young men with that scowl Keith had glimpsed once or twice before. The scowl of practised defiance you always saw in the very small male, and the readiness to transact with cruelty, to absorb it, to transfer it. Adriano, Mr. Punch. Punchinello.

"She said it was like walking along," said Lily, "with her own disturbed child."

"Mm, like a young mum. That's what she looked like from behind."

"It was much worse from in front. She saw herself in a shop window and had a heart attack. Not a nice child. A disturbed child."

"Jesus. And that crowd . . ."

"Jumping up and down in front of her with their tongues hanging out. All through lunch her pulse was raging. About whether he'd do it on the way back."

Overseen, with severe connoisseurship, by Adriano, the meal went on for three hours. And as they gathered in the lobby he again reached towards Scheherazade with an opened palm. She turned away and gave a shivering laugh and said, *Oh don't worry about me. I'm a big girl now.*

"It just popped out. Poor her, she's so confused. Weeping in her room."

"So that's off now, is it? No more doing it for the troops."

"Oh out of the question. It was primal. I mean, you can't get involved with someone who makes you think of your own mad child."

Keith agreed that it was hardly a promising sign.

"And then she went and said that thing about Junglebum's arse."

"Yeah, well, it was worse than that, wasn't it," he said. "The champagne."

"The champagne. So now Junglebum knows we know about her pants getting sucked off by the jacuzzi."

"Mm. I've never seen anyone cry like that. Like a popgun. Both barrels."

"Mm. Poor Gloria. Poor Adriano. Poor Scheherazade."

Well, said the shrill Scheherazade on the terrace—and Keith wanted to shout, *Cut!* But no: keep rolling. It occurred to him, now, that *he* was the director of the film in which she starred; and it was time for a change of genre. No more platonic pastoral. Time for the slatternly shepherdess, the venal wood-nymph, the doped contessa.

"I suppose you're happy now."

"Why would I be happy?"

"Why? Adriano gone. No sign of Timmy. And her getting more and more desperate."

". . . Crappy meal, didn't you think? I thought truffles were meat." Heroines were definitely allowed to do that. "Like pâté or something." Heroines were definitely allowed to get more and more desperate. "Not a five-quid toadstool . . . I was proud of you today."

Keith, and not Hansel, now performed the sexual act with Lily, and not Gretel. Its components, as he saw them: on the terrace, the way she pushed down with her hands on the armrests and rose up into it, and brought peace; and earlier, in Ofanto, the rinsed look in her pale blue eyes, the closed smile of disappointment, even disbelief . . . She must have felt as sore and roused as Adriano, when the young men rose from the stone benches (as if gathering for violence), when the young men came hurrying from under the shade of the palm trees.

3

TICKET OF ENTRY

"Any sign of Gloria yet?" said Scheherazade with a guarded look. "No, I suppose she's still in her room."

Keith settled himself near by, himself and *Vanity Fair.*

"I can't think—I can't believe I was such an absolute *witch* last night."

She lay there wearing her belted monokini, her olive oil, and the fleshy V of her frown. She leant back and said,

"I took her breakfast in bed, but of course she still hates me . . . I suppose everyone hates me. Especially a moralist like you. And this is just a question of common decency. So come on, let's hear it."

Keith produced a fresh packet of Cavallos (a local brand) . . . In *Emma,* it was as Mr. Knightley reproached her for publicly ridiculing a defenceless woman that Emma Woodhouse realised, in the novel's key scene, that she was in love with him. *Realised*—for in the world of *Emma* you could be subconsciously in love. At the picnic on Box Hill, Emma was cruel to Miss Bates (the kindly old virgin), and Mr. Knightley told her so . . . Keith, then, might have paraphrased Mr. Knightley, and said, *Were she your equal in situation—but, Scheherazade, consider how far this is from being the case. She is poor; she has sunk from the comforts she was born to; and, if she lives to old age, must probably sink more. Her situation should secure your compassion. It was badly done, indeed!* But Keith didn't say that. He said,

"Hates you? Not at all."

"Everyone hates me. And I deserve it."

If Keith paraphrased Mr. Knightley, would Scheherazade realise, at last, that she was in love with him? No, because things were different now. And what had changed? Well, Emma's colloquy with Miss Bates, on Box Hill, was not about busts and backsides and (by implication) a day of shame at a sex tycoon's; and as she girded herself for censure, Emma did not face Mr. Knightley topless; and Gloria was not, or not yet, a spinster. All that, and this. In 1970, you could no longer love subliminally: the conscious mind worked full-time on love or what used to be love. Anyway, why would he censure Scheherazade? On the west terrace she had shown a vulgarity and a sexual vanity, and an ordinariness, that at this point he could only commend. He said,

"It was unlike you. But relax. We've all got to toughen up a bit. You're too soft-hearted. You were upset. You had that business with Adriano. I—we felt for you."

"Did you? Thanks. But that's just the other side of it, you see. Sentimental-brutal. Poor character."

She lay back and closed her eyes. There was a five-minute silence, and Keith silently observed it, with increasing strain. He inspected his Italian cigarette, his Cavallo. There was the tube of paper, there was the filter; all it seemed to lack was tobacco. He lit it, and the flare scorched his nose for an instant, and then it was gone.

"That looks like a habit well worth sticking to," said Scheherazade, with her smile, the smile in which her whole face participated. And she went on more lethargically, "Still, there's no excuse for that . . . You see, she couldn't retaliate, could she. Mm, I suppose she'll retaliate when Jorq gets here . . . You know, I think she's slightly on the make, Gloria. A bit of a gold-digger. In my opinion . . . You've met Jorq, haven't you. It can't be his looks that attracted her, can it."

Lighting a Disque Bleu, he wordlessly but emphatically agreed. And it heartened him that Scheherazade's *spots of commonness* (as George Eliot would very soon be identifying the weaknesses in an otherwise impressive young man) were still visible. She said,

"Her dad used to be a gentleman diplomat. And ended up earning a crust on the Census Board in Edinburgh. She used to be rich, and now she isn't. She can't help that. Any more than she can help her backside . . . The champagne, though. Horrible of me. I just showed I'm a worthless bitch. That's all."

And this too filled him with faith. But he said, "No. No. Come on, make allowances. It must've been very confusing, Adriano taking your hand. Like a child. It churned you up. You weren't yourself."

". . . That's nice of you to say, but it's a bit elaborate, isn't it? It was just vanity. Slut vanity. Those boys in Ofanto. I astonished myself. I *minded.* Because I'm supposed to be the centre of attention. Of undivided attention. It's pathetic."

He waited.

"I've never felt like this before and I don't like it. This—catty agitation. Does everyone feel like that? Is that what all this is? A contest?"

What all this is. So it's not just me, he thought. We all sense it: the reality of that frightening thing, social change. What all this is? A contest? *Yes,* he would have said if he'd known. *Yes, my dear Emma, this is a contest that is coming, intersexual and intrasexual: a beauty contest, a popularity contest, and a talent contest. There is more display, comparison, staring, noting, assessing—and therefore more* invidia. Invidia: that which is unfair, and likely to arouse resentment and anger in others. *It is a contest, and therefore some will fail, some will lose. And we will find many new ways of failing and losing.* He said,

"It's a sea change."

"And then," she said with a roll of the eyes that took her whole head with it, "there's *still* Adriano. Equally ridiculous. You can't do that, can you. Sleep with someone because of an idea."

People do, he thought. Pansy did. "Frieda Lawrence did. What will you tell him?"

"I'll just say that I tried, but found that my heart lies elsewhere. Et cetera."

Keith was finding all this very uplifting: *absolute witch, worthless bitch,* plus *slut vanity*—and how good it was to hear Timmy reduced to an *et cetera.* She said,

"Well with Adriano, at least, it never really started."

"Didn't it?"

"No. Just holding hands. Just holding hands—which is ironic, I suppose. He kissed my neck, but it was always then that I told him to stop."

Now Keith reassessed the dependability, and the satiric gifts, of his girlfriend, whom he could see, coming forward in slip and flip-flops on the east terrace. Scheherazade said,

"I thought I'd suddenly relax one night and we'd see how we went. I thought I'd suddenly relax. But I never did. I felt I could've managed it physically, but I never really trusted him. Can't think why . . . If only he'd get someone else. Then I'd feel easier."

Lily moved through the grotto.

"Time to take Gloria her lunch, I suppose. And she'll still hate me. Did you see it? Did you see the way she cried?"

Scheherazade went. Lily came. Keith hoped for instruction from *Vanity Fair*—at the feet of its effortlessly dishonest heroine, Becky Sharp, who lies, cheats, and whores around automatically and by instinct: another of nature's infidels. So Becky helped. But the novel that would guide him into the next phase of his story was one he read six years earlier, when he was fifteen. Bram Stoker's *Dracula*.

The muscular little charcoal birds, thirteen of them, were working, climbing, far above the mountaintops. Nearer the ground, the yellow *canarini* (they were actually much bigger than canaries) gave a sudden unanimous cackle. They weren't laughing at him, he realised, or not at him in particular. They were laughing at human beings. What was it about us that they found so funny?

We're birds*!* they were saying. *And we fly! All day we do what you do in your dreams. We fly!*

Lily was reading a book called *Equity*. She turned the page. They were all of them very young, they were all of them neither one thing nor the other, they were all of them trying to work out who they were. Scheherazade was beautiful, but she was just like everybody else. Tomorrow, thought Keith: the historic opportunity. *Carpe noctem.* Seize the night.

Gloria, in fact, rose up at five o'clock that afternoon. Rose up and came down—grand, ill-used, unblinking. It was impressive, the magnitude of her indignation, and its content ran as follows: this indignation is uncontainable, and you're lucky that it's Gloria Beautyman who's containing it, because nobody else could. Keith, perhaps, and certainly Whittaker were excused from the full sweep of her disgust; but Lily wasn't. *She's hating me too,* she said. *So I'm hating her back.* Woman–woman diplomacy or statecraft was something that Keith knew he would never understand; it was like looking down on a bright sea from a clifftop, the million points of light pinging from droplet to droplet—untrackably. An arcane discipline, like molecular thermodynamics. Whereas male disaffection was mere male sullenness, with its Queensbury rules . . . *It'll all ease off,* said Lily. And it did.

Otherwise, as the inhabitant of the next turret along, Gloria was an invisible and almost inaudible towermate. It became clear—perhaps it was always clear—that she would never forget to unlatch the bathroom door. And, within, no sopping flannels, no stuff in tubs and bottles to slap on your face and no stuff in tubs and bottles to take it all off again, no stockings or swimsuits drying on the rack (and no hot shape in white bathtowels). Lily herself, after a day or two, pronounced the bathroom *usable.* Gloria, seldom seen, and silent. Even her showers were whispers: so might a watering can weep over a flowerbed. And compare this to the mad gossip, the wild rumours, of the showers of Scheherazade.

. . . The stasis of the afternoon is the time for the thick and ponderous longing of the twenty-year-old. What to do with it all? It was everything and nothing, it subsumed death and infinity—what to do with the instrument of yearning? . . . The girls were down at the pool, and Whittaker was out sketching with Gloria, and Keith paid a call on the twin turret, hoping to find a scent or a residue of more interesting times. And the room was now utterly clutterless. Where were the heaps of shoes, the crumpled nighties, the blue jeans trampled out of and still holding, as if in cupped palms, Scheherazade's loins and hips? Madonna hadn't been in for half a week and yet Gloria's sheets seemed ironed into place, with nautical severity, and the pillows looked as solid as slabs of chalk. Then Keith's eyes picked up a bearing. Her passport's still here, he thought—and there it was, beneath the triple mirror. But it was Gloria's passport, of course, and not Scheherazade's.

He flicked through it. Renewed in 1967; Gloria with hair, glossily curved round her smile; Distinguishing Features—none; 5' 5"; not well-travelled (Greece, France, and now Italy, all this year). Wedged into the empty pages were her provisional driving licence and her birth certificate . . . Keith was always eccentrically stirred and moved by birth certificates (and Violet's was a talisman to him, because he was there to issue it and receive her). Your birth certificate was your BC—before Christ, before anything—and your proof of innocence. It was your ticket of entry; it put you inside history . . . Glasgow Infirmary; February 1, 1947; Girl; Gloria Rowena; Reginald Beautyman, Diplomat; Prunella Beautyman (née MacWhirr); If Married, Place and Date—Church of the Holy Virgin, Cairo, Egypt, June 11, 1935 . . .

After a moment he went next door and took out his own entry ticket, kept in a polythene sachet at the bottom of his spongebag, together with another document, in ordinary longhand, which said:

'65 Ella 1	'68 Doris 5
'66 Jenny 5	'68 Verity 12
'67 Deirdre 3	'68 "Dewdrop" (Mary) 8
'67 Sarah D. 7	'68 Sarah L. 11
'67 Ruth 10!	'69 Lily 12*+
'67 Ashraf 12!	'70 Rosemary 10
'68 Pansy 11	'70 Patience 7
'68 Dilkash 2	'70 Joan 11

The key to this chart was kept in Keith's head. I can disclose it: the numeral 1 meant holding hands, 2 was kissing, and so on, and 10 was *it* (Lily's asterisk could be glossed as *fellatio unto orgasm,* and the plus sign as *plus swallowing*). There. Sixteen girls, and eight clear successes, in five years . . . Keith's birth certificate, with its two *deceased*s, was more dramatic than Gloria's. But this other thing, this record, rewritten with every update, also told him who he was.

At five thirty Scheherazade drove in the cabriolet from castle to castle and returned after an hour, looking childishly contrite, with her shoulders raised and locked. Dinner unfolded, its surface tension, its meniscus, casually qualified by Whittaker. After Gloria had proudly taken her leave, Scheherazade told of Adriano, saying,

"He was very correct. Quiet. Rather angry, I think. I don't blame him. I asked him to keep coming over. I stressed that we're still good friends."

"That's what we're hoping Kenrik and Rita will be," said Lily. "Still good friends."

"You're hoping," said Whittaker, "that they stayed in the right sleeping bags."

Keith watched as Whittaker went off. Keith watched as Lily went up . . .

It was now just before midnight in the gunroom. The moose, with its marble eyes, stared out inexorably. On the floor, on the tiger rug, Indian-fashion faced side-saddle: Keith faced the forbidding approachability, the illegible openness of Scheherazade. What was this alphabet that he couldn't read? She wore a close dress of murky pink, with five white buttons down the front at six-inch intervals; she kept scratching at the little red swell on the paler side of her forearm where, the night before, a mosquito had inserted its syringe. Keith was in his usual state, which was this. Every other minute, he could hear heaven snickering at his forebearance; and every minute in between, he blushed white sweat at the thought of the sulphurous tar pit in his soul.

The night was probably about to end, and Keith was blithely (and ignorantly) saying something about the castle, about how the exterior sometimes struck him as more Transylvanian than Italianate (with a haunted slant to it), and he went on,

"The best bit in *Dracula* is when he climbs down the rampart—head first. Coming down to feast on the girl."

"Head first?"

"Head first. He sticks to the wall like a fly. He's already done for Lucy Westenra. He savaged her—in the form of a wild animal. Now it's Wilhelmina's turn. He bites her three times. And he makes her drink his blood. And from then on she's under his control."

"I'm scared now." She lowered her voice. "What if I'm attacked on my way up? I'm scared now."

And *his* blood—it altered thickly. "But I'll protect you," he said.

They stood. They climbed the staircase that wound its way round the ballroom. On the recessed half-landing she said,

"I suppose this is far enough."

"Wait," he said, and placed the three-branched candelabrum on the floor, and straightened slowly. "You stand betrayed. I'm the undead. I'm the prince of darkness."

So he was pretending to be Dracula (his hands were vampirically raised and tensed), and she was pretending to be his victim (her hands were clasped in obeisance or prayer), and he was moving in on her, and she was backing off and even half sat herself on the curved lid of a wooden trunk, and their faces were level, eye to eye and breath to breath. And now they were given a ticket of entry to another genre . . . the world of the heaving bosom and the drooling canine, of bats and screech owls, of fluids and straight razors and blinded mirrors, where everything was allowed. He looked down the length of her: the stretched gaps between her buttons were mouths of smiling flesh. From throat to thigh, it was all before him.

She raised a palm halfway towards his chest—and, as if pushed, he staggered sideways, and something clattered, and there were three rolling tubes of tallow with flickering wicks, and they laughed, fatally, and suddenly it was over.

Then Scheherazade went on up and Keith went on down. He crossed the courtyard under the ridiculous innocence of the moon. He climbed the tower.

And entered the insanity of night.

Oh, I know *now* what I should have said and done. *Count Dracula would want your throat, your neck. But I—I want your mouth, your lips.* Then onward, and all would have followed and flowed. Wouldn't it?

Esprit de l'escalier: spirit of the staircase, wishing you'd said, wishing you'd done. Yet how much more indelible it was when the staircase was *the staircase that led to the bedroom . . .*

Gathering, shadowing, boding, closing over Scheherazade, he felt a near-irresistible force. And an immovable object. What was the nature of the impediment, what was its shape and mass? He turned to the sleeping form at his side and whispered,

How could you do *this to me?*

For weeks Keith had known that his chosen project was something like the opposite of self-improvement. But he honestly never dreamt that he had so far to go.

I expect you're wondering if I'm a genuine redhead. Well I destroyed the evidence, didn't I. Naygo traygace. I'm real enough: look at the stipple on me oxters. Here. You know, *I* know a girl who's *never* had pubic hair. No, never. She—"

—Forgive me, Rita, for this brief interruption, but I've just noticed a vein pulsing its way from left to right across Keith's brow: an idea is being born in him. And I must begin to stand off, to go back, to withdraw . . . Now, as for Dilkash, I made my position clear; and I gave him a truly terrible time about Pansy. If, last night, he had closed on

Scheherazade, well, there would have been one prompt repercussion that he has so far wilfully refused to weigh. But what he is contemplating as I speak (see the vermicular movement, east to west, across his lineless forehead) . . . To put it in words he would plainly understand, he is launched on his own corruption: from L. *corrumpere,* Keith, "mar, bribe," my friend, from *cor-* "altogether" + *rumpere* "to break." Forgive me, Rita, I'm sorry—please proceed.

"No, never. She made war on it the instant it appeared. She never let it get a hold. That's the future, that is. Sorry, girls, but the days of the beaver are over. No more jungle combat. Eh, Rik, it's all right here, isn't it. Day-ghed paygosh. We were on the road all night, and I'm filthy, me. I want a lovely long bath. A long bath," she said, "and I'll be as sound as the mail."

Rita had not been among them half a minute before she was mother naked—she approached the pool drawing her frock over her head and scraping off her shoes; Rita, in her birthday suit; then came the ear-to-ear grin and the racing dive. Kenrik was following slowly in her path with his head set well down.

And where were the police? Where were they? Although Scheherazade, Keith felt, could probably be processed by the constabulary forces (and Lily let off with a warning), Rita, surely, merited a visit from the Serious Crimes Squad. Rita: 5' 8", 32-30-31, not just topless, not just bottomless, but depilated too—pre-adolescent, at twenty-five . . . And Keith himself might have attracted the attention of the authorities, had there been any. His new inkling throbbed like a black flower with a bee feeding on it. Lily, her upper teeth bared, looked on as Rita said,

"So can we go round again? Now you're . . . Say it slow."

"Scheherazade."

"Hey, bird, that goes on a bit, don't you think—the suspense! And after that tongue-twister, after that gobful—it's Adriano, isn't it. Oh and you're a big fella for a little fella, aren't you love. What's your middle name, sweetheart?"

". . . Sebastiano," said Adriano (eventually remembering to be proud about it).

"Then that's what I'll call you. D'you mind? See, Seb, I had me heart broken by an Adrian. He was a fucking animal, he was . . . And you're

Whittaker. Charmed. And you're Gloria. And you, kid—you, of course, are Lily. So. What wickedness have you all been up to under the sun?"

". . . Nothing," said Scheherazade. "It's a bit feeble, but there it is. Nothing."

In a menacing undertone Kenrik had asked to be taken to the nearest bar.

More than once, on the steep path, Keith turned to him with the beginnings of a simple declarative sentence, only to be silenced by a raised hand. And Kenrik called for halts, and sat on a rock, smoking, then on a tree stump, smoking, and kneaded his hair with eight stiffened fingers . . .

Kenrik, too, was the child of a pregnant widow. It happened early in the second trimester (fast convertible, summer rain). So, for five months—the vanished father, the unborn son, and the mother both lamenting and expecting. The black weeds or threads, but also the familiar curve of the silhouette, with the profile poised like a question mark between life and death. And the old order gives way to the new, not immediately, though, not yet: the filled breasts and weakened knees, the cravings, the broken waters, the pumping womb, and labour, labour, labour.

For five months the growing baby was rinsed in the juices of mourning. And this was the difference between the two friends. As she gave birth, Keith's mother believed that the father was still alive; so in his round bath the unborn child never tasted the excretions of grief. Widow—OE *widewe* "be empty"; but they weren't empty, these two women, these two widows.

Kenrik said, "What's that mean?"

"Mussolini is always right."

"The thing is, man, I haven't been alone for twenty days, and I . . . Do you ever get that—when you don't know who you are?"

Well, no, thought Keith. Though I'm feeling, now, as if I'm floating in and out of myself. "Sort of," he said.

". . . All right. I'm in your hands. Lead on."

4

SENTIMENTAL EDUCATION

They entered the cave of carpentry across the alley from the pet shop. The drinkers, in their fleeces, as if disguised as sheep. Kenrik said,

"I'm quite good at this by now. *Buon giorno. Due cognac grandes, per favore.* That's for me. What're you having?"

The two of them stood at the counter, watched by six or seven pairs of ancient eyes. Kenrik drained his first glass in one, and shuddered. They felt no need to lower their voices; they lit cigarettes and Keith said,

"Can we begin?"

"Yeah. Wait. Nicholas sends his love. And did you get that package? Nicholas doesn't like me, does he. He thinks I'm useless. He thinks I'm a useless little prick."

"No," said Keith—but there was something in this. *What is it you see,* his brother often asked, *in that useless little prick? He's a lush, a flop, and a snob. I know. With him you can take a holiday from being high-minded. You are high-minded—it's not a pretence. But it tuckers you out. And every now and then you need a holiday.* There was something in this too. When he answered his brother, Keith emphasised Kenrik's expressiveness— and the fact that he attracted girls. He attracted Lily. Keith's eyes widened over the foam of his beer for a second. "Nicholas," he said, "thinks you're cool. Now can we start?"

"Start."

"You fucked the Dog!"

". . . Yeah, I fucked the Dog. But it wasn't my fault. I *had* to fuck the Dog."

"I knew it. The instant I saw you, I thought—He fucked the Dog! And I told you *not* to fuck the Dog."

"I know you did and I wasn't going to. I mean, I'm not stupid. I saw what fucking the Dog did to Arn. And Ewan. And I was going to be spending forty-two nights with her. I knew how serious it was. We even had a long talk on the ferry and we solemnly agreed I wouldn't fuck the Dog—I mean, we agreed to go on being just good friends. I was determined not to fuck the Dog. But I *had* to fuck the Dog. *Ancora, per favore.* I'll explain."

Their camping trip began sunnily, Rita in her MGB, Kenrik waiting with his kitbags (the pegs, the tarps), bright and early one morning, three weeks ago. They caught the twelve o'clock boat from Folkestone to Boulogne. Taking it in turns, and stopping twice for snacks, they drove until midnight, south. Kenrik said,

"And it was cool. She's an excellent travelling companion, the Dog. A real rattle, but very good fun—and incredibly fearless. And she *pays* for everything. You know my fifty quid? I lost it."

"Horses."

"Roulette. By the time I got to France, I didn't have enough money to get back to England. Anyway. I thought, This was a terrific idea. I like and respect the Dog, and we're just really good friends. And I told myself, All you've got to do is remember one thing. Don't fuck the Dog. Anyway. Then we found a site—you know, you just stick your head out and say, *Cam-peeng?* This was south of Lyon. And then in the tent . . . In the tent it was so *hot.* It was really unbelievably hot." He shrugged. "It was so hot I fucked the Dog. There."

"Mm," said Keith. Keith, too, was twenty years old. And he did see that a really unbelievably hot tent, with Rita in it, would more or less take the matter out of your hands. "Mm. Yeah, in a very hot tent. And what was it like?"

"Astonishing. We were still at it when the Germans started queueing for the showers."

". . . Then what went wrong?"

"I don't want to talk about it."

"Yeah, that's what they all say."

"All right, I fucked the Dog. So what. I don't want to talk about it, okay?"

"Yeah, that's what Arn said. No one wants to talk about it."

"Maybe that's why people go on doing it. Go on fucking the Dog. If word got out, they'd stop . . . I keep trying to see it as a rite of passage. Something you just have to go through in life. Fucking the Dog."

Keith said vaguely, "Or something you do when you're very jet-lagged."

"Uh?"

"Garth. My tutor. When he came back from New Zealand. He said he took his wife to the park, on a lead, and then fucked the dog."

Kenrik said vaguely, "Or something you do at cards."

"Uh?"

"You know. Bridge or something. His high spades put him in an excellent position to fuck the dog."

Keith said, "No, you were right the first time. A test of character. Part of your sentimental education. There comes a moment when every young man has to . . ."

"Has to put away childish things."

"Has to show what he's made of."

"And fuck the dog."

There was a silence. Then Kenrik said thoughtfully,

"You know the way you and me go on about chicks? That's the way she goes on about *guys*—guys she's fucked. Guys don't fuck her. She fucks them. But listen. We don't go on like that about chicks *to chicks,* do we. Jesus."

Kenrik and Keith always told each other absolutely everything (every bra-clip, every zip-notch), so out of sheer habit Keith said, "In the tent, how did you get undressed, or were you already—"

"No, man, I can't talk about it . . . It's all I can think about—I'm kind of *writing* it in my head. But I can't talk about it."

Writing it? Nicholas further despised Kenrik because his mental development came to a halt at the age of seventeen (when he got thrown out of the best school in London). And he never read anything. Looking at Kenrik, many were deceived by the pure jawline and the arty cheekbones. As Lily was deceived . . . With dragging reluctance, Keith said,

"Oh yeah. You know that night you spent with Violet. I just want to ask you one thing. And no details. But did she enjoy it, d'you think?"

"Enjoy it? Uh, yeah . . . Actually, to tell you the truth, I can't remember. I mean, I couldn't remember the next day either. It was after that party. *Signore. Ancora, per favore. Grazie.* When she woke up she said, *You were a bit of a naughty boy last night.* So I suppose something or other must've happened. And then I tried to be a bit of a naughty boy in the morning too. But I couldn't manage it. Sorry."

They talked about Violet, and about the castle; and Kenrik, who was not afraid of feminine beauty, said,

"Is that the exquisite one with the tits? Christ. You hardly ever see a face like that on a figure like that. Well you don't. I suppose that's why she needs all that neck. Imagine how much you'd have to fancy yourself to make a pass at Scheherazade."

"You fancy yourself."

"Up to a point. I quite like the other one too. The one with no hair and the arse. And the swimsuit. Like Mum's."

They finished their drinks, and Keith showed him the village sights (principally the church and the rat), and Kenrik said,

"So how's it going with Lily?"

They started up the steep lane just ahead of a herd of goats—or ewes and lambs, the colour of city snow, shuffling, bobbing, like a loom.

"I want to talk to you about Lily. See, it's to do with her sexual confidence. And I thought you might be able to help me out."

"How?"

It was a Friday, and this was the idea: they'd have a late lunch, or an early dinner, or a meat tea, around five thirty, and then, for the willing, there'd be a trip, sponsored by Adriano, to some sort of nightclub in Montale. So, at any rate, Keith was indifferently informed by Gloria, who sat alone in the courtyard with her sketchpad on her lap.

Kenrik said, "Where's Rita?"

"She's sleeping. Everyone's having a siesta. Shall I show you where?"

"Christ no. I'll just hang around upstairs. If I may. With a glass of something."

Keith climbed the tower. He planned to prep Lily—and to nudge reality in the direction he wanted it to take, eliding with his interests, as he saw them . . . He thought of Rita at the pool, her doubled, tripled nudity. Rita reminded him, most anti-erotically, of Violet at ten or eleven—very slender, but in that sheath of plump flesh, in that birth-day suit.

Lily was standing at the window, looking out. She turned.

He said, "Something's wrong."

"I bet you and your friend think that's very funny. Don't you know what it *means*?"

For a moment Keith felt that he was already thwarted and exposed—because he had never seen Lily as angry as this. She said,

"You *liar. Why's she called the Dog?*"

"What? . . . Why shouldn't she be called the Dog? I mean among friends."

"She's gorgeous!"

"Well," he said, "in her way maybe. All right, she's gorgeous. I never said she wasn't."

"Then *why's she called the Dog?* Don't you know what it *means?*"

"Dog? What?" He listened, and said, "Well it might mean that in America. In England it just means *dog.* We all call Rita the Dog. Nicholas calls Rita the Dog. It's because she—she reminds you of a dog."

"*How?*"

"Christ. She *acts* like a dog." He went on slowly, "Rita acts like a dog. She's all bustle. The way you can see her tongue quivering. As if she's lightly panting all the time. And the way she constantly wiggles her arse. As if she's wagging her tail. She wiggles her arse like a dog."

"She *doesn't* wiggle her arse!"

He wiped the sweat off his lip. ". . . Actually you're right. She doesn't. She's stopped wiggling her arse. She used to, but she's stopped. I'll ask her about it—I'll get her to wiggle her arse for you. And you'll be reminded of a dog. I swear."

"Oh, Keith, *why* aren't I beautiful?"

And she so rarely used his name . . . And there was nothing to say in answer to this terrible question. There was nothing to do but step forward, into it, and hold her and stroke her hair.

"*Why* aren't I beautiful," she said in that circling voice of hers. "Scheherazade's beautiful. Rita's beautiful. Even Gloria's beautiful when she smiles. Everyone's beautiful. Why aren't I beautiful . . ."

You will be, he kept saying. And they lay down together, then she slept. And he too experimented with it—the siesta, the nap, *sleep,* the visit to insanity, in the hours of broad daylight . . . When Lily woke, he attentively watched and gossiped with her as she bathed and dressed; and he kept patiently telling her how pretty Kenrik thought she looked.

"Lovely and brown," he told Lily as they came down the stone steps at half past five. "And you've lost weight. That's what he said. And your eyes shine."

"Mm. I'm sorry. It's just that I was looking forward to a dog."

"I'm sorry too. I honestly didn't know about this *dog* business. By your rule, then, the Dog should be called the Fox."

"She looks like a fox."

"Yeah, but it's too late now." And Rita didn't act like a fox. Ambivalently but unmistakably, Rita was somehow man's best friend. "So the Dog it is."

"Did Pansy talk like that? And was she the one who never had pubic hair?"

"No. But she had Rita's accent. And she had that funny way with her *me*s. Pass me nightie. I'm starving, me. It's nice. I like the way they talk."

"Well half of you's from up there, isn't it . . . I can tell Kenrik's not very happy," said Lily as they came out into the courtyard, "but we still don't know why you mustn't."

"Mustn't? Oh yeah. That's right, we don't. Amazing though, isn't it, in a way. Time and time again I told him. Time and again."

"You drummed it into him."

"I drummed it into him. And he knows perfectly well that you mustn't. And on the very first night, the very first night, what's the very first thing he does?"

"He ups and fucks the Dog."

"Exactly."

"And that's exactly what you mustn't do."

They had the food laid out on the sideboard, and the young ones shuffled along its length—cold meats, salads of spinach and potato and bean, proximities, possibilities, body scents, hands, hair, haunch. One by one, at the table, the various figures subsided into place. And you knew for sure that a line would be crossed: Kenrik, with his leaden eyelids, and Rita, with her coercive vividness, already guaranteed it. Not a slippage of genre but a change of certificate. No unaccompanied minors—this would be rated X. Everyone already knew for sure that a line would be crossed.

Adriano turned to Whittaker. "Propose a toast, my friend!" he cried.

Whittaker shrugged and said, "To heterosexuality."

So for a while, under Rita's superintendence, the girls talked about the number of children they hoped to have, Rita herself wanting six, Scheherazade four, Gloria three, Lily two.

"No," said Rita. "Eight, me. No. Ten."

They all seemed to pause before this vision of prolific maternity. But then Lily said,

"Well you'd better get on with it, hadn't you."

"Oh I am, pet, I am. These are me fucking years. I'll get all that out of me system, and then I'll buckle down. One a year." Rita abruptly gulped and said, "Ooh, Gloria love. How can you wear that bra in these temperatures? Aren't the poor darlings gasping for breath?"

In a rare concession to the heat, Gloria was wearing a light blouse with an elliptical neck; both collarbones were indented by broad straps of a surgical dun. She glanced downward and sideways, and coloured. She said softly,

"It's just more comfortable."

"You won't catch mine up in one of those things." Rita swiped a finger through the air. "Now nobody blurt the obvious. I've got two backs, me—and I'm glad! Tits can be . . . *mwa,* I know, but they're always in the bloody road. Even in bed." Rita turned to Scheherazade with her dolphin smile. "Eh, sort, I wouldn't even want your two. Naygo chay-gance. How would I do me limbo?"

Whittaker said, "I don't think I quite get it about bras. The politicisation of bras. What's this bra-burning business with the sisters? I thought bras were your friends."

"They uh, they impose uniformity," said Lily. "That's why they're meant to be bad."

"Bras make everyone's the same," said Scheherazade. "Breasts vary. Bras turn every girl into a kind of sweater girl."

"And that would never do," said Gloria. "No, we can't possibly have that."

She seemed disinclined to continue, but Rita said, "Go on, duck. Speak."

"All right," she said and gave her cough. "Huh-*hm.* So it's just coincidence, is it, it's just the merest coincidence, is it, that not wearing a bra makes your breasts about ten thousand times more noticeable? Bras keep breasts *still.*"

". . . She's right, you know," said Rita, with a nod at Scheherazade. "I'll be ogling yours all night. And Jesus, kid, when you move—seeing you cross a room's like watching a fucking thriller. Will they, won't they? And you," she told Gloria, "you look like you've got a fair pair swaddled away in that bloody hammock. You ought to whip it off, some nights, bint, and give us all a gawp. If you were in proportion, mind, you'd be even fuller than Schez! You don't drink, do you, love. Me neither. Unlike some. Unlike some miserable little soaks I know . . . Right. Seconds, me. And thirds in a minute. I eat like a pig and I never gain. Girls hate me for that, Lil. And who can blame them? Anyone need feeding?"

Adriano, showing much white of eye, held up his plate.

"What are you on, Sebs darling—the beef? That's the spirit. Anyone else?"

Kenrik sat slumped at the head of the table, with his arm curled protectively round a pitcher of wine. The other hand was conducting a series of very slow experiments with its fork. Keith said,

"Oh yeah, Rita. I was wondering. What happened to your wiggle? You've stopped wiggling. You've lost your signature wiggle. Show Lily. Wiggle your arse."

Rita wiggled. And she did: she reminded you of a dog—she looked like a dog looks when you put on your overcoat and reach for the lead. "Again."

Rita wiggled again and said, "*Ow.* Oof. No, Keith, I've got me reasons. Stay there and I'll tell you for why. I'll just ease meself . . . *Oof.*" She leant forward. "No more wiggling. See, the thing is, Keith, I've never been buggered so much *in me life.*"

Kenrik's dropped fork hit his plate with a crack.

"And it's not just him either," said Rita with a jerk of her chin. "And it's not against me will or anything. Call me a pillow-biter, but all's fair in love and war. Seb, is that sufficient, or could you fancy another chunk? No. It's not just Rik. None of them can seem to stay out of there for long. And I know why. It's because I'm a boy. I'm a boy, me. I'm a boy."

Keith looked round the table. Lily, narrow-eyed and narrow-mouthed. Scheherazade, erectly concentrated. Gloria, emanating a potent coldness. Whittaker, frowning, smiling. Adriano, a child in shock. Rita said,

"I'm a boy. No tits. And no arse."

"And no waist," said Lily.

"Bless you, skirt, I almost forgot. And no waist. So they're more or less duty-bound to turn me over, aren't they. Especially if they're that way inclined in the first place. Like Rik . . . It takes him back to his schooldays, see. He thinks about the captain of cricket. It's the only thing that makes it stiffen. It's the only thing that makes it stir. Isn't it, love . . . Oh dear, everyone's gone quiet. Have I put me foot in it again?"

Kenrik picked up a knife and lightly tapped its blade on his glass. The hum, the soft chime, took three or four seconds to fade.

"The first time it happens," he began, ". . . the first time you and Rita make the beast with two backs . . . you think this is something you've dreamt of all your life. You think: So this is what a fuck is . . . All the others—they weren't fucks . . . *This* is what a fuck is . . . But she's not a boy . . . She's a *bloke* . . . No, not even. Dirty as hell, I'll give her that, and resourceful too—I'll give her that. But no feeling for it . . . The first time it happens, you reach out a hand. Then the next thing you know, she's got her thumb up your bum and one of your nuts down her throat. And the other one tucked behind her ear for later. And all four eyelashes are batting at your tip. Her *eyelashes.* Then you do everything else. That's the first time, and it's great. And then it's . . . You know what she does? She shakes you awake in the middle of the night, and if you're too tired then she seriously tells you you're queer. *You hate women.* Whereas, in fact, *she* hates women. And she hates men too. Keith. Keith. Imagine shaking Lily awake, and if she doesn't come across she's a dyke. Or a snob. Or frigid. Or religious. *No mere guy* behaves like that. No guy who isn't already locked up behaves like that. And she thinks she's such a great fuck. And she is. But she's not. No talent for it. No talent . . . Because no . . . No sympathy. There."

Rita had listened to him with her head rhythmically idling on her neck. She said,

"Ah, he's after sympathy, is he. He's after pity. Because he's terrified. He wants his mummy. You're just old-fashioned, love. You're like second-hand furniture. See, for Rik, what he likes is a nice little simperer—a simperer with a sopping hanky. Ooh, you mustn't. That's rude, that's *bad.* Oh go on then, you animal, do your worst. I promise I won't enjoy it. God, were we ever as dull as that, us birds? Were we ever as *bloody dull* as that? . . . Now who's coming dancing. I want to wag a hip. Time for me limbo."

Italians are intriguers. Italy is a nation of intrigue. This axiom was coined, or passed on, by Adriano—who, in the mid-evening lull (the lull that follows every trespass, every trampling, as the contestants run their damage checks)—lingered in the dining hall: just the two of them, and Rita gazing into Adriano's eyes as if he was the only man who had ever really understood her . . . Italy and intrigue: this was the land of Cesare and Lucrezia Borgia, of Niccolò Machiavelli, of Alessandro Cagliostro, of Benito Mussolini. Keith Nearing, all clogged up with the English novel, had recently entered into that obscure specialism known as non-fiction—specifically, modern Italian history; and he found there a world of make-believe.

Not until this summer had Keith tried his hand at manipulation, and his first finding was that it kept you occupied. Keith was busy. He was not as busy as Benito Mussolini, who claimed to have transacted 1,887,112 items of business in seven years (or a major decision every thirty-five seconds, with no days off), and logged 17,000 hours of cock-pit aviation (as many as a full-time pilot over a whole career), while also reading 350 newspapers every morning, and always finding time, every afternoon, for a pentathlon of violent exercise, and, every evening, for an extended interlude alone with his violin. Keith didn't have as much on his plate as Mussolini (and Mussolini, incidentally, was always wrong); but he had to make his rounds.

And the sensation persisted. He seemed to be floating, drifting in and out of himself . . .

Seated with a glass of *prosecco* on the swing sofa at the edge of the west terrace, Lily was uncharacteristically engaged. She was stargazing— with her face at an angle, and with a frown of mistrust. It was a mistrust he momentarily shared: the constellations looked as though they belonged to another hemisphere. He said,

"Strange to think that they're there in the day. You just can't see them."

"They're not there in the day. They come out at night. Are you going along?"

He said he thought he would.

"Well I'm not. Rita's appalling. Still. At least we know why. Why you mustn't."

"Yes, I suppose we do know why you mustn't."

"You'd better apologise to Scheherazade. Since you had to sick her on us."

"I wonder if you know this, Lily. *Sick,* in that sense, comes from an old dialect version of *seek.* It meant *set a dog on.*"

"You're sick. And what are you looking so—so stoned about?"

"You'll look after Kenrik, will you, Lily? You'll take care of him."

"Don't go. Go on then. Did he mean *sympathy?* Or *empathy?*"

"Uh, it's the same thing. Etymologically. Sympathy. *With* plus *feeling.*"

"Etymologically. Go on then. I'll take care of him."

"You looked wonderful at dinner, Lily. Your beauty is coming in. It's here."

Then of course he had to make it right with his hostess.

She was sitting at the backgammon board in the salon, and steadying with her hands a textbook (its subject was statistics) on the steep bluffs of her thighs.

"Phew," she said. "That was . . . It was like one of those TV plays that carry a warning. So of course you've got to watch. Whittaker adored it too. What's that language she speaks? Is it vernacular?"

Keith said, "It's a sort of code. She talks to her friends in it, and they think you can't understand. They just put an *a* and a *g* in the middle of everything. Day-ghed pay-gosh. Dead posh. Naygo. No. It's easy. Except when they do whole sentences in it."

". . . God, the things people get up to. I had no idea. She makes me feel about three. It's all working out perfectly, isn't it. Rita and Adriano. Tonight I'll sleep the sleep of the just."

"You're not coming?"

"I'm tempted, but I'd be in the way. Won't you be?"

Well, the thing is, Scheherazade, I have to be out of the house. He said, "Maybe nothing'll happen. Maybe Adriano'll have the power to resist."

"Naygo chan-cegg," said Scheherazade.

And finally Kenrik. Who sat at the kitchen table, with a huge pot of coffee and a look of vacant equanimity on his face. He said,

"Sorry about all that. Now here's an interesting theory. I just had a nice chat with uh, the one with the arse, and *she* said—Gloria—*she* said that I never had a hope once Rita started paying for everything. She said women hate men who don't pay for everything. They even hate you if you go Dutch. Girls can't help it. Bred in the bone. Guess what. Adriano just came in and shook me by the hand. They're down in the car."

"I'd better go. You know, maybe she's just too old for you. It was good, your after-dinner speech. But it won't put anyone off."

"The challenge, you mean? Mm. So. Boys are doomed to fuck the Dog. And they *should* fuck the Dog. But only if she's going to Hawaii the next morning. For ever. Watch the way she dances."

"You relax with Lily," he said. "She's nice and sensitive and demure."

"Demure. Now *that's* a turn-on."

Keith made a further suggestion. And Kenrik said,

"Are you really serious? Why?"

N̲ow he hurried down the stone steps, through the pale smell of sweat. *You see, Scheherazade, I have to be out of the house. So that Kenrik can sleep with Lily. And then, with that out of the way, I can sleep with* you . . . There were the stars, with their points looking cold and sharp: the visible tips of the pins God used to tack down the dark backing of the universe. And what of his own system, his personal galaxy, his Virgo, and the seven suns that remained to him? Before the summer is done, how many more will I extinguish?

The Rolls Royce gnashed and bristled. A clear view of the future would have sent Keith up the steps to Lily's side, or into Montale, where he could start to thumb his way back to England. Keith reached for his packet of Disque Bleu. He thought, It's a test of character. He paused. It's my sentimental education. He lit a cigarette. He breathed in.

FOURTH INTERVAL

And breathed out, a third of a century later.

He cleared his throat, not with a growl (his usual method), but with a bark (like a rifle shot). Ten minutes earlier he had returned from an exceptional sortie to a place called the Smokeshack in Camden Town, and now, with a discoloured tongue boyishly extruded from the corner of his mouth, he was trying to attach various printed labels to the various packets, tins, cartons, and wallets that lay strewn all over his desk. *Smoking Makes You Look Sexy,* said one. *If You Give Up Smoking, You Will Probably Go Insane,* said another. Keith had broken up with nicotine in 1994, but now they were back together again, and very much in love.

Coughing and hoicking and retching and slightly out of breath, and again with much play of the smeared tongue and the trembling, haddocky fingers, he pasted a third label (in fact his own adaptation of a common health warning) to his current pouch of Golden Virginia. It said: *Non-Smokers Outlive Smokers by Seven Years. And Guess* Which *Seven.*

He stared at it with smarting, red-rinded eyes.

.   .   .

Recently, when he was out in the street, he used to think: Beauty is gone. He soon moved forward from this position, and thought: Beauty never was—there never was any. Both premises were resoundingly untrue. The draining of it, the draining of beauty, was taking place inside his own flesh and breast.

Beauty, present beauty, sat before him across the kitchen table.

"Well I'm bound to feel a bit of a prick, aren't I," he said to wife number three (they were discussing that encounter, in the Book and

Bible, with wife number one). "Twenty-five years of cross purpose. A whole lifetime. If you hadn't rescued me, my darling." He sipped his coffee. "I could've been a poet."

"You're a respected critic. And a teacher."

"Yeah, but I could've been a poet. And all for what? All for a—all for a *session*."

"Look on the bright side," she said. "It wasn't just any old session, was it."

"That's an extremely positive way of thinking about it. Still."

"It made your eyes come out on stalks for a whole year."

"Two years. Longer. Three. That was part of the trouble."

"Think of it as what you had to go through to get me."

"I will. I do."

"You've got your boys, your girls, and your womie."

"I have my womie. You know, all this started weeks ago. There's something else. There's this other thing. I don't know what it is. It can't be to do with Violet, can it? How can it be?"

And he went back across the garden through the April shower. But now it was May.

·   ·   ·

Encrypted in mirror writing, and placed at the foot of the page, point three in the revolutionary manifesto was a kind of sleeper clause, implicit but unintended and still imperfectly understood. It was this: *Surface will start tending to supersede essence.* As the self becomes postmodern, how things look will become at least as important as how things are. Essences are hearts, surfaces are sensations . . .

As he opened his eyes that morning, Keith thought, When I was young, old people looked like old people, slowly growing into their masks of bark and walnut. People aged differently now. They looked like young people who had been around far too long. Time moved past them but they dreamt they stayed the same.

Waking in his studio, and getting out of bed, and all the rest of it—this was no longer a Russian novel. It was an American novel. So, not much shorter, but with perceptible gains: a general increase in buoyancy, and far less stuff about everyone's grandfathers.

The bathroom area answered to all Keith's sanitary needs. But it had a flaw: two mirror-fronted cabinets faced each other over the washbasin.

He had to keep these cabinets firmly shut when he shaved. If he didn't, he saw his bald patch receding into infinity.

.   .   .

A typical interlude of pleasure and profit with the girls. They played I Spy, and What Would You Rather. They played a card game called Go Fish. Then they counted the freckles on Chloe's left arm (there were nine). She questioned him about his three favourite colours and his three least favourite colours. Isabel questioned him about his three favourite flavours of ice cream—and his three least favourite. Next, Chloe burped the alphabet, and Isabel told him about a swimming pool so deep that even the grown-ups had to wear floaties.

"When the boys are here," said Isabel, "do you feel ashamed?"

"Ashamed? Why, because they're so tall and handsome? No. I'm proud."

And the two girls laughed like the yellow birds . . .

He slipped away to his shed and spent an hour staring down into the thatchy crater of the Heath. Venus rose. What was it, this other thing?

.   .   .

It was better now—in society.

There used to be the class system, and the race system, and the sex system. The three systems are gone or going. And now we have the age system.

Those between twenty-eight and thirty-five, ideally fresh, are the super-elite, the tsars and tsarinas; those between eighteen and twenty-eight, plus those between thirty-five and forty-five, are the boyars, the nobles; all the others under sixty comprise the bourgeoisie; everyone between sixty and seventy represents the proletariat, the hoi polloi; and those even older than that are the serfs and the wraiths of slaves.

Hoi polloi: the many. And, oh, we will be many (he meant the generation less and less affectionately known as the Baby Boomers). And we will be hated too. *Governance, for at least a generation,* Keith read, *will be a matter of transferring wealth from the young to the old.* And they won't like that, the young. They won't like the *silver tsunami,* with the old hogging the social services and stinking up the clinics and the hospitals, like an inundation of monstrous immigrants. There will be age wars, and chronological cleansing . . .

Perhaps this possible future explains a further anomaly of the age system: it meets no dissent. The old don't agitate or propagandise, they don't even complain about it, not any more. They used to, but they've stopped. They don't want to draw attention to themselves. They're old. They're in enough trouble as it is.

But we think it good, we think it meet, the age system, and profoundly and fluidly democratic. Contemporary reality is the taste in the mouths of the ideally fresh. As we lie dying, not many of us will have enjoyed the inestimable privilege of being born with white skin, blue blood, and a male member. Each and every one of us, though, at some point in our story, will have been young.

. . .

The pure cold opal pool, cupped in soft grasses. No boar or stag had ever lapped and slurped at it, no insects had skated on its surface. And here he came, the glassy boy, and stretched himself out and bent his head, and quenched his thirst with his eyes . . .

From the first instant, when love came as swift as light, the boy became his own torturer. His hands sank into the surface, to embrace and caress the essence within—but it vanished in tremors of disquietened water.

"You laugh when I laugh.
I have watched your tears through my tears.
When I tell you my love, I see your lips
Seeming to tell me yours—though I cannot hear it."

Then it happened, but too late: You are me. Now I see that . . . What I want, I am . . . Let death come quickly. *And when he moaned,* Alas, *she moaned it too—Echo, or the ghost of Echo. Or Echo's echo.* Alas. Touch me, kiss me, touch me, kiss me, touch me.

Let death come quickly. This was his last wish. And it was granted.

. . .

Silvia said, "You're a loser, Mum. Not *you*, but the whole first wave. You missed your chance, and it won't come again."

"We went Napoleonic."

"You went Napoleonic."

According to Silvia, the sexual revolution, like the French (perhaps), diffused its seminal energies in expansion, without pausing to secure its base. In her view, the first and possibly the only clause in the manifesto should have read as follows (and Keith could tell it was salient, because he feared it): *Fifty-fifty in the home.*

"Fifty-fifty. All the boring shite with the house and the kids. No hyphen. Fiftyfifty. But you didn't nail that down. You spread your wings in the wrong way. You grabbed the wrong powers. Administration, decision-making. More shite. Some God-awful document comes in the mail, and Pop goes and stands beside you looking lost. And you *snatch* it from his hands. I've seen him . . . I know he's struggling now, but even when he's fully fit he never does a tenth of what you do. *And* you're earning. And you don't even scream at him. You just let him get away with it."

"I'm not like you. It's my background."

"Yeah. So what's your form of protest? Ten minutes of noisy washing-up. You're a loser, Mum."

Accustomed, by now, to being talked about as if he wasn't in the room, Keith said, mildly, and (as usual) rather off the point, "Your mother's very even-tempered. My second wife was slightly bipolar. Like Proserpina. *One moment Gloomy as hell's king, but the next Bright as the sun's mass, bursting from clouds.*"

"Here he goes," said Silvia.

"My *first* wife turned out to be unusually changeable—moment by moment. You know, there's a subatomic particle that turns into the exact opposite of itself three trillion times a second. She wasn't as changeable as that, but she was changeable."

Both women sighed.

"The micro world is womanlike. *You* know what I mean. It's not so proud of being rational. The macro world is womanlike too. You should be pleased. Vindicated. Reality is womanlike."

"He's slipping off to his shed."

"It's only the middle world that's manlike."

"But that's the one we live in," said Silvia.

.   .   .

Keith sat smoking. In it came, and out it went: the familiar blend of benzene, formaldehyde, and hydrogen cyanide. Amen once said that in Libya the cigarette is a unit of time. How far's the village? Three cigarettes. How long will you be? One cigarette.

He thought, Yeah. Yeah, non-smokers live seven years longer. Which seven will be subtracted by the god called Time? It won't be that convulsive, heart-bursting spell between twenty-eight and thirty-five. No. It'll be that really cool bit between eighty-six and ninety-three.

When he walked the grids of the A to Z, through the flowing metal of the city, he gratefully heeded the instructions daubed on the roadside crossings, LOOK LEFT, LOOK RIGHT. But now—and this happened when he was driving too—he kept suspecting that there was a third direction he should be wary of. There was a third direction that things might be coming from. Not right, not left—but aslant, athwart.

Book Five

Trauma

I

THE TURN

Soon came the waiting, then came the metamorphoses, then came *torquere* ("to twist"); but first came the turn.

When he entered the tower bedroom, at half past two, Lily and Kenrik were lying together on the bared bottom sheet. Lily in her satin housecoat, Kenrik in shirt and jeans and gyms. A rhombus of moonlight bathed their bodies in its innocence; but their faces were lost in black shadow. Keith said,

"Are you awake? . . . I drove the Rolls."

Lily unsleepily said, "Where was Tom Thumb?"

"In the back with the Dog. Doing God knows what."

"Was that them screeching off? That was an hour ago."

"I sat up thinking."

"Mm, I bet you did. Now where will *you* lay your head? You can go next door and climb in with Junglebum for all I care."

"What's *he* doing here anyway?"

"Him? What's he doing here? Well. He made love to me, you see. And it was heaven. Some men know how to make a woman feel beautiful. And then he put his clothes back on—because he wouldn't want you to know. Would he. Then he fell asleep. Or maybe he's just pretending."

"I wish I could see your face. Kenrik? . . . Push him over. There's a pillow on the rug. Push."

Then Kenrik rolled. There was a soggy but nonetheless sickening thud, then silence.

Lily said, "By the way. Buggery is the beast with one back. Isn't that right?"

He said, "I wish I could see your face."

"But you don't have to do it that way round."

"I wish I could see your face."

The two visitors were packed up and on their way by mid-afternoon, but nobody who saw it ever forgot it: Rita and Ruaa, in the same frame of vision—Ruaa and Rita, down by the pool.

Meanwhile, Kenrik and Keith lay on the lawn in their swimsuits. Their utterly hairless chests, their flat stomachs, their full brown thighs: not particularly well made, and not innocent, but indubitably young.

Kenrik leant up on an elbow. "It's Eden here," he said nauseously, and sank back with a quavering sigh. ". . . Jesus, those birds look a bit rough. The crows. Not the, not the gaily coloured coolies in the tree— Christ, they like a laugh, don't they?"

"Look at them up there." Keith meant the *magneti,* perforating the horizon.

"They're cool too. No. The crows."

The crows, their bitter, scavenging faces, their hoarse cries of hunger. And Keith, too, croaked out his question: the one about last night and Lily . . . He was no longer all aglitter with cunning; he had begun to suspect that there were certain people who were better at cunning than he was. Keith felt like a tyro physicist who, on his first day, initiates an irreversible chain reaction, and then just stands there and stares. Kenrik said,

"I don't think anything happened. But I can't remember. Again. It's shocking, that. And *rude.* But there it is. I can't remember."

Yes. Keith's scheme contained another obvious weakness: it had Kenrik in it. "I thought you'd sobered up."

"Me too, but after all that fucking coffee I drank another barrel of wine and went back on the Scotch. Jesus. It's a bit better now. When I opened my eyes, first thing, I hardly knew what I was. Hang on. Maybe it'll all come back to me."

". . . Describe hangovers. I don't think I've ever had one."

Showing one of the fragments of a good (Protestant) education, Kenrik said, "They're like . . . they're like the Inquisition. Yeah. Exactly like. A hangover racks you for your sins. And when you confess, it racks you even more. And by the way, if you don't think you've ever had one, then you haven't ever had one."

"Isn't it the same with sex? If you don't think you did, then you didn't."

"Ah but it's a funny mix, sex and booze. You can wake up saying sorry you didn't, when in fact you did . . . Okay. We talked on the terrace. Then we were up in the tower. I remember thinking how nice she was. I remember thinking how loyal she was—Lily."

This wasn't as informative as it sounded: *loyal,* for Kenrik, was a term of broad approval; various drinking clubs, snooker halls, and gambling dens were praised by him as *loyal.*

"Sorry, man. You can't ask *her,* I suppose. Can't check with Lily."

"I can but she—"

Lily in her indigo bikini was coming across the lawn to where they lay, unusually light-footed, Keith thought, like a girl in an ad for something healthy or fragrant—Ryvita, say, or 4711. She knelt at Kenrik's side and kissed him carefully on the mouth. They watched her walk on down the slope.

"Mm, *that* reminded me of something. Change the subject for a bit. Rita. Did you watch her dancing?"

"The whole club watched her dancing." The sweating nightspot, the cleared floor, the circular crowd, the strobes, the mirrorballs, Rita's tank top and Union Jack miniskirt. "The limbo."

"The limbo." Kenrik sank back.

"And Jesus. The last time round, that pole can't have been more than nine inches off the ground."

"See, that's what she wants. Amazing, isn't it. For her that's the perfect state of affairs. Every pair of eyes in the whole place," said Kenrik, "transfixed by her box."

"Would we do that? If we could?"

"Maybe. If we could. I don't see it somehow. Then what?"

"Then outside she said, *You drive, Keith, and I'll pop in the back with Sebs.*"

"Could you see anything?"

"No, I kept the mirror up. I didn't dare look. But I listened." Intense silences, punctuated by movements of demented suddenness—instantaneous joltings, jerkings, snappings-to. "Sort of whiplash effects. From him. Every now and then." Keith sank back again. "When I got out he clambered over the seat. And they tore off."

Kenrik laughed, reluctantly; then unreluctantly. He said, "Whiplash. She's sort of great, the Dog. I'm too young to be doing all that queer stuff. Too young and too queer."

"What's it like, all that queer stuff?"

"It's terrifying really. Cool at the time. Rita's right, you know. I don't think I like it—now that girls like it. I liked it better when they didn't. Or pretended not to. What's the time? Can I start drinking yet? . . . That kiss reminded me of something. There was kissing."

"And kissing was all?"

"Yeah. I think. You know, I'm ninety per cent certain I *wasn't* a naughty boy last night. And I'll tell you why." He came up on an elbow. "See, for about a week I've been thinking . . . I'm going to make an announcement. I'm going to announce that I won't be fucking anyone ever again."

"Anyone. Not even Scheherazade if she asked you to."

"Not even Scheherazade. And I want it *official*. I want it in my passport. A special stamp, like a visa. So in the tent tonight, all I'd have to do is open my passport at the Dog. Christ, did you see the size of that bee? I bet that packs a sting . . . It's Eden here."

The roses pouted and simpered, the scents swayed and swooned. They were talking about the birds and the bees. It was Eden. And Keith, who was feeling very fallen, said, "I'm sorry to hear that. I mean Lily. But would she have, d'you think? *Would* she have?"

At noon, from the pool, they saw the Rolls Royce come cruising round the curl in the mountainside. Lily and Keith went to the rampart and looked over: Rita flying up the stone steps while the car made a gruff three-point turn on the gravel. She paused to wave, on tiptoe, and there was the bronzed forearm, lazily brandished.

"He does a beautiful breakfast," said Rita as she wriggled out of all her clothes. "Served on his balcony. It's not a castle, where Seb lives. It's a bloody *town*."

She was now under the poolside shower, with one hand ready on the grip of the tap. But first she had much to impart . . . There were just the four of them down there, now, and Scheherazade.

"Flowers on the tray. Three kinds of fruit juice. Croissants. Yoghurt and honey. Little herb omelette under a little silver platter. Oh, it was handsome. Except the tea. I couldn't drink it. I can't drink that muck, me. I need me Tetley. I should've brought along a bag or two. Why *didn't* I? I must have me Tetley."

"She travels with it," said Kenrik. "Her Tetley."

"I'm no good without me Tetley. Rik. Go on, star, go and make us a mug. Ooh, go on."

Kenrik climbed to his feet, conversationally saying, "No offence or anything, and don't answer if you don't want to, but what was he like? Adriano."

It was then that Ruaa appeared, beyond, behind, moving sharply round the side of the pool hut, halting, stiffening, tilting back; her sable gown told you only three things about the body there encased: its gender, of course, its height, of course, and, rather more mysteriously, its youth.

"Look at this he gave me," said Rita, all unaware, as her hands sought her throat: an undulant silver necklet with a solid glint to it. "*My serpent of old Nile . . .* You know, Schez, I've never been made love to like that before. He begins so gentle. And just as you're swooning with the tenderness of it all, he changes. And you think, Oof, have I ever felt *that* well plugged? I think it must be the girth of him."

Then she swivelled. And the moment seemed to zoom upward into the gold and the blue: there they were, by a castle on a mountain in Italy, Ruaa and Rita—yes, the Blob in her burkha, the Dog in her birthday suit . . . Rita shouted out,

"Jesus Christ, love, you must be fucking *frying alive* in there! You want to get that tent off, chick, and come and have a splash with us!"

For lunch there were the leftovers from the (very distant) night before. And then they were gone.

"You know," said an equable Scheherazade, "she's better than us."

"Who is?" said Keith.

"Ruaa."

Lily said, "Oh, come on. Why? Because she wears an instrument of torture? And why's it *black*? Black traps the heat. Why not white? Why are they dressed as widows?"

"Well that may be true. But she's better than us."

Keith went on staring out, long after the little sports car had dropped over the slopes of the first foothill. And when he turned away there was no one there, no Scheherazade, no Lily, no one at all, and he felt suddenly empty, suddenly alone under the sky. He stood at the poolside and stared. The water was motionless and for now translucent; he could see the copper coins and a single flipper. Then the light began to change, as a cloud hurried sideways to shield the modesty of the sun, and a shape like a dark starfish came writhing up from the depths. Only to meet its original—a falling leaf—as the surface changed from glass to mirror.

I t was just the two of them on the terrace before dinner, and Lily said,

"Why aren't you angry?"

"About you and Kenrik? Because I assume you're teasing me. *Some men know how to make a woman feel . . .* You sounded like Rita on Adriano."

"And you're like Kenrik listening to her. Utterly indifferent."

"Because you make it sound implausible."

"Oh, you don't believe me. You don't believe Kenrik tried. Because I'm not attractive enough."

"No, Lily."

"What did Kenrik say about it?"

"Well *he* wouldn't tell me, would he?"

"Wouldn't he? . . . Anyway. He didn't. He was very sweet, and we had a kiss and a cuddle. But he didn't try and take it further. That was all."

"Ah, but would you have? That's the point. *Would* you have?"

"What, so you can . . . No. I wouldn't have. Listen. You and I made a vow. We swore. Remember? That we might break up, but we'd never do that to each other. Never be underhand. Never deceive."

He admitted the truth of this.

". . . I don't know quite what you had in mind, but I've been thinking. Is there an animal between a dog and a fox? Because that's what we are. We're not tree rats and we're not red squirrels. We're the grey. You know, it's not the rich who're really different from us. It's the beautiful. You don't get Visions. I *can,* sometimes, because I'm a girl. But it's never on equal terms. And it always hurts. We're Possibles, you and me. We're still quite cute, and we make each other happy. Look, we can't break up *here,* can we. I love you enough for now. And you should love me back."

He coughed, and went on coughing. When you're a smoker, you sometimes have the chance to get rid of the other stuff that's choking you. She knew everything, he felt. So he came out with it. "I can't believe I said that. *Would you have?* Please forget I ever did. I'm sorry. I'm sorry."

"*Love Story.* The one we hated. Remember? Hysterical sex means never having to say you're sorry."

"Good, Lily. That's your first proper one." It would in fact take him not very long to see how completely useless this was, as an axiom. The truth of it being that love meant *always* having to say you're sorry. "I'm sorry, Lily. And yes to everything. I'm sorry, Lily. I'm sorry."

At dinner in the kitchen, with Scheherazade and Gloria, he kept his head down, and told himself, Well at least, now, the bad dreams will stop — the dreams of Lily. There were variations along the way, but these dreams inevitably came to the point where she was crying and he was laughing. These dreams always gave Keith enough power to wake himself up from them. So even in the mad universe of sleep — you passionately wanted something, and it came about, it came true. You woke up. And it was the only time it ever really happened (he thought): it was in this sense and in this sense only that your dreams ever really came true.

That night it was a little better, the indescribable act. You could even say that Jupiter made love to Juno. It was Jovian, it befitted the King of Heaven, in that Juno was not only his sister but also his wife.

"I wish Timmy would come."

"I do too."

"That would be simplest for everybody. Especially for her. So she can stop . . ."

Being desperate, he thought. And then he gave it up.

For now Adriano held back. And, the next morning, it wasn't Timmy's name that was on everyone's lips. No, the advent of Jorquil, long-rumoured, had hardened into a date, perceptibly adding to the prestige and legitimacy of Gloria Beautyman. Jorq, after all, was speeding to her side — while Timmy fecklessly tarried in Jerusalem. Now power changed.

At lunch, fanning herself with the confirmatory telegram, Gloria asked Scheherazade if she would need any help moving her stuff out of the apartment, adding,

"You can't do it all by yourself, and there's no Eugenio—or Timmy . . . We can leave it till Tuesday. Of course, I'd be perfectly happy in the tower. But you know Jorq."

"I know Jorq. Fine. God, it's his castle."

"And the apartment's awfully big for just one person, isn't it."

"Yes."

"And there's no sign of Timmy, is there."

"No."

"I mean, we haven't seen hide nor hair of Timmy, have we."

"No."

"Well, you've got—what?—another five nights all alone up there."

And this.

Keith was grimly transcribing some notes in one of the anterooms (he was tidying up, in readiness for Dickens and George Eliot) when Gloria passed by with her sewing (she was making a patchwork quilt, patch by patch). And she said,

"I expect you're terribly pleased about Jorquil."

". . . Why d'you expect that?"

"Because it means the servants'll be back. This place is turning into an ashtray, don't you think? Haven't you finished with that yet?"

She meant *Pride and Prejudice*. "I nearly have." He was jotting down the details of Charlotte Lucas's *prudential marriage* to the Reverend Collins. "Why d'you ask?"

"I thought I might have a read of it. If you'd be so kind. Or are you the sort of swot who's 'funny' about his books? His uh, Signet paperbacks."

"Wait." He looked at her, and she looked the same—clumping sandals, dull dun smock, tufted black hair. "Does that mean you've already polished off *Joan of Arc*?"

"Oh, irony again. I'd forgotten how ironical you are."

"There's a much fancier set in the library. Leatherbound. Illustrated."

"No, I'll use yours, if I may. Then I can be as grubby as I like. Is it my kind of thing?"

Keith thought of Jorquil, the heavy blond shape under the top hat in the rural marquee. He said (he paraphrased), "It's a novel about the amorous effects of money. Young women of the middle class—revealing with such sobriety—the economic basis of society."

". . . You clever young men. And it's hilarious, really, because you don't know *anything*."

The heat persisted, and there was now something wholly disgraceful in the way it uncurled and revealed itself each morning. They woke up and it was already there, uncurling and revealing itself, like a beast. The kitchen smelled of cabbage and drains. The milk went off. The pool was ninety-eight point four. I will never tire, the sun was saying. I am like the sea. You will tire. But I will never tire.

"Oh come on, Lily. What d'you mean, *keeps* having handjobs?"

"She does. She keeps having handjobs. At least two a day."

"Two a day?" And Keith wasn't sure that girls even *had* handjobs. "Where?"

"In the bathroom. With the showerhead in the tub that's like a mad snake when you turn it on full. She says the one in the apartment isn't quite as good. Less pressure."

". . . How long does it take?"

"It's all over in a couple of minutes. Especially if she rubs her tits. Now they're so tickly and throbby. Guess what she calls the showerhead? She calls it the Rain God."

He said in the dark, "Does she know you pass on all this stuff?"

"I told you. She'd kill me."

"Do you tell her stuff about us?"

"No. Well. A bit."

Adriano, as already noted, hung back. And when he did resume his visits (and his faithful use of diving board, exercise bar, and trampoline), it was with neither a diffident nor a triumphal air. And he brought company with him . . . Keith had *Oliver Twist* unopened on his lap, in the library, when Adriano boldly approached and said,

"Please kiss Feliciana on either cheek . . . She has no English, so we may speak *uomo a uomo*. I hope and trust your friend Kenrik was not unduly put out?"

Keith, who had just kissed her on either cheek, supposed that Feliciana could be thought of as merely very petite. Barefoot (and in a pink cotton dress), she was close to Adriano in height—close enough for Keith to recall the sequence in *The Incredible Shrinking Man* when the hero has the strange flirtation with the girl from the travelling circus. Otherwise she resembled the notoriously depraved little sister of, say, Sophia Loren or even Gina Lollobrigida—much littler, but not that much younger. In later life he would recognise it, the sheeny, masklike look some women get, when they realise that time has started to happen.

"Put out about Rita?" Keith told him no. "Not unduly. In fact, Adriano," he said, "I think it worked out pretty well. From your point of view."

"I believe it did. What with her going away for ever the next morning. But I'm not proud of myself. And obviously this calls for a change of strategy. As regards Scheherazade. I can tell you this because you're impartial. You have absolutely no interest in the outcome."

Feliciana, meanwhile, flowed with condensed allure around the room, admiring the furniture, the spines of books, the view. Once, twice, she moved inward on Adriano, to stroke his shoulder or brush her lips against his jaw. This vexed him, and he seemed to tell her as much (Keith thought he caught the word *superfluo*). Adriano then continued,

"Women, Keach, even unawakened women, as I take Scheherazade to be, despite this *Timmy,* are sometimes excited by the thought of intense sexual activity elsewhere."

With a silent sigh (he feared it might come to this), Keith resolved to step up his attentions to Lily. He said, "You reckon?"

"Sometimes. I gave Rita every encouragement to describe our night together. Did she oblige?"

"Uh, yeah. In her own way."

He nodded. "And as you see, Feliciana hardly suffers from neglect. Scheherazade is of course a different type. That becoming modesty. Pure in word and thought. But she has her needs. Needs which I happen to know are now pressing. Time will tell. Are you coming to the pool? I recommend the spectacle of Feliciana's physique."

Lily was undressing herself in the runny candlelight. She said,

"Did you notice how different she was at dinner?"

This was with reference to Scheherazade. Keith said, "I just wondered why she went up to bed in the middle of it. Did Tom Thumb rub her up the wrong way?"

"With Thumbelina the second?"

Yes. The second. It was not Feliciana who acted as Adriano's partner at dinner. It was Rachele. Lily said,

"It was a bit much, wasn't it. Spoon-feeding him two whole bowls of crème brûlée."

"And sitting on his lap for coffee."

"With her dress yanked up. No. You're completely wrong, as usual. Scheherazade couldn't care less. Didn't you notice how happy she was? I've been sworn to secrecy, but I can't resist. Timmy rang from Tel Aviv. He's en route."

". . . Ah. At last. And when will this be?"

"She thinks tomorrow night. But with Timmy you can never tell. You know Timmy. The happy-go-lucky type. She expects him to walk in the door any minute. With his knapsack on his back. You know Timmy."

"With his knapsack on his back. Yes, we know Timmy. Yes, we know Jorq. They're rich. So you're supposed to accept them exactly as they are."

"Mm. Well. Just think. They'll have a lovely long weekend in the apartment before Jorquil comes. And now she's saving herself up. No more handjobs. Conserving herself for Timmy."

"That's wise."

The next day he kept to his room, and forced himself to finish *Jane Eyre*. He admired it, but resisted it: more orphans and wards and guardians, more ravings, blazings, blindings. Every twenty minutes he went and smoked on the battlements, and experienced what was technically known as *suicidal ideation*. He didn't consider it, suicide; he just imagined it. Gravity, the greed of gravity, the gravity-well of the courtyard below. The doings of extinction were at his disposal. It would be like making a pass (a lunge, a pounce)—a pass at death. You would have no doubt about your reception. Scheherazade and Keith: it was over. He drily acknowledged this. And went back to Miss Eyre and Mr. Rochester.

·

Then came the turn.

Over the course of the afternoon he received three visits from three young women. And it turned.

"Oh," said Scheherazade. She wore the full bikini and had a rolled towel under her arm with more clothes wrapped up in it. "I didn't know you were here. Excuse me. Would you mind if I had a shower? There's a shower upstairs but it's—it isn't quite as good."

Less pressure, he thought.

"Less pressure," she said sleepily. "I like a shower that leaves your skin tingling. Upstairs it's just a drip. In comparison."

He sat at the table trying not to: trying not to try to listen. Then came a knock. He got up. And found the stairwell empty. Her voice came from behind him.

"I have to know."

It was Gloria, a shadowed shape in the passage between the turrets. "What?"

"Does Elizabeth Bennet marry Mr. Darcy?"

He told her.

"And does Jane marry Mr. Bingley? . . . Thank God for that. Sorry to bother."

She turned. She turned again. She said, "Are there *grave* ups and downs? Warn me."

He warned her in non-specific terms about the vicissitudes to be faced, in particular, by Eliza and Fitzwilliam.

"I used to read all the time, but there seemed no point," said Gloria, "once we were poor."

The bathtaps were running. At this distance it sounded like a seashell held to the ear.

"Is that Scheherazade in there? . . . Mm. Fancy that."

He went back in, and there was silence. Then an hour silently passed. During it (Keith later realised), he read a page and a half of Charlotte Brontë.

"I had a soak in the end," said Scheherazade. "And daydreamed."

She now stood over him in her long white shirt; her hair was lank and citric and clung heavily to her neck and shoulders. Glazed yet also unsteady, her eyes reminded him of the encounter with the black silk dressing gown (bumping into things, and the rich smell of sleep). With a look of concern, she said,

"Keith, can I have a word with you later on?"

It was the first time she had used his name. Don't die, he told himself. Not now. No, please don't die.

She said, "Around five thirty? By the feminine fountain. While Lily's in her bath."

Late in the afternoon he had his third caller, who gave him a cup of tea and a kiss on the crown and a letter from his brother Nicholas. He opened the thing with his face at an angle to it. It was quite long, and its subject was Violet Shackleton. *My dear Little Keith, The foul rag-and-bone shop of the heart. My heart aches, and a drowsy numbness pains My sense . . .*

Yes, he thought. *As though of hemlock I had drunk.*

"Aren't you going to read it?"

"Uh, not now," he said. "I'm not in the mood."

He put the letter back in the envelope, which he installed as his bookmark, three pages from the end of *Jane Eyre.*

Unshaped, unprompted by him, it was hardening into a certainty. All he had to do, from now on, was keep his mouth shut. All he had to do, from now on, was not do anything.

He sat by the feminine fountain, around five fifteen, while Lily was in her bath.

In the myths, distressed or aberrant beauties could be transformed into a variety of things and beings. A flower, a bird, a tree, a star, a weeping statue—or a fountain. The fountain in the centre of the courtyard had its own vital statistics, approximately 7' 6", 44-18-48. Water gathered in the topmost bowl or basin, then folded its tresses downward, gathering at the waist, and then folding again, hipward. The shape-change from woman to living ornament seemed to have taken place very recently; but this was the fountain that Frieda Lawrence had leant herself against, fifty years ago. Keith had a book with him. He didn't open it. He just sat there by the feminine fountain, and did the waiting.

2

THE WAITING

She came at him slenderly, in her full peel of youth. So she was wearing that—the bronzed finish of twenty years old; and blue jeans, and white shirt; and an accessory he had seen only once before, in London, that time, as she moved across the lightly puddled parquetry of some college corridor, in her tasselled mortar board and short black gown: a pair of rimless spectacles.

"That's not quite right, is it? Mutual."

"No, not quite," he said. She was referring to the book he had with him—*Our Mutual Friend.* It was possibly the only example in world literature of a solecism enshrined in a title; and it was the author's last novel, not his first. He said, "It should be our *common* friend. Strictly."

"Mm. Strictly."

Don't do anything, he told himself. He was equally half-convinced that, when it came to interlocution with Scheherazade, all he had to do from now on was not say anything. And yet he felt many consecutive sentences massing and jostling, lobbying, in his throat.

"I'm going to intersperse him with George Eliot," he said. "But I thought with Dickens I'd start at the end and work backward. It's strange reading a man. After all those girls. Jane, Emily, Charlotte, Anne. And now George."

Scheherazade sat back and said, "Gloria thinks George Eliot's a man. She said, *Would I like him?* Uh, listen . . . I'll come to the point in a minute. But before I forget. Rita. I know they liked her in the club. How did they like her in the street? The young men of Montale."

Keith took stock. He'd told Lily that Rita was more or less ignored by the young men of Montale. But now he spoke the truth: Rita, in town, provoked the sort of commotion that called for cordons and mounted officers—but not for the water-cannons and rubber bullets demanded by the transit of Scheherazade . . . He said minimally,

"A considerable disturbance. Still, not like you." After a moment he said, "Glasses."

"Glasses. I cleaned my contact lenses and I'm too blind to see where they went. And I wanted to feel studious. It's like the romantic comedy. *Take off your glasses, Miss Pettigrew. Why, you're . . . Who'd have thought it?* All right. Deep breath."

Her bosom rose and so did his, and the castle itself, standing behind her, seemed to inflate while also losing mass and substance. From her top pocket she took a brown envelope and offered it to him. Keith read: "ETA PPONED 8 DAYS STOP YOU SEE THE THING IS . . ." Keith read on. Scheherazade said,

"The other night—why didn't the count kiss me the other night?"

"The count?"

"Count Dracula."

No, don't die—please don't die. He waited. "The count wanted to kiss you," he then said, and registered the abrupt licence of the third person—the proxy being. "He very much wanted to."

She glanced away and said, "It's Lily. Obviously. I hear how things are between you and our mutual friend. When you broke up before, that was mainly her doing, wasn't it?"

He nodded.

"Well it's going to be mainly her doing all over again. As I'm sure you know. After your friend Kenrik. But you don't want to hurt Lily. And neither do I. And she would be hurt. So here's a suggestion for you. How are your feelings? About me."

"I think—under control. Now."

"Are they? I used to sense something coming from you. I liked it in a way. I didn't, I didn't return it, but I liked it . . . Now, I don't know you very well. But I do know this about you. If we, if you and I started something, something open-ended, it wouldn't be in you to disguise it from Lily. Would it."

He saw that this was crucially and forcefully true, and he just said, "No."

"Then here's a suggestion for you."

For me? I, the unkind, ungrateful? He looked out sentimentally at his friends: the ethereal castanets of the butterflies. Keith had the deeply warming sense that Scheherazade was much older—and much wiser—than he was. She put her glasses back on (the brown eyes were now lost in ellipses of white light), saying,

"All summer, what is it—once?—she's come across the courtyard with her lamp? Lily. And found us playing cards. She's had a funny feeling and come looking. Once in—what?—about twenty nights? One in twenty?"

He nodded.

"So. So if it's just once, there's a five per cent chance that Lily'll find out. If it's twice, then that number rises. And not to ten. Because you'll change, and she'll know. There's a maid's room beyond the apartment. She'd have to be awfully curious to find her way up there. So. That's my suggestion. Once."

"Once."

She stood. She turned. She turned her whole body round but went on looking at him through her oval sheets of white.

"What are we now—Wednesday? Saturday, then, Saturday. No Adriano. No Jorquil, yet. And of course no Timmy. Just me and you. And when we play Racing Demon, I'll start with a glass of champagne . . . Quite tiring, saying all that. But you understand. I don't want love. I just want a fuck. Now that didn't sound at all right, did it? But you know what I mean."

Keith thought he might have to be sick; and then it passed. He lit a cigarette, in this green setting, and watched her walk away. With a curious short-stepped tread, risen up in the shoulders, as if on tiptoe; but her heels and soles, and their grass halms, stayed firmly on the earth . . . And now the feminine fountain, punctually overflowing.

It is straightforward, Keith soon thought. It was a necessary adjustment, and he was halfway there anyway. He would have to avail himself of what was already waiting for him: a lower order of being.

"All right," he said.

All right. A lower order of angel. Not the rapt seraph, that adores and burns. A lower order of angel. No, just a man. Adam, and after the Fall.

Seventy-two hours lay ahead of him. And he noticed almost immediately that something was the matter with time.

Why are you staring at your watch like that? You were doing it at dinner. Like an old yokel. As if you've never seen one before."

"It's gone wrong." He shook it and listened to it. "It's almost stopped. Look. It's on the blink. See? The second hand."

"What about it?"

"It's stopped moving. It's hardly moving . . . You mean it's *meant* to be like that?"

The thing he was most worried about doing was this: dying. Apart from not dying, though, all he had to do was not do anything. And keep his mouth shut. He went back to worrying about acts of God, and earthquakes, and nuclear war, and extraterrestrial invasion, and plagues and volcanoes. And Timmy. The unannounced eruption of Timmy—the rolling orange smoke and scarlet hellflames, far more terrible than any Etna or Stromboli. Keith knew that it was only the world that stood in his way. Would the world let him, that was the point. Would the planet permit it?

On Wednesday night, up in the tower, Jupiter and Juno were nowhere to be seen, and Branwell Brontë (somehow located and brought to his senses) made love to his sister Charlotte. No. Charlotte made love to her sister Emily. No. Emily made love to her sister Anne—the sickliest and most enfeebled combination possible, with Emily dead at thirty, and Anne *(Agnes Grey)* dead at twenty-nine . . . Keith made love to Lily—a performance, such as it was, that he vowed to repeat on Thursday night and Friday night. And on Saturday afternoon, to insulate and pre-prolong his time with Scheherazade. He would make love to Lily on Saturday afternoon, he decided. Either that, or he'd have an episode of applied narcissism. Yeah. Either that or a handjob.

She said later, "He didn't even have the nerve to ring her up and tell her. Then he added insult to injury with the telegram. You should've seen it."

In fact Keith found he knew Timmy's telegram by heart. Lily said, "I could barely keep a straight face."

And yes, Keith too had had difficulty not laughing or at least not smiling. ETA PPONED 8 DAYS STOP YOU SEE THE THING IS OLD THING THAT ABDULLAH HAS OFFERED ME A ONCE IN A LIFETIME CHANCE TO TAKE ON THE BLACK BEAR

REPEAT THE BLACK BEAR IN THE RESERVE JUST BEYOND AZ ZARQA STOP YOU SEE THE THING IS OLD ABDULLAH IS PRETTY SURE THAT THEY . . . And so on. But Keith's smile, now, in the dark, was one of awe and infinite gratitude, even before Lily said feelingly,

"And she was *so* full of plans. The first thing she was going to do was sort of squidge her tits over every inch of his body. Then at least an hour of *soixante-neuf*. And there he is messing around in, where is it? Petra?"

"A rose-red city, Lily, half as old as time." Keith's watch was fake-antique but phosphorescent (with three black hands, prettily barbed, like gutting swords): it now asked him to believe that it was not even half past eleven. "What did you think of Claudia? There's a definite pattern. Adriano's girlfriends are getting taller. Not younger, though. They all look like ageing starlets."

But Lily just went on angrily, "He hasn't set eyes on her in three months. He wouldn't even recognise her. Now that she's oozing out all over."

In five days' time I'll be twenty-one (he said to himself). Saturday will be the climax of my youth: the end of the first act. So it's only to be expected—these thoughts of sins and wrongs (Dilkash, Pansy). It's only to be expected—these little fears and enemies, these small fears and tiny enemies.

Thinking about going down on Scheherazade, he had already discovered, made a change from thinking about being gone down on by Scheherazade, and thinking about the two things happening at the same time made a change from both, but now Thursday towered over him, and he felt like a man due to begin a prison term of fantastic duration (unambiguously unsurvivable, such as the half-millennium sentences handed down to the worst possible mass murderers in the USA), or like an ascetic backing into a pothole in Surinam, committed to remain within until the arrival of Christ or the Mahdi (or the End of Time), or like a . . . Keith rolled over and tried to steady his thoughts. He was carefully sunning himself in the garden (touching up the backs of his legs), with *Our Mutual Friend* pressed out on the grass *(Take off your bra, Miss Pettigrew. Why you're . . .)*, and occasionally absorbing the odd sentence, or clause *(Take off your pants, Miss Pettigrew . . . Who'd have thought it?):* he was reading about the scapegrace John Harmon, and that mercenary minx little Bella Wilfer . . .

The main thing he didn't like about Timmy was this business about him being *happy-go-lucky.* I know Timmy. You know Timmy. And that would be just like him, wouldn't it—to scrag a black bear or two, hail a jeep, catch the next plane out of Amman, and stroll in through the door with his knapsack on his back? Keith's watch had now stopped even trying to keep the time. Wait. It gave a tick. And then, after a while, it gave another. Unbelievably, it was still only nine fifteen.

Anticipation, *looking forward,* not as a passive state, but as the busiest and brightest of activities: that was youth. And the waiting taught him something literary too. He now understood why *dying* was for centuries a poetic synonym for the completion of the male sexual act *(And so live ever—or else swoon to death).* In that moment, but not before, it was all right to die.

"How much is that rat in the window?" said Whittaker. "The one with the slithery tail."

"It's not a rat. Maybe a terrier," said Lily. "Crossed with a small dachshund."

"No, it's the eyes that give it away," said Scheherazade. "And the whiskers."

"That chow in its bowl," said Whittaker. "It's not its kind of thing. It wants a nice selection of garbage."

"Served in a little can," said Scheherazade, "that looks like a dustbin."

"You're so horrible," said Lily.

"How much *is* that rat? I'm going to go ask," said Whittaker, pronouncing *ask* like an Englishman and entering the shop to the sound of a chime.

"Lily, if it's cheap you'll have to buy it," said Scheherazade. "You can keep it in a breadbin in your room."

"You're so mean. Dogs have feelings too you know."

"Yeah, but not many," said Keith, who heard the church bells tolling ten. "The humane thing would be to buy it and set it free."

"Mm. The Blob—oops—could take it back to Naples," said Scheherazade. "And set it loose on the wharf."

"Stop it. Look—it hates you. Both of you. You're torturing it."

And indeed a ragged volley of squeaks or snaps now came echoing against the glass.

"Don't laugh at it! That's the worst thing you can do!"

This was Gloria, who stood a few yards away with her sketchbook held out in front of her; she was blinking across the square at the foolish grandeur of Santa Maria.

"You mustn't ever do that," she called out. "You mustn't ever laugh at dogs."

The door chimed again, and Whittaker was uncertainly saying, "It's—it's free. The rat doesn't cost anything at all. It's been there for a year and a half and no one's ever even asked about it."

They stood in silence. To spend your life in a pet-shop window, thought Keith. On sale, with no one buying or even asking. The occlusion, the *virginity* . . .

"And there's worse to come," said Whittaker. "Its name's Adriano."

This wasn't at all funny either.

". . . What's *that?*" said Gloria, who had just approached, with the pad clutched to her chest. "I don't understand. I thought it was supposed to be a dog."

"And oh look, it's crying."

"Those are old tears, Lily," said Keith. "They dried long ago."

While Gloria lingered, the others moved off; and on their way up the steep ascent they got stuck behind a herd of goats. They crept along behind, and the old rams jinked and tinkled to the rhythm of their slowly shuffling shoulders. And what you couldn't help seeing was a truly atrocious array of genital mishaps and deformations. *Look at that one,* they were all silently saying. *Jesus, look at that one.* Seen from the rear, the herd was a lurching pageant of string bags, each containing some blighted vegetable—a rotten tuber, a cratered spud, two black avocados. *Christ Almighty, look at* that *one.*

"The wages of sin," said Gloria, catching up. "Well there you are you see."

Later, much later, much, much later, as they made the coffee, Gloria came into the kitchen with a single sheet of white paper.

"A drawing," she said on her way out, "of your rat."

And there was Adriano, uncannily present, every ripple of close coarse hair, the static energy of the umbilical tail, the white loop of its collar, the pomp of its padded perch.

". . . She's good," said Scheherazade.

"Yes," said Keith, "but it's not quite right, is it."

"No."

"No," said Lily. "You see what she's done? She's made it look like a dog."

They considered this. Scheherazade said,

"Still. Not just a pretty face."

"A pretty face," said Lily. "And a gigantic——"

"Yes, I keep thinking I'm going to start taking it for granted," said Scheherazade. "But every time she turns round, I hear myself saying, *God . . .*"

And just when you thought they might start talking about something else—about (for instance) the currents and mass emotions that still swayed them, about the systems of thought and belief they were not yet free of, about the fact that they all contained crowds within their own being, crowds in conflict that marched, bore placards, chanted slogans, and sang their old, old songs—Gloria Beautyman, down by the pool, sat on a bee.

Unprecedentedly (and she would immediately revert), Gloria was wearing a normal onepiece swimsuit, without the additional skirts or shorts or pleats. And for that liberty she was at once repaid—with a devilish sting on the arse.

This'll get us through the next few minutes, thought Keith, as they all gathered round, he and the girls and Whittaker, and Adriano (and Pia).

"It felt like a *burn*," Gloria was saying. With her ring finger she wiped away a single tear. "Like a really bad *burn*."

The thick dark roots of her hair bathed with moisture her pained forehead; and Keith had the leisure to observe that she looked strangely serious as well as exotic, as if she'd just swum a relay race in a kibbutz on the Golan Heights, or rescued a child from the shallows in some decadent Middle Eastern capital—Beirut, Bahrain. She frowned down and sideways, and with her hooked thumb revealed the quarter-moon. Four colours: the black of the suit, the incensed plume of the sting's circumference, the teak of her tanned thigh, and the paler flesh everlastingly deprived of sun—which wasn't white, by any means (whatever she liked to think), but the colour of damp sand.

"Keith, I'm disgusted with you," said Whittaker quietly, as they settled in the shade. "And you call yourself a het. Even I could barely stop myself. Why didn't you offer to give it a bite and suck the poison out?"

"Yeah well I was distracted." Didn't you see, Whittaker, how Scheherazade's tits looked when she bent over Gloria's arse like that? Squeezed even closer together, as she leant forward to admire the work of the dying bee. "I thought I'd leave that to Adriano. It's his kind of thing."

"You could've at least offered to kiss it better. Mm. Interesting. Maybe you need to be gay. It's a peach, Gloria's arse, but maybe you need to be a fruit to see it."

"Maybe." But the new angle—the new *elevation*—of the tits, Whittaker. "It was widely admired in Ofanto, Gloria's arse."

"I bet. By the local faggots. But you don't get the picture. That is one beautiful arse."

And here she came again, Scheherazade, and her tits were hurrying down the terraces with a bottle of calamine lotion—for Gloria's arse.

Pull the other one, and tell it to the marines, and don't make me laugh, and fuck off out of it, and all that, but the fact remained that it was still only two forty-five. Keith resolved to kill some more time, as best he could, by being very considerate to Lily.

They even went for a walk.

"And she hates him killing birds or fish or foxes, let alone *bears*. Timmy's on a knife-edge. She's got a good mind to let him get here and then boot him straight out again."

And Keith allowed himself to imagine how nice he'd find it, later on—being in love with Scheherazade, living with Scheherazade, marrying Scheherazade, brimming Scheherazade with his children. It was Lily who steered him back to earth, saying,

"God, and what he's missing . . . You know, I think she's picked up some ideas from Rita. Scheherazade's not the Dog, obviously, but still. Remember what Kenrik said about her eyelashes? Using her eyelashes to tickle his tip? She thought that sounded rather sweet."

Adriano's devoted dinner guest that night, Nerissa, was five foot five, and most affectionate. After coffee, Adriano wiped his mouth and confirmed his intention to drive all night, in his Maserati, to Piacenza—pre-season training with *I Furiosi*.

On Friday morning they prepared a picnic and went to the sea.

Not to the Mediterranean. The Mediterranean, literally the world's middle and, metaphorically (according to a famous novel), also its box—the Mediterranean had already tried and failed to impress Keith Nearing. Yes, this'll take a minute: the Italian Mediterranean. Duck-boards, open-air washrooms, foot buckets, deckchairs, parasols, the weary little waves—and the Italians, half amused, half scandalised, and maintaining a careful distance between themselves and the sun and the sand and the saltwater (how they writhed and wriggled under the showers). Everybody, Keith thought, seemed to have far too many clothes on. Only Gloria, coming out on to the porch of the changing-hut in her linoleum petals, looked at ease in it all.

So on Friday, after breakfast, they made the longer journey east—to the Adriatic.

Keith steered the old Fiat. It was just him and the three girls. Lily said,

"Can't you go any faster?"

"Craters," he said. "And mad Italians everywhere."

"We've hardly seen a car all morning. Look. His knuckles are white. At this rate we won't even ever get there."

As they came down the last of the slopes, under sudden cloud, Keith felt he was driving on level land—and felt that the sea was steeply rising, ramping up like a dark cliff . . . They found the place Scheherazade knew. The deserted shore, the towering softness of the air, the sinking softness of the sand. One by one they entered the glitter of a colder brine.

"Let's not just splash around in the waves," said Scheherazade. "Come on, I dare everyone. Come on. Let's go—out there."

So they went—they went out there, way, way out . . . They pushed off and swam and swam, four trusting amphibians heading for the distant systems—the clouds that lived where the sky met the sea. Keith swam at Lily's side. He paid as little attention as he could to all the sharks, barracuda, giant octopi, swordfish, crocodiles, leviathans, and so on, squirming around directly beneath; these creatures, he soon imagined, were now playing eenie-meenie-minie-mo with the four pairs of legs—their legs, toasted, succulent. And soon the terror became abstract, and was qualified by hilarity: the very weight of the water that supported him, the insane distance from the strand, the horizon as sharp and straight as a razor but trying to send an awful message about the curvature of the earth.

It seemed they would swim their way to Albania and its golden sands. But Scheherazade turned back, then Lily, then Keith; and when he finally hauled his great weight out of the water (it was like stepping down from the trampoline), Gloria was still out there, way, way out, a black dot in the greenish blue.

"She's turned," said Scheherazade. "I think she's turned."

Keith sat on the rocks and incredulously reattached the manacle of his wristwatch (it was barely noon) and smoked a Disque Bleu much enhanced by the salt and the ozone . . . His mother Tina: she used to go *out there*—way, way out. On every fine summer day she took the children to the beach, and at some point she would rise from her towel, and go out there, way, way out. Keith always watched with admiration and not anxiety, her self-sufficient breaststroke, as she moved beyond the hulk of the anchored tanker and disappeared from sight just below the edge of the world. Nicholas was seven, and Keith was four, and the sleeping sister, whom they were to guard, was perhaps eleven months. Violet, whom they were to guard, as their mother went—out there, way, way out. And Tina, then, was just twenty-five. Twenty-five years old . . .

Gloria came wading through the shallows—to scattered applause. Five minutes later Scheherazade idled over to the rocks (Lily was lying on her front with her head facing the other way) and said evenly,

"The bedroom beyond the apartment. There's a way to the north staircase . . . If the worst comes to the worst."

He nodded.

"It won't sound very good, but we can say we were out on the north terrace looking at the stars."

She moved, again with the strange tread, levitational, the shoulder blades raised, the heels on the shingly sand . . .

How far away was the horizon? Keith supposed that it must be a constant, this distance, the same for every observer on every level shore: the point of curvature. And that was the awful thing. If you reached it, if you crossed it and looked back, then, as mariners said, you *sank* your point of departure—you sank the land, you sank Italy, and the castle, and the bedroom beyond the apartment.

It was during the journey back from the beach (Scheherazade drove, and fast, as if against time) that Keith got his next important idea: drugging Lily. Now this would be a brazenly purposive act, and a clear violation of the premium rule about not doing anything. But Keith had at last intuited it—the nature of his special scruple.

He thought that Scheherazade's assessment was about right: there was a five per cent chance that as she trembled into unconsciousness Lily would feel a blip on her witch radar—and take up the lantern and come looking. And five per cent, Keith ascertained, was too high. It had also not escaped him that such a phantom, the lady with the lamp, might do more than abbreviate his time with Scheherazade: it might actually preclude it. One in twenty—when all else seemed consummate, when all else shimmered with perfection, wasn't that exactly the kind of thought that reached down and blocked your blood? Reached down to thwart the instrument of yearning . . .

Besides. You see, he had now identified the peculiarity of the impediment, the obstruction, the glass wall. And it had to do with the young men of Ofanto, the young men of Montale. Keith could not add his yea and nay, he could not add his vote to those of the young men. That, in some inexpiable sense, would be to laugh while Lily cried. Betraying her by preferring another: this was something he fully intended to do. But the ballot must remain a secret ballot. The point being that he had to get away with it. Keith wasn't going to hurt Lily. He was going to drug her instead.

There weren't any rapist-style opiates or horse-stunning soporifics he could get his hands on. But Lily herself had some large and smelly brown pills (the label on the bottle said *Azium: for anxiety*) which she took when she travelled—and slept—by air. So on Friday evening Keith test-drove an Azium. He chopped it up with a razor blade, and secreted the shavings into a glass of *prosecco* (this was Lily's aperitif of choice): it was utterly tasteless to his tongue. And as he picked at dinner he felt the dispersal of the little cares and enemies, and his fingertips hummed to the touch of soft materials, and he could barely stay awake during the punctual felony with his identical twin (10:40 to 10:55). Scheherazade, at the table, looked like the handiwork of a salacious but artistic robotician—and generic. Generic, at last, and not especially Scheherazade.

That Friday night, Tweedledum had sex with Tweedledee. Or was it the other way round? Did Tweedledee, in actual fact, have sex with Tweedledum?

"I love you," said Lily in the dark.

"And I love you too."

The drug gave him continuous sleep—and continuous dreams. And after a night spent losing his passport and failing to rescue Violet and missing trains and nearly going to bed with Ashraf (her aunt kept coming to tea) and sitting exams in the nude (with an empty fountain pen), Keith awoke to *criticism* . . .

Where did the criticism come from? Not from Lily, who, as soon as she heard or sensed the freed latch, rose noiselessly from his side and slipped into the bathroom. The criticism, the unusually harsh and personal criticism, came from within. Its source was what he had learnt to call the *superego*. The superego—as opposed to the ego and the id, or the *egoid*. The egoid was the useful bit, faithfully devoting itself to sociosexual advancement. The superego was the voice of conscience, and of culture. It was also the voice of the elders: his forebears (whoever they were) and his guardians, Tina and Karl, both of whom, naturally, were champions of Lily—and of honourable conduct between the sexes. Perhaps, then, the superego was the secret policeman.

In sarong and bikini top, Lily was saying, "Are you coming down? What's the matter?"

"Yeah." He knew this sometimes happened. The present disquiet focused on something that was a knight's move away from its cause; and it was to do with Ruaa, maybe, and it was to do with *time* . . . It was eight o'clock, *ante meridiem;* soon his fateful delectation would slip out of the penumbra of the twelve hours. Scheherazade was coming up on the East Pacific, and heading west over the Yellow Sea. He said, "This is weird. I'm feeling bad about *Dil*kash. All of a sudden."

"Dilkash? Listen. Have you read your letter yet?" Lily had a T-shirt over her head (its neck was snagged on a hairclip) and you could see her smothered lips saying, "But you didn't even fuck Dilkash."

"Of *course* I didn't."

"Well then. So you're innocent of the worst thing. Sex once or twice and then not even a phone call. What does Nicholas say? *Screwed and scrapped. Fucked and forgotten.*"

". . . Of *course* I didn't fuck Dilkash. Christ." He lifted a hand to his brow. "The very idea. But I did—I did forget her. I did that part of it. I did do that."

"Well you needn't look quite so stricken."

"It was Nicholas," he said, "who introduced me to her. He had a holiday job at the *Statesman* and Dilkash was a temp. He said, *Dilkash—so sweet. Come and meet Dilkash.* She was in the—"

"Why d'you think I want to hear about Dilkash? And after Dilkash we'll have an hour on Doris and her pants. Tea or coffee? Are you coming down?"

"In a while," he said, and turned over, trying to ease the ache in his neck . . . Dilkash, Lily, was allowed to "meet" but she was forbidden to "mingle"—to be in public with a man who was not a relative. She was allowed to entertain me in her room, which she did most evenings (six thirty to nine) for almost two months. We feared no interruption, no, Lily, none, from her festively welcoming parents, the senior Khans, who watched TV and drank pop in the big sitting room upstairs. Anyway, at first, there was nothing to interrupt. We just sat and talked.

You're sad, she once said. *You seem happy, but you're sad.*

Do I? I had a—I had a confusing time with a girl. In the summer. She's gone back up north. But I'm happy now.

Are you? Good, then I'm happy too.

Her older sister, bespectacled Perrin, sometimes knocked, Lily, and waited, and then looked in for a chat. But the one we had to watch out for was Pervez, her seven-year-old brother. Little Pervez, richly handsome, ever silent: he threw the door open, he came in and it was always a serious chore getting him out again; he would bunch himself up on the sofa with his arms tightly folded. Pervez hated me, Lily, and I hated him back; but it was impressive, Pervez's frown, made redoubtable by his luxuriant eyebrows—the frown, the scowl (Keith would later think), of the rejectionist.

There came a night—it was perhaps my twentieth visit . . . Her room was dark anyway, Lily (that sodden garden wall), and it darkened another shade as I reached out across a great distance and took her hand. For some time we sat there side by side, staring straight ahead, speechless, and full of emotion. And it was almost a deliverance when, without any warning at all, the door was wrenched open by Pervez.

As she was seeing me out, Lily, and our hands again touched, I said, *I could feel your heart beating.*

And she said, *And I could feel yours.*

There was more, Lily. And this will be a good way of timing the night as it moves across Siberia. And Pakistan. There was not much more, Lily; but there was more.

Now Keith climbed naked from the bed and resumed being happy. It was the day all boys love best. It was Saturday.

3

THE METAMORPHOSES

Apart from the pitifully crippled clock on the wall above the open window, the castle kitchen, that morning, presented a scene of crystallised normality. Scheherazade with her vast bowl of cereal, Lily with her grapes and clementines, Gloria with her toast and marmalade. Until recently, Keith himself was starting the day with a cooked breakfast; but he feared the microbes in the gamey bacon, just as he feared H-bombs, *ejaculatio praecox,* revolution, dysentery, the man strolling in through the door with his knapsack on his back . . . As he leant into the fridge for a plain yoghurt, Scheherazade reached past him for the milk. There were no words or smiles or gestures, yet his eyes were somehow directed to the bottle of champagne half hidden by peaches and tomatoes on the lowest ledge.

"Yesterday we swam the marathon," she said. "Let's have a lazy day today."

Scheherazade in nightdress and flip-flops. She filled her vast bowl yet again. The legs crossed, calf on shin; the innocence of the flip-flops. More constructive, at this stage, to think about the inner thighs, softer and moister than the outer . . . He left her there beneath the slow, creaking loop of the overhead fan. And we don't quite trust the overhead fan, do we. Because it always seems to be unscrewing itself.

Keith sat alone at the stone table, where he unexpectedly succeeded in getting through an hour's worth of *The Mill on the Floss:* the adorable, the irresistible Maggie Tulliver was being led astray by the foppish Stephen Guest. Maggie's reputation—and so her life—was about to be destroyed. The two of them were alone on a punt together, floating down the river on the current, floating down the Floss . . .

So, he asked huskily, drawing deep on his Disque Bleu, *how was it for you?*

And Dilkash said, *It was . . . Of course, I was a bit frightened at first.*

· *Of course. Only natural.*

That's true.

More frightened or less frightened than you expected?

Oh, less.

You're eighteen. You couldn't postpone it for ever. The next time it won't seem such a big thing.

That's true. The next time. And thank you for being so gentle.

What they were talking about, these two, was Dilkash's first kiss—her first kiss ever. He had just administered it. Keith didn't take her by surprise. They discussed the whole question beforehand . . . Her lips were the same colour as her skin, with the transition marked only by the change in texture. These lips did not part, and neither did his, as he kissed the flesh-hued mouth in the mouth-hued face.

The next time, he began—

But then the door was yanked open—by the implacable Pervez, who came and stood over them, satanically handsome, with folded arms. And there was no second kiss. He stopped calling. He never saw her again.

Now Keith sneezed, yawned, and stretched. The frogs and their gurgle of satisfaction. The ratcheting cicadas with their ratcheted question and answer, trying to stutter it out—always the same answer, always the same question.

Where was your father posted?"

The girls were foraging in the kitchen. After the Old Testament of breakfast, the Mahabharata of lunch. The clock, once in a blue moon, ticked. Or tocked. Or clocked. Or clicked, or clucked, or clacked. Gloria said,

"Cairo before the war. Then Lisbon. Then Helsinki. Then Reykjavik. Iceland."

How to sum up this particular diplomatic career? Keith, who welcomed the distraction, was searching his lexicon for the opposite of *meteoric*. He said neutrally (from now on he would confine his remarks to the self-evident—commonplaces, tautologies), "Heading north. Do you remember Lisbon?"

"I was an infant in Lisbon. I remember Helsinki," she said, and gave a genuine shiver. "Colder than Iceland. Cairo's the part he talks about. Mm. The royal wedding."

"What royal wedding?" said Scheherazade. "Who between?"

Gloria sat back in her chair. She said contentedly (Jorquil, in contrast to Timmy, was already racing to her arms, Dover, Paris, Monaco, Florence), "King Farouk's sister, Fawzia, and the future Shah of Iran. Very unpopular in both countries. Because they're different sects. And Fawzia's mother stormed off—something about the dowry. The party lasted five weeks."

Keith watched as Gloria lowered her head beneath the table; it soon reappeared (the straw bag), and she placed before him his corrugated copy of *Pride and Prejudice*.

"Thanks. I enjoyed that. And it's *not* about marrying for money. Who told me it was? Was it you, Scheherazade?"

"No. It was me."

"You? And aren't you supposed to be good at this kind of thing? Reading books? You're quite wrong. Elizabeth turns Darcy down flat the first time, remember. And her father forbids her to marry him if it's just because he's rich—really near the end too. I was aghast."

Pride and Prejudice, Keith could have said, had but a single flaw: the absence, towards the close, of a forty-page sex scene. But of course he kept quiet and only waited. Every ten minutes the clock on the dresser managed another arthritic jolt. Which, he supposed, was *relativity*. Scheherazade said,

"Anyway, it's a happy ending."

"Yes," said Gloria.

"Except for that slag who fucks the dragoon," said Lily.

He took his mug of coffee up on to the battlements. It was half past three.

You can start coming to the office again, said Nicholas on the phone. *Dilkash has packed up her biros and her stencils and has gone on her way. After a month of staring at the phone. Pining. Pining its little heart out for her Keith.*

219

Keith listened philosophically. This was just the sort of thing Nicholas liked best.

Aching. Yearning. Eating its little heart out. Poor Dilkash. Boffed and betrayed by her Keith. Dorked and disdained by her Keith.

. . . Oh sure. Come on. I told you.

All right. Frenched and forsaken by her Keith. Snogged and set at nought by her Keith.

Come on. Not even.

All right. Pecked and repudiated by her Keith. Now you'll have to answer to Pervez and all his cousins and uncles.

. . . I loved her, but what was the point? Dilkash — so sweet . . .

Keith stopped calling Dilkash, without explanation. He couldn't find them — words both true and kind. Or not untrue and not unkind. So he stopped calling Dilkash. As they exchanged goodbyes, on the night of the kiss, she said, *Well I'm glad it happened with someone nice.* And that he wouldn't ever forget. But even then he thought — Dilkash, oh no, no, you'll have to find someone much, *much* nicer than me. To take you all the way to the modern. Imagine. Holding hands — with your heart climbing into your throat. The touch of lips on lips — and the cosmos wheeling on its axle-tree. Is it time, Dilkash, to move on to the next stage?

No, I can't be doing with these religious chicks, he told Nicholas on the phone. *And before Dilkash I had that weird time with Pansy. Christ, I haven't got it wet since the summer. You've seen how pale I am. Listen. This new chick has just moved into the flat, and I'm taking her out to dinner tonight. A single glance at her and you think, Yeah. She knows what the hell it's all about. Little Doris.*

. . . Keith stood on the battlements, stiffly nodding his head yes, and then loosely shaking his head no. Yes, he stopped calling Dilkash, and no, he didn't write. He left her staring at the phone, and wondering what was wrong with it — her first kiss. And that wasn't very nice.

Someone nice. Keith was nicer then than he was now, unquestionably. How nice would he be in September?

So with all that out of the way (it was now a quarter to four), he went down to the pool and immersed himself unreservedly in the near-naked beauty of the wanted one—the every-inch beauty of the wanted one . . . Keith had long ago, oh, long, long ago worked out the best place to sit: behind Lily, and in some neglected and rundown corner of Scheherazade's vision (and unmonitored, incidentally, by Gloria, who, with a spry yet censorious flourish, always turned and faced the other way).

The feminine body seemed to be made of pairs. The hair with its parting, even the forehead and its two hemispheres; then eyes, nostrils, septum, lips, the chin with its dividing indentation, the doubled cords and hollows of the throat; then matching shoulders, breasts, arms, hips, labia, buttocks, thighs, knees, calves. Only the navel, then, was mono-form. And men were the same, except for the central anomaly. Men had all the same dittoes, but also this central question mark. A question mark that sometimes became an exclamation point; and then went back to being a question mark.

Which reminded him. There was a good case for half an hour of vig-orous incest: it might make Lily sleep so much the sounder. On the other hand, the business of detaching her from the group brought with it the danger of indelicacy—and he couldn't have that. So he thought, Ah, fuck, I'll just have a handjob. And he laconically took his leave.

At six o'clock he climbed out of a hot bath, did ten press-ups, and stepped into a cold shower. He shaved, and brushed his teeth and tongue. He clipped and filed his nails, upper and nether. Maintaining a stern expression, he blow-dried and—with formidably steady fin-gers—tonged his pubic hair. He dressed in jeans still warm from the tumble drier, and a fresh white shirt. He was ready.

There is an evening coming in, One never seen before . . . By six forty-five Keith was bent over the salon drinks table, where he smoothly sprin-kled the pre-atomised Azium into Lily's *prosecco* . . . Of course, he had lectured himself about not staring or even glancing at Scheherazade until later on, so he avoided her face (with a puzzling sense that there was something wrong with it—some evanescent blemish) and merely scanned the outward mould and form, the presentation: black velvet slippers, white dress (mid-thigh) with a loose cloth belt, no brassiere of course, and he could see the hip-high outline of what would almost certainly turn out to be her coolest . . . But it was different now. This was the birthday present (farcically undeserved) which he would soon unwrap, and these clothes were just packaging: it would all be coming off. Yes, the reptilian condition was upon him. There was only one possible future.

And he acceded to it. Tonight, he said to himself, I will relieve, I will soothe and salve the desperation of Scheherazade—I will give Scheherazade hope! I am the Rain God, and this is now to be.

At seven twenty, after a soundless approach, a man strolled in through the door with his knapsack on his back.

Keith had the coronary anyway. But it was only Whittaker, with the heavy mail.

"I am here," he said, "and I bring the world."

They were in the dining room, now, and Keith's watch already said seven thirty. This was surprising. In fact, something entirely new seemed to be the matter with time. He glanced again at his wrist. It was twenty to eight. The barbed second hand scurried across the dial like a fleeing insect; even the minute hand looked to be making resolute headway; and, yes, the hour hand itself was perceptibly towing itself northward, heading for night.

"I'm like Atlas," said Whittaker, in his fawn scarf, his horn-rims. "Or maybe I'll settle for Frankie Avalon. I have the whole world in my hands."

The world. And there it was, the mailbag, the convict-woven burlap of the mailbag. And all the *Life*s and *Time*s, the *Spectator*s, the *Listener*s, the *Encounter*s . . .

Keith eyed it, the world. The world was all very well, the world was all very fine and large, but what did it want with the castle in Campania, with Keith and Scheherazade? On top of this, Lily now handed him a thick brown packet, saying,

"For you."

And while he attended to his local concerns (the staples, the cardboard zipper), they all started reading about it—about the planet earth . . . In retrospect, so long as you weren't Charles de Gaulle or

Gypsy Rose Lee or Jimi Hendrix or Paul Celan or Janis Joplin or E. M. Forster or Vera Brittain or Bertrand Russell, 1970 was a fairly mild year—so long as you weren't Cambodian, or Peruvian, or Rhodesian, or Biafran, or Ugandan . . .

"Mm," said Gloria, who sat with her spiked crown inclined over a *Herald Tribune.* "They've passed the Equal Pay Act. But it won't come in for years. Girls' pay."

Whittaker said, "Nixon's telling us it's now or never with the environment. America must—I quote—*pay its debt to the past by reclaiming the purity of its air, its waters.* And then he goes and dumps sixty tons of nerve gas off the coast of Florida."

"And the pitiful helpless giant is expanding the war," said Scheherazade quietly. "Why?"

"And the PLO are claiming they killed the seven Jews in the old folks' home in Munich."

"There. They've banned cigarette ads," said Lily. "What d'you say to that?"

She meant Keith, who was of course smoking. But he wasn't talking. He had so far said nothing at all, not a syllable, not a phoneme. He was surer than ever about the sanctity of his vow of silence. But he had some shop to get through, now, and he said, with a parched rasp that turned every head,

"The date might be awkward." And he explained.

Although he was yet to start his third year at university, Keith (rather unattractively, some may feel) had written to the *Literary Supplement* earlier in the summer and asked to be given a book to review—on trial. As a consequence, he had before him a heap of grey fluff and a loaf-sized monograph called *Antinomianism in D. H. Lawrence* by Marvin M. Meadowbrook (Rhode Island University Press). The stipulated length was a thousand words and the deadline was four days away. Lily said,

"Ring them up and tell them it's impossible."

"I can't do that. You've got to try. You've got to at least *try.*"

"A mere student," said Gloria, "and already you're trolling for work. Oh, *very* ambitious."

"That's what we're all meant to be, isn't it?" said Scheherazade, as she stood and then entered the long corridor.

Keith looked up. Scheherazade entered the long corridor, which was aflame with sunset. The heavens themselves colluded with him, and he saw the last wake of light, cruciform, and burning through the cusp and join of her thighs and arse. And you could see the outward pressure of her tits, too, even from behind. Lily said,

"Do you know what uh, antinomianism means?"

"What? No. But I will when I've . . . when I've read eight hundred pages on it."

Lily's nostrils encouragingly broadened, and her gripped jaw gave a shudder. She said, as if leadenly working her way through a list, "You've read all the Italy stuff. And the poems. What else've you read?"

"Lawrence? Let me think . . . I read a third of *Sons and Lovers*. And the bit that says *cunt* in *Lady Chatterley*."

"Tsuh," said Gloria.

". . . Say *tsuh* again, Gloria. Go on. It's like the tick of a watch. And I'm not swearing. That was just a quote from a pioneering writer."

"Stop," groaned Lily. "You're making that wheedling sound."

"Wait," he said, with care, as Scheherazade returned. "Whittaker's going to London on Tuesday. Aren't you, Whittaker? Would you mind dropping an envelope in a letterbox?" He turned to Lily for a sentence. "I'll speed-read it tomorrow and write the piece on Monday. I'm sorry, everyone, but it just means that I won't be able to come to the ruins."

"On your birthday," said Lily. "On your twenty-first birthday."

"I'm sorry, Lily. I'm sorry, everyone."

Keith regrouped. All seemed calm and clear. It was already eight twenty. Now Whittaker sloped off to join Amen in the studio. More lights came on. One by one they went to the kitchen and filled their plates and returned. The world was all before them, and they ate like students in a JCR, but it was normal, it was social realism, it was kitchen-sink. *Life*s, *Time*s. *Good salad,* said a voice. *Could you pass the pepper?* said another . . .

Very suddenly indeed they were eating their fruit: it was ten to ten. Lily's head dropped another inch, and her mouth was forming its tragic mask. Gloria got to her feet and started stacking plates and magazines. With some nonchalance, Keith put aside *Antinomianism in D. H. Lawrence* (it didn't look that difficult and there was quite a lot about Frieda fucking everyone), and said,

"I was just thinking about sex in the afterlife."

What made him break the second rule? He had broken the first (don't do anything); now he was breaking the second (and don't say anything). What made him? Power, partly. The eastern side of every instant was aglitter with it, with class power and beauty power, infinitesimally added to (let's not leave this out) by the power of inaugurating a vocation, of expressing himself in chosen words (while at the same time settling the immediate career prospects of Marvin M. Meadowbrook). But he couldn't help it anyway. Because every breath he drew was now pure helium, and far, far lighter than air. It is over, and this is the climax of my youth, he thought, saying,

"With reincarnation I suppose it depends what you're reborn as, a tiger, or a hyena, and in Israel they just sit tight, don't they, till Judgement Day, and in Amen and Ruaa's paradise they have girls but no boys, plus a nice kind of *prosecco,* Lily, Whittaker said, and as for us it's not all over, because Gabriel told Adam that even in heaven the angels interpenetrate, and they . . ."

He stopped, he subsided, softly whinnying to himself, and looked round the company from under his brow. No one had listened. No one had noticed. Coolly Keith picked up an *Encounter* and opened it and frowned at it.

"I'll leave you," said Lily slowly, "to your cards. Oh, look. Oh no . . . *Let It Be.*"

"Yes, isn't that sad. The Beatles' last LP," said Scheherazade. *"Let It Be."*

With her hand resting flat on the side of her jaw, Gloria was saying, "The New English Bible. Bad idea, that . . . Tsuh, is that the time? Oh well. Jorquil has reached Monaco. And Beautyman must get her beautysleep. Lily, come on, we'll go arm in arm . . . Trying to make it all chatty and modern. It's sure to be a mistake, that. The New English Bible."

"Gloria, I agree," said Keith. "Bibles, bibles. I'm reading about bibles."

"Oh? And?"

"Listen to this. It's really quite funny. Listen to this. Some busybody, prick, and creep called the Reverend John Johnson got caught smuggling five thousand bibles into Russia through Czechoslovakia. And he'd already smuggled a quarter of a *million* bibles into Bulgaria and the Ukraine. What for? . . . Anyway, the stupid sod's in a prison in Moscow. The very worst prison in Moscow."

Keith felt the fumbling dig of Lily's shoe on his shin. He looked up. And Gloria warmly began,

"Oh, that's priceless, that is. Truly priceless. A little squirt like you saying that about an ordained missionary. And I'll thank you to keep a decent tongue in your head when you talk about such things. To risk prison for your convictions. Excuse me, but I'm a Roman Catholic. And I'm in the country of my faith. Yes that's right, I happen to believe in God. And I think that man's incredibly brave."

Keith said, "Tell me, Gloria, do you happen to believe in Father Christmas? No. Of course you don't. You grew out of it. Of course you did. You know, it's a pity Father Christmas isn't featured in your holy book. Because you could've grown out of scripture too. Yes, a great shame Santa wasn't at least *foretold* in the New Testament." He went on reedily, "You know—There will come a man, at every Nativity, he will wear a red suit, fringed in white, he will ride through the air on a sleigh drawn by flying reindeers . . . It might have helped all you stupid sods to put these things in their true—"

Lily kicked him again. A movement of her head now directed his eyes, not to Gloria, but to the colourless face of Scheherazade. She had changed, altered. Do you know what she looked like? She looked like the photograph of the girl who distinguished herself on the harpsichord, or clocked up five thousand miles for Meals on Wheels, or rescued a cat from the great oak behind the guildhall.

When Keith came to the dark tower, around twelve, after two hours of solitaire in the gunroom, a jagged light was rocking its way downward, and on the steep steps he was met by the lady with the lamp.

"I was coming to look for you," said Lily.

"What for?"

"I don't know. I had a funny feeling."

She turned and climbed. He followed.

"You're early." She was watching him over her shoulder. ". . . And you're *drunk*."

"Mm. Well." Starting at around eleven twenty, Keith had three huge glasses of something called Parfait Amour—pink, sticky, and insultingly sweet. Followed by most of a bottle of Benedictine. He followed her into the room, saying, "Yeah. Well. By my standards."

"I suppose you're relieved," said Lily as she climbed into bed.

"Relieved? Relieved? Why would I be relieved?"

"That you're not out on your ear. After that display. It wasn't just what you said, it was how you said it. Sadistic. You're lucky."

"Oh I'm lucky all right. How the fuck was I supposed to know she's religious?"

"You mean Scheherazade."

"Yeah I mean Scheherazade." He was unbuttoning his shirt, unbuckling his belt. He fell over and said, "She doesn't *look* religious."

"And neither do you . . . It's Timmy, you idiot."

"Timmy? Is Timmy that religious?"

"Religious? He's a practising maniac. Don't you ever listen? Smuggling bibles is *exactly* the kind of thing Timmy does all the time. That's why he was in Jerusalem. They go there to convert the Jews."

He switched off the light and lowered himself downward.

"You offended Junglebum too."

"Oh fuck Junglebum."

There was a short silence. Then she said, "Did you see the difference? Gloria was all roused for the fight. But Scheherazade. Her eyes were ice."

"Pathetic," he said.

"You know, I think there's something wrong with Scheherazade. Don't you think? You saw how pale she was."

"Pale?"

"You mean you didn't notice? Gloria said she looked like Casper the Ghost. How could you not have noticed?"

He said, "Well I didn't. And she doesn't *look* religious. Her *tits* don't look religious. And anyway, why aren't you asleep?"

There was a long silence. Then her torso stiffly and frighteningly rose all at once and Keith was clenching his eyelids in the electric light.

"Why aren't I asleep?" she said. "Why aren't I asleep? You mean after being *drugged*?"

I'm not here, he thought. I'm not here, and, besides, this isn't me anyway.

"Christ. It was like drinking a glass of *barium*. I thought I must be ovulating. I only realised what it was when I got back here and burped."

And burped? You see, Lily, I'm actually rather disappointed about how things seem to have turned out tonight. Well I am. I had other ideas—I had other plans and hopes.

She said, "Azium gives you smelly burps."

Smelly burps? Do you perhaps sense, Lily, that there's been a slight falling-short? From my point of view, admittedly. Let me explain. Around now, I should be in the shape of a reef knot with your friend Scheherazade, in the bedroom beyond the apartment; I should be wiping my mouth, around now, on a silken thigh before getting down to my second pint of her bodily fluid. And instead? Instead I find myself in a world of arraignment—of accurate arraignment, of ovulation, and smelly burps. He said,

"Wait." His eyes gradually opened. "I mixed the glasses up—that's all. Yours was meant for me."

". . . What do *you* need tranquillising for? Dilkash? No," she said. "You *liar.* You had some sort of sex date with Scheherazade, didn't you. And you fucked it all up by shitting on God."

This went on until half past three. Keith's story was not actually falsifiable (or so he then supposed), and he stuck to it. This went on until half past three. Then Lily switched off the light and left him to his thoughts.

Keith Nearing awoke from troubled dreams and found himself changed in his bed into a monstrous vermin. His room, a regular human room, lay quiet between the four familiar walls; and he had his human eyes. But that was what he was—an enormous insect with human eyes.

4

TORQUERE "TO TWIST"

Go on, get your staring done with. The air shuddered and juddered around him in phonebox-sized volumes, it gonged and twanged around him, but he had to enter the kitchen. He had to enter the kitchen because he had to have coffee. And he had to have coffee to fuel the nicotine sobbed for by his foul mouth . . .

The three girls, as he approached, didn't actually scream out loud, or climb up on their chairs, or fight their way, like little Miss Samsa, to the wide window for a lungful of breathable air. They stayed in their seats and stared. *Get it done with.* Lily looked at him with a kind of infinite weariness, Gloria with the contempt due to a crushed enemy, and Scheherazade's flat glance made Keith feel invisible—morally invisible, in the way that poverty and sordor are said to be invisible to Hindus of the higher castes. *Go on, get it done.*

. . . He sat sweating and swearing and trembling and weeping, and smoking, in the loveseat on the west terrace, with Professor Meadowbrook, and Antinomianism, and Nottingham and Sardinia and Guadalajara, and D. H. Lawrence, and Frieda von Richthofen. If the terrible theory was true, and looks were shaped by happiness (if surface was determined by essence), then Keith did indeed have the six wavery limbs, the toothlessly drooling jaws, the vaulted brown belly, the metallic carapace, and the hurled apple rotting and reeking in his back. A storm was on its way, and too late. Not the sky but the air itself was a gangrenous green. The air itself was about to throw up. And he could hear the yellow birds in their tree—pissing themselves laughing.

So there was self-pity: in the mirror that morning he was foetal with it, his face a foetus of crapulent self-pity. And with regard to the other business, the business with Lily, he could smell about himself the effluent of ingratitude. And he felt his bastardy too. *"Why bastard? wherefore base?"* he kept whispering. *"Why brand they us With base? bastardy? base, base?"* Here, in Italy, Keith was Salò, in 1944—the republic of dissolution and defeat, of impotence and emptiness . . .

But men are shifty. Shiftier than they know. Shifty even within their own shifty beings. Life had pronounced him dead, but somewhere within, in his groin, perhaps, was a pulse of hope. And he felt the lucidity that comes with doom.

Keith had a stratagem for Lily. The back pocket of his jeans now contained Nicholas's letter about their sister, Violet—still unread. Tactical prudence demanded that he acquaint himself with its contents; once or twice he unfolded the envelope and considered it. But his resolve could not survive the sadistic interdiction of his gut, his craw, and he simply took what courage he could from the firm curves of his brother's hand.

So Keith had a stratagem for Lily. And he had a stratagem for Scheherazade.

It came again: from the far distance, the supposedly cleansing rumours of thunder.

Around noon he raised his head and saw that Lily was staring at him through the French windows. Her face wore a much more distilled version of the forensic look he had seen often enough the night before; and Keith could tell by the sharpness of her movements, as she opened the glass doors, that she came to him with a case much fortified by research. He felt reasonably frightened; but he somehow hugged it to himself, the airy clarity of doom.

"You—look—*terrible,*" she said. "Listen. I'm missing two. I count my pills, and I'm missing two. Now why's that?"

He didn't answer.

"You don't answer. Two. You tried one out, didn't you. And you thought it didn't taste of anything. Because you smoke a carton of French cigarettes every day, you thought it didn't taste of anything. You tried it out. And then you drugged me so you could sleep with Scheherazade."

Keith lit a Disque Bleu. He had a tight balloon of gas—laughing gas and tear gas—in his solar plexus; this gas was sweetish and colourless and made him want to sob and cackle. For even he could see the quiet artistry, the hushed equipoise of his fate: here he sat, squaring up to the consequences of sleeping with Scheherazade—*without* sleeping with Scheherazade. And (he thought exhaustedly) is there any any, is there none such, nowhere known some: some credit, some moral recompense on this earth, for *not* sleeping with Scheherazade?

"Lily, I mixed the glasses up. That's all."

"Mixed them up? How could you mix them up? They weren't the same . . . I asked Gloria and she said you had a beer before dinner."

He had not been looking forward to this thrust, but he had anticipated it—this thrust into the very crotch of his defence. Gloria was right. Beer, and in a hefty beaker, and not a long-stemmed flute of tempered glass. "That was later," he said. "I had a *prosecco* first. Like I did the night before."

"I seem to remember you just went and got a beer."

He said, "Seem to remember, Lily? How would you remember? You were drugged. I'm sorry, but there it is."

"Yes, drugged. For your sex date with Scheherazade."

Keith exhaled and thought about male anger: male anger as a tactic. He had an opening phrase ready in his mind. *Lily, how dare you even—* and so on . . . The underexperienced but observant Nicholas once advised him that anger was still worth trying: when your position was truly dire, it was still worth trying male anger—because some women still instinctively feared it, even the best and the bravest of them. Even the most accomplished terrorists, Nicholas said, were still vulnerable to male anger—because it reminded them of their fathers. Keith, now, a bent shape on the loveseat, under the tundra of Lily's stare—no, Keith was not about to reach for male anger. He had no talent for anger, anger, which is only in command of the power to postpone.

Lily said, "Not a date. Not a fuck. She isn't like that. It's not in her . . . No. You felt she'd been flirting with you, and you were planning to make your move. That's why you were douching yourself in the bathroom for an hour and a half."

Keith stirred. It was of course axiomatic, according to Nicholas, that you seized on it—the moment when the witch radar showed its first false reading. He said (having given a curlike sneeze that left his palm secretly coated in snot),

"Come on, Lily. You're so proud of being rational. Think. I've had—

what?—twenty evenings alone with Scheherazade. If I was that kind of . . . If I was that type, I'd have made my move long before now. Christ. I like her, she's a lovely girl, but she's not my type. You're my type, Lily. You."

She examined him. "And the pills?" She examined him further. "Mm. Your story'd sound better if you looked less suicidal."

Now Keith chose to take the two necessary risks (did she inspect *Jane Eyre* last night? how often did she count her pills?). He said, he recited,

"So you *have* noticed. Listen. I took the first pill after I read the first letter from Nicholas. I took the second pill—or I tried—to prepare myself to read the second. Okay?"

"You haven't even glanced at it. It's still in *Jane Eyre*."

"No it isn't." He reached into his back pocket. "I had it with me last night. I read it last night. That's why I got drunk. I'm speechless, Lily. Violet. It's really very seriously terrible. Help me. I need you to help me think it through, Lily. Help me."

She consented to be led by the hand to the swing sofa, where he flattened the letter out on her lap.

My dear Little Keith,

The foul rag-and-bone shop of the heart. My heart aches, and a drowsy numbness Pains my sense. So the heart be right, it is no matter which way the head lieth.

"Yeats, Keats," he murmured. "And Sir Walter Raleigh." Keith was now in the curious position of hoping that the news about his sister would indeed be really very seriously terrible. "Those were Raleigh's last words," he said. "He was putting his neck on the block at the time."

They began. And Violet, not always the most dependable of young women, didn't let her brother down.

A little later Lily reappeared with a cup of coffee, meant for him, and he thanked her, and drank in silence, while she stood looking out, with her hands joined and a freshened sheen in her eyes.

"All right. Gloria said she wasn't sure about the beer. Not at all sure. So I suppose I . . . Now what have we here? Well isn't that a sight."

In wasp-waisted charcoal suits, and arm in arm, Scheherazade and Gloria were making their way across the terrace, heading for the steps that led to the lane and the village.

"Church."

"It's pitiful, isn't it," said Keith. "Absolutely fucking pitiful. Gloria's RC, right? Scheherazade isn't. What's Scheherazade?"

Lily told him that Timmy, at least, was Pentecostalist—and it should be admitted that this was something that Keith thought he still needed to know. He said,

"So. Santa Maria. Catholic. Any port in a fucking storm, eh?"

"Why are you so het up about it? You should have heard yourself last night. Groaning and wailing in your sleep."

"All this hypocrisy."

"Squealing you were. Like a pig having an operation."

"Lily, it's the principle of the thing. They believe in Father Christmas. Why? Because the present he brings is eternal life."

". . . What's antinomianism?"

"It means doing whatever the fuck you want all the hours there are. *With 'should' and 'ought' I have nothing to do.*" Keith felt his body relax, and he went on, "It means *anti-law,* Lily. I'm surprised you didn't know that. Frieda was the same. German, see. Nudism and yoghurts. Eros-worship. Nietzsche. Otto Gross. *Repress nothing!*"

Lily said, "Aren't you hungry? I was just thinking. You've lost weight. You haven't eaten all week."

"Yeah, come on. While they're down there on their lousy knees. Jesus. On their knees. You don't know whether to laugh or cry."

Left alone for a moment, he went to the wall and peered over it. You could see the two tight and bustly little forms moving over the cobblestones. Children criss-crossed their path, but no swirling coils of young men took shape in the rear of Gloria or in the van of Scheherazade.

In the library he put Professor Meadowbrook aside and pored over a semi-literate paperback called *Religions of the World,* which eventually referred him to the Book of John. Then he unsheathed the Olivetti and typed out a note on it: *Dear Scheherazade, May I say something to you? I'll be reading in the gunroom after dinner. Just a few words. K.* With that accomplished, he crept out into the salon, and moved through the precincts of his demotion—like an intruder, or like some menial and futile phantom, one worthy of a decrepit cottage, perhaps, but not a fortress on a mountainside in Italy . . . It seemed that eternal excommunication was the sentence he'd been given, and it came like a summons from outer darkness when Gloria turned in the corridor and said with a matronly air,

"Oh, Keith."

"Yes, Gloria."

"There's a choice tonight—meat or fish. I tried the fish earlier, and I thought it was a bit off. Have the meat."

"Thank you, Gloria, That's very thoughtful of you. I will."

"Do," she said.

And that was all. Fractionally emboldened, Keith offered Scheherazade his folded note as they passed in an anteroom, and she accepted it without meeting his eye.

The four of them took their seats in the kitchen: one Catholic, one Protestant, one Atheist, and one Agnostic. Yes, Keith, unlike Lily, was an agnostic: he knew that he would die all right, and that heaven and hell were vulgar insults to human dignity, but he also knew that the universe was very imperfectly understood. In his opinion, it would be an outcome mainly notable for its banality—but God might turn out to be true. Claiming otherwise, as he told Lily when they argued about it, was crabbed, presumptuous, *and not rational, Lily. I'm teetering on the edge of it*—of godlessness, Lily. But that's what you have to do. Teeter. Now he said to her,

"Not for me." And covered his wine glass with his hand.

During the salad course Gloria said to Scheherazade, "When shall we swap rooms? Not tonight. I'm too . . . weak. I think I've got what you had last night. Queasy."

"It soon passes. I'm fine now. Tuesday morning. Eugenio can help."

"Jorquil's in Florence. Poor you. Oh I do wish Timmy were here."

Keith's stratagem for Scheherazade, then, was only ninety-nine-point-nine per cent dishonest: it contained its mote-sized blind spot. He was going to tell her that he had experienced a change of heart and mind. *Yes, Scheherazade, I have. And is there, perhaps, some vicar . . .* No, not vicar. Luminary? . . . *perhaps some spiritual counsellor I could go and talk to, when we all get back to London?* Keith knew that success was not much more likely than the cosmic manifestation, that same night, of an omnipotent being. But he had to try. And now he sought comfort in harmonial themes, how they spring eternal, the tender leaves of hope—and so on.

"Mmm," said Lily as she tasted her sole.

"Mmm," said Scheherazade as she tasted hers.

"I'm sure the fish is perfectly fresh," said Gloria. "But Keith and I are very happy with the lamb. Now Whittaker said half past seven. An early night, I think. So that we're all bright-eyed and bushy-tailed," she concluded, "for the *ruins.*"

*A*ntinomianism in D. H. Lawrence was finished with and tossed aside by a quarter to twelve.

Scheherazade had in fact stuck her head round the door of the gun-room, on her way upstairs, and Keith did in fact manage to announce, from a seated posture, that he was suddenly open to persuasion about the existence of God and, more particularly, the merits of the Pentecos-talist persuasion (with its emphasis on prophecy, miracles, and exorcism).

"I know the Bible quite well," he said, "and I've always been very moved by that verse in John. And it's central, isn't it, to the born-again idea. You know—*The wind bloweth where it listeth, and thou hearest the sound thereof, but canst not tell whence it cometh, and whither it goeth; so is everyone that is born of the Spirit.* That resonates, I find."

He kept this up for a couple of minutes. Scheherazade frowned lev-elly at him. As if his words were not necessarily implausible but merely obtuse and irrelevant. And boring—don't forget boring. Keith couldn't construe her: the one visible hand on the one visible hip, her shifts of stance. Her indifference. There was something—there was something almost un-Christian in it. He said,

"I was very wrong to be dismissive like that. That was trivial of me. And I'd like to give the whole thing a lot more thought."

"Well," she said with a dutiful shrug, "since you ask, there's a man called Geoffrey Wainwright at St. David-in-the-Field. I'll drop him a line about you. If you like."

"Right. Fine."

Right. Fine. And now we've got all the religious shit out of the way, Scheherazade, how about a game of cards and a glass of champagne? This much at least was clear. In fact it had never in his life struck him with such force: religion was the antichrist of eros. No, the two themes, Racing Demon and God, God and Racing Demon, did not combine. Or so he then thought.

"Timmy swears by Geoffrey Wainwright," said Scheherazade. "Goodnight."

"Goodnight. Don't tell Lily," he said as she closed the door on him. "She wouldn't approve."

So to round out the panoply of the weekend's achievements, its moral and intellectual breakthroughs and triumphs, he reached into his back pocket and read the thing again, without Lily's breath on his neck.

My heart aches, and a drowsy numbness Pains my sense. So the heart be right, it is no matter which way the head lieth.

It was a dull day at work (August) and I thought I'd liven up the evening with a violent film. I fancied A Man Called Horse— two hours of torture at the expense of Richard Harris. I wanted a couple of powerful ones to get me in the mood, so I looked in at the Saracen's Head in Cambridge Circus, a place described to me, by Violet, as "good." Why, I wondered, did Violet think it was good, apart from the fact that it sold alcohol? What is this business with Violet and alcohol—with England and alcohol?

It was by no means the worst of all possible pubs, the carpets not much damper than bathmats, the tureens of the ashtrays not yet brimming over, the clientele not audibly planning your murder. I ought to say at this point that I'd been on the evening news two nights running that week (Vietnam). As I was ordering, I felt a waft of yeast on my cheek and a tap on my shoulder, and even before I turned I felt the arrival of violence (violence at my expense). It's a funny feeling. The shift of type, of category—the arrival of the radically unfamiliar (well caught, I think, in Augie March, when he watches his brother pistol-whip the drunk: "My heart went back on me when the cuts were torn, and I thought, Does it make him think he knows what he's doing if the guy bleeds?"). I wasn't scared. As you know, I don't get scared. But it was a funny feeling.

I turned, and found myself staring into a big, rhomboidal, bottom-heavy face, and trap-mouthed, with the tongue idling on the lower teeth. This face undoubtedly wanted to hurt me. But it

wouldn't be needing physical force. He said, "Have you got a little sister called Violet?" I said slowly and emphatically, "Yeah?"—
because I knew what was coming.

He bared his upper teeth, now, and gave a nodding sneer. And
then he started laughing. Yes, he had a good laugh about it all.
Then this fucking berk looked me up and down, and backed off to
join all the other fucking berks by the pie-warmer, and they
started doing it too. Staring, sneering, and laughing. By the way,
the berk's status, as a berk, was far from irrelevant. I hardly need
to point out that I didn't disdain the berk qua berk. But when it
comes to the extreme sexual delinquency of your little sister, only
a fucking berk is going to tell you about it.

My dear Little Keith, I invite you to consider some of the
implications. 1) Imagine the kind of guy you'd have to be to enjoy
passing that on to a brother. 2) That's the kind of guy Violet
thinks is good. 3) He was being implicitly violent to me (Well,
big brother, what are you going to do about it?), for reasons of
class—the revenge of the berks; so it's a fair bet that he's implicitly violent to her too. 4) Their response was unmistakably communal. In other words, Violet is the kind of girl who dates football
teams.

Remember when we were young we used to say we'd kill anyone who laid a finger on her? We used to get very emotional about
it. And that's what we used to say, again and again. We'd kill.

After that, A Man Called Horse didn't quite seem up to it. So I
went to the Taboo and did what I could with The Dungeon that
Dripped Blood.

I sort of raised it with her, obliquely, and she said, with some
indignation, "I'm a helfy young girl!" Why can't she talk properly
any more? Why does she sound like someone who's accustomed to
being in prison?

You're the only one who knows about this. Hurry home.

And then Keith crossed the expectantly starless courtyard and
climbed the steps of the tower.

"Hear that?" said Lily in the dark. "Not the rumbling. Santa Maria. At
a stroke you're—twenty-one."

He did not respond. She kissed his ear, his neck. He did not respond.

Her hand caressed his shoulders, his chest, and moved downward. Now would be the time to show gratitude to Lily. Now would be the time to be grateful to Lily. But Keith wasn't grateful any more.

"I can't," he said. "Violet."

His body, now embarking on its twenty-second year, gave its reflex. Yet Keith did not respond. Lily held it. Then she flung it aside.

"Do you know something? Your cock," she said, "is much smaller than average."

He at once resolved not to take this too seriously. Then again, he knew that anything a girl said to you on this subject was by definition unforgettable.

"Oh really," he said. "Fascinating. Much smaller than everyone else's. That's well worth knowing."

"Yes, much smaller," she said, turning over. *"Much."*

Up above in the firmament, great weights were being wheeled around on sets of titanic castors: the rolling stock of heaven, mobilised for civil strife . . .

Lily's quiet flurry; in the dawn—he was intermittently aware of it; and there was a small packet of time (he sensed) when she stood over him and looked down, and not with liking either. There had just been a disastrous spillage (he had accidentally poured a two-pound bag of sugar into the intimate workings of a grandfather clock)—but someone else could clear it up, the dream could clear it up, he left it there for the dream . . .

Now Keith heard the car doors slam shut and the slow and monstrous snarl of rubber on gravel. And he began the task of separating the real from the imaginary, separating fact from fiction. Feminine shapes and configurations, then thoughts like the clues of cryptic crosswords—these slowly scattered, and he reversed himself, with many misanglings, into his opening sentence. *It must have been a considerable relief to D. H. Lawrence—the formulation of a . . . The formulation of a creed of unadorned self-centredness must have come as a . . .* Keith reared up and sat there with his feet on the floor. All was bare. He was neuter, loveless, sexless; and he was twenty-one years old.

Naked, he pushed at the bathroom door. It was locked. He listened

to the silence. Then he fastened a towel round his waist and rang the
bell. He heard ticking footsteps.

"Ah there you are. Good morning," said Gloria Beautyman.

With pinched thumbs and fingertips she was holding up a light-blue
summer dress at shoulder height, as if assessing it for length in front of
a mirror.

"You didn't go," he said.

"Mm. I pretended to be ill. I hate ruins. I mean they're *ruins.*"

"Exactly." He said, with prescience, "You're made-up."

"Well I had to retouch it. I wanted to look all feverish. A bit of purple eyeshadow usually does the trick."

"You find?"

"Mm. I even hid a rotten apple under the bed. For the tang of the
sickroom. I'm airing it even as we speak . . . I'm terribly good, you
know. No one will ever guess."

"Well."

"Well. I'm sorry I kept you waiting. I was just saying my prayers
before putting some clothes on. You see I always pray naked."

"And why's that?"

"For the humility. Do you have any objection?"

"No. None."

"I thought you might have some objection . . ."

And a voice said to him, *There's no need to hurry. Everything is as it
should be. Everything is just as it should be.*

"Yes, I thought you might have some objection."

"To praying, or praying naked?"

"To both."

"What do you say in your prayers?"

"Well first I praise Him. Then I thank Him for what I've got. Then I
ask for a little bit more. But it's probably pointless, don't you think?"

"Is it?"

"Tell me. If you had to give just one reason. What is your quarrel
with those of us who believe?"

Never worry. Proceed. It has all been decided.

"All right. It's a failure of courage."

239

"Not true in my case."

"Why's that?"

"It's simple. I believe. And I know I'm going to hell."

Remain silent. Go on looking into her eyes, and remain silent.

"So!" she said. "Then I had a quick shower and I was just putting on some clothes."

"How far did you get?"

"Shoes," she said.

They both looked down. White high heels. He said,

"So. Not very far."

"No. Not very far at all."

She tipped her head at an angle and gave him a flat smile. The polite cough: "Huh-*hm*." Then she looked him up and down in a way that made him feel, for a moment, that he had come to fix the loose tiles or see to the plumbing. She turned and slowly walked.

Jesus Christ. Say, No bee sting. *Say it. No bee sting.*

He said, "No bee sting."

She halted, and ran a hand down the small of her back. "To tell you the truth, Keith, I put a dab on that too. While I was at it. You know. Concealer."

He thought, I am in a very strange place: I am in the future. And this is the strangest thing of all: I know exactly what to do . . . Lit by the innards of the storm, all the colours in the room were lurid, torrid, morbid, even the whites. Another strange thought: the vulgarity of the colour white. *Step forward.*

Stepping forward, he said, after a while, "So pale. So cold."

She moved her feet apart.

His towel seemed to make a lot of noise when it fell—like a collapsing marquee. Her dress made no sound at all. The first thing she did, with her gaze on the mirror, was attend to her breasts in a way he had never seen before. She said ardently,

"Oh, I love me. Oh I love me so."

Neither blinked as thunder split the room. He went even closer in.

She brought her legs together. "Kadoink," she said.

Make a joke. Make two jokes. It doesn't matter what they are, but the first one has to be dirty.

"You forgot to dry yourself."

Her spine quivered and arched.

"Because you were distracted by higher things."

"Look," she said to the figures in the glass. "I'm a boy. I've got a cock too."

Say, You *are* a cock. *Say it.* You *are* a cock. "You *are* a cock," he said.

". . . How on *earth* did you know? I *am* a cock. And we're very rare— girls who are cocks. Stand back a minute."

She leant over with parted legs and her small left fist tightened on the towel rack.

"Look. The sting's actually quite far in. Look."

She was doing something, with her right hand, that he had seen before, but never at this angle. *Say something about money.*

"I want to buy it a present. Your arse. Silk. Mink."

She was doing something, with her right hand, that he had never even heard about.

"Look what happens," she said, "when I use two fingers."

It was then that he had his moment of vertigo. I'm too young, he thought, to go to the future. Then the vertigo passed and the hypnosis returned. She said,

"Look what happens. Not to the arse. To the cunt."

He stared on at it leadenly—at the far future.

". . . Some might say that it's a bit droll—to *start* with this. But we're having a black mass, you and I. You know—backward. Every-thing the wrong way round. Stay still, and I'll do it all. Understand? And try your hardest not to come."

"Good," she said, as, some minutes later, her knees settled on the bath-mat. "Now. The only way to spin this out is for me to be a bit of a chat-terer for a while—do you mind? . . . You can talk while you do most other things . . . Often to no great purpose, in my opinion . . . But you can't talk while you . . . while you . . . Now here's something you've probably never seen before . . . Big as this is, and very hard. As hard as the towel rack. I can make it completely disappear. And then come back even bigger. Oh look. It's even bigger already."

Yeah, he thought. Yeah, that's the spirit, Gloria. If you want it big, just *tell* it it's big.

"Completely disappear. Watch. In the mirror . . . Again? . . . Again? . . . Right. In a minute I'm going to speed up. Now listen carefully."

He listened carefully—as she issued a set of instructions. He had never heard about this either (he would later characterise it as the *sinister refinement*). He said,

"Are you sure?"

"Of course I'm sure. Right. I'm going to speed up. I won't be doing any more talking. But I will be making rather a lot of noise. And afterwards, Keith, we'll have a light breakfast and go to my room. Agreed? Then at last you can feel my breasts. And kiss my lips. And hold my hand . . . We'll make a day of it. Or would you rather get on with your trial review?"

FIFTH INTERVAL

They were the children of the Golden Age (1948?–73), elsewhere known as *Il Miracolo Economico, La Trente Glorieuses, Der Wirtschaftswunder.* The Golden Age, when they never had it so good.

What you could hear in the background, during this period, was progress music. The sort of music you heard, for instance, in Cliff Richard's *The Young Ones* (1961). We don't mean the songs. We're thinking of that long sequence when, with a tap-tap here and a knock-knock there, and to the sound of progress music, the young ones transform a derelict building into a thriving community centre—a youth club, for the young ones.

In the Golden Age progress music was heard in the background by nearly everybody. The first phone, the first car, the first house, the first summer holiday, the first TV—all to progress music. Then the arrival of sexual intercourse, in 1966, and the full ascendancy of the children of the Golden Age.

In the First World, now, *the greying of the globe,* as demographers put it, *will constitute the most significant population shift in history.* The Golden Age turned into the Silver Tsunami, the Sixties Crowd became the sixties crowd, and the young ones, now, were all old ones.

"With the sole exception," he told his wife, "of Cliff Richard. He's *still* a young one."

.   .   .

"I used to have a birthday suit," he continued. "But something's gone wrong with it. It doesn't fit any more. And it's all worn out. I could take it to Jeeves's, I suppose. But this needs to go to the invisible menders."

"See the doctor again," she said. "See the one you quite liked at St. Mary's."

"Great. From Club Med to Club Med."

The first Club Med, or Club Mediterranean, was the name of the network of attractive resorts that dedicated itself to those between the ages of eighteen and thirty. The second Club Med, or Club Medico, was the name of the hospital cafeteria at St. Mary's. There were no age restrictions at the second Club Med, though it did seem to cater to a more mature clientele. He said,

"I didn't tell you. Last time I went, the guy said I might have CFS. Chronic Fatigue Syndrome. Uh, myalgic encephalo . . . encephalomyelitis. Or ME. A virus in the cerebellum. But apparently I don't. Anyway. You know, Pulc, I think I'm getting better." He hadn't called her that for some time (a diminutive of Pulchritude). "It was just psychological."

"What makes you think that?"

"Not sure. Touch wood. And it *is* depressing. Think. From the Me Decade to the ME Decade. From Club Med to Club Med. Great."

. . .

We come to item four in the revolutionary manifesto, and, yes, this was the one that caused most of the grief.

. . . In the seventeenth century, it is said, there was a *dissociation of sensibility*. The poets could no longer think and feel at the same time. Shakespeare could do it, the Metaphysicals could do it; they could write brainily about feeling and sex. But it went. The poets could no longer naturally think and feel at the same time.

All we are saying is that something analogous happened while the children of the Golden Age were becoming men and women. Feeling was already separated from thought. And then feeling was separated from sex.

So the position of feeling found itself (again) shifted. This was the one that almost did for him, and for scores of thousands—perhaps tens of millions—of others.

. . .

When the end came, and closed the eyes that had loved themselves too much, the glassy youth entered the Land of the Dead.

> He ran straight to the banks of the Styx
> And gazed down at the smear of his shadow
> Trembling on the fearful current.

A shadowsmear: that was all. That was all the mirroring water was ever going to give him—a shadowsmear.

The nymphs of the forests and fountains cropped their hair and wailed. And Echo, or Echo's ghost, or Echo's echo, echoed his last words: Farewell, farewell. Alas, alas, alas. *No one found his body. What they found was a flower: a yellow heart in a ruff of white petals.*

We are given to understand that the dissolution—the fading, the shrivelling—of the glassy youth was completed in the course of a day and a night. In this he differed from his children, the children of the Golden Age.

. . .

Silvia said she'd be dropping in to show them her new uniform. Her new uniform—as a feminist. And Keith prepared himself for a surprise, because Silvia was like that. In the kitchen, with a torpid flourish, she removed her woollen overcoat (it was May 15, 2003), and said torpidly,

"It's a joke, isn't it." She was wearing a white miniskirt daubed with the red cross of St. George, a halter top with HOOKER stamped across the chest—plus several items of (detachable) jewellery in her navel, in her lower lip, and in both nostrils. "I give it six months. But it's a *joke.*"

"I hope that washes off."

"Come on, Mum, of course it washes off. D'you think I want a nest of snakes all over my hips when I'm ninety? I'm going on a strip-club crawl. With the sisters. We're all got up like this. I hope you're proud."

Before she left, she asked Keith something—how he learnt about the birds and the bees.

"Uh, in stages. And different versions. A shitty little kid at school who scared the life out of me. Then Nicholas. Then a biology class. While we were dissecting a worm."

"And you know how I got *my* sex education? How Nat and Gus got theirs? How Isabel and Chloe'll get theirs? We're *porny.*"

He said, "Can't we improve on *porny*, Silvia? . . . How about *pornoid*?"

"All right. Pornoid. Yeah, that's good. It's more like *paranoid.* And when you're with a new guy, that's what you are. You're paranoid about how pornoid he's going to be. You know, Pop, we're the spiders of the Web. We got everything we know from the infinity of filth. He's better, Mum, don't you think? Pop's a bit better."

He used to admire them, but Keith was no longer sure how he felt about spiders. Spiders ate flies; and flies ate shit. And if, in any sense, you were what you ate—if you were what you consumed every day— then what were spiders?

And yet spiders were alive and flies were not, somehow. And Keith still thought that killing a fly was a creative act—because a fly was a fleck of death. Little skull and crossbones, little jolly roger. Armoured survivalist with gas-mask face: but not here in London, perhaps, in the twenty-first century. There was only one instance so far—when the fly snarled up at him from a patch of birdshit on the garden paving, and applied its suckers, and stood its ground, and just snarled up at him through the spray.

Silvia left. Husband and wife processed their young daughters, and Keith, prolonging his experiment with fiftyfifty, helped assemble a modest dinner—salad, spaghetti bolognese, red wine.

He said, "I don't want to think about *me* any more." About my self: two words. "That's a good sign, isn't it? And it's physically easier too."

"How?"

Well, I could put it this way. Two months ago, Pulc, waking, and then getting up, was a Russian novel. One month ago, it was an American novel. And now it's only an English novel. An English novel of about 1970—concerning itself with the ups and downs of the middle classes, and never any longer than two hundred and twenty-five pages.

"That's progress. And beauty is returning. Thanks to you. As always."

·   ·   ·

Sex is bad enough, as a subject, and the *self* is pretty glutinous too. The *I*, the *io*, the *yo*, the *je*, the *Ich*. The *Ich:* Freud's preferred term for the *ego*, for the *I*. Sex is bad enough (but someone's got to do it); and then there's the *Ich*. And what does that sound like—*Ich*, the *Ich*?

Book Six

The Problem of Re-entry

I

ELIZABETH BENNET IN BED

We'll have a light breakfast, and then go to my room. And make a day of it. Or would you rather get on with your trial review? . . . I'm very rare, you know. We're awfully rare.

Thirteen hours later, in the pentagonal library, Lily was saying,

"You're no good? What d'you mean you're no good?"

"I'm no good. I'm just no good. Look."

He gestured at the page of foolscap, held upright by the crossed struts of the Olivetti. During a brief interlude, around five, Keith ran barefoot from the tower (under the skyquake, the zig and zag, the sudden cracks in heaven's floor) and rattled out a couple of paragraphs. The break had been called because Gloria Beautyman needed ten minutes to dress up as Elizabeth Bennet. You see, they'd had a difference of opinion about *Pride and Prejudice,* and Gloria wanted to prove her point.

"Read that bit," he told Lily. "It's been like this all day. Read that bit. Does it make any sense?"

"*. . . Lawrence believed,*" she said, "*that the great disaster of the civilisation he inhabited was its poisonous hatred of sex, and this hatred carried with it the morbid fear of beauty (the fear best epitomised, in Lawrence's view, by psychoanalysis), fear of 'alive' beauty which causes the atrophy of our intuitive faculty and our intuitive power.*"

"Does it make any sense at all?"

"No. Are you *insane*? . . . And your hair's wet."

"Yeah, I had a cold shower. To try and clear my head. I'm no good. I can't do it."

"*. . .* Oh, God. Just—just think of it as your weekly essay."

He paused and said, "Yeah. Yeah, like my weekly essay. No, that's good, Lily. I feel better about it already. How were the ruins?"

"Oh, completely miserable. You couldn't even tell what they were ruins *of*. Baths, supposedly. And it poured. What about Gloria?"

You see, it was Gloria's contention that Elizabeth Bennet was a . . . *She can't be,* Keith objected. *There weren't any then. Surely.* But Gloria insisted it was so. And as she led him through the novel (with her pertinent emphases, her telling quotations) Keith began to feel that even a Lionel Trilling or an F. R. Leavis would be reluctantly obliged to take the Beautyman interpretation on board. And the outfit, too, was deeply convincing—she even had a bonnet, an inverted wicker fruit bowl, kept in place by a white silk scarf that fastened under her chin.

"I'll do what Lawrence kept doing with whole novels," he told Lily. "I'll chuck it out and start again. Gloria? What about her? I didn't even know she was here." He recalled Gloria's lesson on lying *(Never elaborate. Just pretend it's all boringly true),* but he nonetheless heard himself say, "Not till she came limping over to get herself a cup of broth. In a duffel coat. She looked terrible."

"Well she dodged a bullet with the ruins."

You see, in their discussion of Jane Austen, Gloria rested her case on two key scenes: Elizabeth's physical appearance on her arrival at Mr. Bingley's (in the early pages), and the much later exchange when Mr. Bennet warns his daughter against a loveless marriage. *No,* Gloria decided, as if washing her hands of the matter. *She's as bad as I am, she is. Ooh, I bet she is.* The dressing-up was followed by a session of what might be called practical criticism. Then she said, Now *do you believe me? I was right and you were wrong. Say it. Elizabeth's a . . .*

No, okay. You've proved your point.

"Well I haven't got any choice, have I," he told Lily. "I'll just have to stick with it till it's done."

"I suppose I'd better make you something. To keep you going. Anyway. Happy birthday."

"Thank you, Lily."

He finished his review not that late—a little after one. A little after one, and Keith felt wise and happy and proud, and rich, and beautiful, and obscurely frightened, and slightly mad. And unbelievably tired. Jorquil was expected in twelve hours' time. And how did our hero feel about that? Only this: Jorq, in his eyes, stood for tradition, for social realism as he knew it, for the past. Keith, after all, had spent the day in a genre that belonged to the future.

Lily—Lily had waited up.

"Can't close my eyes. Don't know why."

All day (he imagined) Lily's probes and sensors, her magnetic needles, had been about their work; and now she wanted reassurance. Keith, to his surprise, was able to give it. And the act, the interchange, while pleasurable (in very faint continuation), and emotional (in utter contrast), was almost satirically antique, like a round of morris dancing, or like rubbing two sticks together—in one of the very earliest attempts to create fire.

"Scheherazade took her a tray," said Lily as she trembled off into sleep. "Lying there with a thermometer in her mouth. And an ice pack on her head . . . Hear her sneezing? It's a bit . . . You watch. Tomorrow she'll be fit as a fiddle."

The next day Keith looked around for at least some sedimentary suspicion—and there wasn't any. Because Gloria, in her own phrase, was *terribly good.* Keith already knew that he was in another world; knew, too, that he was in quite serious trouble—but only psychologically. And for the time being he just lay back and thought, with pure admiration, This is more like it. This is how duplicity's *supposed* to be done.

For example, at breakfast he had the pleasure of hearing Scheherazade say,

"Quite frankly, I admire her pluck. Well I do. You know, she was talking about the ruins all afternoon? Even in church. She kept reading out bits from her guidebook. And right through dinner she seemed to think she'd somehow be able to manage it. Half dead and still trying to be a sport. I call that game."

And with Lily herself, on the subject of Gloria and her indisposition, Keith had the mindless luxury of being rebuked for his incuriosity (and self-centredness): Gloria's Sunday—hadn't he even noticed?—was a continuous stop-start of dizzy spells, hot flushes, and woeful hastenings to the bathroom.

"How could it've passed you by?"

"Well it did."

"Christ," said Lily. "I thought I was watching *Emergency Ward 10.*"

Not satisfied with that, Gloria was now putting it about that her condition had deteriorated overnight. She asked for, and duly received, a visit from the doctor, who drove over from Montale; claiming to detect the presence of a famous Campanian virus, he sluiced out her ears with garlic and olive oil. And when Jorq arrived, and at once insisted on the change of rooms, Gloria was more or less stretchered from the tower to the apartment.

"Poor Gloria," said Scheherazade. "Such a slender reed."

Would it actually happen? Would he one day open his copy of *Critical Quarterly,* and see the article entitled "A Reassessment of *Pride and Prejudice:* Elizabeth Bennet Considered as a Cock"? By Gloria Beautyman—*and* (or perhaps *with,* or possibly *as told to*) Keith Nearing. And he believed that her exegesis, while certainly controversial, could not be easily dismissed.

Can't you read English? she asked him. *Listen. This comes ten pages from the end. Concentrate.*

"Lizzy," said her father, "I have given [Mr. Darcy] my consent . . . I now give it to *you,* if you are resolved on having him. But let me advise you to think better of it. I know your disposition, Lizzy. I know that you could be neither happy nor respectable, unless you truly esteemed your husband . . . Your lively talents would place you in the greatest danger in an unequal marriage. You could scarcely escape discredit and misery."

"I know your disposition," Gloria reiterated. *"Your lively talents." "Discredit and misery." "Neither happy nor respectable."* Not respectable. *What d'you think* that *means? I ask again. Can't you read English?*

Yeah. Mm. There's nothing remotely like that in any of the others. So does Mr. Bennet know *she's a cock?*

Not exactly. He knows she's unusually interested in sex. He doesn't know she's a cock, but he does know that.

I think I see.

And when she causes a scandal by walking three miles across country to Mr. Bingley's. Unaccompanied, mind. The fine eyes, the face "glowing with warmth of exercise," looking "blowsy" and "almost wild." Then the soiled stockings.

And her petticoat "six inches deep in mud." Her underwear covered in dirt . . . Bloody hell, aren't you supposed to be quite good at this kind of thing? "Symbols" and so on?

Keith lay there and listened.

And the very good teeth. That's a sign of virility. Look at mine . . . So we're agreed. Elizabeth's a cock. And the only way to deal with being a cock, then, was marrying for love. Good sex had to follow the emotions. It's not like that now. . . . So on their first night?

I'll show you. Go and amuse yourself for ten minutes. And I'll start looking for some wedding wear.

On his return—the white cotton dress with its improvised empire-line bust, the white shawl, the bonnet fastened by the white silk scarf.

I pray you remember, sir, I am not yet one and twenty.

A few minutes later he was near the bottom of the bed, working his way through a phenomenal density of slips and underslips and clasps and hasps, and she leant up on her elbows and said,

All Mr. Bennet knows for sure is if she married for money then she'd certainly stray. The cock bit's really just an extra. It's to do with what you're like naked. How you look.

How you feel to the touch (a hardness within a softness). And how you think, too, he thought, and worked on.

It's just an extra. Being a cock. But it's very rare.

When the whole thing was over Keith lay back and imagined a future almost blotted out by leisurely seminars on every heroine and anti-heroine in world literature, starting with *The Odyssey* (Circe, then Calypso). In a thickened voice he said,

I'm going to give you Sense and Sensibility.

How're you going to do that? she asked in all innocence, her eyes directed upward while she smoothed her cheeks and temples with her hands. *By fucking my arse off? . . . And would you mind not smoking in here. It's evidential, and it's a filthy habit anyway.*

The delicate wafers of the tickets told them plain enough: their summer was coming to an end. Lily said,

"Then what'll happen? To you and me? I suppose we'll break up."

Keith met her eye, and went back to *Bleak House.* Oh yeah, Christ—

Lily, and all that. He applied himself to the question. *Breaking up will be her idea all over again,* said Scheherazade. *After your friend Kenrik.* It was like a chess problem: he (Keith) now thought that he (Kenrik) had let slip that he (Keith) wanted him (Kenrik) to sleep with her (Lily)—not so that he (Keith) could sleep with *her* (Scheherazade), but just to improve her sexual confidence. Or something like that. It was like a chess problem, a contrivance, quite separable from the dynamism of the actual game. He said,

"In some ways that's a very frightening idea. Let's not decide anything now."

"Frightening?"

He shrugged and said, "Gaw, this Lady Dedlock. Honoria. She's great. A proud schemer with a murky past."

"So you fancy Lady Dedlock now."

"She makes a nice change from Esther Summerson. Who's a do-gooder. And such a fucking saint that she's *proud* of being disfigured by smallpox. Imagine that."

"Who was the other one you liked?"

"Bella Wilfer. Bella's almost as good as Becky Sharp. Can you believe that Jorquil?"

"Jorquil? He's not such a bad chap."

"Yes he is. He is such a bad chap. I mean, who cares? But he is."

The summer was over. They would be returning; and Jorquil, in his person, was a rumour of what they'd be returning to. In Keith's eyes, old Jorq was a terrible compendium of Upper England, he was Ascot and Lord's and the Henley Regatta, he was hay-wains and ha-has and cowpats and sheep dips. And it was in his scrutiny of Jorquil, over several days, that Keith discovered something extraordinary: the profound, the virtuoso, the almost hilarious fraudulence of Gloria Beautyman. She's terribly good, he thought. She's very clever. And she's insane.

What genre did I visit, on my animal birthday? This was the question he couldn't answer. What mode, what type, what *kind*?

In the bathroom with Gloria it wasn't just the colours that were wrong—all Day-Glo and wax-museum. The acoustics were hopeless too. And so was the continuity. One moment the thunder felt no louder than a plastic dustbin being dragged across the courtyard; the next, it was all over you like a detonation. And the human figures—him, her? Gloria was much better at it than he was, naturally (she played the lead); but he kept having his doubts about the quality of the acting.

The light and the atmospherics were a bit more normal in the bedroom, later, but not much more normal, with the heavy yellow flashes, then darkness at noon, then intense silver sunshine, then biblical, world-drowning rain.

Again and again he thought, What category am I in? In its lustres and static facets it often reminded him of the pages of a glossy magazine—fashion, glamour. But what was its type as drama, as narrative? He was sure it wasn't romance. Every few minutes it occurred to him that it might be science fiction. Or advertising. Or propaganda. But this was 1970 and he didn't know it—he didn't know the mode.

It seemed to make sense only when you watched it in the mirror.

Something had been separated out. He did know that.

Jorq? *It can't be his looks that attracted her, can it,* Scheherazade had said. No, not his face (albinoid, with sore red lips), and not his body (fat-strong, with heavy bones). And it couldn't be his mind either. For this clear reason: to be stimulated by Jorquil's company, you would have to be abnormally interested in cheese. His boundless estates in the West Country produced great quantities of cheese. And that's all he ever talked about: cheese.

During the day he looked like a cumbersome gentleman farmer (twills, trilby, tweeds, swagger stick); during the evening he looked like a cumbersome gentleman farmer in a tuxedo (his invariable dinner wear). Keith never once saw him when he wasn't both eating and talking; and both activities produced in Jorquil a kind of oral inundation—a deluge of drool. On the other hand, old Jorq was wronged by Keith's first impression. His chat wasn't all of Double Gloucester, of Caerphilly, of Lymeswold—of *torolone,* of *stracchino,* of *caciocavallo.* As a kind of sideline, Jorq turned out to be laboriously right-wing.

Early afternoon was his chosen time for going upstairs with Gloria. As he forced a final reeking wedge of *parmeigiano* or Dorset Blue into his mouth, he maintained his slobbered diatribe about the wealth tax or the rise of the trades unions; then he held out a downturned hand, and

Gloria would accompany him to the ballroom and its orbital staircase with an air of contrition and industriousness.

At that point Lily and Scheherazade always looked at each other with a lift of the chin.

Adriano was back. Back from pre-season training with *I Furiosi*. On his left cheek, from eye to jawline, he had a purple bruise that bore the faithful impression of a rugby boot (you could count the studs). It was gone the next day. Consolata, Adriano's latest, incidentally, was the same height as Gloria Beautyman.

"What are you talking about? He doesn't dribble. He just enjoys his food."

Lily had embarked on the first, exploratory phase of her packing—the jerseys folded in their moth-proof polythene bags, the shoes berthed in their tissue paper . . . The conversation idled along at sixteen rpm.

"Enjoys his food?" Keith turned the page. "Show him a cheddar roll and it's like that submarine film. *Ice Station Zebra,* remember?"

"Rock Hudson."

"Yeah. Remember the best bit? The guy opens the fucked-up torpedo bay. And half the Arctic Ocean comes poling into the hold. Show Jorq a Dairylea and that's what you get."

"He just likes his food . . . You know what Adriano's doing now? He's playing it cool."

"I ask again. How can four foot ten play it cool? Play *what* cool?"

"Well all these other girls seem to like him. And when they're smoothing his thighs or giving him a kiss curl he turns to Scheherazade with a certain look."

"What kind of look? Do it." She did it. "Christ . . . Jorquil's eyelashes."

"His eyelashes? What about them?"

"They're not eyelashes—they're just two sets of whiteheads. Each of them speared by a bristle. And he's a fascist. He voted for Heath."

"He votes Liberal. He said."

"*Lib*eral . . . And his smutty jokes. When he takes her upstairs. *Time for a visit to the Cape of Horn. Time for some Egyptian PT.*"

"That's just slang for sleep. Egyptian PT. That's army slang. Because Arabs are meant to be lazy . . . Look. Rich men have a constituency with girls. It's just a fact of life."

"Agreed. But why are you sticking up," he slowly asked, "for that fat brute?"

"He's not even fat. Not particularly. He's just big. And some girls like big men. It makes them feel secure. You're just a chippy little guttersnipe. That's all."

Keith said, "It's the aesthetics of it. Her all dark and small. Him like a huge loaf of white bread. I mean, who cares, but doesn't it chill you to think of them lying down together?"

"She probably just isn't very interested in sex. Not everyone is, you know. You think everyone is, and they aren't. Look at her background. Girls aren't meant to enjoy it. So she just lies back and thinks of England."

"Scotland."

"And he doesn't *only* talk about cheese."

That night at dinner, Keith closely monitored him—the village idiot in the dinner jacket. And it seemed to Keith that, yes, Jorquil did indeed talk about cheese all the time (when he wasn't being laboriously right-wing), and he looked outlandishly fat, too, and he came close to drowning in his own saliva, and he . . . Such an impression, if distorted, was not distorted by envy or possessiveness. He wished it was, in a way, but it wasn't. The distortion remained eerily otherwise. When he gazed at Jorquil's lips, chafed, flayed, peeled, he saw and felt those lips in the act of kissing. And Keith thought, He's not kissing Gloria. He's kissing me.

Are you better? At last you're venturing out of doors."

"Quite recovered, thank you."

"You had some of us very worried there for a while."

"Yes. It was touch-and-go, I admit."

". . . God he's a Dud."

Keith had caught her alone, with her patchwork quilt (the squares and triangles of cardpaper, the scraps of satin and velvet), on the south terrace. She now looked up and said, quite unintimately (an observer on the far side of the French windows might have thought she was talking about the morning weather—which was fresh and brilliant—or the price of yarn),

"Yes, isn't he. *Mon*strous. Those lips. Those lashes. Like a row of pimples."

Keith carefully sat himself down on the swing sofa. "So we see eye to eye on Jorq," he said. Was that what was happening? Was he seeing Jorquil with Gloria's eyes? "And the drool."

"And the drool. And the *cheese . . .* Of course, that's why I prolonged my uh, my ailment. To stay out from under him for another day or two. But I was pushing it. As far as he's concerned I've been ill for months."

"Months?"

"Ever since I drank that glass of champagne. Remember? And got caught messing around with the polo pro." Slowly and solemnly she shook her head. "I'll never forgive myself for that. Never. It was *so* unlike me."

"Messing around with the polo pro?"

"No. Getting caught. I mean it's unheard of."

Keith continued to swing on the swing sofa, and there seemed no reason not to ask (because everything was now allowed), "What's he like? Up in the apartment?"

Gloria reached for another shaped template, another scrap of plush. "The same as he is everywhere else. Jorq's a bore. And bores don't listen . . . I was going to say that he's not too bad in bed when he's fast asleep. But of course he snores. He's like a great white whale. And he saturates all the pillows."

"Still. Come on. It's hardly a blind date, is it. And aren't you two getting engaged? Well I suppose old Jorq has other attractions."

She said quietly, "Listen, you fool. Moving down to London costs money—and I haven't got any, you fool. You boring fool."

"All right. I hear. I listen."

Now Jorq's face (which was chewing something) established itself on the other side of the glass. Gloria rippled her fingers at it; and gave it a startling false smile. She said,

"Well originally I thought I'd make him marry me and then get the divorce going as soon as possible after the honeymoon. But I don't think I can even bring myself to do that . . . There's already someone else."

"Who?"

"You," she seemed to say.

She seemed to say, *You.* Keith had misapprehended, and it was quickly cleared up. But we might step back from him here, at this revolutionary moment . . . Men have two hearts—the upper, the nether; and convention tells us that when all is well they act in concert. But here, in this case, the two hearts responded antithetically. Keith's upper heart sank, quailed, sickened; or it fearfully subsided into a certain kind of future. It was his underheart that felt poetic—not bursting, as hearts are said to do, but filling, rising, aching. He said,

"Me?"

"*You?* No, not *you*. Huw. Aitch you doubleyou."

"Huw."

"Huw. He's Welsh. He's got a castle too. Now isn't that a coincidence. You see, the trick is to find someone who's rich *and* pretty. And who listens."

"I thought for a moment you meant me."

"You? Well you listen, I suppose . . . You're just a student."

"That's what you are too."

"I know, but I'm a girl."

Jorq started rattling at the handle. Gloria said,

"Can't the stupid sod see the catch?"

"It's tricky. You have to pull then push. It's an IQ test."

"Then he won't pass it. God, help the stupid sod out, somebody." She gestured at Jorquil's baffled image—pointing, tugging, shoving. "And I've got to keep him happy. If you please. Or I get the gorgon look from Oona. Oona scares the hell out of me. I sometimes have the terrible feeling she knows what I'm really like."

After a moment he said, "Elizabeth Bennet."

"Yes? What?"

"You're not really the same, you two. She's from the past. And you're from the future."

"Well," she said. "Cocks naturally adapt. Down through the ages."

Jorquil was now beating the door frame with the flat of his hand.

"Uh, Gloria—you know there's a maid's room beyond and above the apartment."

"How did you hear about the maid's room?"

"I could come up the north staircase. We might be able to slip in there for a minute or two. When he's out."

"Whatever for? Look at you," she said, and laughed, "you're terrified. You're already out of your depth. And you know it." She turned to watch Jorquil throwing his shoulder against the glass. "When they're that stupid, I hate rich people, don't you? I hate rich people. But the trouble is, they're the ones who've got all the money. I'll look into it. The maid's room. Ah, *here* he is!"

Jorquil stumbled out and steadied and straightened up; he surveyed the sky, the slope, the descents, the grotto, the white sheet of the pool; his chins settled and he gave a soft grunt of ponderous entitlement. Keith saw that Jorq had a scattering of cheese puffs in his cupped left palm. Now he smeared the remainder into his mouth and said,

"Airy nothings, that's all they are." He licked his hand. "Like so much in life. Airy nothings. Come on, my darling. To the pool with you."

"I don't think I'm quite well enough for the pool."

"No no. On with your togs. Or should I say *off* with them."

"Jorquil's brought me some decent clothes at least."

"Oh here," said Keith, passing it over. And *Sense and Sensibility* disappeared into Gloria's straw bag.

"Now come along. I want you turning all heads," said Jorq, "with your pretty titties. Those pretty titties of yours. I want everyone to see them and weep."

Could he really have said that, Jorquil? But what Keith was left with, on the terrace, was a sudden memory of his sister. *Vi,* he asked her, in the wood-framed Morris 1000, *why are you sticking your feet out of the window?* And Violet (eight, nine) said, *Because I want everyone to see my lovely new shoes. I want everyone to see them and weep.*

And then haphazardly came other memories. Like the time she ran the length of the garden and returned to him the lofted cricket ball, and then ran back again, and weeping throughout—weeping about something else.

And then came other memories. Needing to be rescued. What was he to do with them all? In this new world he had entered (it was very developed, very far advanced), thinking and feeling were rearranged. And this, he thought and felt, might show him another way.

Oona was back. On that much everyone agreed: Oona was back—with Prentiss and Conchita (Dodo having been jettisoned somewhere over the Alps). With difficulty Keith made room for them in his mind.

Oona, yes, quietly watchful, and her experienced eyes did indeed closely follow the movements of Miss Beautyman. Perpendicular Prentiss, all joints and hinges, like an Amish hatstand. And Conchita, who had changed. With Jorquil here, and Whittaker back, and Timmy due, and all the servants present, the castle no longer felt spacious. Or perhaps he just meant that there seemed to be no room for manoeuvre.

They had to vacate their turret, Lily and Keith, and were transferred to a forbiddingly dark but curiously congenial room on the dungeon floor. Here Keith threw himself into his work, itemising, systematising, and eventually alphabetising the vast archive of his twenty-first birthday. He wanted to enter it now, in the list that lived with his birth certificate, under *Jean 7*. Not *Scheherazade 10* or even *Scheherazade 12a*, but *Gloria 99z*!* There were so many things he hadn't known you were allowed to do.

"But I feel defenceless," said Lily, "when you pin my arms."

"That's the point . . . And if it's so small, why can't you get it all in your mouth?"

". . . Why should I *want* it all in my mouth?"

"Go on. Keep trying."

"Now my head's upside down . . . No. I won't. You even look different. What's *happened* to you?"

Lily said these things, but not in the dark — not any more.

Gloria Beautyman had a secret. A secret of titanic dimensions. Gloria was secretly married with three children. It was something of that size. Gloria was secretly a boy. It was something of that size.

2

OMPHALOS ·

"What would you call it? A monokini, I suppose."

"But it's not like yours, is it. Yours just looks like a bikini without the top."

"She does it to humour Jorq. He insists. But she's come on at least a generation, hasn't she. It's like having a whole new guest around the place. A thong?"

"It's very narrow at the front . . . Does she wax it? Has she done a Rita?"

"A G-string? No, you can sometimes see a little fringe just above the band."

"So she barbers it."

"Trims it."

Correct, Scheherazade. The triangle is isosceles in shape. Unlike your undesigning equilateral (I assume)—or yours, Lily.

"A loincloth? But it's not the front, is it."

"No, it's not the front. It's the back. Billowing out of it like that."

"It's hardly more than a glorified wedgie, is it. The back. I know. A fig leaf."

"A tailored fig leaf."

"Yes. A very expensive fig leaf. A fig leaf is what it is."

Correct, Lily. Who was it who said, And the eyes of them both were opened, and they knew that they were naked? *That was in Eden, after the Fall; you didn't need a fig leaf until after the Fall. And consider another observation (made two thousand years later):* I never yet touched a fig leaf that didn't turn into a price tag. *Correct, Lily. That's all correct.*

Grazia, Adriano's latest (and last), who was five foot ten, was blowing iridescent bubbles at him as he sprawled on his lounger, her mouth a thick pout behind the soapy monocle. Lily said,

"I see what you mean about Gloria's tits."

"Mm. She makes me feel sort of clumsy . . . Anyway, her arse is still enormous."

"Mm. It's still a *farcical* arse."

And now Timmy was here. Timmy arrived, not on foot, but in a brace of taxis. And not with a knapsack on his back. He had with him an extended dynasty of monogrammed leather suitcases, plus his cello. His cello, like an encoffined Ruaa, with vast brood-bearing hips.

But it was a good entrance—Timmy's. Long, slender, loose, vague, and somehow limply stylish—like a doodle from a talented hand . . .

Brrr. Mmm," said Scheherazade, settling herself on the sofa. "Lovely fire."

"Lovely fire," said Keith.

Ah yes: Scheherazade. He bestirred himself. Sitting there before the flames with his wine glass, Keith gave up trying to parse his altered state. He gave that up, and went back to doing what he did when he had nothing better to do (a now-frequent state of affairs): he was cherishing the thirteen hours. The thirteen hours comprised his secret. Nothing much, in scale, compared to Gloria's double life or parallel universe. How was it for her? *The secret,* as a distinguished student of the mind once put it, *produces an immense enlargement. The secret offers, so to speak, the possibility of a second world alongside the manifest world.* Keith said to Scheherazade,

"You know, in Dickens, when the good characters look in the fire, they see the faces of their loved ones. And the bad characters, they just see hell and doom."

"What do you see?"

Keith swung his neck around, all the way, like Adriano in the Rolls Royce. Strangely, he and Scheherazade were in the room's still centre: all were otherwise engaged, with the senior ladies away to one side, and Jorq and Timmy presiding over a noisy school of cards (a game called Loo, with much betting, raising, doubling, scooping).

"Neither," he answered. "Something in between. Look, I'm sorry about what I said the other night. But don't despise me for ever for it. I didn't know you were religious."

"I'm not." And she too turned to see. The turret of her neck, the pink shirt, the tea-brown cardigan. "I'm not religious. I mean, I believe, in a way. But that's all. I'm not like Timmy . . . And I don't despise you. It's me. It's just me."

Keith inclined his head.

"I discovered something about myself. I couldn't—I couldn't do it. All right, on holiday, a moment, an impulse. Maybe. But not with . . . premeditation. Bit feeble, isn't it. But it seems I'm not the type."

"There has to be love."

"It goes beyond that. I'm just stuck. I think it's to do with Dad dying when he did. I'm just stuck with what I've got."

"And what do *you* see when you look in the fire?"

"It's true. I sometimes see my father's face."

"Mm," he said. Last month, last week, he would have been moved and honoured by such a confidence—from those lips, under those eyes and that level brow. Now he thought, So you're not the type: well you should've done some premeditation about *that*. "It makes sense, I suppose."

"It's best, I think. Even if it means I'll miss out on all the fun. Maybe when I'm more grown up I'll be braver."

This made his eyes widen; but he also had an unfamiliar, commissarial impulse, something like—Scheherazade, you belong to the old regime. You are not equipped for what is now to be. "Well, Timmy's here. And I've got no complaints."

"Good. Fine."

Adriano and Conchita, like a little married couple, came to warm themselves, and for a moment there was silence.

What did Keith see when he looked in the fire? Fire, he thought, was the amorous element, neurotic, corrosive, devouring. Fire was the amorous element; and a fire of logs was an *orgy*—throw on another one and watch all the snakes, all the copperheads, as they arch and veer; then they came in over it, under it, round the back of it, with lips and fingertips, and spitting and licking with their serpent tongues.

Conchita was saying, "What's Italian for *fire*?"

"*Fuoco, incendio*," said Adriano, who, these days, wore a haggard look. "*Inferno*."

And Keith sat on with his wine and his fire and his secret.

Gloria Beautyman was out of occultation—bodily, anyway.

Her fig leaf, down at the pool (there were in fact several fig leaves, silver, gold, pale platinum), introduced an erotic emphasis not yet explored by Scheherazade or by Lily or by Feliciana/Rachele/Claudia/Pia/Nerissa/Consolata/Grazia. This was *looseness*. As if the elastic of the waistband had been deliberately distressed. When she showered, under the hut's eave, you felt that any second the flimsy sliver—the *airy nothing*—must surely slip to the floor. All you needed to do was stay around long enough. And when she dived, if you clambered to your feet in time, you could see it down there under the slippery fathom, the great wet whiteness, and then her hands reached back and tugged.

Jorquil would come staggering down in his crofter's kit and cheer her on from the shadows (he himself never disrobed: after five minutes in the sun his face went the colour of an inner tube). And there was Timmy, suavely shoulderless, unconcernedly engrossed in his pamphlets and brochures (hunting, Pentecostalism). And there was Adriano, now unaccompanied (and somehow doubly solitary, as he applied himself to his new discipline: yoga). More unexpected was the steady presence of white-shirted, umber-skinned Amen. His dark glasses stared at you in the light.

Stared, occasionally perhaps, at Keith's dark glasses: he had got hold of a spare pair of Lily's, so he could contemplate—without inhibition and without blinking—the navel of Gloria Beautyman. This was the latest thing: Beautyman's abdomen. It wasn't concave, like Scheherazade's, or a smooth continuation, like Lily's. It was the central panel of Gloria's design, a luxurious protuberance. The *omphalos,* as poets called it, representing the centre of the earth, like the soft swell of the Mediterranean Sea.

There was also a qualitative distinction in her. Gloria's body was completed, entire, the final version. It was her colouring, he thought. Whereas with Lily, and even with Scheherazade, there was something feverish and unstable and open to change. Sudden blotches, alarums. What they were still in, she was already out of. Or was this just the candour of blondes?

And it was all perfectly manageable. For an hour or so he took pictures with his photographic memory, then it was up to the castle—

with the omphalos alive in his head. There followed ninety seconds of practical narcissism, behind closed eyes. Which seemed to solve everything. Wanting Gloria wasn't like wanting Scheherazade, in the old days: it came and went, but it didn't accumulate. Love (he knew) made the world expand; this (whatever it was) reduced the world to a single point. The physical act with Gloria had produced nothing more than a primitive desire to repeat it. A desire more or less exactly balanced by a primitive fear.

The navel, that shadowy hollow, was the site of Gloria's last connection to her mother. It also marked the area, of course, where her own children would one day grow.

"Now how did you get wind of the maid's room? . . . That's where you were going to go with Scheherazade, wasn't it. Until she lost her nerve."

Gloria, poolside, was packing up her straw bag. All the others were climbing the garden path, in Indian file. She spoke unsmilingly, uncollusively. She said,

"Yes, I followed your blunderings with Scheherazade. I'm curious. What was this Dracula business?"

"She told you?"

"She just said she was worried about vampire bats, now, because you pretended to be Dracula. One night. Describe."

He told her something about it. She stood up, shouldering her bag with a rustle, and he came on behind.

"You see, Keith, that's why old-fashioned girls like the *idea* of ravishment. Not the reality, the idea. Because if they want to, and then enjoy it, it's not their fault."

"It's not their fault?"

"No. It's Bela Lugosi's or Christopher Lee's. Typical Scheherazade. So Dracula missed his chance," said Gloria, "to suck her blood. And that's a terrible shame."

"I've got no complaints. You were wonderful . . . A shame why?"

"A terrible shame." She paused on the slope and turned to him with quiet earnestness. "That thing boys do with girls with big tits. Huh-*hm*. When they fuck the tits."

". . . *Do* they?"

"Ooh, I bet they do. You know, I can manage that if I squeeze them together. Though of course you'd have to watch out for my cross."

Keith waited for a voice to instruct him. None came, but he said, "You could show me. In the maid's room. When Jorq goes for one of his drives."

"I've reconnoitred the maid's room. Await my instructions. Quiet now."

"You know, Gloria, *you're* old-fashioned. Futuristic, too, but old-fashioned. Living off men. You could be a great dancer."

". . . Now you've read a lot of books, but do you know *Little Pink Ballerina*? Little Pink Ballerina prays to be able to whirl, twirl, and leap, like a fairy princess, graceful as a feather floating through the air. I'll never be a dancer. My arse is too big. I just can't get it all in a tutu. Quiet now."

"Or a painter. Your drawing's phenomenal."

"There's something—unclean about drawing. Quiet now."

"You've got a secret. Isn't that true?"

She paused. ". . . Lily told me she hates dancing. She hates it when she has to dance. What does that tell you about her nature?"

"I don't know. What?"

"Well. I'm sure your sex life was in need of some gingering up. But I've noticed that Lily has an ill-used look about her in the mornings. Don't take her out of her nature. Don't do that. Quiet now."

He stayed and let her move ahead. So he could watch her go: two different women joined at the waist.

Flowers: Lily didn't know a lot about many of them, but she did know a lot about some. And she said you could tell that autumn had come to Italy—when the cyclamens bloomed in the shade. Having none of the frankness of the primrose (its second cousin), the cyclamen hid its stigma in purple folds. Garden wisdom—in the shape of Eugenio—maintained that the wild swine loved the cyclamen for the acridity of its roots. The flower's scent was chilled: an icy fragrance. It smelled of all the seasons, but the autumn was its time.

"The summer's going," said Lily. "You can feel it in the air."

Yes. The aftermath of autumn. The silence of September.

They walked on.

Now Lily was packing. Having sketched it out, in note form, she had begun her first draft. She folded T-shirts, folded T-shirts . . .

"I've worked it out," he said.

"Worked what out?"

"Timmy's a ninny. The count's a cunt. And Jorq's a joke."

"And Keith's a kid," she said (uncharacteristically, he felt). "And a kook."

"Yeah. By your lights, Lily, you're the only person here who's not insane. Of our age. Adriano's nuts, understandably enough, and everyone else's religious. Or not an atheist. To you that qualifies as nuts."

"Whittaker's not nuts."

This was all she'd say . . . Packing, Keith thought, was Lily's art form. In fact it was the only art form that she didn't privately disapprove of. Her finished suitcase was a finished jigsaw; she brought the same precision to bear on a picnic basket; even her beach bag looked like a Japanese garden. This was her nature.

"Autumn's here, Lily. Time to get back to some real people."

"Who're they?"

"Ordinary people." Yes. Ordinary people like Kenrik and Rita and Dilkash and Pansy. Ordinary people like Violet. "Normal."

"Why aren't *you* normal any more? Your new stunts. The dressing-up and pretending."

"But normal's changing, Lily. Soon all that *will* be normal. In the future," he said (he was actually plagiarising Gloria), "sex will be play, Lily. A play of surfaces and sensations. Anyway. Summer's over. The project's over."

"And have you read it at last?"

"What?"

"The English novel. You didn't give Hardy much of a go. Though of course you liked that slag in *Jude*."

"Arabella. *A mere female animal.*"

"And I'll never forgive you for Rosamond Vincy," she said (picking up on their discussion of her favourite novel—*Middlemarch*). "There's the lovely Dorothea, and you lust after that grasping bitch Rosamond Vincy. Who ruins Lydgate. Slags and villains. That's all you like now— slags and villains."

"Yeah, well I couldn't be doing with Hardy. I bow to his poetry. But I couldn't be doing with his fiction."

· No, he couldn't be doing with Thomas Hardy's fiction—with Tess, with Bathsheba. It sometimes seemed to Keith that the English novel, at least in its first two or three centuries, asked only one question. Will she fall? Will she fall, this woman? What'll they write about, he wondered, when *all* women fall? Well, there'll be new ways of falling . . .

"I couldn't be doing with him. No, on to Lawrence. No. Give me DHL."

"But you're always writhing around when you read him."

"It's true," he said and sat up. "*He's* nuts, but he's also a genius. So he's very turbulent. The fucks in Lawrence—they're more like fights. Anyway. This one's not much cop."

She said, "Women in Hysterical Sex."

"That's not a proper one. Hysterical Sex Among the Haystacks. That's a proper one."

"What shall we do with Adriano?"

"Tom Thumb?"

"No. Not the count. The rat." She held up the sheet of thick white paper. "Junglebum's Adriano."

He felt himself alerted. Keith hadn't called Adriano Tom Thumb in a while; and Lily hadn't called Gloria Junglebum either. Their duolect, like everything else, was growing old. He said,

"Let me have a last look . . . Mind you, in his later stuff he gets very anti-box."

"Anti-women?"

"Yeah, but also anti-box." And pro-arse. "Mellors calls Connie's box *her beak.* And then he stops being normal."

". . . That hurts."

"You tried it with Gordon, and it hurt. But Gordon's got a big cock, Lily, like all other boys. It wouldn't hurt with me. Okay. Forget it. But why can't you get the whole thing in your mouth?"

"Christ, I told you."

"Ah. The retch reflex." This was actually Gloria's name for it. *That's the challenge now facing womankind,* she said. *Rising above the retch reflex.* "Just make yourself mistress of the retch reflex, Lily, and we'll—"

"What's in it for me?"

"Ask not what—"

"Oh shut up, you little shit. You used to say you hoped to be *normal* in bed. You said it's like being sane. Sanity is being *normal.*"

"That's true—I did use to say that." He did use to say that. Freud, after all, wrote that sexual oddities were *private religions.* "Up to you, Lily. And I don't like it if you don't like it."

"Well I don't like it."

"Fine . . . I suppose we just chuck this out. She can certainly draw."

"Junglebum? Weird, isn't it. All that ladylike stuff. And now in her sex-shop fig leaf."

"Mm. It's Jorq. He's vain about her."

"Well he must've brought a whole trunkful of those slinky black dresses. And the slit skirts and the satin tops with her tits pushed up around her chin. And she looks the part, doesn't she."

Another of Gloria's qualities: you gazed at her now, and always wondered what was happening on the other side of her clothes. Lily said,

"My mother has a name for the type who dresses like that. Cocktail waitress."

". . . Come and lie down for a bit," he said. "With that sarong. And the halter top on the chair there." Her eyes went heavenward. "And that hat," he added.

When it was over he pronounced the usual sentence: subject, verb, object. And she gave no answer. His eyes went to the window—half banked with mist and soil in the low yellow sun.

Lily said, "That's what Tom Thumb's telling Scheherazade."

"Love again? He can't be. With Timmy here?"

"He's dead serious. Not flowery any more. She thinks Adriano's going to declare himself."

Keith said indifferently, "The count? Are you sure you don't mean the rat? Yeah, what if the rat declared itself, Lily? I mean to you. You'd have to say yes. Or you'd hurt its feelings."

"Very funny. You little shit. She's worried. She's worried Adriano's going to do something rash."

Left alone, he contemplated Gloria's drawing of Adriano the rat. Everyone agreed. Hand followed eye with uncanny facility: the weak pomp of the chest, the cylindrical ribbing of the tail. There was the rat; but you had to say that she had missed its this-ness. Gloria's Adriano looked far more dignified—looked far less disgraceful—than the thing in the pet-shop window. Gloria's Adriano had been promoted in the chain of being. Gloria's rat was a dog.

During one of their lulls, on that animal afternoon (Gloria was

changing), Keith leafed through her sketchbook: Santa Maria as grand
as St. Peter's, village streets cleansed of accident and clutter; Lily with
her beauty long-ensconced, Adriano with Mark Antony face but his
torso misleadingly full-scale, topless Scheherazade unembarrassed by
her "noble" breasts; and Keith himself, perfunctorily furnished with a
Kenrik-like elaboration of the eyes and lips.

Was that magnanimity or was it sentimentality? Was it perhaps even
religious—an absolution that promised ascendance? To Keith, in any
event, the prettification seemed inartistic. He thought, then, that art
was meant to be truthful, and therefore unforgiving. But hand followed
eye with uncanny facility. And that's the way she was in the bedroom:
phenomenal concordance of hand and eye. How, he wondered, would
Gloria draw Gloria? Looking in the full-length mirror, naked, with
pencil and pad, how would she choose to represent it? The physique of
course would be standardised. And the face would be honest, and unse-
cretive.

The cold breath of the cyclamens. Evanescent, like the season, now, a
cold dissolution. This summer was the climax of his youth. It had come
and gone, it was over, Lily, his first love, his only love, was probably
over. Yet much had been gained (he felt, in the September silence) from
the example of Gloria Beautyman. Now he thought of London and its
million girls.

W̲hittaker was arranging the white pieces on the table in the salon.
He was doing this out of the goodness of his heart, because Keith no
longer played chess with Whittaker. Whittaker was relieved about
that, and so was Keith, at first. But Keith now played with Timmy.

"Do you know what I am? I'm a frustrated parent. I'm not even a
fruit. I'm a pop. Amen. There's been a development."

Keith looked up: Whittaker, who so often seemed to fill the same
space as his brother Nicholas. In seventy-two hours' time, Keith would
be in his brother's arms, and would tell him everything . . .

"Amen's fallen in love—in his way. Not with me, of course. It's one
of those hopeless passions. And you know something? I couldn't be
more touched. I spoon him and nurse him. And he's so sweet to me. I'm
a frustrated parent."

"Who's he in love with?"

"In fact it's awfully good," said Whittaker. "Three days ago he took Ruaa to the bus. And I thought he'd escort her to Naples, like he always does. But no—he just slung her on board and came straight back. To be near the loved one. It's a love that dare not speak its name. Gloria."

There was no longer any doubt. Keith had to get back to some normal people. And quickly too. "Gloria?"

"Gloria. He says he's going straight for Gloria's arse."

". . . Say again?"

"I'll rephrase that. Amen's considering going straight—for the sake of Gloria's arse."

"With, uh, does he have ambitions?"

"No. It's too exalted for that. He's considering going straight in the *name* of Gloria's arse. To honour Gloria's arse."

"I think I see."

"He doesn't like her face or anything. Or her personality. Or her knack with a pencil. Just her arse."

"Just her arse."

"Just her arse. Though he quite likes her hair."

Keith lit a cigarette. "Well I noticed he's always down there suddenly." Amen, poolside, legs neatly crossed, on a director's chair, his dark glasses strangely prominent, like antennae. "And I was wondering. Has he made his peace with Scheherazade's tits?"

"On the contrary. He thinks they're more violent than ever. But he braves Scheherazade's tits—for Gloria's arse. And now he's in a kind of tender despair. It's made him humble. He's in despair. He says he'll never find a guy with an arse like that."

"And he won't, will he," said Keith with confidence. "I mean it's a very feminine arse."

"As feminine as Scheherazade's tits. And it's weird. The arses we like are muscular—kind of cuboid. And Gloria's is . . ."

Like a prize tomato, pronounced Scheherazade, that time—referring to the red corduroys so contentiously unleashed on the young men of Ofanto. Later that same day, playing solitaire, Keith made an exact visual match: the ace of hearts. In two dimensions, then. And hearts: hearts. Which wasn't the right suit.

"Then I don't get it, Whittaker. Why's the arse okay? The arse and not the tits?"

"There's a basic difference."

". . . Ah Christ. Excuse me for a while. What's the basic difference?"
"Boys have arses."

Keith did not need reminding that boys have arses. All the slow burns inside him, the flickerings and reorderings, like logs succumbing to change in the core of a fire—these brought with them an upheaval in his gut. To the cold-sweat undertaste of the dungeon floor he added the smell, not of his dead concerns, his yesterdays: it was his present, and his stake in it, that he seemed to be evacuating. He crouched there. He waited. The last tugging reminder of pain. It was going away . . . And where does pain go, he wondered, when it goes away? Does it disappear, or does it go somewhere else? I know, he thought. It goes into the well of your weakness; and it waits.

He lay in the pale green tub, in the wintry acre of the dungeon bathroom. This was a place for pain, for torture and trauma, with its pendent meathooks, its drainage channels, buckets, duckboards, and its great slum family of caked rubber boots. The bathroom in the cloudy tower was the place for pleasure (look at the human shapes in the glass), the place where, nonetheless, he had learnt that pleasure could burn and sting, could throb and stab.

His talk with Whittaker had reopened a line of unease—the counter-intuition that his day with Gloria Beautyman was in some sense *homoerotic*. And the evidence for this was still mounting. First, Gloria was a sexual tomboy: she liked to climb all the trees and get her kneecaps scraped and dirty. Then there was the business (no small matter) of her being a cock. *Jorquil had the nerve to call me a* coquette, she said with what seemed to be genuine indignation. *D'you know what that word means? It's ridiculous. I'm five foot eight in my spikes.* And, so saying, she got off the bed and walked naked from the room; and Keith imagined her buttocks as a pair of gigantic testicles (from L. *testiculus,* lit. "a witness"—a witness to virility), not oval, but perfectly round, and sloping upward into the hard-on of her torso and the helmet of her head. Third, her name: Beautyman. Fourth, and most obviously, there was the beast with one back. Plus the sinister refinement. He had heard and read that women could be masochists. Gloria, though, had no interest in pain. She was not a masochist. But it prompted a question. Could a woman be a misogynist—in bed?

There was a sixth element too; it was revolutionary, and perhaps that was why he couldn't yet grasp it . . . Her secret. Her middle, the omphalos, like the smelted convexity at the centre of a shield.

Timmy, as White, played P-Q4; and so did black. White played P-QB4. The offered pawn: this was known as the Queen's Gambit. Timmy's long and shapely fingers, each with independent life, it seemed, now withdrew, and selected two items, a magazine and a pamphlet, from the stack of reading matter beside his chair. The pamphlet was called *One God;* the magazine was called *Gun Dog.* For the time being these periodicals remained unopened on his lap.

"So how did it go in Jerusalem—your work?" asked Keith, who was already stalling for time. In their penultimate game he had accepted the Queen's Gambit; and after Timmy pushed his king's pawn to the fourth rank, Keith's centre instantly disappeared; and five moves later his position—his mocking kingdom—was in ruins. Now he meekly played P-K3 and said, "Any joy?"

Timmy played N-QB3. "Sorry?"

"Converting the Jews."

"Well if you go by the figures, it all looks a bit of a frost. You see, our priority was to get those chaps with, you know, the chaps with the little berets on their heads. And the funny sideburns. And you see they're very narrow-minded."

Keith asked him how he meant.

"Well you go up to them, and you tell them, you know, there's another way. There's another way! And they just look at you as if you're . . . Are you sure you want to do that?"

"Touch."

"You see, they're *so* narrow-minded. It's amazing. You wouldn't believe."

Which might have been all very well. Except that Keith, for the fifth game in a row, was being given a terrible time on the chessboard; except that Timmy, that same summer, had taken a starred first in mathematics at the University of Cambridge; except that those long fingers of his, the night before, had raced and wriggled over the shaft of his cello, while the other hand carved out an impossibly agonised fugue (by J. S. Bach; Oona listened to it with tears seeping from her closed eyes). Keith said,

"Ooh that's sharp."

"And your bishop's *en prise* . . . You don't mind, do you? Some people find it offensive."

"No, I don't mind."

And Timmy sank back—and opened *Gun Dog* with a sudden grunt of interest . . . Keith, after much hesitation, put another helpless bodyguard in front of his king. Then Timmy looked up and instantly gave him the dreadful present, the dreadful friend, of his next move.

They heard the call for dinner.

"Draw?" said Timmy.

Keith took a last look at his position. The black pieces were huddled or scattered; and all of them broken-winged. Whereas White was in full array, like the massed hosts of heaven, burning with beauty and power.

"Resign," he said.

Timmy shrugged, and bent down to restore cohesion to his pile of periodicals. Periodicals of urgent interest to the born-again crowd, to the hook-and-bullet community . . . Chess and maths and music: these were the only spheres, Keith had read, in which you encountered *prodigies*. Human beings, that is to say, who were capable of creative originality before the onset of adolescence. There were no prodigies anywhere else. Because these closed systems did not depend on life: on experience of life. Religion too, maybe, was prodigious, when children dreamt, with all their authentic force, of Father Christmas and his sleigh.

Scheherazade came for Timmy's arm, and bore him off: her stately tread, his loutishly elegant sidle. Oona, Prentiss, and Gloria Beautyman were the last to filter from the room.

"Are you making progress," Keith asked, "with *Sense and Sensibility?*"

"No," said Gloria (in brocaded black velvet trousers, in waisted silk shirt), "I gave up after seven pages."

"Why's that?"

"She makes me feel like a child. All that truth. It frightens me. What she knows."

Oona was still half listening, as she moved off, so Keith said, "Can you believe she was younger than you when she wrote it? They think she wrote her first three novels when she was not yet one and twenty. The first at eighteen."

"Impossible."

"With so little experience of life. Why do you pinch your tits like that?" he said. "In the mirror. Why d'you do that? Because it feels nice?"

"No. Because it *looks* nice. The maid's room," she said matter-of-factly. "It's pretty well perfect for us. We could slip in there and I could do that thing we talked about. Where I push them together. Or are you too frightened of me? You should be, you know."

"I'm not too frightened of you."

"Yes, well there's only one catch with the maid's room," she said, and smiled. "It's got a maid in it. Madonna. Count your blessings. Think of yourself as Adriano to my Rita. You've had your birthday present."

He watched her go, in tight black: the ace of spades, this time. But now the ace was upside down . . .

The serial, day-long saturnalia with Gloria had not reminded him of anything in his past—except for that moment of disconnection, early on, in the bathroom, when the vertigo came (*Look what happens when I use two fingers*) and he felt the evaporation of all his courage. For just a moment, he couldn't face what was now to be. It reminded him of a much-pondered episode, in another bathroom, in 1962, with a certain Lizzyboo, the magically transgressive daughter of one of his mother's older friends. He was thirteen; and Lizzyboo was the same age as the emergent, the dawning Jane Austen. And she locked the door from the inside and said she was going to strip him for the shower. Little Keith was weeping and giggling as she went for his buttons—it was like being tickled to death. Then Lizzyboo put the key down the V of her sweater and leant towards him: *If you're in such a panic to run away, you can reach in and take it.* He sent out his hand on its mission—its mission to enter the future—and it wouldn't go. His hand was the hand of the mime artist when it runs up against the wall of invisible glass. He was thirteen, then; and she spared him (he was allowed to flee). And now he was twenty-one.

"Timmy's about to say grace," said Lily from the doorway. "And you wouldn't want to miss that."

Keith's attitude to religion was evolving, it seemed. He now had cause to thank God—to thank religion. *Ah, mille grazie, Dio. Aw, tantissime grazie, religione.* Many times, in her themed fantasies, Gloria returned to the idea of blasphemy. *In half an hour they're taking me to the church,* she soliloquised, slipping into her white cotton dress. *I'm getting married to an older man. How very fortunate that I'm still a virgin. Just so long as I don't crack now. Oh, hello. I didn't see you lying there . . .* And then again, at the very last, in the bathroom, in front of the mirror. Religion aroused Gloria Beautyman. And who could quarrel with it if it did that?

On his way to the dining room he remembered something else about Lizzyboo. It wasn't relevant to anything, he supposed; it was, on the other hand, true. She had a special skill—demonstrated on three or four occasions, in front of the family and other visitors, and once at a party (students, academics, professors of sociology and history), to general admiration and applause. Seated on the carpet, with her arms folded at shoulder height, with legs raised and bent, and using muscle power alone, Lizzyboo could bounce at speed across the length of the room on her arse. All the other girls tried it; and none of them could even get off the ground. Lizzyboo had a different relationship with gravity—gravity, whose desire is to get you down there in the centre of the earth.

Shaking his head (experience of life, life!), Keith took his place at the table between Gloria and Conchita, facing Jorquil, Lily, and Adriano.

3

THE POOL HUT

Mysteriously blasé about Frieda (and, later, about the likes of Scheherazade and Rita and Gloria Beautyman), the police were always abnormally interested in D. H. Lawrence. It wasn't only *Lady Chatterley* that caught their attention: so did *The Rainbow* (obscenity), and so did *Women in Love* (libel). And so did a very late book of verse (*grossly indecent,* according to the Home Secretary; *nauseous and disgusting,* according to the Director of Public Prosecutions). Sufficiently gay, deep down, to be thrown behind bars in the first place, Lawrence nonetheless ignored the ridicule of his friends and called this collection *Pansies*—a pun, he said, on *pensées.* There were two editions of *Pansies:* the expurgated and the original, in which the eleven dirtiest poems were preserved.

It was of course the unexpurgated version that Keith was looking for—and he found it, high up in the infinite library. Down below, Conchita sat at the davenport with her colouring books. He surveyed her: the tight black bun of her hair, the round shoulders, one hand flat on the sloping leather surface, the other reaching out to the simple prism of her pencils and crayons. Colouring books—seasides, ball gowns, flowers.

"Found it . . . How was Berlin?"

She shrugged and said, "We went to the Wall."

Unlike everyone else, Conchita had grown younger during the course of the summer. The precocious luminosity had passed over, and it no longer looked unusual—when she hastened to her colouring books, or when she attended, with the tenderest and most pitying of smiles, to Ducky and Lamby, to Patita and Corderito.

He climbed down, saying, "And how was Copenhagen? I've been there."

"Cold. And expensive. That's what—that's what Prentiss said."

". . . Say *expensive* again?"

"Expensive."

"Two months ago you'd have said *esspensive.* Say *magazines.*"

"Magazines."

"You've changed. You're an American now. And you're slimmer. It suits you."

The example of the apoplectic Dodo, he imagined, had taught caution to Conchita's appetite (at meal times she no longer asked for more). Yet the loss of weight, he thought, was also a loss of trouble, of inner heaviness; she no longer wore the weeds of mourning; Conchita wore white.

"Thanks . . . You've changed too."

"Oh really? Better or worse? . . . Worse, right? In what way?"

She was smiling as she dipped her head. "Your eyes are funny."

". . . Oh yeah. Conchita. Up in the tower. Does Scheherazade sometimes forget to unlock the bathroom door?"

"All the time."

After a moment Keith took his leave, and stepped out into the garden. The bees were gone, and nearly all the butterflies. The frogs no longer gurgled in their swamp. The sheep were gone, but the horses loyally remained. Keith flexed his brow. Beyond the paddock and on a higher slope he could see the figure of Adriano, slowly walking, with his neck bent down and his hands joined behind the small of his back.

"Oh, what can ail thee, knight-at-arms," Keith whispered—

> Oh, what can ail thee, knight-at-arms,
> Alone and palely loitering?
> The sedge is wither'd from the lake,
> And no birds sing.

I see a lily on thy brow, With anguish moist and fever-dew . . . The vines were bare and the lemon-houses shut. The squirrel's granary was full.

There's nothing *sinister* about it," said Gloria. "You're obsessed by this."

"No I'm not. I remarked on it at the time, and I'm mentioning it now."

"You've got a thing about it. What's the matter with you?"

"I don't think *I've* got a thing about it."

"Oh and I have, have I? God, you can certainly drone on . . . It's something a lot of girls do."

"In my limited experience," said Keith, giving a terrified thought to how the *refinement* would be greeted by, say, Lily, "it's not something a lot of girls do."

"Well that must be pure ignorance on their part. And they're fools if they don't know about it. They're fools. You're obsessed by this. All right. Ejaculate," she said, with a full-circle roll of the eyes, "con—"

"Wait. Isn't it ejacu-*late*? You say ejacu-*lut*."

"That's because it's the noun, not the verb. You fool. I'm *surrounded* by fools . . ."

Which was quite possibly the case. But this was certain: Gloria was surrounded by Italians—and Italians of the provincial bourgeoisie. Keith was in Montale, at the *casa signorile* of the *sindaco,* or the mayoral mansion. It was a lunch for fifty or sixty. Oona had prevailed on them to make up a contingent (Prentiss and Jorquil were paired together about twenty Italians away). They had all just sat through two long speeches, one by a hoary dignitary (whose chin was the size of a medium-length beard), and one by a fat soldier in full uniform (whose oxbow moustache reached up to the whites of his eyes). Now, with great weariness, Gloria was saying,

"*Ejaculate* . . . contains many of the same ingredients as face cream. And I mean expensive face cream. Lipids, amino acids, and proteins that tighten the skin. It's not a good moisturiser, which is why I wash it off after ten or fifteen minutes. But it's a very good exfoliant. And what does *exfoliant* mean?"

"I'm not sure. De-leafing?"

"Wrong again. The walking dictionary is wrong again. An *exfoliant* is something that removes dead cells. Ejaculate is the secret of eternal youth."

"I suppose that's logical in a way."

She said vindictively, "*Now* are you satisfied? . . . Oh, see that? Oh *no*. He's having the fish." And she rapped her palm on the cloth. "I give up. The stupid sod's having the fish!"

Keith glanced out across the diagonal length of the table. Jorq was watching with an appreciative loll of the chin as the waiter spoon-forked a wedge of salmon on to his plate.

"I despair. He just doesn't *listen*."

Feeling a frown forming on his face, Keith said, "The fish. Why . . . ?"

"Don't you know anything? Fish makes ejaculate smell *awful*. There. You didn't know that either, did you. Well then."

"Christ. I remember. *I'm sure the fish is perfectly fresh. But Keith and I are very happy with the lamb.*"

"What are you banging on about now?"

"You planned that part of it too. The night before my birthday. You planned it."

"Of course I planned it. Otherwise you'd have had the fish. Of course I planned it."

He said, "Well, planning's very important. You've shown me that."

"Naturally you can't control everything," she said sleepily (and even more affectlessly than usual). "It's a mistake to think you can. You know I get so furious, I get *so* furious when I go to a dinner party and they serve fish. And you're not given a choice. It means all the men are *hors de combat*. In effect. And of course you can't *say* anything. You just have to sit there and seethe. The presumption of it—it's unbelievable. Don't you think?"

"You make me see it in a new way. You often make me see things in a new way."

"Lord Jesus meek and mild. He's having seconds."

Keith finished his glass of champagne and said, "I tell you what, Gloria, you ought to have a drop of this. Then we can go in that room over there."

". . . Yes. Yes, you're well on your way. You're well on your way to being a thoroughly repellent young man. With your fizzy new eyes."

"Do you secretly work for the CIA or the KGB?"

"No."

"Are you secretly from another planet?"

"No."

"Are you secretly a boy?"

"No. I'm secretly a cock . . . In the future every girl will be like me. I'm just ahead of my time."

"Every girl will be a cock?"

"Oh no. It's given to very few," she said, "to be a cock. Now shut up and eat your meat."

He said, "The pool hut."

"Shut up and eat your meat."

Later, as he drank his coffee, he said,

"That was the best birthday present I ever had." He spoke for about five minutes, ending, "It was unforgettably wonderful. Thank you."

"Ah, a hint of appreciation at last . . . The pool hut, you say. Mm. It'd have to rain."

Of the many things Dodo suffered from (Dodo was a good example), narcissism would not be among them, Keith reflected, as he sat by the feminine fountain with *Pansies* on his lap. In all his adult life Lawrence never drew a breath without pain, and his lungs throttled him out of existence at the age of forty-four (last words: *Look at him on the bed there!*). The late poems in *Pansies* were about the opposite of narcissism, the end of narcissism—the human closing of it. Self-dissolution, and the feeling that his own flesh was no longer fit to be touched.

Lawrence was once handsome. Lawrence was once young. But to how many is it given, to stand naked before the mirror and say, with ardour, *Oh, I love me. Oh I love me so*—to how many?

Now Lily was asking if she could take the uniform off (and she also found fault with the blazing overhead light). The uniform, that of a French maid, was in many ways a success. But it left something to be desired. What? This. It didn't matter, in the new world, whether Lily loved Keith Nearing. The thing that mattered was whether Lily loved Lily. And she didn't—or not enough.

"Yeah go on then," he said.

"You didn't exert yourself, I notice," said Lily, throwing the fluffy duster aside and plucking at the bow of her white apron. "You didn't pretend to be a butler or a footman."

"No," he said. "I'm normal."

Why are uniforms good?

Two reasons, said Gloria. *It makes you less specific. I'm not Gloria Beautyman. I'm an air hostess. I'm a nurse. Nuns are best, but it's a lot of effort and hopeless without the buckly shoes and the wimple.*

"Lily. Let me tell you about Pansy. See if you think *that's* normal. I want your legal opinion." The expurgated Pansy, or the unexpurgated? He would see. "And in return," he said, "you can tell me about your switch to cool pants. Who suggested it? Harry? Tom?"

What's the other reason uniforms are good?

Well she's supposed to be doing something else, isn't she. She's already being very bad just by talking to you. You're keeping her from her work.

"No one suggested it," said Lily in the dark. "I decided."

"So you just thought, I know—I'll switch to cool pants."

Lily, during the sexual act (in her uptugged black skirt, her black stockings), did some sighing. Not high sighs, not low sighs—sighs at ground level. But now she was doing her sighing on the dungeon floor. She said,

"Well if you're going to go to bed with people just for the hell of it . . . If you're going to act like a man. You want to show you've thought it through. The pants send a signal."

He said, "And the signal is—we're coming off. Only uncool pants stay on." And this wasn't strictly true, he realised. Gloria herself had introduced him to a new technique: the retention of the lower under-garment during full intercourse. And Pansy also (in the unexpurgated version) contravened this rule. He said, "There's the self-cosseting as well. A signal of self-love. That's good."

"Funny," said Lily, "that Scheherazade had to be told about cool pants."

"And didn't just wisely decide on them. As you did, Lily. Pansy probably had to be told about cool pants—by Rita."

"Was she pretty, Pansy?"

"Not conventionally. But sweet. Long brown hair and a sweet face. Like a woodland creature." And a powerful body, Lily. With long brown legs in the incredibly short dresses and skirts mandated by Rita. "And it was the most amazing moment, Lily. In this entire . . ." He meant the revolution or the sea change. "In this entire thing, it was the most amazing moment of all."

Lily sighed and said, "Go on then."

"Well. Arn took me round to their place. And on the third date, Lily, I helped Pansy undress. And as I scrolled down her pants—she arched her back and I scrolled them down, and guess what."

"I knew it. She's one who never had pubic hair."

"*No*, Lily . . . The strange thing was—I could tell she didn't want to.

Even as she arched her back. She was going to. But she didn't want to. No volition. No I-wish."

"And she did? . . . Why?"

"She was—I don't know. Going along with the spirit of the times."

Lily said, "And you went through with it?"

"Of course I went through with it." To be perfectly frank with you, Lily, I'd had a very bad run. Which was set to resume, with Dilkash and then Doris. "Okay. Far from ideal. But of course I went through with it."

"And what was it like?"

"Straightforward." And then we lay there for about three hours, Lily. And listened to Rita putting Arn through it next door. "Straightforward."

"What you did. That's something like a breach of trust. In my legal opinion. You should have talked to her . . . I'm surprised you were *able.*"

"Oh fuck off, Lily. Talked to her?" Trying to get girls to do the next thing—that's taken up half my life. "I wasn't going to tell Pansy to put her pants on."

"It was sort of rape, in a way."

"No." This accusation had of course already been levelled at him. By the superego: by the voice of conscience, and culture—by the voices of the fathers and the presences of the mothers. "No. I suppose I was just poncing off the spirit of the times. That's all."

"And you went on going round there."

"Yeah. For months." I was in a situation. And to be completely honest, Lily, I reckoned I could plate my way out of it. I thought, I'll go down on Pansy a lot—and plate my way out of it. "I tried everything. I wrote her letters. I gave her presents." I tried to plate my way out of it. "And I told her I loved her. Which was true."

"Yeah. Slag for love . . . Maybe she liked you. She was just very shy and undemonstrative. Maybe she wanted to, really."

"That's kind, Lily. And I'd like to think it's true." But it wasn't, and Pansy proved it. That addendum, for now, Keith shelved. He lit a cigarette and said, "In Montale in the nightclub I asked Rita what happened to Pansy. My great hope was that she'd turned out to be gay. But the Dog said—scathingly, mind. Scathingly. The Dog said she was back up north and going to get married to her first love."

"So you and her . . . So it wasn't really in her nature. That's awful in a way, isn't it."

"Yes."

"People doing it when it's not in their nature. When they don't want to. It's worse, isn't it, than people not doing it when they do. Want to. Somehow."

"Yes."

"Silly name, Pansy."

"No it's not. It's just the name of a flower. Like your name."

". . . Hush now."

. . . When he was a child—nine, ten, eleven, twelve—every night, every single night, he put himself to sleep with fantasies of rescue. In these vivid, eager thoughts, it wasn't little girls he rescued but grown women: huge dancers and movie stars. And always two at a time. He waited in his rowing boat by the pier of the island fortress. Through the creaking and trickling he would make out the sound of their hurrying high heels on the lowered drawbridge, and then he would be helping them aboard—Bea in her ball gown, Lola in her leotard, and Keith in his school blazer and shorts. They fussed over him, and perhaps stroked his hair (no more), as he faithfully oared them to sanctuary.

Violet herself never appeared in these imaginings, but he always knew that she was the source of them—that she was the innocent captive, the wronged prisoner. The thoughts and feelings that had given him his aspirations of rescue he now cancelled. They were bitter to him.

He had been trying to enter it, for hours he had been trying to enter it, the world of dreams and death, from which all human energy comes. Around five he heard light-fingered rain as it dotted the thick glass.

Timmy, in a soiled silver dressing gown, sat unaccompanied at the kitchen table; he was doing the moron crossword in an old *Herald Tribune.* Gloria, in white T-shirt and her red cords, stood at the kitchen sink . . . As usual, Keith was amazed to see Timmy—Timmy going about his business on the ground floor. Why wasn't he always upstairs with Scheherazade? The same applied to Jorquil. Why wasn't he always upstairs with Gloria? But no. These two did other things. They even went out for long drives together, if you can credit it, in Jorquil's Jaguar, prospecting for churches and cheeses . . .

Keith wanted to ask Timmy a question. *This may sound funny, Timmy.*

But can you think of anything *religious about the pool hut?* Because Keith knew that this was the theme he needed. Now he came up behind Gloria and threw on both the taps. The weather, all by itself, was nearly noisy enough. He said,

"Look out there, Gloria. Brown sleet. And Jorq'll be gone all afternoon."

She glanced over her shoulder. Like Keith struggling with *Mornings in Mexico* or *Twilight in Italy,* Timmy was twisting around and scratching his hair.

"It's my last day. Please. Meet me in the pool hut. Please."

Gloria said politely, "What, to suck you off, I suppose." With high efficiency she went on sloshing out glasses, Edinburgh-style perhaps (palm cupped over rim). "I know. There'll be a brief smooch, and then I'll feel these two hands on my shoulders. *I* know."

Keith listened, but no inner voice counselled him. Where was it, that inner voice? Where did it come from? Was it the id (the *that:* the part of the mind that dealt with instinctive impulses and primary processes)? "I just want to kiss you *here,"* he said, and touched her midriff with his fingertips. "Once. You can come dressed up as Eve."

". . . Now that's an interesting question. How do you dress up as Eve?"

"Eve after the Fall, Gloria. In your fig leaf."

"Well. Terrifying weather, I admit. And it's not even white any more, is it. Dirty snow. Now let's think . . . I'll fly down there in my swimsuit and you can fuck me on the bench—get some towels laid out. Then I'll plunge in and fly back up. And Keith?"

"Yeah?"

"Speed will be of the essence. Ten thrusts, and that's all. Ten? Am I insane? No. Five. No, four. And for God's sake—be down there early and *get ready.* And hope the weather doesn't clear. Half past two. Let's synchronise our watches . . . Oh and Keith?"

"Yeah?"

"Which fig leaf?"

He told her the gold, and looked on as she walked away; then, weak with unreality, he poured himself a mug of coffee and stood over Timmy for a moment—the moron crossword, the virgin squares.

"Heinz," said Keith.

"I beg your pardon?"

"One across. *Big name in baked beans.*"

"What?"

"Heinz," said Keith, who, in his time, had eaten a great many baked beans. "Beanz Means Heinz."

"Spelt? . . . Good. Aha! Five down. *Alphabet's twenty-sixth.* Three letters beginning with zed . . . No, but that's a trick question, Keith. You see, this is an American newspaper. And that's a trick question. It looks simple, but it's not."

Keith's watch was quite normally going about its business. The hands said five to ten. Reasonably soon, then, it would be time to start getting ready in the pool hut.

"It's fiendish," said Timmy. "Here. One down. *Pluto's realm.* What *are* they on about? Four letters. Beginning with aitch."

He drew up a chair and said gently, "Let me help you with that."

Adriano was alone in one of the stiff, still anterooms.

And Keith, pacing past, might have hurried straight on; but he was caught and held by it—the vision of deliquescence. Adriano quietly weeping, like a child, with his face in his soaked hands; behind him, the window, and the wet hailstones splatting the leaded glass, and then the shivering diagonals of their tails; and beyond that, the third echelon, the bamboo curtain of soiled snow. The tears were creeping out through Adriano's bunched knuckles and even dripping on to his thighs. Who would have thought that the count had so many tears in him? Keith said his name and sat at his side on the low settee. Fairly soon it would be time to start getting ready in the pool hut.

After a moment Adriano looked up vaguely. There were his eyes, the lashes matted and dotted with droplets. "I—I laid it all before her," he said.

"No good?"

Hesitantly Adriano reached out a moist hand for Keith's cigarette; he puffed, he drew in, he coughed. And Keith wanted to put his arms around him—and even felt the urge to gather him on to his lap. Only the day before Keith had seen Adriano up on the high bar. Putting aside, for now, the frozen severities of his yoga, Adriano climbed the steel scaffold, where he folded himself tight, and whirled. And Keith thought of the large fly he had recently dispatched, and how it seemed to disappear into the maelstrom of its own death.

"I am not an innocent," said Adriano, and gave a long rippling sniff. "It may surprise you to hear, Quiche, that I have known well over a thousand women. Oh yes. A handicap, in such matters, may turn out to be no handicap at all. And great wealth helps, of course. I do try very hard, you know."

Keith was sceptical, but he wondered whether Adriano had had *time* to keep a list. "I'm sure you do, Adriano."

"Oh, I am not an innocent . . . At first, with Scheherazade, my concern was purely carnal. 'Love' was merely the trusted stratagem. Our visit to Luchino and Tybalt in Rome seemed to have its usual effect. Oh, I make no apologies. A very stubborn case, Scheherazade. Then Rita, and the necessary change of tactic. A slender hope—but worth trying, I thought. Oh, I make no apologies."

And Keith saw it all. Adriano's girls were hired actresses. Luchino and Tybalt were hired actors: in reality, in kitchen-sink, Adriano came from a long and unbroken line of midgets—rich and noble midgets, no doubt, but necessarily non-combatant. Keith shrugged and said, "And then, Adriano?"

"Then suddenly love surprised me. It was as the proverbial lightning strike. Gusts of feeling such as I have never known. Scheherazade. Scheherazade is a work of art."

"And now, Adriano?"

"What will I do? . . . I know that I cannot rest. Well then. I will go on a journey. In the wind I hear the word *Africa* . . ."

And Keith, steadying, thought, Oh yeah, you're a "character," aren't you. Go on then: join the Foreign Legion, the Legion of the Lost . . . Who were these *characters,* with their applied eccentricity? Jorquil was a character, and Timmy was turning into a character. Was high birth a prerequisite of being a character—giving you the latitude? No. Rita was a character. Rita was rich. Did you, then, need money to be a character? No. Because Gloria was a character; and Gloria, as she herself put it, was as poor as a church mouse.

"Goodbye, my friend. And please convey my respects to Kenrik. We may never meet again. I thank you for your kind words."

"Fare thee well, Adriano."

Already self-dosed on Azium (she would take another on the way to the airport), Lily was in their room on the dungeon floor, reading and resting and polishing her packing (which, tomorrow morning, she would duly sub-edit). The clock said twenty to twelve: very soon, then, it would be time to start getting ready in the pool hut. In the thrumming, pumping heat of the pool hut. It was no longer snowing and was now only raining. But raining with diligence and drive.

In fact the day cleared at the very end of the afternoon, giving way, after a final curtsey of drizzle, to a rose-and-yellow dusk. Keith took more notice of the sky that evening, conscious, perhaps, of having recently neglected it. Its pouting pinks, its brothelly oranges. The sun put in a guest appearance, with a beaming smile, then exited stage left. Just before curtain-fall, a ripe, hot, fully limbed Venus climbed up into the darkening blue. And he was thinking that there should be a sky for every one of us. Every one of us should have our own peculiar sky. What would mine look like? What would yours?

Gloria was out there sketching the graph lines of the mountains, on the west terrace, and Keith went and joined her with his beer. He said,

"Good evening, Gloria."

"Good evening, Keith."

". . . I was down there for four hours."

She didn't actually laugh, but she closed her eyes and tightened her lips and repeatedly cuffed her thigh with her hand. "Four hours. For four thrusts. No, that's good." She worked on with her head down.

"It's warm again," he said, and registered her low-cut emerald dress, the almost frivolous intricacy of her clavicles, and the warm hollows on either side of her throat.

"Now I wonder how it went," she said musingly. "Let's think. Down there nice and early, of course. Half past one? Making it all comfy with the towels. And quite hopeful until about half past three. Then less hopeful. Till you finally finished your wank," she said, using the eraser and brushing the flecks away with her little finger, "and came back up and told Lily how much you loved swimming in the rain."

In a voice of quiet concentration she went on,

"You're lucky. You're lucky she didn't come down and give you a nasty surprise. You'd have had a bit of explaining to do. Sitting there with your cock out in the middle of the afternoon. But that's your style, isn't it."

"My style?"

"Yes. Getting caught without even doing anything. Like with Scheherazade. And you didn't even have the nous to see she'd changed her mind. Then a great smelly drug in a glass of *prosecco*. Pathetic."

It was true: Lily's witch radar was by now an obsolescent contraption—compared to the great array, the transcontinental NORAD deployed by Gloria Beautyman. And Keith himself? The radio ham with his lone aerial, his ginger beard, his weight problem, his diabetes . . . And he parenthetically wondered: In the whole post-Marconi period, worldwide, has a radio ham *ever* had a girlfriend? Gloria, still drawing, rubbing, shading, said quietly,

"Sometimes, at breakfast, Lily looks at you, and then looks at me, and then looks at you again. And not fondly. What are you doing to her at night?"

"Oh you know. Livening things up a bit."

"Mm. On your birthday, I happened to bring off a perfect little crime. And now you're trying to get caught *after* the event. Trying to get caught . . . what's the word? Retroactively. Keith, you're a proven incompetent . . . Getting the *drinks* mixed up. You should be grateful I went quiet about your beer."

"Yes, thanks for that. I was surprised. I had no idea you even liked me." She said, "I don't."

". . . You don't?"

"No. You're very annoying. I just thought, Oh, *he'll* do. I had reasons of my own."

"What reasons?"

"I had some mental scores to settle. Put it this way. I saw an opportunity. Call it . . ." They heard Jorq's Jag on the gravel below. "Call it self-expression. Now I expect the stupid sod'll just fling his tuxedo on over his sweaty jumper. I'm going in. Is there anything else?"

Keith had the use of Gloria—of her divinatory powers, of what she knew—for another two or three minutes. And he wanted to ask her about Violet. But he chose an analogue, a shorter short story: he gave her the unexpurgated version.

"And then Rita and Pansy," he was soon saying, "kissed us goodbye in November and went back up north. Eight months later, Arn and I were going back to his place one night, and they were waiting for us on the street." Girlless Arn, girlless Keith—and Rita and Pansy in the open-topped MGB, like starlets at the Motor Show, like a vulgar dream. "We went up. There's only one room and one big bed and we all got into it."

"And was it—communal?"

"No. Pairs. Though we were all naked . . . Except for Pansy. Who kept her pants on."

"Oh dear."

"Yes. Oh dear. Yes very much oh dear."

"So you—so you cuddled Pansy, while inches away . . ."

"Yeah." While inches away, Gloria, the Dog was fucking the arse off Arn. "For four hours." It was the worst night of my life. Maybe it's why I'm here. Here with Lily in Italy. "And they did it again in the morning. While Pansy and I pretended to be asleep."

"Well what d'you want to know? Eight months up north. All the old stuff took hold. Not with Rita, obviously. With Pansy."

"But why'd she do it in the first place? Earlier. When she didn't want to."

And Gloria, ever surprising, said, "Echolalia. The meaningless repetition of what others say and do. Sexual echolalia. Pansy slept with you for one reason. Because if she didn't, Rita would sneer at her for not acting like a man."

Keith sat back.

"I was just thinking," she said as she closed her pad and sheathed her pencil. "Remember Whittaker? When he talked that night about the politicisation of bras? Well this was the politicisation of pants. The politicised pants were the ones that came off."

They stood. "Let me call you in London. Please."

She gathered the green dress around her. The square face with its pointed chin, the whiteness of eye, the whiteness of tooth. "Be sensible," she said. "Whenever you think of me, just think of yourself—in the pool hut. D'you want more of that? Or less?"

"Well. Less pool hut. More birthday."

"I thought so. Look at him. Wrecked for life. Keith, your birthday never happened. You imagined it. I went to the ruins."

Dinner-jacketed, beige-jumpered Jorquil, after not much huffing and shouldering, succeeded in freeing the glass door.

"And they were so romantic in the rain. Ah, here he is. We were just admiring Venus. Isn't she pretty tonight?"

He sat on under a sky now crazed with stars—stars in such wild profusion that the night had no idea what to do with them all. Actually, it did. Actually of course it did. We don't understand the stars, we don't understand the galaxy (how it formed). The night is more intelligent than we are—many Einsteins more intelligent. And so he sat on, under the intelligence of the night.

Gloria had a point. No, Keith wasn't at his most personable and convincing in the pool hut. Crouched on the bench with his swimsuit round his ankles. The pine cabinet as loud as an engine room. And as hot as a bakery . . .

She had a point about Pansy too. It was an important principle, and he assented to it: don't do *anything* for the crowd. And not *that,* not that, especially not that: the intimate, the innermost. It worked both ways. With sex, don't do it, and don't *don't* do it, for the crowd.

And Adriano—he was right too. When he said that Scheherazade was a work of art. In her whole being, in the way she looked, thought, and felt, ingenuous Scheherazade was like a work of art. And the same could not be said of Gloria Beautyman. Because a work of art has no designs on you. It may have its hopes, but a work of art has no designs.

It was already obvious that every hard and demanding adaptation would be falling to the girls. Not to the boys—who were all like that anyway. The boys could just go on being boys. It was the girls who had to choose. And ingenuousness was probably over. Maybe, in this new age, girls needed designs.

4

WHEN THEY HATE YOU
ALREADY

And life, for its part, went on behaving impeccably right up to and
including the last day of the summer. There were to be revelations,
recognitions, about-turns, come-uppances, and so on. And life, gener-
ally indifferent to these things, went ahead and obliged.

After breakfast they swam, and there was the occasion for a final dark-
spectacled glare at the two girls and their bodies, and he undertook it in
the spirit of an archivist—to shore up memory. The face and breasts of
Scheherazade filled him with grief; and the arse and the legs and the
arms and the tits and the omphalos and the box of Gloria Beautyman
filled him not with feelings so much as a set of impulses. The impulses
of the raptor. From L., lit. "plunderer," from *rapere* "seize." Keith had
entered the world again. Or so he liked to believe.

It was Timmy's first time to go and get the coffee; and when he
returned about an hour later, descending with the tray, he looked
slightly more puzzled than usual, and he said, as he slouched by in his
slippers,

"Someone telephoned. It was that chap Adriano. He's in Nairobi.
Very bad line."

"Nairobi?"

"You know, big game. The Serengeti. And now he's banged up in a
hospital in Nairobi."

"That's terrible," said Scheherazade.

Yes, true to character, Adriano had gone and coptered himself to
Kenya. And now Keith was wondering which way it would go. Half

eaten by headhunters or soldier ants? Or chomped practically in two by a hippopotamus. And for several seconds he thought that Adriano's fate was an artistic disappointment, because Timmy was saying,

"No, nothing very dramatic. It happened last night. He checked into the Serengeti VIP. *I* stayed at the Serengeti VIP. Don't you remember, old thing, when I came to rescue you in Bagamoyo? Marvellous place. Not Bagamoyo. I mean the Serengeti VIP. They wake you up at night with these little signals. Two chimes for a lion. You know, visible in the lit area. Three for a rhino. You know."

"But what happened to Adriano?"

"Oh Adriano. Oh, he pranged his jeep. Trying to find the car park. You see, it's on a hill, the Serengeti VIP. And it's, it's maddening because the car park . . . Anyway. He found it in the end, the car park. In a bit of a bait by then, no doubt. And he ran his jeep into a brick wall. And the poor chap's gone and shattered both his knees."

After a moment Keith's head gave a jolt of consent. That was Adriano. Forever brought to grief by the mere furniture of the high life. Timmy said,

"Is there anyone staying here called Kitsch?"

"That must be me."

"Sends his regards. As I say, it was a very bad line."

Then there were farewells, down at the pool, with Whittaker and Amen, and then, up in the castle, with Oona, Jorquil, Prentiss, and Conchita. And with Madonna and Eugenio.

Now travel, and the business (hardly less onerous in art than in life) of getting people from one place to another place.

Their taxi came exactly an hour early, while the church-goers were still at Santa Maria; the driver, Fulgencio, who had no forehead at all (flat black hair sloped directly into his eyebrows), drove them down to the deserted village and then cheerfully disappeared.

"Let's go and pay our last respects," Keith told Lily, "to the rat."

But when, on the sunken street, they drew level with the pet-shop window, they were greeted, not by the crimson eyes and the vermicular tail, but by a startling void.

"Sold!" said Lily.

"Maybe. Or maybe it just escaped."

"It's been bought. Somebody bought it."

The sign on the door said *chiuso*. Keith peered in and saw a woman in black with a mop and a red plastic bucket. He said, "Give me the . . ." He reached into Lily's bag for the pocket dictionary. "Here we are. *Il roditore*. The rodent."

"You're so horrible."

"Stay here." He went in to the sound of the chime. And he came out saying, "You're right. The lady, she mimed it—doling out banknotes. Imagine. Someone paid good money for a rat."

"Quite right. Poor little Adriano. Just think."

"Just think. It's lying on its back in some little parlour."

"With all the children stroking its little tummy. Just think."

And now the bells of Santa Maria declared peace in heaven, and Gloria and Scheherazade stepped out on to the leafy courtyard, their faces bright with immortality and joy, in their Sunday best. And with Timmy, too, sidling along behind.

Scheherazade (whom, very soon, Keith would touch—Keith would lightly kiss—for the first time), Scheherazade walked straight up and said, "You *missed* it. Oh, it was so tragic. *So* moving." She turned to Gloria with pleading eyes. "Tell them."

"Amen. At the pool."

"He came up to her at the pool. With his dark glasses off. He has such soulful eyes."

"And?"

"He told me he loved me," said Gloria drily, "and would always be my friend."

"And that he'd love her for the rest of his life. He looked so sad! Such spiritual eyes. And then Whittaker sort of helped him away."

While Scheherazade and Lily wept and necked and whispered goodbye, goodbye, goodbye, Keith fell into step with Gloria Beautyman.

"*Spiritual*," she said. "I humoured her, but really, Scheherazade's a sap. *Such soulful eyes* . . . Amen's just obsessed by my backside, that's all. I can tell. That's normal for queers—they've got some taste, God bless them. *Spiritual*. Spiritual, *my arse* . . . Well take a good look. You won't see me again."

They turned a corner and were miraculously alone—in a narrow square full of low-flying yellow birds and nothing and nobody else.

And the voice spoke. *Don't try and kiss her. Take her hand.* And put it where? *There. Go on. Just for a second.* There? Are you sure? Is it all right?

It's all right. The black gloves and the church bells make it all right. What do I tell her? And the voice spoke.

"Gloria, that's your power," he said. "That's *you.*"

She bared her teeth (those mysterious blue-tinged moonstones) and said, ". . . *Ich.*"

Then Italy was streaming past the windows with its strontian yellows and edenic greens and cobalt blues and madder-browns, madder-reds. At length Fulgencio's humped shoulders straightened them out on to the highway, raw mile upon raw mile, and knots of contorted factories periodically grew slowly nearer, with their cuboid flatblocks, where you saw half-naked children playing happily in the dirt.

Just before take-off Lily called for a pillow in a thick voice, and reached for Keith's hand. Then the plane trundled and raced, leant back and climbed, with the towers of the airport losing their balance and teetering over rearward, as Keith and Lily left behind them the land of Franca Viola . . .

They were not yet clear of the clouds when the plane seemed to settle. Lily's head struggled for comfort in the cusp of the porthole. Keith lit a cigarette.

"Conchita had an abortion in Amsterdam."

"What? Oh don't tell me that, Lily . . . Please don't say any more."

"Conchita had an abortion in Amsterdam. Four months. You must've noticed the bump was gone."

"I didn't think it was a *bump.* I just thought she'd lost weight. Please. Enough."

"Everyone was on tiptoe. I wondered if you'd ever twig. She was raped. Only Prentiss and Oona know who by."

"Please don't say any more."

"You didn't notice. You often don't see things very clearly. Do you . . . Oh for God's sake, why are we still in the clouds?"

He slumped back in his seat, and noticed, as an irrelevance now, that he was no longer afraid of flying. And this was just as well. When Keith closed his eyes he believed himself to be on an aircraft in heavy weather, with wind shear and muscular thermals; then he was on a boat, cresting up and sliding down, and scooping itself through violent seas; then he was in an express elevator that rocketed and plunged—but made no headway. On the horizontal line, they seemed, if anything, to be going backward. He looked out. The white wing strained, as if made of flesh and sinew. A winged horse, a horse with wings. Like the wings of the horse that took the Prophet to heaven. He again closed his eyes. Trying as hard as it could, the little plane laboured to take them up into the blue . . .

K*eith . . . Keith!*

It was eight fifteen in the evening, and he was in the shower of the significant bathroom. All the day's work was on his flesh, as the old order gave way to the new—all the repudiations and alterations, the riots and mutinies, all his seraphic sins. Would they ever come off? Like Pyrrhus at the fall of Troy, his

> dread and black complexion smeared
> With heraldry more dismal; head to foot
> Now is he total gules; horridly tricked
> With blood of fathers, mothers, daughters, sons,
> Baked and impasted . . . roasted in wrath and fire,
> And thus o'ersized with coagulate gore,
> With eyes like carbuncles, the hellish Pyrrhus
> Old grandsire Priam seeks.
>   Anon he finds him . . .

Keith stepped out. She was kneeling on the tiles, naked except for her velvet hat, her black veil, her crucifix.

In ten minutes they're taking me to a beguinage. *A* nunnery*—Nostra Dama Immacolata. I'm to become a bride of Christ . . . Come here.*

I can't.

Come here in front of the mirror. Yes you can . . . You know, the vulgar call me Shesus. Because I can raise you from the dead.

He went and stood dripping over her, dripping over her shoulders, her outcurved belly, her thighs: over the elastic soundness of Gloria Beautyman . . . Did he hear the scrape of wheels on gravel?

Watch. There! *Fuck me now and you'll never die.*

Yes, it was good in the mirror, realer in the mirror. You could see

297

what was happening very clearly. Uncluttered, unsullied by the other dimensions, which were those of depth and time.

"Keith . . . Keith!"

His eyes opened—Lily's face, grey against the grey. Of her bones were coral made: those were pearls that were her eyes.

"How can you sleep? Where's the blue sky for God's sake?"

"There isn't any. Not today."

"In ten minutes we'll both be dead. Tell me—"

The air hostess hurried by. "Seatbelt," she said.

"Can he still smoke?"

"He can still smoke."

"Are you sure?"

"Lily. You're keeping her from her work."

". . . We're both going to die. Tell me what happened with Gloria."

He said, with the assurance of perfect boredom, "Nothing happened. I was getting on with my trial review. She was sick."

"Okay, she was sick. Anyone could see that. But something happened. Sick as she was. You changed."

"Nothing happened."

"You changed."

"Why aren't you asleep?"

"Yes, why aren't I asleep. Listen. I'll help with Violet if you need me. But it's over."

He felt his Adam's apple rise and fall.

"You know, I still loved you. At first. Till you started looking like an undertaker around bedtime. Then you changed. Staring like a stick insect. It was quite hard work, getting to hate you. But I managed it. Thanks for a horrible summer."

"Oh don't be theatrical," he said coolly. "It wasn't all bad."

"No. It wasn't all bad. I slept with Kenrik. That was the good part."

"Prove it."

"All right. I said, *Tell him you can't remember.* Is that what he said? . . . I thought of you in the middle of it. I thought, Hysterical sex—that's what this *really is.*"

He lit another cigarette. On the night of their reunion, and at other times in the past, Keith had known hysterical sex with Lily. He had not known hysterical sex with Gloria Beautyman. Her voice changed, seeking a deeper and smoother register. But her composure was not otherwise inconvenienced (and around noon he himself stopped moaning and whimpering and started to concentrate). And it came to Keith now—her essential peculiarity. She went at it as if the sexual act, in all human history, had never even been suspected of leading to childbirth, as if everyone had immemorially known that it was by other means that you peopled the world. All the ancient colourations of significance and consequence had been bleached from it . . . Whenever he thought of her naked body (and this would go on being true), he saw something like a desert, he saw a beautiful Sahara, with its slopes and dunes and whorls, its shadows and sandy vapours and tricks of the light, its oases, its mirages. Keith said,

"Fair enough, Lily. If you want to play it that way. Adriano's been put down. All right? The rat's been put to sleep. The woman in the shop—she didn't mime cash. She put her finger to her throat and went like *that*. With a wet sound. Yes, I'm so horrible."

"Which is true?"

"Oh go on. You decide."

". . . You do have a bond with Conchita. Both her parents died on the same day."

"Please don't say any more."

Three or four times Lily took his hand. But only out of fear. Then the plane levelled out into the blue.

Gloria's voice changed, and once she bared her white teeth in what seemed to be savage indignation, and two or three times, as he lay waiting, she came towards him in some new combination of clothes and roles with a certain smile on her face. As if she had entered into a conspiracy with herself to make him happy . . .

How would you explain it: why couldn't you smoke in dreams? You could smoke almost anywhere you liked—except in churches, and rocket-refuelling bays, and most hospital delivery rooms, and so on. But dreams were non-smoking. Even when the situation would normally demand it, after moments of great tension (after a chase sequence, say, or while recovering from some horrific transformation); or after a long episode of strenuous swimming, or strenuous flying; or after a sudden bereavement, a sudden subtraction; or after successful sexual intercourse. And successful sexual intercourse in dreams, though rare, was not unknown. But you couldn't smoke in dreams.

They got off the bus at Victoria, and shallowly embraced, and went their different ways.

What do you do in a revolution? This. You grieve for what goes, you grant what stays, you greet what comes.

Nicholas always got there early.

And he didn't really like it if you got there early too. Half an hour, alone at the table with a book—this was also a component of his evening. Therefore Keith walked slowly. Kensington Church Street, Bayswater Road and the railing-girt northern border of Hyde Park, then Queensway—the Arab quarter, with its veiled women, its sceptical moustaches. And there were tourists (Americans), students, young mothers pushing on the crossbars of tall prams. It was now that Keith began to feel unfamiliar to himself, and faint, and disorganised in thought. But he shook his head with a shiver and blamed it on all the travel.

It was eight o'clock, and bright as day, yet London had assumed a sheepish and apprehensive expression, as cities will, he supposed, when seen with new eyes. For a moment, but only for a moment, the roads and pavements and crossings appeared to him to be full of movement and thrilling variety, full of different people going from one place to a different place, needing to go from that different place to this different place.

He wasn't to know it, of course. He wasn't to know it, but one humble and unsonorous adjective comprehensively described the London of 1970. Empty.

I've taken you there before, said Nicholas on the phone. *The restaurant that's only big enough for one person.* And his brother was already present, in the Italian grotto facing the cupola of the Greek Orthodox church in Moscow Road. Keith stayed outside for a moment and looked through the bloated glass—Nicholas, the single seated customer, at the central table, and doubtfully frowning over the page, with his drink, his olives. There was a time in Keith's childhood when Nicholas was absolutely everything—he filled the sky like a Saturn; and he still looked godlike (Keith thought), with his solid height, his determined face and his thick and longish dirty-blond hair; and with the aspect of someone who, apart from everything else, knew all about Sumerian pottery and Etruscan sculpture. He looked like what he would soon become—the foreign correspondent.

"My dear Little Keith. Yes. So *sweet* . . ."

Then there was the usual hugging and kissing, which often went on long enough to draw stares, because there was of course no reason on earth why they should look like brothers—the two Lawrences, T. E. and D. H.. Keith took his seat; he naturally intended to tell Nicholas everything, everything, as promised, as always—every bra-clip and zip-notch. Keith took his seat. And he had a one-second warning before he picked up a paper napkin and sneezed. He said (as only a brother would),

"Christ. Look at that. I came halfway by Tube. Two stops. And look at that. Black snot."

"That's London. Black snot," said Nicholas. "Welcome back. Listen. I was thinking—let's leave the Violet stuff for a bit later. Do you mind? I want your *Decameron*. Only there's . . ."

He meant the distraction of the tall young couple in the middle of the room—the young man and the young woman, whom Keith had slipped past or between on his approach. The restaurant, no bigger than the pool hut, with its four or five tables, seemed stalled or immobilised by the couple in the middle of the room. Giving a smile of irritation, Nicholas said quietly,

"Why don't they go away or, failing that, why don't they sit down? . . . Hearing about you and girls reminds me of reading *Peyton Place* when I was twelve. Or Harold Robbins. How long will you need?"

"Oh about an hour," he said. "It's terribly good."

"And you got away with it."

"I got away with it. Christ. I'd given up hope and then all my birthdays came at once. See, she was the—"

"Wait." He meant the young couple. ". . . Well let's get my side of it out of the way. Oh yeah." And Nicholas said stoically, "*The Dog* made a pass at me last night. And no sign of your Kenrik."

"He's back. We talked." And Kenrik, who was very dishonest but utterly undevious (a combination that would not serve him well), merely reiterated, on the phone, that he couldn't remember. Keith was happy to leave it at that—though *he* remembered Lily's light-footedness as she came across the lawn and kissed Kenrik on the lips . . . But the disquiet Keith felt was not connected to Kenrik or Lily. It was new. He had the sense that he would soon be pushing on a door, pushing on a door that wouldn't open. He sat up and said, "Kenrik *did* fuck the Dog, of course."

"Of course."

"In the tent on the very first night. And now at last we know why you mustn't. What kind of pass?"

"Oh. Oh, she just rammed her hand up my skirt, so to speak, and said, *Come on darling, you know you love it.*"

"She's a bloke, the Dog. And you made your excuses."

"Of course I made my excuses. *I'm* not going to fuck the Dog." He looked out (the young couple) and said, "Nothing's changed really. Still very happy with Jean. I'm a bit more famous now. I've decided I'm perfect for television."

"How's that?"

"Very well informed. Handsomer than any man has the right to be. And more left-wing than ever, by the way. Even more committed to putting the berks in the saddle."

"Rule by berks."

"Berk rule. I live for that day. Jean and I live for that day."

"You're interested in the wrong revolution, mate," said Keith. "Mine's the one that makes the world go round."

"So you keep saying. Christ."

He meant the young man and the young woman. Who must now be described, because they wouldn't sit down and they wouldn't go away. Like Nicholas, they were in their early-middle twenties: the man tall and long-haired and wearing a waisted black velvet suit, the woman tall and long-haired and wearing a waisted black velvet gown. They were unignorably tiptoeing and signalling and pointing and whispering, with their seating-plan and their questions for the solitary waiter. An evolved air was what they disseminated, and conscious gracefulness, and something of the lambent light of the fairy tale. Their shapely faces were of similar cast and you might have taken them for brother and sister if it wasn't for the way they touched, with long and lingering fingers . . . The tiny restaurant knew it was being found wanting, and the expression it wore was increasingly strained.

"Here they come."

Here they came, here they were. Stylishly they both sank to their haunches and gazed up at Nicholas and Keith, the woman with her second-best smile, the man—the man seeming to pout through the fine strands of his fringe. The crouch, the smile, the fringe, the pout: these had clearly enjoyed many successes in the matter of bending others to their will.

After a flirtatious pause the young man said, "You're going to hate us for this."

And Nicholas said, "We hate you already."

She was in disgrace, see—Gloria. She'd made a spectacle of herself at this lunch at the sex tycoon's." Keith itemised Gloria's trespasses. "But when she came she seemed incredibly prim. You know—Edinburgh. Old-fashioned. And not topless, like the others. These Victorian swimsuits. She told me later she'd made her mother bring them down from Scotland. Severe little thing with short black hair and an absolutely stupendous arse. Like you'd see on a billboard just before Valentine's Day . . ."

The foster-brothers, quite good-naturedly in the end, had obliged the tall young couple, and moved to a corner table—where they took delivery, five minutes later, of a terrified bottle of Valpolicella. So Keith was drinking a bit of that, and eating olives, and smoking (and Nicholas was of course smoking). And talking. But he was also experiencing a difficulty he did not understand. It was something like a liver attack—a thick presence had rigged itself up in the air above them. Keith could look at it, this presence. Keith could even look at himself. Keith saw Keith, sipping, gesturing, urging his narrative forward— the tight red cords, the young men of Ofanto, the bee sting by the pool, and then he was saying,

"I thought I was alone. With the castle all to myself. And I got out of bed and I . . . I got out of bed and I . . . She was in the bathroom."

What was it? He felt he had a bolt or a plug of hard air in his chest. He gulped, and gulped again.

"Gloria was in the bathroom. Holding up this light-blue dress. And she turned . . . But she was sick, see, Gloria. Reaction to the bee sting. That's what the doctor said. She turned and walked. And she wasn't wearing anything except her shoes. Amazing sight."

"Could you see it?"

"Her arse?"

"Well I'm assuming you could see her arse. The bee sting."

"Oh. No. I think it must have been quite far in. No. No, the real saga of the summer was something else. Me having my cock teased off," he said, "by Scheherazade."

And he told Nicholas about that, the glimpses of Scheherazade in T-shirt and ball gown, and about Lily giving her the cool pants, and about Dracula, and about the time he apparently fucked it all up by shitting on God—and he also managed to enliven things a bit, he thought, with some stuff on Kenrik and the Dog, and on the Dog and Adriano, and, oh yeah, on why you mustn't fuck the Dog.

"That's all?" said Nicholas, and glanced at his watch. "I don't understand. Forgive me, but what was it you got away with?"

Keith leant forward with sharp interest and heard Keith say, "I was leading up to that. There was another chick there all along—little Dodo."

Two cups of coffee and two torched sambucas were now brought to their table. The conversation had already turned to Violet, and Keith was no longer feeling very frightened. There was no longer a screen, like a gossamer washing line, between himself and his brother, between himself and the foreign correspondent. There was no longer a plug of air in his chest. Nicholas absented himself, and Keith stared into the twinned flames of the glasses: one fire for each eye. Across the way, the young man and the young woman, entwined in one another's limbs, presided over a party of ten . . .

One day in Italy Keith read about an alternative version of the myth of Narcissus. The variant set out to de-homosexualise the story, but introduced (as if in recompense) an alternative taboo: Narcissus had a twin sister, an *identica,* who died very young. When he leant over the untainted pool it was Narcissa whom he saw in the water. And it was thirst, and not self-love, that killed the glassy boy; he wouldn't drink, he wouldn't disturb that rapt reflection . . .

Keith now ran a check on his own reality. The person in the alcove with the telephone was his foster-brother. The book on the floor was about someone called Muhammad ibn Abd al-Wahhab. The waiter was fat. The young woman was kissing the young man, or the young man was kissing the young woman, and what was it like, when the other was the same, and you kissed yourself?

"Well let's see if we can draw things together." He regularly did this, Nicholas: he drew things together. "It's in the air that girls should act like boys. Now. There are some girls who *try* to act like boys. But they're old-school in their hearts. Your Pansy. Scheherazade perhaps. And there are girls who just—who just feel their way forward. Jean. Lily. And then there are girls who act more like boys than *boys* do. Molly Sims. And of course Rita. And—Violet."

"Yeah but . . . The other girls are aware of a kind of wave. And Violet's not a part of anything."

"Unless it's the wave of the healthy young girls. Violet marches with the healthy young girls."

Keith said, "She probably got that out of a magazine at the hairdresser's. Jesus, can she still read? Agony column. You know."

"Yeah. Dear Daphne. I'm seventeen, and I've had ninety-two boyfriends. Is this normal?"

"Yeah. Dear Violet. Don't worry. That's normal."

"Mm. It would've had to go something like, *A lively sexual appetite is normal. After all, you're a healthy young girl.*"

"You can see her staring at it. And feeling incredibly relieved. There it is in print."

"It's in print. It's official. She's a healthy young girl," said Nicholas. "That's all."

"Is she just extreme? Or is she *sui generis?*"

"*Sui generis?* You mean nuts."

"Well she's not nuts, is she. She's a lush, and a dyslexic, but she's not nuts when it comes to anything else. Still. The fact remains that Vi rapes fruits and dates football teams."

"She acts like a boy. Nature without nurture. Like Caliban. Like a Yahoo."

Keith said, "She acts like a very *bad* boy. And it's not in her interests. We've got to make her act more like a girl. And how do we do that? We can't. She's uncontrollable. We'd have to—we'd have to be the police."

"The secret police. Like the Cheka or the Stasi. With informers. The Committee for the Promotion of Virtue and the Prevention of Vice. Men with whips on street corners."

"We'd have to do nothing else. Is that what you're going to do? Do nothing else? Listen," said Keith. "I've decided what *I'm* going to do about Violet." I'm going to stop loving her, Nicholas. Because then it won't hurt. "Look, I'll muck in with my share, but I'm backing off. Emotionally. Don't get angry."

"I'm not. And I won't say it's because she isn't your blood. Because I know for a fact that you love her more than I do."

Keith sat there. Nicholas said,

"It won't work. What do you think you're going to do? You're just going to watch. Unemotionally. While Vi gets fucked to death."

". . . I'm not even going to watch. If I can help it. I'm not as brave as you are. I'm going to close my eyes. I'm going to *withdraw*."

"What?"

"I'm going to withdraw."

And Nicholas said, "Where to?"

There was a minute's silence. Then Nicholas looked at the time and said,

"Give it some more thought. Anyway. I haven't asked. How's that Lily?"

"Oh. Lily. The trial reunion was a mistake. Italy was a mistake." He looked around. The fishing nets tacked to the walls, the thatched Chianti bottles, the fat waiter with the outlandish pepper-grinder (the size of a supergalactic telescope), the framed photographs—churches, hunting scenes. "I wouldn't have missed it, not for the world. But Italy was a mistake. In the end. Anyway Lily dumped me. On the plane."

"My dear . . ."

"She said I'd changed. And she upped and dumped me on the plane. Don't worry—I'm relieved. I'm delighted. I'm free."

"Lily will always love her Keith."

"I don't want love. No, I do. But I want hysterical sex."

"As with Dodo."

"Forget Dodo . . . Why're you frowning like that? Listen, Nicholas, do I *look* any different?"

"Well you're lovely and brown . . ."

"My eyes." Keith felt himself tauten. Conchita, Lily, Gloria herself: *Look at him, with his new eyes.* And what about the eyes of Gloria Beautyman? Her ulterior eyes: from L., lit. "further, more distant." Gloria's ulterior eyes. "Has anything happened to them, my eyes?"

"They look—very clean. Against the tan. I don't know, slightly more protuberant. Now you mention it."

"Christ. More protuberant. You mean like a fucking stick insect?"

"Well they're not actually on stalks, your eyes. It's probably just because the whites are brighter. So no more Lily. Now a cleansing beer, and then . . ."

Nicholas drank his beer, called for the bill, queried it, paid it, and left. Keith sat on.

Some wine remained in the second bottle, and he poured himself a little of that. He leant forward, with his brow cupped in a cold hand. He supposed he was very tired . . .

The story about Gloria, the Beautyman myth, it just collapsed in his head, like a mocking kingdom made by sleep, and now all he had was its echo, a reverberating pang in the core of his mind.

Across the way, the table of ten, like a single creature, got to its feet. Out they all processed, in three pairs and a quartet. The waiter, in his tormented waistcoat, stood nodding and bowing at the door. Last to leave was the tall couple, the twins, in their ebony velvet.

Narcissus's sister. That version was not only incestuous—it was literalistic, and sentimental. The older story was the one that hurt and connected. Was he, was Keith, guilty of the disgusting vice of self-love? Well, he loved the rose of youth in himself, such as it was. That was forgivable. On the other hand, a surface, something of two dimensions, had transfixed him—not his own shape in the mirror but the shape that loomed at his side. *Oh, I love me.* Through her, for a day, he had loved himself, which he had never done before. Because there he was in the mirror too, standing behind her. The reflection—and also the echo: *Oh I love me so . . .*

With his broad back turned and a fat little fist on his hip, the waiter was staring at the abandoned tablecloth, which stared back up at him, soiled and conscience-stricken, now, with dozens, scores, of dirty glasses, with cigarettes crushed out in coffee saucers, with wrinkled napkins dropped in half-eaten ice creams . . . The waiter shook his head, sat down hard, and unbuttoned his vest. Then all fell still.

Gloria was *sui generis,* probably, no, come on, she was: not just a cock

307

but a religious cock—and a religious cock with an exorbitant secret. Now Keith, too, had a secret, also unrevealable. Could this be called trauma? A trauma was a secret you kept from yourself. And Gloria knew her secret; and he knew his . . . She had taught him much, he believed, about the place of sensibility in this new world. She had promoted him, he believed, in the chain of being. He was a laureate, he believed, a valedictorian, of the academy of Gloria Beautyman; and he was now poised to pass on her teachings to the young women of a grateful capital. I'm free, he thought.

The waiter's shadow told him that it was time to leave. I'm very tired, he said to himself. Italy, the castle, the summer months, and the events of that same morning (the church bells, the black gloves, the bared teeth, the *Ich*) seemed inconceivably distant, like childhood. Or like the time still earlier than childhood—infancy, babyhood. Or like 1948, when he wasn't even born.

But now Keith Nearing had freedom.

And so it was that he went out among the young women of London. Over the coming days, weeks, months, years, he went out into London, the streets, the lecture halls, the offices, the pubs, the caffs, the gatherings, under its roofs and chimneys. Under the urban trolls of the trees, under the city skies. And it was the strangest thing.

He went out among the young women of London. And it was the strangest thing. Each and every one of them hated him already.

CODA. LIFE.

I suppose it's only human. It's only human—the need to know what happened to them all.

Well, in 1971, Scheherazade . . . Wait. The old order gave way to the new—not easily, though; the revolution was a velvet revolution, but it wasn't bloodless; some came through, some more or less came through, and some went under. Some were all right, some were not all right, and some were somewhere in between. There were three orders, it seemed, like Dud, Possible, Vision, like the three grades of distance chosen by the mountains, like the three kinds of birds, the black, the yellow, and the magnets of the upper air, shaped like the head of an arrow . . . Some came through, some more or less came through, and some went under, but they all had their sexual trauma—all those present. All those who took the strange ride with the pregnant widow.

There will be more on their particular fates, but here, for now, are the abridged versions. Scheherazade was all right (with one qualification), and Timmy was all right, and Jorquil was more or less all right, and Conchita (he hoped and trusted) was all right, and Whittaker and Amen were all right, and Nicholas was all right, and Lily was all right in the end.

On the other hand, Adriano was somewhere in between, and Rita was not quite all right (and Molly Sims, incidentally, was not quite all right in the same way), and Kenrik was definitely not all right, and Violet was definitely not all right, and Gloria, too, was not all right. Dodo (this is only a guess, because nobody ever saw her again) was not all right. Prentiss and Oona were all right until 1994 and 1998 respectively. Then they were dead.

As for Keith . . . Well, it is 2009, now, not 2003, when, reasonably novelistically, 1970 caught up with him, all at once. This unfortunate crisis—his "N. B.," as his third wife so gently and aptly called it—was in the past, and he was all right.

The Italian summer—that was the only passage in his whole existence that ever felt like a novel. It had chronology and truth (it did happen). But it also boasted the unities of time, place, and action; it aspired to at least partial coherence; it had some shape, some pattern, with its echelons, its bestiaries. Once that was over, all he had was truth and chronology—and, oh yes, the inherently tragic shape (rise, crest, fall), like the mouth on a tragic mask: and this is a face that is common to everybody who doesn't die young.

But it turns out that there's another way of doing things, another mode, another *genre.* And I hereby christen it Life.

Life is the world of Well Anyway, and Which Reminds Me, and He Said, She Said.

Life has no time for the exalted proprieties, the ornate contrivances, and the intense stylisations of kitchen-sink.

Life is not a court shoe, with its narrowing heel and arched sole; Life is the tasteless trotter down there at the other end of your leg.

Life is made up as it goes along. It can never be rewritten. It can never be revised.

Life comes in the form of sixteen-hour units, between waking up and going to sleep, between escaping from the unreal and re-embracing the unreal. There are over three hundred and sixty such units in every year.

Gloria Beautyman, at least, will be giving us something that Life badly needs. Plot.

Some of the Things That
Happened Between
1970 and 1974

For forty months, beginning with that September when his eyes were very clear, Keith lived in Larkinland — fish-grey, monkey-brown, the land of sexual dearth. The most salient feature of Larkinland is that all women, after a few seconds, can tell that that's where you live — in Larkinland.

At first, all his moves on girls were met by a rearing-back or a twisting-away or an emphatic shake of the head. One very articulate postgraduate, having rebuffed him, went on to say that he exuded a strange mixture of electricity and ice. "As if you've got PMT," she said. That phase passed. His advances became tentative (he reached out a hand), then quietly vocal, then impotently telepathic. That opposites attract is not among the rules of amatory physics. In 1971, and again in 1973, he had successive entanglements with two nervous wrecks from the Poetry Society (round the corner from his dank flat in Earls Court): its treasurer, Joy, and then Patience, the most glazed and tenacious attendee of its twice-weekly readings. In 1972, and again in 1973, he became familiar with the narrow staircase that led to a certain attic flat in Fulham Broadway. Inside it was a publisher's reader of a certain age called Winifred, with her cardigan, her sweet sherry, her John Cowper Powys, her tic.

He trolled through his past of course, but Ashraf was in Isfahan, Dilkash was in Islamabad, and Doris was in Islington (and he had a drink with her there, in a pub — with her and her boyfriend). Every five or six months he spent a celibate night with Lily (while she was briefly between affairs). He tried to get her back, naturally, and she pitied him; but she wasn't coming back.

1974 was seven days away (it was Christmas Eve) when he had his first re-encounter with Gloria Beautyman.

It is the kind of gathering convened by the more bohemian sector of the moneyed young—the kind of gathering at which Keith is by now very seldom to be seen. I won't describe it (humid pools of velvet and luxurious heads of hair). Gloria arrives late, and tours the room, moving through a thoroughly grasped and mastered milieu. Physically she makes you think of Viola in *Twelfth Night* or Rosalind in *As You Like It*: a girl transparently and playfully disguised as a boy. Hair up under the cocked hat, a tight silk trouser suit of Lincoln green.

He is waiting in a passageway. And this is their opening exchange.

"Are you pretending you don't remember me? Is that what you're doing?"

". . . I find I fail to understand your tone."

"Did you get my messages? Did you get my letters? How about dinner one night? Or lunch. Keep the afternoon free. Suppose there's no chance of that."

". . . No. None. To be honest, I'm astounded you've got the nerve to ask."

"Yeah, stick to your own kind. Okay. Tell me. How's the world of cheese?" She takes a step back. And for four or five excruciating seconds he feels himself being *painted* by her radar—not just scanned, but exactly targeted. "Wait," he says. "I'm sorry. Don't."

"My God. The curse of Onan is upon him. My God. You can almost smell it."

Keith's new suit (which cost six quid from Take Six) hugs him in its fire.

"Ooh, I want to talk to you," she says. "Stay here. This is fascinating. I feel—I feel like someone slowing down to look at a car crash. You know. Ghoulish curiosity."

Gloria turns and walks . . . And yes, it is too big, *much* too big, as Lily always insisted; but it now strikes his famished gaze as an achievement on an epic and terrifying scale, like the Chinese Revolution or the rise of Islam or the colonisation of the Americas. He watches her move from guest to guest. Men looked at Gloria, now, and automatically wondered what was happening on the other side of her clothes—the concavities and convexities on the other side of her clothes. And yes, she is astronomically remote from him, now, far, far beyond the capabilities of his naked eye.

She keeps going away and coming back again, but she tells him many things that night.

"Oh *dear . . .* And you were quite sweet to girls in Italy. Because girls were quite sweet to you. But it's all gone terribly wrong, hasn't it. With you and girls. And this is only the beginning."

Beyond a certain level of sexual failure, she goes on to explain, a part of the male mind gets to work on hating women. And women sense this. It's like a self-fulfilling prophesy, she says. And this he already knew. Larkinland, it self-fulfils, it self-perpetuates, it self-defeats.

"And it can only get worse. Ah. Now see that beautiful youth who's just come in, the tall one with the golden hair? That's Huw. The one with the castle in Wales."

"Typical, that is. Yeah. The economic basis of society."

". . . You can't help yourself, can you. You only *sound* as if you're being a nightmare on purpose. One's instinct is to walk away. My legs want to walk away. But it's the festive season. Goodwill to all men. Are you ready for some advice?"

He stands there, smoking, with his head down. "Tell me. Help me."

"All right. Take a turn round the room. Hover near the girls you like most. I'm going to go and kiss my fiancé, but I'll be watching."

Ten minutes later she's telling him something that at least sounds quite symmetrical: the prettier the girls are, the uglier he looks—the more furtive, the more rancorous.

"You seemed perfectly at ease near Petronella. The one in the smock with the port-wine stain. And Monica. The one with the slight harelip. Mm. Your eyes aren't fizzy like they were, but something's gone wrong with your mouth."

"Show me," he says. She shows him. "Christ. Gloria, how can I get out?"

"Well you're so far gone, that's the trouble. Are you still a student? No? Then I'm sorry, but I'm assuming you're a complete flop at what you do."

This was actually very far from being the case. On graduation, with his exceptional degree, Keith applied for jobs more or less at random— he worked in an antique shop, an art gallery; for two months he worked in an advertising agency, Derwent and Digby, in Berkeley Square. Then he stopped being a trainee copywriter, and became a trainee assistant at the *Literary Supplement.* He was now a full editor there, while also publishing uncannily mature pieces on critical theory in the *Observer,* the *Listener,* and the *Statesman and Nation.* About a dozen of his poems had appeared in various periodicals, and he was the recipient of an encouraging note from Neil Darlington, editor of *The Little Magazine* and co-publisher of a series of pamphlets called Slim Volumes . . .

"Oh I see. Hopeless," she says. "You've got to earn more, Keith. And lose that dank look. There are exceptions, but girls want to go up in the world, not down. Do you remember that touching ballad? 'If I were a carpenter and you were a lady.'"

"'Would you marry me anyway, would you have my baby.'"

"Well the answer to that question is *certainly not.* The funny thing is, all you need is one pretty girlfriend and the others'll follow."

He asks why this is.

"Why? Because the rules of attraction are vaguer with girls. Because men's looks matter less. So we keep an eye out for the smoke signals. We listen to the tom-toms. If one of us—a pretty one—thinks you'll do, then we take notice. Here and now I could make you halfway attractive. A walk round the room would do it."

He sighs. "Oh Robin Hood. In your Sherwood green. You take from the rich and give to the poor. Walk me round . . . I'll pay you a hundred quid."

And Gloria, ever surprising, says, "Have you got it on you? Mm. No. It's quite a performance, and Huw'd get vexed."

"Then I'm going home. So it's to be Huw, is it?"

"Probably. He's perfect. Apart from the hellhag mother. Who hates me . . . I'm twenty-six you know. Tick-tock goes the clock."

"Which reminds me." And in a weak voice he tells her about Scheherazade. Already married (to Timmy), already the mother of two (Jimmy and Millie), already devout (according to Lily). She shrugs, and he says, "Time to go." The voice within him (Christ, what a croak it is) makes a suggestion. It doesn't sound much to Keith, but he says, "Well, festive wishes. Uh, it's traditional, isn't it, to leave something out for Santa. Don't bother with a mince pie. Just give him a beautiful sight. You praying naked on your knees."

Her colour, her shadowy bronze, intensifies. "How d'you know I pray naked?"

"You told me. In the bathroom."

"What bathroom?"

"You remember. You turned, holding the blue dress. And I said, 'No bee sting.' "

"Oh what nonsense. Then what?"

"You bent over the towel rack and said, 'It's actually quite far in.' "

"So you still think that really happened? No, Keith, you dreamt it. I remember the bee sting, though. How could I forget? And it's true that I really do genuinely hate ruins. Good luck. You know, all this stuff is like conkers. Do you remember conkers? A mere oner beats a twenty-fiver, and suddenly it's a twenty-sixer. You see, you can't get a pretty girlfriend until you get a pretty girlfriend. I know. It's a right bastard."

"Yes, isn't it. And how's your secret? Still well?"

"Happy Christmas to you."

He walked in the snow down Kensington High Street. What kind of poet was Keith Nearing, so far? He was a minor exponent of humorous self-deprecation (was there any other culture on earth that went in for this?). He wasn't an Acmeist or a surrealist. He was of the school of the Sexual Losers, the Duds, the Toads, whose laureate and hero was of course Philip Larkin. Celebrated poets could get girls, sometimes many girls (there were poets who looked like Quasimodo and behaved like Casanova), but they seemed to evade prettiness, or shied away from it because it was just too obvious. Larkin's women had their world,

> where they work, and age, and put off men
> By being unattractive, or too shy,
> Or having morals . . .

So, with a kind of slothful heroism, Larkin inhabited Larkinland, and wrote the poems that sang of it. And I'm not going to do that, Keith decided, as he turned left towards Earls Court. Because otherwise I'll have nothing to think about when I'm old. Anyway, he didn't *want* to be that kind of poet. He wanted to be romantic, like Neil Darlington ("The storm rolls through me as your mouth opens"). But Keith didn't have anything to be romantic about.

In those days the capital shut down for a week, at midnight, on Christmas Eve. It went *black*. God had his hand poised above the switch: any second the lights would go out and wouldn't come on again until 1974.

A Certain Occasion
in 1975

To his personal assistant, and then to his secretary, Keith bids good-bye, and rides down in the soundless cube of mirrors from the four-teenth floor of Derwent and Digby. On the flat plain of the atrium Digby in his bomber jacket and Derwent in his silk poncho are waiting for their car. Derwent and Digby are first cousins, and wrote a first novel each, long ago . . .

"No, I can't," says Keith. "I'm meeting a pretty girl. My sister Violet. In Khartoum."

"Wise man. Try the Zombie."

And Keith steps out into the sparsity and human colourlessness of rush-hour London in 1975.

When he tendered his resignation at Derwent and Digby, in early 1972, first Digby and then Derwent took him out to lunch and spoke of their sadness at losing someone "so exceptionally gifted"—i.e., some-one so good at peddling non-essentials. "The money's the same at the *Lit Supp,*" he said, for something to say. "Believe me," said Derwent, and Digby, "it won't go on being." There was truth in this. Keith now had a mortgage on a sizeable maisonette in Notting Hill, he drove a new German car, he wore—this night—a scarf and overcoat of black cashmere.

By far the worst bit of the transition was telling Nicholas. Oh, no, Keith wouldn't want to go through that again. Part of the trouble was that he couldn't quite tell Nicholas *why.* "Well. You're still my brother," said Nicholas, at four o'clock in the morning. Keith, these days, still wrote criticism, but the verse stopped coming almost imme-diately, as he knew it would. He was still a rhymer, of sorts. You don't have to wait—till After Eight. Hey, fella, Fruitella. His salary had octupled in nineteen months. The only poet who still gave him the time of day was the charming, handsome, litigious, drink-drenched, debt-ridden, women-infested Neil Darlington, the editor of *The Little Magazine*. Keith told Neil why. *Why* might not have impressed Nicholas anyway.

There were girls now. There almost always was a girl. Colleagues—a temp, a market researcher, a typist, a junior account manager . . . This remained the import of Gloria's imitation of him (of his mouth) on Christmas Eve, 1973: the beak was back. Now the beak was gone again. Out of Dud-dom, he was gradually surfacing as a Low Possible, but a Low Possible equipped with patience, humility, and cash.

He was out of Larkinland. Sometimes he felt like an ecstatic refugee. He had sought asylum, and found it. A lengthy process, getting out of Larkinland (he dispensed many bribes). The months in the border holding-camp, the hostile interrogations and health checks; and for many hours they frowned at his documents and his visa. He walked through the gates under the watchtower, the searchlights and the razor wire. He could still hear the dogs. Someone blew a whistle and he turned. He kept walking. He was out.

His celibate nights with Lily had evolved into weekends—not dirty weekends exactly, but not celibate either—in Brighton, Paris, Amsterdam.

As he walks through Mayfair and then across trafficless Piccadilly and past the Ritz, to St. James's, swinging a pair of soft leather gloves in his right hand (it is early October), he finds himself looking forward to seeing his younger sister. More in his heart than in his person, he has been keeping his regulated, geometrical distance, unlike his brother, who actually had Violet come and live with him in his two-room flat in Paddington for three terrible months in 1974.

"Every morning—the crowbar," said Nicholas. In other words, the first thing you did each day was lever her out from under the burglar/builder/beggar/bouncer (or—last resort—the cabbie) she'd brought home with her the night before. Violet, it seemed, was moving on from the proletariat and heading for the underclass (or what used to be called the residuum). Next, early in the summer that had just ended, she turned the colour of English mustard (jaundice). There was a hospitalisation followed by a costly convalescence at a dry-out spa in Kent called the Parsonage, paid for by Keith. Keith paid for all the shrinks and therapists too (until Violet put her foot down and said it was a waste of time). He was always giving Violet money. He did it eagerly. Writing a cheque only took a few seconds, and it didn't hurt.

He had gone to visit her in September, the train, the fields, the motionless cows like pieces of a jigsaw waiting to be put together, the manor house with the green gables, Violet in the refectory playing Hangman with a fellow recoverer, the walk in the grounds under the alerting blue, where she took his hand, as of course she used to do in childhood . . . Whereas Keith's minimal handsomeness had been entirely erased by his years of famine (his years of want), Violet's beauty was fully restored, her nose, her mouth, her chin, smoothly eliding into one another. There was even talk of a possible marriage — to someone twice her age (forty-three), an admirer, a protector, a redeemer.

Tonight there would be fruit cocktails, a show (she loved a show, and he had good tickets for *The Boy Friend*), then dinner at Trader Vic's.

Now Keith enters Khartoum, pushing on the tinted glass door. Their evening, as a familiar and intelligible event, will last a single minute. And the single minute isn't any good either. No, untrue, unfair: the opening three seconds are perfectly fine, as he spots her soft blonde shape (a whiteclad profile) on a stool at the circular steel counter.

What is happening to her face? What is happening to its sinews and tendons? Then he sees that she is in fact engaged in a more or less recognisable human activity. The first word that comes into his head is an adjective: talentless. The second is an intensifier: fantastically. Because what Violet is accomplishing, or imagines she's accomplishing, is this: the sexual bewitchment of the bartender.

Who, with his ponytail, his sleeveless black T-shirt, his ugly muscles, keeps turning to glance at her, not in reciprocation, but in disbelief. To see if she's still doing it. And she's still doing it, still doing it, still hooding her eyes and leering and sneering and licking her lips. Keith steps forward.

"Violet."

"Hi Key," she says and slides from her stool.

"Oh Vi!"

Like a globule of yolk and albumen freed from its shell, Violet drops all at once, and lies there, forming a circular pool — the egg-white now flat in the pan, with her yellow head in the middle of it. Five minutes later he has at last installed her in a leather armchair, and she is saying, "Home. Home."

Keith goes and calls Nicholas, who gives him three different and widely separated addresses. As he is paying the bill ("Can this be right?"), he sees that the leather armchair is empty. The barman points. Keith swings the glass door open, and Violet is under his feet on her hands and knees, head tucked down, being copiously and noisily sick.

Soon afterwards they are in a series of taxis, going to Cold Blow Lane in the Isle of Dogs, going to the Mile End Road, going to Orpington Avenue, N19. She badly wants her bed, she badly wants her room-mate, Veronique. But before she can go there she needs her key, they need to find the key.

The bar bill at Khartoum — it was the kind of tab he might have settled after two hours with Nicholas or even Kenrik. "Can this be right?" The barman widened his eyes (and then pointed). Violet had drunk seven Martinis in less than half an hour.

Entering his bed, in the attractive maisonette, he parted Iris's Irish hair (like thick marmalade) at the back of her neck — so that he could rest his cheek against her rusty down.

Apart from Violet (Violet's shadow in his mind), was he happy? He wanted to say yes. But the two hearts, his upper (fixed or steady-state), his lower (extensile, or supposedly so), were unaligned. His had become a traitorous eros. The question, sad to say, of the *hard-on:* he couldn't get one, or when he got one he couldn't keep one. And he didn't love them, his girls. And he used to love them all. I'll say this for myself (he thought): I am no longer a bully in the bedroom, I no longer try to force girls out of their nature. You need a proper hard-on to do that. And so he subsisted, with his cross-purposed blood.

All these flowers, the irises, the pansies, the lilies, the violets. And himself — and his rose of youth. O rose, thou art sick . . .

> Oh rose, thou art sick;
> The invisible worm
> That flies in the night,
> In the howling storm,

Hath found out thy bed
Of crimson joy,
And her dark secret love
Doth thy life destroy.

. . . Keith rolled onto his back. Out in London that night, he and Violet had to find something. They had to find Violet's key. That took until half past midnight. They found out where the key was, they found the key. Then they had to find out where it was the key to.

A Couple of
Developments in 1976

In July 1976 Keith hired Gloria Beautyman for a thousand pounds a week. Her job was to pretend to be his girlfriend . . .

It's April, and Gloria is walking across Holland Park, with briskness and address, to get from one end of it to the other; whereas Keith is just walking, and going nowhere. He hails her. They fall into step.

"Nice *hat,*" she concedes (as he tips towards her his charcoal Borsalino). "Have you lost your bedsit blues?"

"I took your advice." And he explains. His curriculum vitae, his course of life.

"Mm," she says. "But earned money never lasts."

"Are you married yet? . . . Well I expect you'll be off to Canterbury anyway."

"What are you talking about?"

"When that April, Gloria, with its showers sweet, the drought of March hath pierced to the root, then people long to go on pilgrimages."

"Do they now."

"No they don't. Not any more. That's the trouble. They just sigh and think, April is the cruellest month. Breeding lilacs out of the dead land, Gloria. Mixing memory and desire."

". . . You ought to stop all that, you know. It just makes girls feel ignorant."

"You're right. Anyway, I've given up poetry. It's given me up."

For the first time her pace slows, and she smiles his way—as if he's done a good thing. And even Lily, utilitarian Lily, was saddened by this news. When he visited the part of his mind where the poems used to come from, he was met with the kind of silence that follows a violently slammed door.

"Because it only works if you're penniless?" says Gloria. "There've been rich poets, surely."

"True. But the Earl of Rochester didn't work at Derwent and Digby." Whose corridors, he reflects, are thick with silenced poets, blocked novelists, concussed playwrights.

"And how's it going with the girls?"

"Not too bad. But I can't get the girls I really want. Girls like you."

"What are girls like me like?"

"Girls who look in the mirror and say 'I love me so.' Girls with glossy black hair. Shoeshine hair. Your hair's like a mirror. I could see my face in it. This is the first time you've shown it to me, your hair. Girls with glossy hair and a secret."

"Just as I foretold. Ruined for life."

"You spoilt me, but I'm over you now. I want Penny in Public Relations. I want Pamela in Personnel. Are you married yet? My sister's getting married. Are you?"

"It's hot suddenly."

And suddenly she stops, turns, and opens her coat . . . In novels, weather and landscape answer to mood. Life isn't like that. But now a warm breeze, a hot wind, sweeps past them, and there is minute precipitation, like a humid vapour, and within seconds Gloria's white cotton top is a clinging transparency, the complementary breasts the shape of teardrops, the artistic omphalos. Memory and desire come up from the ground, from the paved path, from the dead land, and take him by the back of the knees. He says,

"Remember—remember you told me something. You could walk me round the room, and girls would look at me differently. Remember?"

And he made his offer.

"Penny. Pamela. There are two office parties coming up. I want Penny in Public Relations, I want Pamela in Personnel. Come to the summer parties. And come and have lunch with me in Berkeley Square—just once or twice. Collect me from work. Pretend to be my girlfriend."

"It's not enough money."

"I'll double it. Let me give you my card."

By now he had been to America—to New York, to Los Angeles—and he knew much more about the genre (the type, the mode) that Gloria in some sense belonged to.

Here is the youngish woman, apparently held together by the cords of her scars and the lattice of her cellulite, and sometimes tattooed to the thickness of a tarot card. Here is the youngish man, with his brute tumescence, his lantern jaw, his ignoble brow.

Now fade. Here is Keith, a towel round his waist. Here is Gloria, holding up a blue dress as if assessing it for length. Then the look she gives him just before she turns. As if he has come to deliver the pizza or drain the swimming pool. Then the physical interchange—"the act by which love would be transmitted," as one observer put it, "if there *were* any."

Of course, Gloria was non-generic in two vital respects. The first was her use of the humorous, the droll (with Gloria sex had been *funny*—because of what it told you about their natures, his, hers). Up there on the screen, with its gruesome colours, Day-Glo and wax-museum, a single genuine smile and the whole illusion would flee with a shriek. Gloria's second anomaly was her beauty. She combined beauty and dirt, like city snow. And then there was the religion.

"We have a deal," she said on the phone. "The thing is, Huw's seeing too much of an old girlfriend. Not what you think, but he needs a good fright. Now when should I start pretending?"

Keith replaced the receiver and thought of the white T-shirt in Holland Park. The meteorological or heavenly connivance. No-see-um raindrops, and her torso moulded by the pornodew.

Violet was a June bride.

Karl Shackleton, all atremble on his walking sticks, gave her away. There was a lunch at the house of her faithful admirer, unexceptionable Francis, kind, educated. "We've no choice," said Nicholas, "but to see him as a force for good." Francis's widowed mother was present, among furnishings as gaunt as her person. Then they all waved the newly-weds off on their honeymoon—the Austin Princess with its white streamers. Violet was twenty-two.

There were some difficulties early on, Keith heard. Then the marriage seemed to settle. But by July the house was undergoing renovation. Violet had the builders in.

"Huh-*hm*," says Gloria, by way of polite introduction, as he drives her to the first summer party—whose setting is an opulent "hermaphrodite brig" (a two-masted sailing ship) on the River Thames. "It may embarrass you to learn what the trick is. I'll do all the usual stuff like stroking and nuzzling. But this is the trick. I have to stare adoringly all the time in the general direction of your cock."

Keith, at the wheel, says, "Are you sure?"

"Of course I'm sure. Funnily enough there was a . . . I thought I was the only one who knew about this, but funnily enough there was a programme about it the other night. They wired up everyone's eyes with laser beams or whatever it was. When a girl is introduced to a boy at a social gathering, she glances at his cock about every ten seconds. He does the same, only he includes her tits. Newly-weds' eyes are *glued* to each other that way. Which are the girls you like?"

"Penny and Pamela."

"I'll be flirting with them too. Don't be alarmed if you see me kissing them or feeling them up. People don't know this yet either, but girls go weak for that if it's done in the right way. Even the straightest of them."

"Really?"

"Trust me."

At midnight he pulls up outside Huw's double-fronted townhouse in Primrose Hill. A tuxedoed Keith Nearing opens the passenger door and extends his hand towards a cheongsamed Gloria Beautyman.

"That was rather fun," she says. "Now. What are you doing wrong?"

"I think all girls with bedroom bodies are cocks."

"That's right. And as I was at pains to tell you, long ago, hardly *any* girls are cocks. Here. Shake my glove."

"Cocks. Staring at cocks. Don't be offended, but are there boys who are cunts?"

"No. It's all cocks. Goodnight."

Smoothed, pawed, squeezed, nibbled, and adoringly stared at, Keith drove home and had an unqualified fiasco with Iris.

Three weeks later, the envelope containing the second half of her honorarium (Gloria's preferred term for it) gets handed over in the BMW. Keith in white tie, Gloria in a starkly abbreviated version of her Sunday best. The second works outing consists of cocktails and dinner in the revolving carvery on top of the Post Office Tower.

"That was wonderful. You know, for an hour or two I really and truly believed you were my girlfriend."

"Mm, and then you came on so suave. Right. To summarise. Forget Penny. She's tight-lipped, but I can tell she's wearing down a married man. And Pamela, I think, is borderline gay."

"You and her in the bathroom. How could you tell? The kissing?"

"No, they all do the kissing. No. The *breathing*. Maybe you'd be better off with Alexis."

"Alexis?" Alexis is Digby's secretary. "She's too—isn't she too worldly for me? She's married."

"No she's not. She's advantageously divorced. She's a very decent forty, and by now she's good fun in the way we mean. Ooh, I bet she is. But remember: she's not a cock."

Keith says that he'll bear this in mind. "But I'd never get off with Alexis."

"You might. She likes books. And I don't know if she reads it, but she sees that guff you write in the *Lit Supp*. Send her some flowers and ask her to lunch. Now. When you drop me off, we'll stand at the garden gate and you're to give me a sex kiss lasting about a minute. Because Huw'll be watching. Actually no. A minute can be an absolute age, don't you find? Ten or fifteen seconds. But make sure you put your hand up the back of my skirt."

Conclusions. It wasn't long before everyone at Derwent and Digby knew that Derwent had left his wife and moved in with Penny. Pamela came back from her summer holiday in New York with her head shaved. Soon afterwards, Keith started seeing Alexis. He felt as if Gloria was directing his life, like a general on a hill.

And he had no complaints. Something new was going wrong sexually, but he had no complaints. What he couldn't forget was that his sex kiss with Gloria went on for at least an absolute age.

What Came Down in 1977

Violet's marriage was already over. An improbable sister and an impossible daughter, Violet turned out to be an inconceivable wife.

"She fucked the builder?"

"No," said Nicholas on the phone. "She fucked the builders. With an ess."

"She fucked two builders."

"No. She fucked *all* the builders."

"But there were lots of builders."

"I know."

It's spring again (May), and now Keith is at his desk, with Ed looking over his shoulder. Ed (short for Ahmed) is the visual wunderkind from Communications, and the two of them are "midwifing" an original product (a kind of choc-ice sandwich). Keith's new secretary, Judith, buzzes through to say that a Mrs. H. Llewellyn is here to see him.

"No, I'm not married," says Gloria when they're alone. "Not quite. Not yet. And do you realise I'm *thirty*?" She pauses while Judith brings in her tea. "There's a problem with Huw."

"He's keen on drugs," says Keith, repeating the rumour.

"Huw's not keen on drugs. He's a heroin addict."

This makes perfect sense. Huw is tall, handsome, and rich—so naturally he can't bear it. He can't bear it *another second.*

"Every couple of months," Gloria continues, "he checks into the Parsonage for a fruit juice and a back rub. Then it happens all over again. He won't go to the place in Germany." She describes the place in Germany—its bedstraps, its singleted male nurses. "We haven't had sex for over a year."

Keith's interest becomes acute. "So what do you do about that?" he asks her. "I mean, you're a healthy young girl."

"I relied on Probert," she explains (Probert is Huw's younger brother). "And that's what I've come to see you about."

He lights a cigarette. She assumes a long-suffering expression.

"Now Probert's gone and knocked up one of the milkmaids at Llangollen. And he's religious. So that's that."

". . . Are you still religious?"

"More than ever. Actually I'm getting fed up with Rome. It asks so little of you. I need something with a bit more bite."

". . . Did you ever think of switching to Probert?"

"Good God no. The way they do it, Huw gets it all. Probert lives in the castle but he's like a farmhand. Humping bags of manure about the place. Rescuing sheep."

"Forgive me, but does Huw know you fuck his brother?" She gives a sideways nod, and Keith is suddenly aware of how very passionately he doesn't want Gloria to fuck *his* brother, or any of his friends, or indeed anybody at all. Ever. "And now the farmhand is marrying the milkmaid."

"Yes. So there's a kind of opening for you here. It'll be temporary. Are you free tomorrow evening between six thirty and eight? Come and see me. Primrose Hill."

"I'll be there," he says, as she gets up to go. "What does seeing you mean?" He hopes it just means having an affair without going to restaurants. She says,

"You'll see what seeing me means."

Violet was still religious. But she no longer consorted with young builders. To win Violet's favour, or so it seemed for a while, you needed to be in your twenties, with a visible bumcrack, a hod in one hand and a trowel in the other. But Violet no longer consorted with young builders. She consorted with old builders. The latest builder, Bill, was sixty-two.

Nicholas maintained that builders weren't just cheats and botchers and all the rest of it. He said that builders were violent criminals at one remove, or psychopaths manqué. They devoted their lives to the torture of inanimate objects—the banging, the clacking, the whining, the grinding. Keith and Nicholas didn't need to say that Violet would soon discover this.

At Primrose Hill she receives him in a black satin housecoat and gold sandals with kitten heels, and leads him at once into a bedroom. And through the bedroom into a bathroom.

"Sit on that chair. There's some wine in the bucket if you want." She unfurls the sheath at her waist. "This is what seeing me means."

And there it is again, seven years later: the elastic soundness of Gloria Beautyman. She attends to her breasts, and stands stock still for a second. Keith's eyes make the expected tour but then settle on the oval convexity, the creature or genie that lived in the core of her—and he almost looks for the staple in the middle of its static sheen.

"You're more muscular."

"Am I?" She steps into the filled tub and sinks back with a moan. "I need your help. Coming up there's a fancy-dress ball at Mansion House, and you've got to be someone from Shakespeare. And you're the very man to ask."

He says in a voice gone deep, "I am that man. Well." For some reason the first name that comes into his head is Hermione—the wronged Hermione. "From *The Winter's Tale*. She spends sixteen years as a statue in a chapel."

"Are there any other religious ones?"

Against the background of soft sluice and splash, as Gloria raises small handfuls of water to her shoulders, her throat, he says, "Ophelia. She's not really religious. But there's talk of her going to a nunnery."

"Pretty name. But I think I've seen that one and doesn't she go mad?"

"She drowns herself in the end. 'There is a willow grows aslant a brook . . .' Sorry."

"No. Go on."

"'There with fantastic garlands did she come, Of crow-flowers, nettles, daisies . . .'" And, no, Gloria doesn't go all still and silent. Her splashes and sluices grow louder ("'When down her weedy trophies and herself Fell in the weeping brook'"), and then there comes the drop-rush of water as she stands ("'Her clothes spread wide, And, mermaid-like, awhile they bore her up'"), and then she was wielding the hissing serpent of the showerhead ("'but long it could not be'"), with dips of the knees and the widening of the angles between her thighs.

"'Till that her garments, heavy with their drink, Pulled the poor wretch from her melodious lay To muddy death.'"

"I hate mad people. Don't you? . . . Apart from 'To be or not to be' there's only one line of Shakespeare I know. 'I that am with Phoebus' am'rous pinches black.' "

"Cleopatra. You could go as her. You're dark enough."

"I am *not* dark enough."

"All right. You could go as Viola or Rosalind and dress up as a boy. She's pretending to be a boy. Passing as a boy. Wear a sword."

"Now that's a brilliant idea." With her back to him she reaches for the white bathrobe in the avocado light. "I'd be a very good boy."

The second half of seeing Gloria consisted of a reverse striptease that lasted for almost an hour. But he didn't feel like a teased man. She was showing him things—this was how they washed, this was how they dressed. And there were moments of near-innocence in it: he remembered how he felt as a boy of ten, reading Violet's copies of *Bunty*.

"It's soft-core this time," she said, showing her blue-white teeth. "But it's still a black mass. We're doing everything the wrong way round."

As he walked over Primrose Hill and across Regent's Park, Keith thought of India, of Bollywood, where films with religious themes were called "theologicals." Maybe that was the genre he had entered. The pornotheological farce.

August. Keith enters the office and has his secretary place a call.

"I have just got out of a bed," he says, "that contained Gloria Beautyman."

"My dear Little Keith."

"Now I'm going to tell you *everything,* okay? Wherever in the world you are. Everything."

"Don't you always?"

"I don't tell you much about my failures. Like the fact that I can't come with Alexis."

"Oh. So not like with Iris."

"No, not like with Iris. I can commence, with Alexis, but I can't conclude. And I get a completely different kind of hard-on with Gloria. A different order of hard-on. It's like a towel rack. Anyway. I need to tell you everything about Gloria. To help keep my grip."

"Well tell."

"It was surprising. She's a very surprising girl. She came to my place and she said, 'Right. Where d'you want it?' I said I wanted it in the bedroom. And I didn't get it."

"That *is* surprising."

"We got into bed and guess what. No tomfoolery about keeping her pants on or anything like that. But we got into bed and guess what. Just a handjob."

". . . What kind of handjob?"

"Well, Nicholas, you know there are certain poets who are—who're so plangent and yet technically advanced that they're known as poet's poets? It was like that. A handjob's handjob. But just a handjob."

"She gave you a handjob. And your rights and privileges, Little Keith?"

"I had rights and privileges. I gave *her* a handjob. First."

In the morning he brought Gloria breakfast in bed, tea, toast, yoghurt, a quartered orange. He said, "Believe me, I'm not complaining. But it seems almost quaint. After Italy."

"Italy," said Gloria, holding the teacup with both hands (the upper sheet across her chest like a bed-wide bra), "was a holiday fling. And whatever this is, it isn't that. Now lie back."

She said he could go on seeing Alexis (who knew about and accepted Gloria)—but no one else. "I'm a terrible hypochondriac," she said. "And I need to know where you've been."

That was the only time she ever spent the night.

September. "Gloria just left. She came over for a light dinner."

"Oh," says Nicholas. "So I suppose you're well whacked off."

"We've moved beyond that. I go down on her. And then she goes down on me. She disapproves of *soixante-neuf.* She says, 'You can't give the thing the undivided attention it so richly deserves.'"

"What could be more agreeable? A swallower, I presume."

Keith tells him about the sinister refinement.

"Christ."

October.

"Gloria popped round again. For a mineral water."

"Oh. So I suppose you're well sucked off."

"We've moved beyond that. Now you can do whatever you like. As long as you can do it in thirty-five minutes." He talks on for quite a while. "She said, 'An arse like mine soon learns to take its chances.' Imagine . . . Do you think the police know about Gloria?"

"Obviously not."

"No. Because otherwise . . ."

"They would've acted. They're bound to catch up with her in the end."

"I suppose that's true. Poor Gloria. We'll visit her."

Nicholas says, "No, *I'll* visit her. I'll visit you too. You'll be in a different prison. One for men."

This was Gloria's considered verdict on poetry: "In my view that kind of thing is best left to the Old Man. Honestly. With all that in your head, I don't know why you're not in floods of tears all the hours there are."

In late November he visited Violet in the Church Army Hostel for Young Women on the corner of Marylebone Road and Cosway Street. Church Army: he thought that this denoted a joint effort. But Church Army was a specific sect, the Church Militant—the body of living Christian believers striving to combat evil on earth. Violet sat in the common room, a silenced girl among all the other silenced girls, and wearing an enormous and very black black eye. She was out by Christmas, and the process of her life resumed.

There is a—there is a willow. There is a willow . . . There is a willow grows aslant a brook.

The Kind of Stuff They
All Got Up To in 1978

"Keith," said the machine. "Gloria. I am to be found in room six-one-three of the Heathrow Hilton until about nine fifteen. My flight's delayed. Kiss."

"Keith," said the machine. "Gloria. There's a perfectly decent little inn called the Queen's Head on the road from Bristol to Bath. Wait there on Saturday afternoon. They have rooms. I asked. Kiss."

"Keith," says the machine. "Gloria. Where—"

He picks up.

"Where on earth have you been? Anyway. Tonight's the Shakespeare ball. I can't be Viola. They've assigned everybody one play per group. They're scared everyone'll come as Romeo or Juliet. And we got *Othello*."

"So you're Desdemona."

"No. Priscilla bagged Desdemona," she says (Priscilla is Huw's elder sister). "So I had to go to the library and read the whole thing. Because you were off somewhere."

"Sorry, I had to go and bail out Violet. Nicholas is in Tehran. Where they're having a revolution."

"Stick to the point."

"Well it's a bit thin on women, *Othello*. I suppose you'd better be Emilia. Mrs. Iago."

"Why would I want to be that old boot? I settled on Bianca. You know—Cassio's slag. I want to show you my outfit. I'll be there about six forty. And I'll have to keep the cab at the door. Bianca was an inspiration. So much the better if I look as though I've just been had. Six forty. I'll be covered in rags and grease. And d'you know what? Othello was queer for Cassio. Kiss."

Six forty came and went. This happened about every other time. Keith once drove to Coedpoeth in North Wales, where he checked into the Gamekeeper's Arms, ate lunch alone, and drove back again. On the other hand, he once flew to Monaco and had a whole hour with her in a golfing ranch in Cap d'Antibes . . .

That night he is awoken at four in the morning. So Violet's dead, he decides as he reaches for the phone.

"They've just served the kedgeree and the porridge. I'll be there in twenty minutes. I've got my keys. Kiss."

Twenty minutes later she says, "Who was that biddy who passed me on the stairs? Bloody hell, that wasn't *Alexis* was it?"

"I asked her to wait in the spare room, but she wouldn't have it. And she didn't have time to put her make-up on."

"Oh God. I suppose I'll send her flowers . . . They're all down there in the car. Funny-looking lot we are too . . . Probert in blackface, Priscilla in a silk chemise . . . and Huw unconscious in a ginger wig. And Bianca at the wheel. Does my grease still shine? . . . Huw? Roderigo . . . Oh, I told Othello and Desdemona I had to pick up Roderigo's drugs . . . No more questions. Concentrate, Cassio. Listen to your slag."

This sort of thing went on for over a year.

Since 1970, Nicholas Shackleton had had two changes of girlfriend. In 1973, Jean was replaced by Jane. In 1976, Jane was replaced by Joan. Your future looks limitless, Keith kept telling him: there's still the possibility of a Jan or a June.

"Or a Jen," said Nicholas, over a glass of Scotch in Keith's kitchen. "Or a Jin. I know a Jin. She's Korean."

"But Jen or Jin would have to be very left-wing, like Jean and Jane and Joan."

"More than that. Jen or Jan or June or Jin would have to be terrorists. *You* should get a terrorist. Gloria—you call her the Future, but she's retrograde. Non-independent. Man-pleasing. God-fearing. You should get a nice terrorist. A feminist with a job who screams at you."

"Gloria's not a screamer. But she *can* be terrifying. Listen to this," says Keith with a nod. "She weaned Huw off heroin by having him switch to methamphetamine. 'That way,' she says, 'I get the sex weapon back.' Meth's not like heroin. Meth gives you a permanent towel rack."

"She certainly thinks these things through."

"And she won't let him near her until he agrees to go to Germany. Three months in a dungeon. Forty thousand quid. Ninety per cent success rate . . . She's weird, Gloria, but she's absolutely standard on marriage and children. In a panic. Because she's turned thirty."

"Mm, the cusp of hell. I thought the sisters might've pushed that up a few years—say to thirty-three or thirty-four. But they're all like that the minute they're twenty-eight. Even the terrorists."

". . . She's coming round at seven."

"That's all right," says Nicholas (this has happened before). "I'll go down the Shakespeare for half an hour."

"No. Stay here. *I'll* go down the Shakespeare for half an hour. With Gloria."

"Oh. So. Not the usual."

"I could be wrong. But I think the usual's coming to an end."

They talk on, about family matters, until they hear the keys in the door.

Nicholas says quietly, "I'll slip off. You might get a going-away present. You never know."

"Go to the restaurant that's only big enough for one person. With your book. I'll be paying tonight. You'll have to hold my hand."

"I hope you're late. Don't forget. She's a surprising girl. The Future is surprising."

Keith listens to their exchange in the entrance hall, which is full of comity, even gallantry, on both sides. Then she enters, with a smile he's never seen before.

But his eyes were already going past her—and he saw the future plain enough. The inability to enter a bedroom without fear; fumbling, dreamlike, trameled by strange impediments; and the deep weave, the deep stitch of self-doubt. Gloria, he wanted to say: Tell me your secret and whatever it is I'll beg you to come and live with me. But he said nothing as she stepped towards him.

Nicholas of course is already there, with his book, and Keith comes in and drops his hat on the tablecloth.

"The Future's fucking the dog."

"Come on. She's not *that* surprising."

"Dog with a little dee. I mean in general. She's making her move. Everything's fixed. Huw's sworn to go to Germany *on the Bible.* Jesus. I'm in shock. I'm also drunk. I had two huge glasses of vodka on my way out."

"Vodka? You told me the last time you drank spirits was in Italy. After you fucked it all up with Scheherazade by shitting on God."

"It's true. But I was so scared. I'm so scared. And you know what? Gloria was happy. I've seen her cheerful before. But never happy."

"A pretty sight."

"Yes. And I told her so. You'd have been proud of me. I said, 'I'm miserable, but it's good to see you looking so happy and so young.' And I got a kiss out of it too."

"A sex kiss?"

"Sort of. For the record. And I felt her up. But that's not how you do it with the Future."

"How d'you do it?"

"I'm not telling you . . . Christ, I almost tried, but then I didn't. Too demoralised. Oh yeah, and high-minded. I suppose I'll have to go back to being high-minded. And to being a gimp in the boudoir. A high-minded gimp in the boudoir. Nice."

"Call Alexis."

"Call Alexis, and give myself a heart attack trying to finish. Call Iris. And give myself a heart attack trying to start."

"That never happens to me—except, of course, when I'm unusually drunk." Nicholas attends to the menu. "It's no fun, all that. Cupping your hands over your shame. Or fighting to come. The trouble is, when that happens, they take it personally."

"Mm. The only one I'm normal with is Lily."

"And that's what—an annual event? . . . Maybe you're normal with Lily because she precedes your obsession with the Future. Wait. How did you get on with the two nutters from the Poetry Society?"

"I couldn't raise it with them either."

"But maybe there's a simple explanation. They were two nutters from the Poetry Society. And John Cowper Powys?"

". . . On the way here I thought, I'll chuck my job and go back to being a poet. Which means going back to Joy and Patience. And John Cowper Powys. Christ, what is it, Nicholas? What went wrong with me and girls?"

"Mm. The other night I ran into your Neil Darlington. He's delightful, isn't he. Very drunk, of course. He said you should try and marry Gloria. 'Enter the labyrinth.' "

"Typical Neil. He's addicted to complication. The reason I'm normal with Lily is that there's still some love. There's no love with Gloria. No talk of love. No talk of like. In fifteen months the prettiest thing she's ever said to me is 'kiss.' "

"You say love frightens you. Well then. Settle for sex. Marry her."

"She'd laugh in my face. I'm not rich enough. She curls her lip when she hears the word 'salary.' It has to be old money. Old money. What *is* old money?"

"It's what you get when you did all your gouging and skanking a couple of centuries ago."

"Huw's lot were Catholic grandees. Mine were servants. And they weren't even married. I'm shit."

". . . You know, I've only heard you talk like this once before. When they were teasing you at school. Before Mum put a stop to it. Think of Edmund in *Lear*. 'Why brand they us With base?' Remember, Little Keith. You've got more in you than a whole tribe of fops, Got 'tween asleep and wake."

". . . You're a good brother to me."

"Please don't cry. You look eight years old again."

"This time next week . . . this time next week, he'll be pegged out on a cellar floor in Munich. Bind fast his corky arms. And I'll be . . . Fuck Huw. Fuck *Huw*. I hope something very horrible happens to him before his wedding day."

Raising his glass, Keith summons the gothic, the Grand Guignol.

And Nicholas says, "That's the spirit. Now, gods, stand up for bastards."

In September the two of them went to Essex to see Violet, who was shacked up with a comprehensively humourless ex-sailor in Shoebury-ness. His name was Anthony—or, in Violet's rendering, Amfony or Anfony. Nicholas, who had been there before, called him Unfunny (with the stress on the first syllable). Keith drove. He was hungover. He was drinking more. That week he had spent two lunchtimes in a May-fair escort agency, with catalogues, with *Who's Who*s of young women on his lap. He was looking for a certain face and a certain shape . . .

"So how long's she been with Unfunny?"

"A whole three months. He's a hero. You'll see. A whole free mumfs in Unfunny's arms."

Scrawny, bearded, and bald, in a typhoon-proof rollneck sweater, and with eyes of Icelandic blue, Anthony lived in the cabin of a boat called *The Little Lady.* His sea-roving days were at an end, and he was permanently and grimly moored up a tributary of the Mersea River. *The Little Lady* was in fact no longer water-borne, but wedged porthole-deep in a great expanse, like a solid ocean, of riverine slime; you boarded her by means of a warped gangplank as twangy as the diving board at the *castello.* They had electricity (and a noisy generator), and the taps quite often worked.

Anthony no longer sought adventure on the high seas; but he could somehow manage Violet. How? Well, as an able-bodied swabbie of twenty years' service, he was used to entrusting his life to a monster. He knew the contrary currents, the heaving swells. And he needed to. Because every morning Violet walked the plank and continued on into town, where she picked up men in pubs, returning in various stages of undress and incapacity in the early evening, to be bathed and fed.

There would be a surprise, or a reversal, but Violet was very good on the day her brothers came. Now let's see—what do normal people do? The three siblings went to Clacton and had lunch at an Angus Steak House; they waved off Nicholas on the train to Cambridge (a Union debate about Cambodia); and Keith took Violet to the funfair. Then there was a hearty fish stew on *The Little Lady,* fondly prepared by Anthony. Who talked all evening about his years as a maritimer (all of them spent gutting fish in the hold of a North Sea trawler). The two men got through most of a bottle of rum, while Violet drank pop.

At eleven Keith readied himself to drunk-drive back to London. He gave thanks and farewells, started off down the gangplank, and, with a perceptible spring, as if helped on his way by the toe of a boot, leapt into the brown ocean of riverine slime . . . Which wasn't so remarkable, perhaps—except that an hour later, after Violet, with buckets and towels, had stripped him and sluiced him and somehow reassembled him, he went out and did it again.

Hooked out by Anthony for a second time, Keith sits reeking in the tiny galley while Violet refills the buckets.

"Vi, you must've done that once or twice by now."

"Oh I lost count ages ago," she says.

And attends to him, with patience, with humour, with infinite forgivingness. With sisterly love, in short. And it makes him think that if their roles were reversed then *Violet* would go all the way—that it would be possible, all your life, to do nothing else but lift someone out of the mire, clean them up, lift them out again, and clean them up again.

On October 15 Keith received an embossed invitation to Gloria's wedding (he would not attend), and also received, that same morning, a phone call from a tearful Anthony (who couldn't take it any more). Violet disappeared for a while, but she was back in London in time for Halloween.

The Way It Panned
Out in 1979

It is 7 p.m. on the day of Gloria Beautyman's marriage, and Keith is halfway through his fourth game of Scrabble—his opponent is Kenrik. And all this time Gloria has been desperately trying to reach him. But he isn't to know that, is he (nor is he to know that she is now alone on the platform of the train station in Llangollen—the fine rain, the cold, the floating haloes of the lights): as Keith places his moves, and lays out the letters on his rack, and occasionally consults the dictionary, he is also on the phone with Violet.

"So Gary said go on then, scrub the bloody floor. And I said no fanks mate, *you* scrub the bloody floor if you love it so clean. And he beat me up! Wiv a cricket bat fanks very much."

Keith cups the receiver and says, "'Wrentit?' First, 'krait,' then 'wrentit.' Seven letters."

"I said. Krait's a little shit of a snake. Wrentit's a little dope of a bird," says Kenrik, who, the next day, will attend preliminary criminal proceedings on the charge of assaulting his mother—the diminutive yet remorseless Roberta.

"And he called me a slag and I'm *not* a slag! I'm an elfy young girl! Then he says guiss your money. And muggins here give it him. And what's he do? He buggers up!"

"Off," Keith reflexively reminds her. It really is remarkable: to attempt so little in the way of language—and to bugger *that* up. Wiv, fanks, elfy: the explanation for all this would belatedly occur to him. "Off, Vi. Buggers off."

"Pardon? Yeah he goes and buggers up!"

The call somehow comes to an end. They play three more games (like Timmy at the chessboard, Kenrik always wins), and they walk out to

339

dinner—just as Gloria changes trains at Wolverhampton and is once more speeding south-east.

"So what happened with Bertie?"

"The usual. Bertie was screaming in my face, I gave her a push, and she threw herself down the stairs. No. She did a backward somersault. I might get off with a warning, but I'll need a cool judge. It's just a domestic."

This is not the first time Kenrik has faced trial: credit fraud, VAT-avoidance, drunk-driving . . . Believing as he does that all magistrates are a) right-wing and b) homosexual, he always stands in the dock with a *Daily Telegraph* under his arm, and gives the magistrate a steady pout of conspiratorial submissiveness.

"I'll be all right. Unless Bertie comes to court in a wheelchair. Or on a stretcher. She wants me in jail, you see."

". . . Are you still with Olivia?"

Now things take a prophetically pertinent turn (as things, in Life, very seldom do), and Kenrik says, "No, she kicked me out. See, she's very pretty, Olivia, so she gave me an ultimatum. The rougher ones don't bother with ultimatums, because they're used to being passed over. Olivia says: me or booze. Then she screamed in my face about something else, so I got drunk. And she kicked me out. She *loathes* me now. The very pretty ones can't believe, *cannot believe,* they've been passed over. For something the shape of a bottle."

"You're a very pretty one," says Keith, and thinks of Kenrik in Pentonville, in Wormwood Scrubs. Kenrik would not go on being a very pretty one.

"It made me realise something. How much Bertie must've hated my dad when he died. Bertie was a very pretty one. And he went on a three-day bender and killed himself in his car. And made her a widow."

"A pregnant widow. Mm. Mine never knew she was a widow."

"I suppose all widows grieve. But some widows hate."

And Keith thinks of all that hatred coursing through fierce little pretty Roberta. And Kenrik inside her, drinking it.

"That's why she wants me in jail," says Kenrik. "To punish him. Because he's me."

They are eating their main course as Gloria's train enters the thickening city.

Keith walked home through a fog the colour of withered leaves—through the sere fog, and its smell of the churchyard. He was remembering the time Kenrik rang him at two in the morning: Kenrik was in the process of getting arrested for the first time. You could hear the voices in the background. Put the phone down, sir. Come on now, sir. That was a phone call from another genre—another way of doing things.

She is standing, now, a solid but altered shape, in the cold darkness of the porch outside his building.

"Mrs. Llewellyn. Are you *very* pregnant?"

"No, I'm still Miss Beautyman. And no again. I've just got all my clothes on. The train was like a fridge. Feel my suitcase. There's nothing in it. I've got *all* my clothes on. Are you going to take pity on me?"

"Why aren't you in Wales?"

She says, "I've had a very bad dream."

For this hinge moment, then, Gloria is disarmed, or neutralised: not just with all her clothes on, but with *all* her clothes on.

These she now takes off, or fights her way out of, standing in front of the ornamental coal fire, overcoat, leather jacket, two sweaters, shirt, T-shirt, long skirt, short skirt, long skirt, jeans, stockings, socks. Then she turns, her flesh stippled and goosebumped, and marked by indentations and crenellations, like scars. He hands her the warmed robe . . . She bathes, and drinks two pots of sugary tea. Now she sits folded on the sofa; he crouches on the facing chair, and listens to the wintriness of her voice.

"It wasn't a good time to have a very bad dream. I was getting married in the morning."

Gloria and Huw, she briskly explains, were the occupants of the bridal suite at the Grand, in the border city of Chester. Huw had his stag night, and Gloria had her doe night, in two different dining rooms at the hotel. She went to bed at nine—for, as everybody knew, Beautyman must have her beautysleep. Briefly waking her, Huw came in at a quarter to ten.

"You yourself have remarked on how hot my breasts get in the night. I went to cool them against his back. And it stung, it burned. Like dry ice. And you know what he was doing? He was dying. Keith, stay where you are . . . No, unfortunately not. They found a pulse. The two words they're using to describe his condition are 'serious' and 'stable.' And when you think about it, that's really very funny. Huw? Serious? Stable? . . . As I imagine it, his heart stopped beating for nine minutes. One for every year he stole from me. He's damaged his brain. Not that anyone'll see the difference. Now what've you got to say to all that? . . . I'll think about it. Come here. I wish Huw could watch me doing this. But he's probably blind."

Nicholas was in South East Asia, and it was a couple of weeks before they spoke. He called collect from a sepulchral echo chamber in Calcutta.

"Imagine that," said Keith. "You wake up on your wedding day. You're trying to separate fact from fiction. And there's this snowman lying beside you. Your groom." There was a silence. "Nicholas?"

"I'm still here. Well she bounced back quick enough."

"Look, uh, ethically it's far from ideal, I admit, but it's not quite as bad as it sounds. God, that night I was petrified. And so was she. Her eyes were as hard as rocks. Like jewels. But it makes sense in a way."

"Does it? How?"

"See, she's not a woman bereaved. She's a woman scorned." See, Nicholas, her body, with its hollows and rises, its feminine exaggerations, was passed over for something the shape of a needle. "In her heart she's been hating him for years. Ever since he first went on it. A woman scorned. She's had, she says, 'dozens of flings,' but she's been nursing Huw along since 1970. The lost decade. She's in a deep frenzy about the lost decade."

"And don't tell me. This has made her *more* religious. They all do that. Something shitty happens and they just double their bet."

"Yeah, but not in the way you'd think. She believes God's punishing him—to her specifications. Or she did. Huw's all fucked up and can't walk or talk or anything. And she was ticking off his faculties one by one. Then suddenly he was out of danger."

"And that shook her faith."

"It did a bit. The poor little thing was very low for a day or two. But she's rallied."

"I can't tell whether you're being ironic or not."

"Neither can I. Not any more. And get this. Huw's been disinherited, right? I mean, he's a vegetable. And get this. The other morning we had sex—topped off with the sinister refinement. And she's sitting at breakfast with it all over her face. Eating toast. Drinking tea. And she looks up and says, 'This should've happened two years ago. Then Probert would've been perfectly fine.'" There was a silence. "Nicholas?"

"I'm still here. So she's in residence."

"Yeah, on one condition. She said, 'We'll have to get engaged. It doesn't commit you to anything. Or me either. It's just for my parents.' I said okay. She's here. She's penniless. And she's desperate. It's great."

"Keith. Don't marry the Future."

"No. You know, she never levels with you. Her secret's still brewing away in there. And I don't get it. What's left to be ashamed about in this day and age?"

"Don't marry Miss Towel Rack."

"Of course I won't. You think I'm nuts?"

One of the first things he did, after Gloria moved in, was take her to prison. "I don't want to go to prison," she said. But she came. They went to see Kenrik, who was in Brixton on remand. Gloria was strong throughout, but afterwards she wept. "So pretty," she said in the car (with fellow feeling, Keith thought), "and so afraid."

Then he took her to the Church Army Hostel for Young Women. To see Violet (who had another black eye). Gloria was strong throughout, but afterwards she wept. "The place is like a library," said Keith in the car. "Except no one's reading. Why are the girls so silent?" And Gloria said, "Because they've been shamed beyond words."

The only thing they rowed about, in the first few months, was money. Oh yeah—and marriage. The two themes were related in her mind.

"If we break up now," she said, "I get nothing."

"I don't want to break up now."

"But what if I meet Mr. Christmas?"

"You're being illogical. If you meet Mr. Christmas, you won't need my money. Which is new money. You'll have Mr. Christmas's money. Which'll be old money."

"I want to be able to put something aside. Triple my allowance. Most of it goes on bedroom stuff anyway. You're so selfish."

"Oh all right."

In April she took him to Edinburgh to meet her parents (this was a preposterous occasion), and in May he took her to Spain to meet his.

La casita de campo—the little house in the country. Travel is almost always art in motion (a journey is almost always a reasonable short story), so, first, there are animals. Edinburgh had its animals: the parrot in the kitchen, the elephant in the living room. And the *campo* has its animals: the birds and the bees, the busybody chickens with their strict neurotic faces, and their gaits, like clockwork nurses, the ursine Alsatian, old Coca, who nuzzles your groin and gives out great groans of debility and despair. All around and up above, the craters and graters of the sierras.

"Can I help you with that?" says Gloria.

"It won't come out," says Tina. "What on earth did she do?"

Nicholas used to say that he got on so well with his mother because they were exactly the same age. But Tina is a little older than Keith: she is fifty-one. Karl, nine years her senior, has been placed in the shade.

"How'd she do it?" wonders Tina, who has a plastic bucket before her, and is washing one of the dresses that Violet, after her recent visit, left behind. The dress has a deep coating of dirt all over its seat. "I suppose she might've fallen on her bum in the mud. But that looks really *worked in . . .*"

There is a silence.

"Where does she go, Mum? When she's here?"

"She just goes to the bars. She used to go to the Gypsy camp. For days, weeks. Until they threw her out."

Gloria says, "Gypsies are actually quite puritanical. People think they aren't, but they are. And they're not from Egypt either."

". . . I'm her mother and she's a complete mystery to me. When she's here, she's so sweet with Dad. Devoted. I think she's got a very good heart. But then why?"

In the garden of the Hotel Reina Victoria there is a statue of Rainer Maria Rilke, who took sanctuary here while sleeping out, while dreaming out, the First World War. The poet—his subject was "the decay of reality"—is here etched, chipped, out of black bronze, and looks jagged, frazzled, like someone undergoing electrocution. The statue makes him think of the later Kenrik, his face medieval, Druidical, and carved out of rock . . . Keith feels the reproachful gaze of Rainer Maria's sightless eyes.

"My oldest friend," he says carefully, "is sharing a cell, and a toilet, with a man who probably knifed a family of five. Just a couple of days ago, my sister was screwed in a ditch. Gloria, nothing could possibly shock me. So go on. Tell."

A minute passes by. They stare out at the ramped mountains, with their three strategies of distance.

"All right, I will. My father's not my father."

And he thinks, That's not a secret. The elephant in the living room: one feels it is important to know what the elephant is *doing*—when it's in the living room. Is it jouncing and trumpeting and shivering its flanks? Or is it just standing there, as still as a cow under a tree in the rain? The Edinburgh elephant was house-trained. That was the trouble. Keith had been expecting one or both of Gloria's parents to be Celt-Iberian. And they were both dairy products—pure and simple. And then there was the flurried visit from the younger sister, Mary: like the mother, she seemed to be two different women joined at the waist; but she too was flaxen-haired, and when she smiled she revealed, not Gloria's strips of spearmint Chiclets, but the barnyard balcony of the unadulterated Scot. It was so palpable that Keith didn't even mention it—the elephant in the living room, with its African ears.

"I'll go into detail," says Gloria, under Rilke's gaze, "so you'll know I'm not lying. I usually tell everyone that my mother's parents were swarthy, and it skipped a generation. I've even got a photograph I show."

"And it isn't true."

"It isn't true. Listen. In the Sixties there was only one other proper consulate in Iceland. Portuguese. Because of the fishing. There was a man who was always around. Marquez. Pronounced Markish. He kept looking at me oddly, and one day he stroked my hair and said, 'I followed you from Lisbon.' I was fourteen. And he wasn't even Portuguese. He was Brazilian. So there."

"Why would *I* worry about your parentage? Or anyone else's?"

"No. You're worried about my sanity. My father never held me as a real father would. So something's missing. And all through my childhood it was dawning on me. *He can't be my father.* So I'm not normal."

"Neither am I . . . Gloria, that isn't your secret. It may be true, but it isn't *it.*"

"Oh shut up and marry me. Give me children."

He says, "I'd rather wait a while for children. And marriage is old-fashioned."

"Well so am I. It's what women want."

And Edinburgh, black granite under the mean rain. As if, this far north, nature was itself an industry, a night shift that manufactured murk, and the sky was just the site where it dumped its waste . . . There was adoration, or worship, and there was addiction, but there wasn't any love. That would be the state of true terror—loving Gloria. No.

"I was thinking about Vi's honeymoon," said Tina. "They came here for their honeymoon." ·

"Oh yeah. Remind me?"

"They arrived, and Vi went back to her Gypsy."

"What, quite soon?"

"Oh immediately. The minute they got here. She went flying over the fields. I was shouting at her. But she had no more thought in her head than a puppy. She wanted Juan."

"Oh yeah. Juan. She loved him."

"He wasn't quite right in the head either. He always had people with him in case he did himself an injury. But she seemed to love him. And he loved her."

"What did Francis do when she ran off?"

"He just stood there holding his suitcase. Twenty minutes later Vi came running back, but she just ran past us. Running the other way. With her chest really heaving. Looking for Juan."

"But she loved him."

"Yes. Then she came crashing in five nights later. And then went back to Juan."

Keith drove Gloria up to town . . . By then he knew about the poetic content of mountains, but first he said, "I heard you crying in the bathroom. Again. Why?"

"I was crying about Huw."

He waited.

She said, "I cry with anger too, you know."

He thought for a moment. "Because he didn't die."

"No, it's better that he didn't die. Because it tortures the mother. What makes me cry is the time. Ten years."

By then he knew about the poetic content of mountains. Young mountains are ridged and jagged. Old mountains are smooth and even, made sleek by billennia and weather. Mountains are not like human beings. The sierras were young mountains—no older, perhaps, than five million years: round about the time that *Homo sapiens* diverged from the apes. The young, the sky-shearing, the heaven-grating sierras.

What Came About in 1980

And very early in 1980 too.

"What may I ask," he asks, "is the meaning of those pants?"

"You know perfectly well."

". . . I don't believe it. Ten years later, and I'm back on the pants!"

"What d'you mean, *back* on the pants?"

"I'm back on the pants! . . . Wait. Look. This is—the seventh night running. So it can't just be your *period,* can it."

"God you're disgusting. I told you. I'm off the coil."

". . . It's very you, that is, Gloria—the coil. It suits your nature." With that mystery coiled up in her omphalos. "And the coil's the best too. Better than the Pill. Let alone the fucking cap."

Over the past year Keith's morals, I should stress, have undergone a certain . . . Wait. Is this the time to clear up the question of who *I* am? Not just yet, I don't think. But I would like to put some distance between the "I" and the being propped up on the pillow—whose gaze now roams the cathouse of the shared bedroom, the screens, the outfits, the uniforms (nun, flight attendant, health visitor, policewoman), the wigs and hair-extensions, the two Polaroid cameras, the two camcorders, and mirrors everywhere.

"I want children. And I'm not going to have a bastard, thank you very much. We've already got a bastard. Therefore . . . no contraception."

"Oh don't worry. There must be an old pack of dunkers around here somewhere."

"God you're disgusting."

"We hardly ever do it there anyway."

"God you're disgusting. And that's off the menu, all that. The only thing on the menu is normal intercourse."

"Fine. I'll take it out at the last minute."

"God you're disgusting. Normal reproductive intercourse. Marry me."

And his thought was: Girls who are cocks are very rare and very great. But you can't *marry* a cock.

"Okay, I will. If you tell me your secret."

Seven nights later she said,

"Have you got Neil Darlington's number?"

"Why do you ask?"

"He's very attractive. I thought he might like a fuck. Is Nicholas in the country?"

There was a lot of He Said, She Said. Then she said,

"A major concession. We needn't have children immediately. Say in a year or two. All right? But you've got to make an honest woman of me *now*."

. . . Kenrik, just out of Pentonville for living off immoral earnings, was best man.

Violet, six months pregnant by she wasn't sure who, served as bridesmaid.

No one gave Gloria away.

Sample declarations by Violet on the phone. "I'm going to adopt it, Key. I fink that's the best fing, don't you?" And: "Nuffing's going to take that baby away from me, Keith! Nuffing! *Nuffing!*" And: "I'm going to adopt it, Key. I fink that's the best fing, don't you?"

Keith and Gloria went to see the baby, who was named Heidi (after Heidi, Violet's alcoholic housemate). Another alcoholic, a young man in a City suit, came to dinner, and another alcoholic, a middle-aged woman in a kaftan, looked in for coffee. And the baby was beautiful, Keith thought or imagined; but her nappy was soiled and cold, and she was pale, with chapped lips (Violet was giving her milk straight out of the fridge). And everyone was drunk. The house, a normal-seeming house, was drunk.

"I think you'd better adopt her, Vi," he said, up in Vi's room.

"But it hurts," said Violet. "It hurts. I feel it in my froat."

Heidi was not submitted for adoption. When she was six weeks old the social services came and took her away.

Three months after the wedding, the pants treatment was resumed.

Gloria said, "I told you. A year *or* two. Well I've chosen. And it's not two. It's one. It'll be exactly a year."

Ten nights later, after much sophistical evasion about the secret, and after renewed threats about Neil and Nicholas, she said,

"Please. Oh *please* . . ."

"Oh all right." Come to think of it (and he was thinking of Heidi), I *do* want to see a fresh face around the house. "It's agreed. Now let's have normal reproductive intercourse."

"Yes let's. Would you help me off with these? . . . And I know you won't have any objection," she said, arching her back, "to the child being raised in the faith."

Well anyway. There was a further month on the pants; and then she left him. Three months later she returned, but different.

What Came to Pass
in 1982

This particular married couple, in its time, had tried out many modes and genres, many different ways of going about things—pornotheological farce, cat-and-mouse, sex-and-shopping, Life. They saved the worst for last: psychohorror, in la Place de la Contrescarpe, in Paris.

"And she never threatens to commit suicide?" Nicholas says on the phone (from Beirut).

"No. She won't do anything unoriginal. Like she never got pregnant on the sly or anything unoriginal like that. She doesn't threaten to commit suicide. That's unoriginal. So what she does is, she threatens to go to a nunnery."

"Christ. Are you still sleeping together?"

"Once in a blue moon she lets me. And it's completely straight. Not that I mind that, funnily enough. The only extra is the sinister refinement. Which, it goes without saying, is the only one I never liked. All she talks about is money, and religion and how I'm going to hell."

". . . In a way, religion's the most interesting subject on earth."

"Yeah but not if you believe in it. Here she is. Talk soon."

Keith and Gloria were staying for a week in the rented flat where they spent their long honeymoon, two springtimes ago. Only now they had no maid (as Gloria kept reminding him), and the weather remained uniformly dreadful. It was quite an achievement, to quench Paris of all its light, but God or some such artist had managed it. That afternoon they were drinking coffee in a bar on la rue Mouffetard. They had just come in from under the dripping tarp . . .

"Remember when we were arrested in here?"

"Arrested? What can you mean?"

"What can I mean by arrested? I mean arrested by the police. The plainclothes man, remember? *Il faut prendre votre passeport.* And he slung us in the van. Then you explained, in your perfect French, Gloria, and he let us out again. You said, *C'est incroyable, ça!* Remember?"

"I wish you'd never been born. No. I wish you'd die. You're going to go to hell. Shall I tell you how it is in hell? What they do to you?"

He listens for a while and says, "All right. I understand. There I am all scorched and peed-on. And to what end exactly?"

"To punish you. To scourge you. You ruined my life."

Because of course he never did give in—about the child being raised in the faith. About the child being raised without courage, without having to understand what death really means. She left him that time; and when she returned it was in defeat (you see, she didn't have any-where else to go); and there was no more talk of children.

He said, "You should've settled for a baby agnostic."

"What, and raise someone disgusting like you? Someone who thinks that killing and eating animals, and fucking and dreaming and shit-ting, and then dying, is good enough all by itself? . . . Quite ruined. Utterly. *Merci pour tout ce que tu m'as donné. Cher ami.*"

That night they had sex for the first time in nearly a month, and there was a sour caloricity to it, as if they both had fevers and all their bones ached, with savoury breath and savoury sweat. It drew to an end. And with embarrassing copiousness he followed her four-word instruc-tion. Gloria rose and went to the bathroom, and when she returned she was dressed in black.

"Notre Dame," she said through her veil. "Midnight mass."

He awoke at three in an empty bed with the image of a black shape in the brown Seine, the drifting tresses, the open eyes . . . She was in the other room, kneeling naked on the window seat and looking out at the moonlit square. She turned. Her face was a deathmask, encrusted with dried white.

"I need it to be stronger," she said. "Much stronger. It's just not strong enough."

Gloria wanted a stronger god. One who would strike her down, there and then, for what she wore behind her veil.

We would like this to be over quickly: this particular cosmology of two.

The next day she was all ice and electricity, all electricity and ice. In a white cotton dress and with narrow white ribbons in her hair, she darkly established herself on the white sofa. She neither spoke nor stirred. She stared.

He sat at the mirror-topped dining table, bent over *The Denial of Death* (1973), a book about psychology by Ernest Becker. Who argued, inter alia, that religions were "hero systems." Which, in the modern setting, could only be revitalised if they set out to work "against the culture, [and to] recruit youth to be anti-heroes to the ways of life of the society they live in" . . .

Just after one o'clock Gloria stood up suddenly. Her mouth opened and stayed open in disbelief and what seemed to be glee as she looked down at the sudden sarong of scarlet that swathed her hips. And on the sofa behind her, not a shapeless patch but a burning orb, like a sunset.

"That's all finished with," she said. "I'm going to go."

"Yes, go." He took her in his arms and, doubly, triply hatefully, whispered in her ear, "Get thee to a nunnery . . . Why woulds't thou be a breeder of sinners? Get thee to a nunnery, and quickly too. To a nunnery, go."

1994

They were all there, pretty much. Timmy and Scheherazade with their four grown-up children, in perfect-family formation—girl, boy, girl, boy. Born-again Scheherazade looked unglamorous but very young, as you would do, no doubt, if you thought you were going to live for ever. Whittaker was fifty-six; his friend/son/protégé Amen, now a quite celebrated photographer (with good Americanised English), was forty-two. Oona was perhaps seventy-eight, superfat Jorquil (already married six times, Keith learnt, to a succession of grasping starlets) was fifty-three, and Conchita was thirty-seven. Keith was there with his second ex-wife, Lily: they were both forty-five. The occasion was the memorial service for Prentiss. Amen asked tenderly after Gloria, who (the last Keith heard) was in Utah. And Adriano wasn't there either. Adriano had married a Kenyan nurse; then he divorced her, and then (after another much more serious accident) remarried her—the nurse who had tended to his shattered knees in Nairobi, back in 1970.

Keith supposed he felt strengthened in his view that it ought to be very easy to get divorced, and very difficult, boring, painful, and expensive to get married. But that's Life, and we never learn. Divorcing Gloria was very difficult, boring, painful, and expensive. Divorcing Lily was easy; she wanted it, and he quite wanted it too.

A week later he had lunch with Conchita, and it was all decided in the first ten minutes.

"My father in a bus crash on his way to the hospital," he said, "and my mother in childbirth."

"My mother of leukaemia," she said, "and my father, suicide, two hours later."

He reached out a hand—to shake on it. Then she briefly told Keith what happened in between, between the death of the one and the death of the other: the event that took her to Amsterdam. They shook hands anyway. Within half an hour he briefly told Conchita what he had never told Lily (or anyone else), despite her bi-weekly interrogations over an entire decade: the truth about his birthday in Campania.

"This was how it's been going for me," he said as they were finishing up, "and it's simple. I'm kind now. My vices got me absolutely nowhere. So for years I've been working on my virtues."

"All right. Then give up smoking," she said. "And give up your job at Derwent and Digby. All right?"

The next afternoon but one they met again, and he drove her to Heathrow to pick up Silvia, who had just spent the statutory month with her father in Buenos Aires. Silvia was fourteen.

So first Keith married Gloria, then he married Lily, then he married Conchita. He didn't marry Scheherazade or Oona or Dodo. But he married all the others.

With Gloria it was just sex, with Lily it was just love. Then he married Conchita, and he was all right.

At the Book and Bible in 2003

It is April Fool's Day, and he is sitting in the snug of a pub called the Book and Bible. After the kaleidoscopic detail of the street, with its beautiful flesh tones, the Book and Bible is like a groaning relict of a vanished England, all white, all middle-class, and all middle-aged— England before the invention of colour. The shove-ha'penny board, the Scotch eggs and pork scratchings, the sodden carpet, the furry wallpaper. Keith hates it in the Book and Bible; but this is where he has started coming, ever since the great heaviness descended on him, eight or nine weeks ago. He is fifty-three. He is drinking tomato juice, and smoking.

The unsuspected sensuality of stasis, of stillness, the expert caress of the cotton sheets. In normal times a combination of greed, boredom, and curiosity got him out of bed by nine o'clock (he wanted to know what had happened, while he slept, to the planet Earth). But now he stays horizontal until keeping his eyes shut is harder work than keeping them open. His body deeply needs this. And every night, for about an hour, he weeps and swears. He lies on the bed and swears with stinging eyes. When fully awake, he retains a stunned feeling. And he doesn't know why. What has happened to him that he should have to carry all this weight?

He doesn't understand. Because Violet is already dead. She died in 1999. And the last section of her life, spent in cohabitation with the last of her terrible boyfriends, was comparatively quiet, much of it dedicated to Karl. She spoon-fed him. She clipped his toenails. She would put on a swimsuit and guide him into the shower. Then Karl died, in 1998. Then Violet died. The woman doctor, in intensive care, spoke of "a failure cascade." When Keith dragged his eyes over the autopsy report, the only phrase he registered was "purulent urine" (not just alliterative but somehow onomatopoeic), and then he read no more.

After Violet died, Nicholas went insane for a while, and Tina went insane for a while. Keith did not go insane. His symptoms were physical: the three-month collapse of his handwriting (the pen just shot about the page); and then the year-long sore throat. That's where she got him, Violet—in the throat. And since then there were other deaths. Neil Darlington seventeen months ago, at the age of sixty-three, and Kenrik in 2000, at the age of fifty-one. Violet died in 1999, at the age of forty-six.

There is a palpitation, now, in the Book and Bible. Because someone ultramundane is entering it: a lady in a black veil (not the burkha, but the hijab, with the eyes stylishly displayed), hand in hand with an unexotic little boy of eight or nine—Isabel's age. They come with their soft drinks and settle in the snug, and it is anomalous, he supposes, a child and a quite elderly Muslim woman in a public house made of taupe and ash.

"What shall we play?" she asks him (in an accentless voice). "I Spy?"

"Let's play What Would You Rather."

Keith has three thoughts, and in the following order. First, that he no more wants to tell this woman to remove her veil than he wants to tell her to wear it in the first place. Second, that two major wars are now being fought between the believers and the infidels (and the first war, the older war, had "female equality" as one of its stated military goals). The third thought comes from the ex-poet in him: But we seemed to be getting on so well . . . He sentimentally has in mind Ashraf, and Dilkash, and Amen, and many others, including the widow Sahira. In 1980 Neil Darlington, limitlessly louche, converted to Islam, in order to marry Sahira—a Vision, a poet, and a Palestinian.

"What would you rather?" he hears the woman say. "Have twenty children or none at all?"

Which brings on a further thought. Silvia, the other night, said that Europe was destined to become a Muslim-majority continent by about 2110. "The feminised woman only has one child," she said. "So the end result of your sexual revolution might be sharia and the veil . . . Of course it won't work out like that. That's a whole century away. Imagine what else'll happen in between." Now Keith rolls another cigarette and lights it, and wishes Violet had adopted Islam rather than Christianity. At least she'd be alive.

"Let's play World's Most Expensive Hotel," he hears the boy say.

"Yes, that's enough What Would You Rather. In the bar, the—"

"Me first . . . The peanuts all cost a million dollars each."

"The olives are two million. Plus five hundred thousand if they're on toothpicks. The toilet paper costs a hundred thousand dollars a segment. The coat hangers—"

"Auntie, who stays in the world's most expensive hotel?"

"Oh. Well, when it opened, George Soros filed for bankruptcy after the very first night. On the second afternoon the Sheikh of Dubai was arrested because he couldn't pay for his lunch. And on the third day even Bill Gates was out on his arse."

Keith looks up. She winds off her veil, saying, "I was born in Cairo in nineteen *thirty-seven.*"

Gloria Beautyman. Who is now—how old?

His thoughts are not in order any more, as his past recalibrates like a Rubik's cube. I that am with Phoebus' am'rous pinches black, *not* dark enough for Cleopatra, I'm just years ahead of my time, Census Board (her father: birth certificate), Gypsies aren't from Egypt either, there's something unclean about drawing, the secret of eternal youth, and the lost, the stolen decade. Keith remembered what she said, in the car, in Andalucia ("I cry with anger too, you know . . . What makes me cry is the time. Ten years"). And the nightsweats and the animal birthday in Paris ("That's the end of it"), when her body was suddenly *happening* to her.

"Reginald, you go and play shove-ha'penny for a minute," she says, "while I make a little speech to this very nice young man."

She watches the boy hurry off—her face is still square, her chin is still curved to a point, her eyes are still deep; but all of her is sixty-six.

"My great-nephew. Mary's daughter's boy . . . Oh, Keith! Can you imagine what *heaven* it was, living your twenties twice? Knowing what you know at thirty, and doing it all over again? It was like a dream come true. It was like a wonderful game."

He finds he can speak. "That's what it felt like. Like a game." Yes, it was better in the mirror, realer in the mirror. "Like a game." The body in the mirror, reduced to two dimensions. Without depth and without time.

"A game, Keith, that you were too young for. I was like one of those chocolates. With the liqueur centres. Nice, but not good for the young. You needed another ten years on you. To even have a chance. I take what solace I can," she says, "from the fact that I ruined you for life. *I* was right. It was time that was wrong."

358

"Your plan. It had a weakness."

"Yes. When my twenties were over—I was forty. Goodbye."

"Goodbye. Kenrik's dead. Neil's dead. Vi's dead."

"Vi? *Oh.* You must feel so horribly guilty! . . . But that's all right, because you never loved her anyway. And you never loved me."

"No. And you never loved me. Of course. You never even *liked* me."

"No. As I took the trouble to tell you, years ago. You're very annoying."

". . . All right. But I'll tell you something. And it's true. My memory loves you. Goodbye."

And he dazedly wondered (and went on wondering): Did it mean anything, historically? That Gloria was born a Muslim, that Gloria Beautyman was born in the land of Hasan al-Banna, and Ayman al-Zawahri, and Sayyid Qutb? Did it connect to anything? To New York, Madrid, Bali, London, Baghdad, Kabul? Only in this, perhaps. Gloria was a visit from outside history. She was a visit from another clock.

2009

Valedictory

There is a—there is a willow. There is a willow grows aslant a brook . . . But long it could not be. Till that her garments, heavy with their drink, Pulled the poor wretch from her melodious lay To muddy death.

And so it was that on this night (September 7), ten years ago, Keith was alone in the room with a panting corpse.

She had been unconscious for over a hundred hours, and he told his mother and brother that there was no point in coming, she would not be waking up and there was no point in coming, coming from Andalucia, from Sierra Leone . . . It was nearly midnight. Her body was flat, sunken, on the raised bed, all buoyancy gone; but the lifeline on the monitor continued to undulate, like a childish representation of the ocean, and she continued to breathe—to breathe with preternatural force.

Yes Violet looked forceful. For the first time in her life, she seemed to be someone it would be foolish to treat lightly or underestimate, ridge-faced, totemic, like a squaw queen with orange hair.

"She's gone," said the doctor and pointed with her hand.

The wavering line had levelled out. "She's still breathing," said Keith. But of course it was the machine that was still breathing. He stood over a breathless corpse, the chest filling, heaving, and he thought of her running and running, flying over the fields.

"Why should Vi have been interested in Woman's Liberation?" he said to Silvia late one night.

Silvia was now twenty-nine, and married to a journalist called David Silver (she used her maiden name), and they had an infant daughter, Paula (pron. *Powla*), and it was fiftyfifty.

"Vi wasn't a woman," he said. "She was a child." A grown child in a world of adults: a very terrifying situation. You would need all the false courage you could possibly find. And she offered herself to men (at least at first) for childish reasons: she wanted them to keep her safe from harm. "That's why she talked like a little girl. She wasn't even a woman."

They sat on for another hour; and Silvia, as she often did late at night, returned them to what she felt was the great subterranean question. With her dark rose colour somehow not affecting her lunar purity of brow, she said, "Violence. Against the gentler sex. Why?"

"I don't know."

"Even here, in England. We're always going on about the other stuff. Honour killing and genital mutilation and all that. And nine-year-old brides."

"Mm. Who aren't marrying nine-year-old grooms. Imagine *Isabel*, at nine, getting married to anyone, let alone an old man. That's *violent*. I can't think of anything more violent. More richly violent."

"Yes, but what about here? I saw it the other day. I quote. 'The most common form of death for women between sixteen and forty-five,' here, now, 'is murder by the male partner.' Now that's really weird. That they only need to kill us when we're of childbearing age."

"I don't understand. I never have. I suppose those are the men who've just run out of words. Long ago. But I don't understand."

"Well it's the caveman asset, isn't it. It underlies everything. Bigger and stronger. What are we going to do about *that*?"

One night a week, David took Paula to his parents' house. One night a week, Silvia came with Paula to the house above the Heath. It was all fiftyfifty. None of this twentyeighty or thirtyseventy or fortysixty. None of this forty-fivefifty-five.

"Your fiftyfifty," said Keith. "I could tell it was good because I feared it. It hurt. I've got another one for you . . . There's more wine in the fridge. Screw-top wine—screw-top wine has improved the quality of life by about ten per cent, wouldn't you say? But it's not a screw-top. It's late. You're young. Would you mind?"

And Silvia rose lightly from her chair, saying, "And I'll check baby."

Fiftyfifty, he thought, must hurt a lot, because twentyeighty hurt like hell. Everyone, now, was talking about torture. Well, Keith would be easy to torture. Make him show up at a PTA meeting, make him spend fifteen minutes with his accountant, make him go with a list to

Marks & Spencer—and he'd tell you everything he knew . . . Children feel boredom—childish boredom, once described by an aphoristic psychologist (and corroborated, years ago, by Nat and Gus) as "the absence of a wish." Nothing bores the twenty-year-old, the thirty-year-old, the forty-year-old. Keith, in 2009, felt that boredom was as strong as hate. There was of course another very popular kind of torture: non-judicial, and preludial to death. That kind of torture, he was confident, would show up later on.

"Thank you," he said. "Okay. There's this other asymmetry." A little girl who vows to marry her father, he said, is smiled at and chucked under the chin. In most cultures. In most cultures, a little boy who vows to marry his mother will wake up in hospital, or recover from his beating or at least his bawling-out, and then decide never to renew that offer. "You know," he said, "Chloe's first declarative sentence was 'My yoff Daddy.'" Perhaps better rendered as "mI yoff Daddy." "Why? What was she doing? Thanking me for twentyeighty? . . . *You* love Daddy."

And Silvia said, "I do. He wasn't always kind to Mum, but he was always kind to me. It's the way they hold you when you're tiny. Your milky mum's one thing—she's you, and you're her. But your father. He's bigger and stronger, and you smell a man. It's the way they hold you when you're tiny. You never in your entire life feel as safe as that."

"Yes, but we've got to work on this special love for the fathers." Karl died in 1998, Violet a year later. And if those two events were closely connected, then he thought it the saddest thing in the universe. "The fathers have got to stop holding the daughters and making them feel so safe."

"That'll hurt," she said. "Mm. I suppose it's no good unless it hurts."

With a ragged groan of the tenderest despair, Keith still thinks, Keith still briefly broods, about that night in Italy with Dracula and Scheherazade. But nowhere near as often as he used to. Only a few times a week. One morning long ago, he was in the local caff with Isabel (then not quite six), and as he was paying at the till she made the unprecedented announcement that she would wait for him in the street. She walked to the door with that same levitational tread—not on tiptoe, but levitational: just like Scheherazade in the time of the waiting. Isabel walked to the door; she did not go through it.

And the other year he ran into Rita. He was in the household-goods warehouse in Golders Green, buying a circular shower mat (it looked like a steamrollered octopus, with gaping suckers). "You just watch out for your first big fall," Tina said to him in the year 2000, sitting outside her *casita* (where she still sits, now newly widowed, at eighty-one). In the year 2000, I'm pleased to add, Keith was accompanied, not only by the usual three girls, but also by Heidi, now named Catherine (she emerged at Violet's funeral, with her foster-parents), and filling the same physical space (in what he thought was a kind of remission) as her mother used to do . . .

So here was Rita: the mouth, the jaw, the powerful bones were all there, but her biomass had increased by about a factor of three. She was looking for various playroom accoutrements to send to Pansy's first granddaughter.

Keith said, "And you, did you have your ten? One a year?"

"I never did. No babies . . . I never did."

And he hugged the new slab of her body as she started to weep, among the breadbins and fleeces, the Thermoses and abacuses.

"I sort of forgot to." She kept trying to wipe her nose. "I just seemed to miss it."

He quite often met women his age who had just seemed to miss it.

A topic sentence. Pornographic sex is a kind of sex that *can be described.* Which told you something, he felt, about pornography, and about sex. During Keith's time, sex divorced itself from feeling. Pornography was the industrialisation of that rift . . .

And how was it going with the mirror?

It is the fate of all of us to fall out of love with our own reflections. Narcissus took a day and a night to die—but we take half a century. It isn't vanity, it was never vanity. It was always something else.

Keith looked at the shadowsmear in the mirror. And the most amazing thing of all was that this, this in the glass (the perfect, the finished ghoul), would be remembered by him as something actually not that bad—comparatively. This, even this, very this . . . The video nasty, to put it in plain words, the horror film, was set to become a snuff movie, but long before that he would be its trailer. He would be an ad for death.

Death—the dark backing a mirror needs before it can show us ourselves.

It isn't vanity, it was never vanity. It was always death. This was the true and universal metamorphosis: the agonising transfiguration from one state to another—from the state of life to the state of death.

Yes, we're close again, he and I.

. . . I? Well, I'm the voice of conscience (which made such a dramatic comeback between his first and second marriages), and I perform other duties compatible with those of the superego. No, I am not the poet he never was. Keith could have been a poet. But not a novelist. His provenance was too peculiar for that. He couldn't hear what others hear—the reverberation, the echo of humanity. Confined by truth, by Life, I'm nonetheless the part of him that always tried to listen out for that.

"My breasts are getting smaller," said Conchita in the bathroom.

This was not said insanely cheerfully—though Conchita continued, in general, to be insanely cheerful, Keith thought. And that was the more remarkable, in his view, because it was given to her, and not to him: the hourly nightmare of living with someone who was born in 1949.

"They are. My breasts are getting smaller."

"But that's all right," he said. "Because mine are getting bigger."

". . . So it all works out in the end."

Yeah. Fifty's nothing, Pulc. Me, I'm as old as NATO. And it all works out. Your hams get skinnier—but that's all right, because your gut gets fatter. Your eyes get hotter—but that's all right, because your hands get colder (and you can soothe them with your frozen fingertips). Shrill or sudden noises are getting painfully sharper—but that's all right, because you're getting deafer. The hair on your head gets thinner—but that's all right, because the hair in your nose and in your ears gets thicker. It all works out in the end.

There will be guests tonight. Silvia and her husband, Lily and her husband, Nat, Gus, and Nicholas and his wife. Lily's third husband. Nicholas's second wife. His first marriage lasted until 1989 (one daughter). Then for fourteen years Nicholas lived the youth he had somehow deferred, and the women no longer needed to be left-wing, and Keith became the listener, and not the teller. Then Nicholas married again, in 2003; and they have a five-year-old son. The occasion, tonight, is a dinner party in celebration of Keith's recent birthday.

He was now in his study, finishing up . . . His trouble with Violet, the hard, hard work with Violet, rested on this. Keith was someone who had to make his family love him. And with Violet alone he suffered no disadvantage, no displacement. It wasn't difficult to make her love him. There he always was, the small, beaked, fascinated face staring and smiling over the brow of her crib; and then, like a personal trainer, helping her crawl, walk, talk. And reading to her, and telling her stories, the parables, the miracles. You see, Vi, they only had five loaves of bread and two little fishes . . . It wasn't difficult for her. And for him it was easy. It was love at first sight.

So he was there at the beginning and he was there at the end. But where was he in between? He was following his strategy, his strategy of withdrawal. And then he went and had it anyway, later, and worse— his breakdown or crack-up. And there never was the slightest chance that he could evade the strength and also the violence of those early feelings ("If anyone ever touches her . . ."). Which began when he looked down at her newborn body and saw an angel. That's what he actually saw, in his hallucinatory state—smashed on love and protectiveness. So all right. He was there when it began and he was there when it ended.

We live half our lives in shock, he thought. And it's the second half. A death comes; and the brain makes chemicals to get us past it. They numb you, and numbness is an identifiable kind of calm: a false one. All it can do, numbness, is postpone. Then the drugs wear off, and the voids, the little oblivions, come and get you anyway. Where does pain go when it goes? Somewhere else? Or into the well of your weakness? I'll tell you: the latter. And it's the deaths of others that kill you in the end.

Time to go in. Venus was rising over the dark well of the Heath. Keith Nearing, Conchita, Isabel, and Chloe (often accompanied by Silvia) had by now spent several Christmases in southern South America (where Conchita had in-laws and dozens of cousins); and he was going to ask Nicholas about his time with its tutelary spirit. For two days running, in 1980, Nicholas read to the great Borges. When they parted, the blind seer, the living Tiresias, offered him "a present," and recited this quatrain, from Dante Gabriel Rossetti:

> What man has bent o'er his son's sleep, to brood
> How that face shall watch his when cold it lies?
> Or thought, as his own mother kissed his eyes,
> Of what her kiss was when his father wooed?

In Keith's peculiar case, he registered positive to the first question, and a negative to the second. But he believed that Borges universally understood about Time: "Time is the substance I am made of. Time is a river that carries me away, but I am the river . . ."

Venus: when he looked at her with his glasses on, she seemed to be wearing eyelashes. The daughter of Jupiter and Dione, the goddess of love, in false eyelashes. Its gossamer wings—what a fly would look like if born and raised in Elysium . . . The poet Quevedo described the planet Venus: *lucero inobediente, ángel amotinado.* Defiant star. Rebel angel.

Who were these extremists and self-destroyers, these despiters, the people who couldn't stand it another second in heaven? Yes go on, Kenrik, get caught after a long chase for driving five times over the limit at nine o'clock in the morning for the fourth time in three weeks (and serve a year in Wormwood Scrubs). Yes go on, Gloria, place yourself outside history, and live your twenties twice, and do it as a game, while in that way somehow making yourself invaluably dear to the memory. Yes go on, Violet, let the honeymoon last at least half a minute, and then run out over the fields, with no more thought in your head than a puppy, panting, heaving, running, flying, looking for someone you love.

He drew the blinds and shut everything down, and went in.

ACKNOWLEDGEMENTS

First I offer my enraptured thanks to the memory of Ted Hughes. His *Tales from Ovid* is one of the most thrilling books I have ever read. My debt to it goes well beyond the exquisite "Echo and Narcissus," which I quote from and paraphrase throughout.

The "distinguished Marxist historian" is Eric Hobsbawm, and the quotes are from his seminal *Age of Extremes.* The details about Mussolini are from Denis Mack Smith's brilliant and quietly and persistently comical biography. "Action is transitory—a step, a blow. / The motion of a muscle": this is from Wordsworth's *The Borderers.* "Love bade me welcome": George Herbert. "Words at once true and kind": this (and much else) is from Philip Larkin ("Talking in Bed"). "The economic basis of society": Auden's "Letter to Lord Byron." The "aphoristic psychologist" is Adam Phillips. "The means by which love would be communicated if there *were* any" is from Saul Bellow's *More Die of Heartbreak;* the line about the fig leaf and the price tag is from *Humboldt's Gift.* "Oh, what can ail thee, knight-at-arms" is of course from Keats. "The Sick Rose" is by William Blake. "The storm rolls through me as your mouth opens" is the last line of Ian Hamilton's "The Storm."

I would also like to give my thanks to Jane Austen. Childless, like so many of the great feminists, she is nonetheless the mother, I believe, of "the line of sanity" that so characterises the English novel. To demonstrate this penetrating sanity of hers, I quote her last words. Dying of unalleviable cancer, she was asked "what she needed." She said, "Nothing but death." Or, to put it another way: Nothing but nothing. D. H. Lawrence, whose last words I have also quoted, was forty-four when he uttered them. Jane Austen was forty-one when she uttered hers.

Shakespeare, defying all rules and proprieties as usual, needs no thanks from this writer. As Matthew Arnold said of him (meaning something very slightly different), "Others abide our question. Thou art free."

And this still strikes me, almost daily, as a magical fact: the most plangent evocation of the time I lived through (I, and hundreds of millions of others) was written in 1610. Ariel's song appears in that masque-like romance *The Tempest,* Shakespeare's last play, and I quote the second verse yet again:

> Full fathom five thy father lies;
>   Of his bones are coral made:
> Those are pearls that were his eyes:
>   Nothing of him that doth fade,
> But doth suffer a sea change
> Into something rich and strange.
> Sea-nymphs hourly ring his knell . . .

London, 2010

A NOTE ON THE TYPE

The text of this book was set in Garamond No. 3. It is not a true copy of any of the designs of Claude Garamond (ca. 1480–1561), but an adaptation of his types, which set the European standard for two centuries. It probably owes as much to the designs of Jean Jannon, a Protestant printer working in Sedan in the early seventeenth century, who had worked with Garamond's romans earlier, in Paris, but who was denied their use because of Catholic censorship. Jannon's matrices came into the possession of the Imprimerie nationale, where they were thought to be by Garamond himself, and were so described when the Imprimerie revived the type in 1900. This particular version is based on an adaptation by Morris Fuller Benton.

Composed by Creative Graphics, Allentown, Pennsylvania
Printed and bound by Berryville Graphics, Berryville, Virginia